The Bombmaker

Stephen Leather

CORONET BOOKS
Hodder & Stoughton

Copyright © 1999 by Stephen Leather

First published in Great Britain in 1999
by Hodder and Stoughton
A division of Hodder Headline
First published in paperback in 2000
by Hodder and Stoughton

The right of Stephen Leather to be identified as the Author
of the Work has been asserted by him in accordance with the
Copyright, Designs and Patents Act 1988.

A Coronet Paperback

10 9 8 7 6 5 4 3 2 1

A CIP catalogue record for this book
is available from the British Library.

ISBN 0 340 68956 0

Typeset by Hewer Text Ltd, Edinburgh
Printed and bound in Great Britain by
Mackays of Chatham PLC, Chatham, Kent

Hodder and Stoughton
A division of Hodder Headline
338 Euston Road
London NW1 3BH

For Nongsam

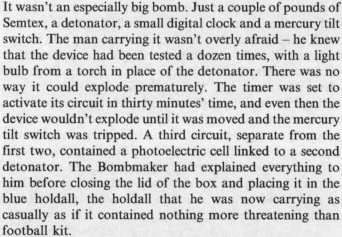

It wasn't an especially big bomb. Just a couple of pounds of
Semtex, a detonator, a small digital clock and a mercury tilt
switch. The man carrying it wasn't overly afraid – he knew
that the device had been tested a dozen times, with a light
bulb from a torch in place of the detonator. There was no
way it could explode prematurely. The timer was set to
activate its circuit in thirty minutes' time, and even then the
device wouldn't explode until it was moved and the mercury
tilt switch was tripped. A third circuit, separate from the
first two, contained a photoelectric cell linked to a second
detonator. The Bombmaker had explained everything to
him before closing the lid of the box and placing it in the
blue holdall, the holdall that he was now carrying as
casually as if it contained nothing more threatening than
football kit.

The man looked left and right, then squeezed through a
gap in the railings and went down the embankment to the
railway tracks. He walked along the sleepers, confident that
there wouldn't be a train for at least an hour, by which time
he'd be long gone. He took a quick look at his wristwatch.
Plenty of time. Plenty of time to place the bomb at the
designated location, then to get to the phone box and make
the coded call. This wasn't a bomb designed to kill, it was
meant to disrupt. To tie up the police, the army and a bomb
disposal team. That's not to say that it wasn't a serious

bomb, but the men who turned up to deal with it would be experts. They'd X-ray it before touching it and they'd see the circuits and then they'd blow it up with a controlled charge. In effect, they'd be blowing up the railway line themselves. Hours of disruption. Great publicity. And a reminder that they had the ability and the supplies to do harm. A nudge, that's all it was, though the man carrying the holdall knew that it was a nudge capable of leaving a crater twenty feet wide.

Ahead of him was the entrance to a tunnel. He walked up to it and left the holdall a few feet inside. The fact that it was in darkness and close to the tunnel wall would make it that much harder to deal with. They'd need lights, and they'd know that if it did go off the tunnel would direct the blast outwards. Plus they'd also have to close the road that ran above the railway line. Two birds with one stone.

He went back along the tracks and climbed up the embankment, then walked along the road. A blue Fiat pulled up alongside him and he climbed in. 'Okay?' said the driver, a cigarette sticking out of the side of his mouth.

The man nodded but didn't say anything. The driver was a driver, nothing more. Told where and when to pick him up and where to take him. The man looked at his watch again. Everything was going to plan.

Lucy Metcalfe hated it when her brother played rough. She was a year older than Tim but he was bigger and stronger and lately he seemed to take great pleasure in pushing her around. He was worse when his friends were with him. They were kicking a football, but every time Lucy got it, Tim would immediately tackle her, charging in with his shoulder and pushing with his elbows. 'Mine, mine,' he'd shout, before taking the ball off her. It wasn't even as if they were trying to score goals – they were just passing the ball to and fro, on their way back from school.

'You're a bully!' she shouted at her ten-year-old brother as he barged into her for the umpteenth time and dribbled the ball away. She stood rubbing her shoulder and glaring at him sullenly.

Tim stopped and put a foot on top of the ball. 'Yeah?' he said.

'Yeah. It's supposed to be a game.'

'Yeah? Well, I'm better than you are.'

'No, you're not better. You're bigger. And uglier. And stupider.'

Tim's friends giggled and his cheeks reddened. He kicked the ball at her, hard, but missed her by several feet. The ball bounced on the kerb and skidded across a strip of grass before disappearing through a line of rusting metal railings. 'Now look what you've done!' Tim shouted. 'Go and get it.'

'Why should I get it? It wasn't my fault.'

'I was kicking it to you.'

Lucy shook her head and folded her arms across her chest in the way she'd seen her mother do when she was insisting that they go to bed early. 'You were kicking it at me, not to me,' she said. 'You were the last to touch it. You get it.'

Tim clenched his fists and took a step towards her. Lucy turned and ran, her school bag banging against her hip. 'Chicken!' Tim shouted, and started making loud clucking noises. His friends joined in. Tim waited until his sister was out of sight before ducking through the railings and sliding down the embankment. His friends followed him, shouting and screaming and flapping their arms like demented crows.

The ball was at the mouth of the tunnel. Tim ran over to it and picked it up. As he bent down, he saw something a few feet inside the entrance. A blue holdall. 'Hey, there's something here,' he yelled. He kicked the ball over to his friends and walked into the tunnel. He was surprised how much colder it was and he shivered. He turned to look at his friends as if to reassure himself that they were still there. He suddenly felt a lot less brave. 'Come on!' he said, and waved them over.

They ran towards him. Tim's confidence returned almost immediately, and he grabbed at the holdall, wanting to be the first to open it.

The man replaced the receiver and left the call-box. He slid into the passenger seat of the blue Fiat. The driver was lighting another cigarette, and the man pointedly wound down the window. 'You don't mind me smoking, do ya?' asked the driver.

The man shrugged but didn't say anything. He motioned with his finger for the driver to move off. As the driver's hand reached for the gear-stick, they heard a dull thudding sound off in the distance. The two men knew immediately what the noise was. They were both Belfast-born and bred and were no strangers to the sound of exploding bombs.

'Jesus fucking Christ,' said the man.

The cigarette dropped from the driver's lips. He fumbled for it as it rolled between his legs, cursing loudly.

The man stared out of the open window, a sick feeling in the pit of his stomach. Something had gone wrong. Something had gone very, very wrong.

TEN YEARS LATER

It had been a long and uncomfortable flight and Egan rubbed his knuckles into the small of his back as he waited for his luggage to appear on the carousel. The men from Beijing had booked him a first-class ticket, but Egan hadn't used it. People were noticed in first class, and Egan had gone through most of his life without being noticed. That was the way he wanted it. His features could best be described as nondescript. He was in his early thirties, a little below average height with receding hair, cropped short. He had pale blue eyes and a squarish face with thin lips that formed an almost straight line unless he smiled. The only distinguishing features Egan had were concealed by his dark blue suit. There was a thick scar that ran from the base of his neck to just above his left breast, a phosphorus burn on his right thigh, and two old bullet wounds in his right shoulder. Anyone who saw Egan naked would never forget the man, but most people would have difficulty describing him an hour after meeting him.

Egan's suitcase was as bland as he was. A grey Samsonite with an Air France tag. He picked it up and walked through Customs. Egan had started his journey in London but had taken the Eurostar train to Paris and flown out of Charles de Gaulle airport. The flight to Hong Kong had taken a little under twelve hours and he'd spent most of the time reading *A Tale of Two Cities*. He was working his way through the complete works of Charles Dickens and hoped to have finished by the end of the year.

As he walked out into the arrivals area he saw a liveried chauffeur holding a piece of white card with 'Mr Egan' written on it. Egan shuddered. He knew that his employers were trying to impress him, and that face was all-important to the Chinese, but Egan had no wish to be impressed. He considered ignoring the chauffeur, but decided not to in case the man had him paged. Egan wasn't his real name, but he still didn't want it broadcast throughout Chek Lap Kok airport. He went over to the chauffeur and nodded.

The chauffeur touched the brim of his cap in an attempt at a salute and reached for Egan's suitcase. Egan let him carry the case. It contained nothing of importance – it was as much a prop as the suit he was wearing, to give him the appearance of a businessman or banker or any of the other vultures who were flocking into Hong Kong to take advantage of the economic crisis that was wreaking havoc in South-East Asia.

The chauffeur was in his sixties and bow-legged, and he was breathing heavily by the time they reached the top-of-the-range Mercedes outside the airport terminal. Egan climbed into the plush interior and settled back for the ride to Hong Kong Island. It was his third visit to the former British colony in six months, and he was as impressed as always by the sheer magnitude of the new airport and its transport system, ferrying thousands of passengers an hour from the outlying island to Hong Kong proper by road, rail and helicopter. It didn't have the character or the white-knuckle approach of the old airport at Kai Tak, but it was considerably more efficient, and if there was one thing Egan admired, it was efficiency.

There was a copy of the *Hong Kong Standard* in the seat pocket and Egan read the business section. The stock market was continuing its downward plunge and the Hang Seng Index was down more than thirty per cent year on year. There were rumours that the government was considering devaluing the Hong Kong dollar, and inflation was climbing. Egan smiled to himself as he scanned the list of stock prices. The days of the so-called Asian miracle were long gone.

The Mercedes drew up in front of the Mandarin Hotel and a red-liveried bell-boy carried Egan's case inside. Egan checked in, showered and put on a clean shirt, then watched CNN until it was time for his meeting.

The men from Beijing had booked a room large enough to hold fifty, even though there were just four of them. It was face, Egan knew, something the Chinese regarded as one of their cultural strengths but which Egan knew was a major weakness. They were already in the room when Egan arrived, sitting in a line at one end of a long apple-wood table. There was only one other chair, at the opposite end, and Egan sat down and studied the men facing him. Three were in their seventies, with watery eyes and lined parchment-like faces. The fourth was middle-aged, in his late forties, and was the only one wearing glasses. His name was Deng, and he was a distant relative of the former Chinese leader, the one they still called the Butcher of Tiananmen Square. The other three had never been introduced to Egan, but he had made enquiries and knew who they were and how much they were worth. One was a general in the People's Liberation Army, the other two were bankers. In the United States they'd be well past retirement age and would be enjoying their twilight years on the golf course, but careers were handled differently in China.

'Good to see you again, Mr Egan,' said Deng. He spoke with an American accent, the result of three years studying for a master's degree at Harvard University.

Egan nodded but said nothing.

'Everything is proceeding satisfactorily?'

'It is.'

Deng's three companions stared at Egan with unblinking eyes. The PLA general's mouth was open and Egan could hear every breath the man took. According to Egan's file on the man, he was suffering from emphysema and was a regular visitor to a lung specialist in London's Harley Street.

Egan leaned forward and interlinked his thick fingers on

the table's surface. 'The teams are now in place – we're in a position to move to the next stage. But before we do proceed, I want to make quite sure you realise the ramifications of what you're asking.'

'What we're paying for,' said Deng.

Egan nodded, acknowledging the point. The four men in front of him had already transferred half a million dollars to his bank account in Zurich, and following today's meeting a further one million would be paid. If everything went to plan, Egan stood to receive a total of seven million dollars.

'Nairobi, 1998. More than two hundred dead, five and a half thousand injured. What I'm organising – what you're paying for – is bigger, much bigger, than what I did in Kenya. Timing is the key. It can be done late at night and casualties will be minimal. It can be done at lunch-time and they'll be digging the bodies out for weeks.'

Deng nodded, but the other three men remained impassive. Egan knew that at least one of the geriatrics spoke fluent English and that the other two had a reasonable grasp of the language.

'I have no qualms either way,' Egan continued, 'but I want to make it clear before we go any further that if you do decide to go ahead with a daytime event, hundreds of office workers could die.'

Deng nodded again. He turned to his three companions and spoke in rapid Mandarin. All three men nodded. 'We have no problems with matters as they stand, Mr Egan. If anything, it adds credibility to our scenario, does it not?'

'It could be taken either way,' said Egan. 'I was thinking in terms of the degree of backlash. Africans are one thing, Europeans are something else.'

'Nevertheless,' said Deng, 'we are of the opinion that we should proceed as planned.'

'No problem,' said Egan. 'As soon as the next tranche is deposited in Zurich, we'll move on to the next stage.'

The PLA general wheezed and then leaned over to Deng and whispered to him in Mandarin. Deng listened, pushing his spectacles higher up his nose. When the general had finished whispering, Deng nodded and then looked at Egan. 'Time is still of the essence, Mr Egan. Do we have your assurance that everything will be completed on time?'

'You do,' said Egan. He was well aware of how anxious the men from Beijing were that his mission be completed without delay. He knew that their lives would be forfeit if he failed.

'The money will be in your account within the hour,' said Deng.

DAY ONE

There were two of them, stocky men wearing matching blue track suits, black Reebok trainers and black ski masks. They vaulted over the back wall and ran, bent double, along the grass to the kitchen door of the house. They crouched at the door for several seconds, then one of the men nodded and reached for the door handle. It opened. They weren't surprised. They'd been watching the house for two weeks and they knew the routine of the occupants. The kitchen door was never locked until the family's golden retriever had been allowed out just after midnight.

The men slipped into the kitchen and gently closed the door behind them. They stood for a while, listening. They could just about hear the television in the sitting room. A comedy programme. Loud studio laughter. They reached into their track-suit tops and pulled out guns. Black automatics with bulbous silencers. The men didn't expect to have to use them. But they were prepared to, if necessary.

Their biggest worry was the dog. People could be threatened, people knew the damage that guns could do, but dogs would just growl and bark, maybe even attack to protect what they considered to be their territory. The dog was in the sitting room, so if they moved carefully they wouldn't be heard.

One of them eased open the door to the hallway. More studio laughter. They moved on the balls of their feet, hardly breathing as they crept to the stairs. The stairs would be the dangerous part. Stairs creaked. They went up two stairs at a time, keeping close to the wall, guns at the ready.

They froze as they heard a police siren, but then relaxed as they realised it was on the television. Somebody had changed channels. They heard a roar. A football match, maybe. Then muffled voices. Then studio laughter again. The men moved along the upper hallway and knelt down at the door to the back bedroom. One of the men was wearing a small rucksack, and he slipped it off and placed it on the carpet. From the rucksack he pulled out a cloth and a small glass bottle containing a colourless liquid. He unscrewed the top and doused the cloth with the liquid, turning his head to avoid the worst of the fumes. When the cloth was soaked, he nodded at his companion, who opened the door and stepped inside.

They moved quickly through the darkness to the bed. A small girl was asleep, her blond hair spread across the pillow, a cuddly Garfield toy clutched to her chest. The man with the cloth held it tightly against the girl's face. She stopped struggling after a few seconds, but he kept the cloth pressed over her mouth and nose for a full minute before releasing his grip on her.

The other man put a white envelope on a bedside table and gathered up the little girl. The Garfield toy slipped on to the floor. The man who'd drugged the girl picked up the cuddly toy, hesitated for a second, and then put it and several other toys into his rucksack. The man holding the unconscious girl made an impatient clicking noise. Even with most of his face covered by the ski mask, it was clear he was glaring at his companion. He nodded at the door.

The two men moved down the stairs as silently as they'd gone up, and two minutes later they were in a Ford Mondeo, driving south with the little girl hidden under a tartan blanket. The chloroform would keep her unconscious for the best part of thirty minutes, and they didn't have far to go.

'Coffee?' asked Martin Hayes.

His wife grinned at him. 'Are you making it, or are you asking me to get one for you?'

Martin pushed himself up off the sofa. The golden retriever at his feet wagged its tail hopefully. 'Okay, Dermott – I'll let you out.' He looked pointedly at his wife.

'You're all heart,' said Andrea Hayes. Martin leaned over and planted a kiss on the top of her head, then ruffled her soft, blond hair. 'Woof,' she said. 'I'll go and check on Katie.'

Martin went through to the kitchen and let the dog out before switching on the electric kettle. The coffee was in the freezer. If it had been up to Martin, he'd have made do with instant, but Andy was fussy about her coffee. And she could tell the difference. Martin had long ago given up trying to test her. She didn't think his attempts to palm her off with Nescafé were funny.

'Martin!'

'What?'

'Martin, come here.'

Martin could tell from her voice that something was wrong. He ran down the hall and up the stairs. 'What? What?' he shouted, a tight feeling in the pit of his stomach.

He found Andy standing at the foot of the bed. He put his hand on her shoulder. She was trembling. The bed was empty. Katie had gone. He looked around the room. Nothing. He turned around and went to the bathroom. The door was open and he could see immediately that Katie wasn't there, but he pulled back the shower curtain to assure himself that she wasn't hiding there, that she wasn't playing some sort of crazy game.

'Katie!' he called.

'She's not here. I looked everywhere.'

Martin fought to stay calm. Katie was a seven-year-old girl, and seven-year-old girls didn't just disappear. He knelt down and looked under the bed.

'I did that,' said Andy, her voice quivering. 'I looked there.'

'She has to be here somewhere,' said Martin. 'Maybe she's sleepwalking.'

'She doesn't sleepwalk.'

'Maybe she's started.'

Martin straightened up. They both jumped as they heard a noise downstairs.

'Thank God,' said Andy.

They rushed downstairs, shouting their daughter's name. Andy went into the sitting room. A stand-up comedian was telling a joke but she couldn't follow what he was saying, her thoughts were too jumbled. She couldn't concentrate. Katie wasn't there. Andy even checked behind the sofas. Nothing. The TV laughter annoyed her and she switched the set off.

'Katie, if you're doing this on purpose, you're in big trouble,' she shouted. Her voice echoed around the room.

The dog came scrabbling along the carpet, pink tongue lolling from the side of his mouth.

'It was Dermott,' said Martin. 'He was scratching at the door.'

'She's not in the garden?'

Martin shook his head.

'Oh, Jesus.' Andy put her hands up to her face, her fingers splayed across her cheeks. 'This can't be happening.'

Martin went over to her and put his arm around her shoulders. 'We don't know that anything's happened,' he said. 'There's got to be an explanation for this. She's fallen asleep somewhere, that's all.'

'Jesus, Jesus, Jesus.'

Martin shook her gently. 'Come on, love. Pull yourself together. Let's search the house from top to bottom. She'll be somewhere. She has to be. We'd have heard her if she'd gone out.'

'We were watching TV,' said Andy.

Martin closed his eyes and tried to quell the rising sense of panic that kept threatening to overwhelm him. 'It's going to be all right,' he whispered, but he could hear the doubt in his voice. He opened his eyes again. 'You check upstairs. I'll check the rooms downstairs.' Andy didn't move. He put his hands on her shoulders and moved his face up close to hers. 'Okay?'

Andy nodded uncertainly. Her eyes were brimming with tears and Martin brushed them away. 'We'll check the house and if there's still no sign of her then we'll phone the police, okay?'

'Police?' she repeated.

'We'll find her,' said Martin. 'Go on, up you go. Check the bedrooms. When I've finished down here, I'll come up and check the loft.' He knew they were clutching at straws but he wanted to do something, anything other than picking up the telephone and calling the police. Calling in the police meant that their daughter was missing. Up until the moment he picked up the phone little Katie was sleepwalking or hiding, somewhere in the house. She wasn't lost. Or worse. Martin was prepared to clutch at any straw within reach before he picked up the phone and dialled 999.

He took Andy by the hand and half led, half pulled her into the hallway. He waited until she was climbing the stairs before he went through to the study. Nothing.

He closed the study door and went to the kitchen. He began opening all the kitchen cupboards, knowing that it was useless but wanting to check nevertheless.

'Martin!'

Martin's head jerked round. 'What? Have you found

her?' Even as he said the words he knew that she hadn't. He dashed upstairs. Andy was walking down the landing, an envelope in one hand, a sheet of paper in the other. 'What is it?' asked Martin. 'What's happened?'

'They've take her,' gasped Andy. 'They've taken my baby.'

Her legs gave way beneath her and she fell. Her head smacked against the banister, smearing it with blood before she crashed to the floor and rolled on to her back, the letter still clutched in her fist.

The man in the passenger seat of the Ford Mondeo twisted around and lifted the corner of the tartan blanket.

'Is she still out?' asked the driver.

Katie lay on her back, snoring softly. 'Yeah. You think I should give her more chloroform?'

'Nah. We're almost there.'

'Do you think they'll have read the note yet?' He draped the blanket back over the child.

The driver looked at the digital clock on the dashboard. 'Maybe. They'll let the dog out first, then check on her.'

The passenger settled back in his seat. 'I'm not sure about being so close to their house.'

'Makes no odds,' said the driver. 'Here, the North, over the water – they're not going to know where to look.'

They drove in silence for a while. The passenger spoke first. 'What if . . . you know? What if they don't do what they're supposed to?'

The driver shrugged but didn't reply.

'Would you . . . you know?'

'Would I what?'

The passenger made a gun with his forefinger and thumb. 'Would you?'

'It won't come to that. The threat'll be enough.'

'Are you sure of that?'

The driver threw him a quick look. 'Are you having second thoughts, Mick?'

'No, but . . .'

'There can't be any buts. Buts are what get people killed. We've been told what we've got to do and we do it.'

Another silence, longer this time. Again, it was the passenger who spoke first. 'George?'

'Aye?'

'Have you ever . . .?' He made the gun with his hand again. 'You know?'

'You know I have,' said George McEvoy.

'Nah, I mean a kid. Have you ever offed a kid?'

McEvoy shrugged. 'Man, woman, kid. A life's a life, Mick.'

Mick Canning nodded. He twisted around in his seat and lifted the blanket again. The little girl's mouth was wide open and a thin trickle of frothy dribble was running down her chin. Canning reached across and used a corner of the blanket to wipe the mess away.

'Stop fiddling with her,' said McEvoy tersely. 'You don't want to get too attached.'

Canning frowned and did as he was told.

Andy opened her eyes and blinked. For a second or two she thought she'd been asleep, and then the horror of it all came rushing back and broke over her like an icy wave. Martin was dabbing at her forehead with a damp cloth. 'Easy, love, you had a nasty fall.' Andy tried to sit up, but as she did so her head swam and she felt consciousness slip away again. Martin helped her lie back on the sofa. 'Take it easy,' he said, pressing the cloth to the bridge of her nose.

'What happened?' she asked.

'You fainted.'

Andy took several deep breaths, trying to gather her thoughts. She'd been in Katie's bedroom. The letter. Oh my

God, the letter. She pushed Martin away and forced herself up. 'The letter,' she whispered.

'I've got it,' said Martin.

Andy held out her hand. 'Give it to me.'

Martin gave her the sheet of paper and she read it quickly, even though she could remember it word for word.

ANDREA HAYES

WE HAVE YOUR DAUGHTER. SHE WILL NOT BE HARMED IF YOU DO EXACTLY AS WE SAY. YOU ARE TO TAKE FLIGHT EI172 TO LONDON TOMORROW. A ROOM HAS BEEN BOOKED IN YOUR NAME AT THE STRAND PALACE HOTEL. WAIT THERE FOR FURTHER INSTRUCTIONS. IF YOU CONTACT THE POLICE YOU WILL NEVER SEE YOUR DAUGHTER AGAIN. YOUR HUSBAND IS TO CARRY ON HIS NORMAL ROUTINE. YOU WILL BOTH BE WATCHED. IF WE BELIEVE YOU HAVE CONTACTED THE POLICE YOUR DAUGHTER WILL DIE.

Andy blinked away tears. 'Why?' she asked. 'Why us?'

Martin took the letter from her. It was typed, all capital letters. It looked as if it had been done on a laser printer. The same typeface was on the envelope. Just two words there. ANDREA HAYES.

Martin read the letter again. 'It doesn't say how much,' he said.

'What?'

'It doesn't say how much they want us to pay.' Martin ran his hand through his hair, frowning. 'What sort of ransom demand doesn't mention money?'

'Maybe they'll phone,' said Andy.

'But then why do they want you to go to London? Our money's here, in Ireland. Everything we own is here. If they want paying in London we'd have to fly over with the money. This doesn't make sense.'

'Sense? Why should it make sense? They've kidnapped Katie, they came into our house and took her, why should anything they do make sense?' She could hear the hysteria in her voice and she fought to stay calm.

Martin took her hands in his. 'Don't worry, love. We'll get this sorted. We'll get Katie back. I promise.'

'You can't promise something like that, Martin.'

Martin shook his head. 'They've obviously planned this, Andy. They've thought it all out. They knew where Katie was, they knew where we were. They had the note ready. They've got the hotel room booked in London. It's all been well planned. Kidnapping is a straightforward business transaction. That's what I'm good at, business. We give them money. They give us Katie. That's business. There's no profit in either side trying to screw things up. Okay?'

Andy nodded. What he was saying made sense. It was horrible, it was frightening, but it was logical. It wasn't a pervert who'd stolen her child, it wasn't a sex killer or a paedophile, it was a kidnapper. It wasn't about sexual thrills or sadism, it was about money, and she could just about cope with that. 'What do we do?' she asked.

'We do what they say in the note. You go to London and I guess they'll contact you there to tell you how much they want.'

'Why us, Martin? Why us? We're not rich.'

'We're not short of money, Andy. There are plenty of scumbags out there who'd class us as wealthy. They don't take mortgages and loans and overdrafts into account. They see a couple of new cars and a four-bedroomed house and they think we're rolling in it.' He stood up and went into the kitchen, returning a short while later with two tumblers of whisky. He gave one to her. 'Drink this,' he said.

She swallowed the whisky in two gulps. Martin sat down and read the letter again. He sipped his own whisky thoughtfully. 'I don't understand why they haven't said how much they want. There are things that have to be arranged. We've got to get the money together, they've got to take the money from us. That's all got to be sorted out, and until they tell us what their demands are, there's nothing we can do.'

'We do have the money, don't we?' asked Andy.

Martin stroked her hair and brushed several stray strands away from her face. 'Whatever it takes, we'll get it. I can increase the mortgage, there's cash in the business, we've got friends. It'll be all right.'

Andy nodded through her tears, desperately wanting to believe him.

Egan took off his headphones and leaned back in his chair. He stretched his arms up above his head and rolled his head from side to side, trying to ease the tension in his neck. On the desk in front of him were five digital tape recorders, each linked to radio receivers, one for each of the five listening devices in the Hayes house.

He'd planted the devices three weeks earlier while Andrea Hayes had been out walking her dog. There was one in the smoke detector in the upstairs hallway, one in the phone in the master bedroom, another in the phone in the sitting room. A fourth device was in an electric socket in the downstairs hall and a fifth in a light fitting in the kitchen. They gave him virtually complete coverage of the house.

Egan stood up and went through to the kitchen where he poured himself a mug of black coffee. The studio apartment was in a block just a half-mile away from the Hayes house and he'd rented it for a full twelve months, even though he only expected to be using it for another week. Once the Hayes woman was in place, Egan planned to fly to London to oversee the final phase of the operation. He took his mug back into the sitting room and sat down at the desk. So far everything had gone to plan. Martin and Andrea Hayes were reacting exactly as he'd anticipated.

George McEvoy drove the Mondeo down the rutted track that led to the cottage. The car bucked and swayed and they slowed to a walking pace. The single-storey building was in darkness, and he put the headlights on full beam. 'Home sweet home,' he muttered. 'How is she?'

Mick Canning leaned over and lifted the tartan blanket. Katie was still fast asleep. 'Out like a light,' he said.

McEvoy drove around the back of the cottage and parked by the side of a wooden garage. He climbed out and unlocked the back door of the cottage and switched on a light before waving at Canning to carry the girl in. The nearest house was a hundred yards away and they weren't overlooked at the back.

Canning gathered up Katie, still covered with the blanket, and took her through the kitchen to a white-painted hallway. A wooden door warped with age opened on to a flight of concrete steps that went down into the basement. The underground room had been sparsely furnished with a small camp bed, two wooden chairs and a small Formica-covered table. On the floor was a wool rug that had originally been in front of the fireplace in the sitting room, and in one corner was a bucket, covered with a towel. Canning placed Katie on the bed, then turned her so that she was lying on her side. Still asleep, Katie murmured and put her thumb in her mouth. Canning gently took her thumb out.

'You all right, Mick?' asked McEvoy. He was standing at

the door, looking down into the basement, an expression of barely concealed contempt on his face.

'Yeah, no problem. Do you think we should be with her when she wakes up? She'll be scared, she might start yelling.'

'No one'll hear her,' said McEvoy.

Canning went up the stairs. 'Do you think we should leave the light on?' he asked.

'For fuck's sake, this isn't a hotel,' snapped McEvoy. He closed the door and slid the bolts across.

DAY TWO

Martin Hayes awoke with a start. It took him a few seconds to realise where he was. He was in the sitting room, sprawled on the sofa. He rubbed his face. He was exhausted. How long had he been asleep? He looked at his watch. It was just after seven. 'Andy?' No answer.

He stood up and his knees cracked. He felt stiff and his shoulders ached. He didn't remember coming down to the sitting room. He'd been upstairs with Andy, lying on their bed, propped up with pillows, hoping that the phone would ring. Martin went upstairs. Their bedroom was empty. Martin was still half asleep. Part of him didn't want to wake up, didn't want to accept the reality of his situation. At least when he was asleep he didn't have to think about Katie and what she was going through. Martin just wanted it all to be over, for the kidnappers to tell him how much they wanted and for them to give him back his little girl.

Andy wasn't in the bathroom, either. The door to Katie's room was closed, and even before Martin pushed it open he knew that he'd find his wife sitting on their daughter's bed. She didn't look up as he went over to her. She was clutching a pillow to her chest and was resting her chin on top of it, her eyes closed. Martin sat down next to her.

'They've taken Garfield,' she said.

'What?'

'Garfield. They've kidnapped Garfield, too.'

Andy kept her eyes closed. Tears glistened on her cheeks. Martin looked around the room. Katie's collection of soft toys lined the shelves on the wall that faced the end of the bed, and others were crammed on to the windowsill. Martin knew that Katie had given them all names, but he knew only a few of them. Bunny. Babe. Foxy. Wilkinson the badger. Andy was right. There was no Garfield, and Garfield was the favourite of late – he was the one she cuddled when she went to sleep. There were two gaps on the windowsill, too, but he wasn't able to remember which toys, if any, were missing.

Martin knelt down beside the single bed and peered under it. No Garfield.

'There's a teddy bear missing, too. The one my father got her two Christmasses ago. And the monkey. The one we got at Regent's Park Zoo. In April. The one with the silly grin and the banana.' Andy's voice was flat and emotionless.

'That's a good sign, Andy,' said Martin.

She looked up at him and opened her eyes. They were as devoid of emotion as her voice. 'A good sign?' she repeated.

He sat down on the bed and put his arm around her. 'They wouldn't have taken her toys if they were going to hurt her,' he said. 'They want her to be happy so they took along some toys. Trust me, it's a good sign. We'll have her back soon.'

She nodded but her eyes were still vacant. She was in shock, Martin realised. 'Come on downstairs, you need a cup of tea,' he said.

Andy nodded. 'I guess,' she said, but she made no move to stand up.

Mick Canning was breaking eggs into a frying pan when Katie started shouting and banging on the basement door. 'Help!' she yelled. 'Let me out!'

George McEvoy looked up from his copy of the *Irish*

Times and scowled at the door. 'Her ladyship's awake,' he said.

'I'll see to her,' said Canning, handing a spatula to McEvoy. 'You look after the eggs, yeah?'

'Don't forget your . . .'

'Balaclava, yeah, I know,' interrupted Canning. He picked up his rucksack and went down the hall. From the pocket of his track-suit top he pulled out a rolled-up ski mask and put it on before unbolting the door. 'Katie, stand away from the door,' he said.

There was a short silence. 'Who is that? I want my mummy.'

'Your mummy's not here, Katie. I'm a friend of hers. Look, I'm opening the door now, be careful.'

Katie was standing four steps down, staring wide-eyed up at Canning. The basement was in darkness. Canning unfastened the neck of the rucksack and took out the Garfield toy. 'I brought this for you,' he said, holding it out to her.

She looked at the soft toy, then back at him. 'I want to go home,' she said.

'You can't. Not right now.'

She glared at him and put her hands on her hips, her chin thrust up defiantly. 'You can't tell me what to do.'

'Yes I can,' he said patiently. 'And I'm telling you that you have to stay here for a few days.' He held out the soft toy again.

Katie looked as if she was going to argue, then she reached for Garfield. 'Thank you,' she said.

Canning was about to say 'You're welcome' when she hurled the toy at his face and scrambled up the stairs, slipping by his legs before he had the chance to stop her. Canning cursed and tried to grab her, but she was too quick for him. Her bare feet padded down the hallway towards the kitchen.

Canning ran after her, cursing. He caught up with her in

three strides and grabbed her by the scruff of her nightie. He yanked her off her feet, then scooped her up. She began to wriggle and scream.

McEvoy opened the kitchen door with the frying pan in his hand. Canning span around so that Katie couldn't see McEvoy's face. 'What the fuck are you playing at?' McEvoy shouted.

'Nothing,' said Canning. 'It's not a problem.'

'It looks like a fucking problem to me,' said McEvoy. 'Put her in the basement and make sure she shuts up.' He slammed the kitchen door.

Katie continued to struggle as Canning carried her down the basement steps. 'I want my mummy!' she screamed. 'I want my mummy and I want my dad.'

'Please, be quiet,' hissed Canning.

'I'll be quiet if you let me go,' she said.

'I can't let you go . . .' Canning began, but he'd barely got the words out of his mouth before she began screaming again. He dropped her down on the camp bed and put his hand over her mouth. It smothered her screams, but Canning had a sudden flash about what he was doing and jerked his hand away as if he'd been burnt. Jesus Christ. He'd had his hand over a child's mouth. He could have killed her. Smothered her. He took a step back, his hands up as if surrendering. Katie seemed as shocked as he was.

'What?' she said.

'I'm sorry,' he said. 'I didn't mean to . . . you know . . .'

'What?'

'I didn't mean to put my hand over your mouth. I wasn't trying to . . . I wasn't trying to hurt you.'

Katie swung her legs over the side of the camp bed and sat looking at him curiously. 'Why are you wearing a mask?' she asked.

'So you won't know who I am,' he said. 'That way, when

26

we send you back to your parents, you won't be able to tell the police what I look like.' Canning crouched down so that his head was on a level with hers. 'Look, I'm sorry if I scared you. But you have to do as we say, okay? You have to stay down here for a few days, then you can go home.'

'You promise?'

Canning made the sign of the cross on his chest. 'Swear to die.'

Andy Hayes put down the phone. 'They'll hold the ticket for me at the airport,' she said.

Martin nodded. 'I'll drive you.'

'You can't,' she said. 'You have to carry on as normal, that's what the letter said. You have to go to work.' She looked at her watch.

'I think I should stay by the phone. They might call.'

Andy shook her head fiercely. 'They said you had to carry out your normal routine. That means going to work, Martin. We mustn't do anything that makes them think we're not co-operating.'

Martin shrugged. 'I guess so.'

Andy's face hardened. 'No, there's no I-guess-so about this. I want you to promise me that you won't call the police.'

'Oh, come on, do you think I'd do anything that would put Katie in danger?'

'Promise me, Martin. Promise me that you won't do anything out of the ordinary.'

Martin took her in his arms and kissed her hair. 'I promise.'

She hugged him tightly. 'I'll call you from London. They didn't say that I couldn't do that.'

Martin stroked the back of her neck. 'It's going to be all right, Andy. I promise.'

*   *   *

McEvoy put on his ski mask and picked up the tray. On it was a paper plate of spaghetti hoops, a slice of bread, and a plastic fork.

'I'll take it,' said Canning. He was sitting at the table working on the crossword in the *Irish Times*. Like McEvoy he'd changed out of his track suit and was wearing a sweatshirt and jeans.

'That's all right, Mick. I'll handle it. Where are the scissors?'

Canning gestured with his chin. 'By the sink. You should give her some milk.'

'Milk?'

'To drink. She'll need something to drink.'

McEvoy put the tray down. He picked up the scissors and slipped them into the back pocket of his jeans.

'You haven't got kids, have you, George?' said Canning, looking up from his crossword.

'Not that I know of,' said McEvoy. 'Your point being?'

He chuckled, went over to the fridge, opened it and took out a carton of milk. He poured some into a plastic cup and then put the carton back in the fridge. 'Anything else I should take her ladyship?' he asked.

Canning ignored him and concentrated on the crossword.

McEvoy went over to the door that led to the basement and juggled the tray as he slipped the bolts. He eased the door open with his foot and peered down the stairs. Katie was sitting on the camp bed, her Garfield in her lap. She looked up and watched him walk down the stairs. He put the tray on the bed next to her and she looked at it disdainfully. 'Spaghetti hoops?'

'Leave it if you don't want it,' said McEvoy curtly.

'What else is there to eat?'

'Nothing. It's spaghetti hoops or nothing.'

Katie sniffed and rested her head on top of Garfield.

McEvoy took the scissors from his back pocket. Katie looked at him fearfully.

'Please don't,' said Katie, clasping Garfield tightly.

'It won't hurt if you don't move,' said McEvoy.

Andy opened the suitcase and stared at its interior. What was she supposed to pack? She didn't even know how long she was going to be away. She closed the suitcase again and went over to the wardrobe. The front was mirrored and she stared at her reflection. Fly to London and wait, the letter said. Wait for further instructions. Did that mean they would send her somewhere else? Or would she collect Katie in London? Should she pack for Katie, too? She opened the wardrobe and ran a hand along the dresses and jackets hanging there. Maybe she shouldn't take anything with her. If anyone saw her leaving the house with a suitcase, they'd wonder where she was going. What would she say? That she was going away for a holiday? On her own? What if she met anyone she knew at the airport?

She heard Martin climbing the stairs, a heavy footfall as if every step was an effort. He walked up behind her and put his hands on her shoulders. 'I don't know what to take with me,' she said.

'Pack for a couple of days,' he said.

'Pack what?'

'Jeans. Shirts. Underwear. Hell, Andy, I don't know.' His fingers moved around her neck and he massaged her slowly.

'Why me, Martin? Why do they want me in London and you here? Why haven't they told us what they want?'

She felt her husband shrug. 'Maybe Katie's already in London. Maybe they took her over the water and that's where they'll give her back to us.'

Andy turned to face him. 'Do you think that's it?'

'It's possible. Dublin's a small city – it'd be easier to hide her in London. They could have taken her over on the ferry, in a car. Hidden her in the boot or . . .' His mouth snapped shut when he saw the look of horror on her face.

'Boot? Oh my God . . .' Tears welled up in her eyes and Martin hugged her.

'Oh, Jesus, Andy, I don't know what I'm saying. I'm just guessing. I don't know where she is or what they're doing. Don't get upset. Please.' He wiped away her tears with his thumbs, smearing them across her cheeks. 'I'll drive you to the airport.'

Andy shook her head. 'You can't,' she said. 'You have to go to work.'

'The airport's on the way.'

Andy reached up and held his wrists. 'We talked about this last night. You have to do everything as normal, Martin.'

'This is different,' said Martin. 'They know you're going to the airport – they'll expect me to take you.'

'I don't know . . .'

'I want to,' said Martin.

Andy sat down on the bed, too tired to argue. She'd barely slept, and it was as if she was thinking in slow motion. 'Okay,' she said.

Martin sat next to her and put his arm around her. 'Look, I'll drop you at the airport, then I'll go straight to the office. I'll talk to the bank, see how much we've got on deposit.'

'I hope it's enough,' she said.

'If it isn't, we can raise more,' said Martin. 'We've got the cash flow, we've got assets. The house alone is worth twice the mortgage. We can raise a hundred grand on a phone call.'

Tears began to stream down Andy's cheeks. 'Why us, Martin?' she asked. 'Why our Katie?'

'I don't know. I really don't know.'

She put her arms around his waist and buried her face in his neck, her body racked by silent sobs. Martin held her, feeling more helpless than he'd ever felt in his life.

* * *

30

Canning walked through the arrivals area, tapping the copy of the *Irish Times* against his leg. He bought a coffee, sat on a stool and surveyed the terminal. Eager faces watched the sliding doors that kept opening and closing, disgorging a stream of passengers. Canning cast his eyes over the paper's headlines. Government figures showing the Irish economy was booming. Rumours that the American President might make a flying visit to Dublin during his trip to Europe. A supermodel overdosed on heroin. Canning sipped his coffee. He flicked through the pages to the crossword. Only six clues to finish.

A woman pulled out the stool on the other side of his table. 'Do you mind?' she asked. She was slim in a pale grey business suit, carrying a burgundy briefcase and a mobile telephone. Her shoulder-length hair was blond, but the dark roots suggested that it had been dyed. There was something unnatural about her eyes, too. They were almost too green, as if she were wearing contact lenses.

Canning waved at the stool. 'Help yourself,' he said. He took a small padded envelope from the inside pocket of his jacket and slipped it between the pages of the newspaper, which he then folded and placed on the table.

The woman ripped the corner off a pack of sweetener and poured it into her coffee. Canning slid off his stool, nodded at the woman, and walked away. He didn't see her take the newspaper and put it in her briefcase.

Andy couldn't bear to say goodbye to her husband. She forced a smile and then walked away from the car. She could feel Martin watching her but she didn't turn around. She walked through the doors into the departure area. There was a queue of half a dozen people ahead of her having their luggage checked. A uniformed policeman ran some sort of detector over her suitcase. He was in his fifties with the sunburned skin and broken veins of a sailor. He smiled at her and waved her through. Andy wondered what he'd been checking for. Guns? Explosives? Drugs? The check had seemed cursory at best, as if he wasn't expecting to find anything.

The ticket was ready for her at the Aer Lingus sales counter. She took it over to the check-in counter and a young man in shirtsleeves checked her in. He asked her about her case – had she packed it herself, had it been out of her sight, did it contain electrical items? Andy barely listened to the questions. They seemed naïve. If she hadn't packed it herself, would they open it and go through her belongings? If it contained a bomb, would she tell them? The security precautions seemed as ridiculous as the middle-aged policeman with his detector. Her daughter had been kidnapped, for God's sake. Taken from her bed in the middle of the night, and she was being asked if she had batteries in her luggage. She had to fight to stop herself from screaming.

McEvoy tensed as he heard the car pull up outside. He looked at his watch. It was too soon for Canning to have got back from the airport. He picked up his Smith & Wesson, cocked the hammer, and moved on tiptoe to the back door. Outside, a car door opened and then slammed shut. Footsteps crunched along the path, towards the cottage. McEvoy flattened himself against the kitchen wall, the gun at the ready. The footsteps stopped. McEvoy breathed heavily, his mouth half open, his ears straining to hear what was going on outside. Someone knocked on the door. Three short raps. Then silence.

'Who is it?' McEvoy called, his finger tense on the trigger. There was no reply. 'Who's there?' he repeated. No answer. McEvoy took the door key from his jeans pocket and slid it into the lock. He turned it, wincing at the loud metallic click, then pulled his hand away. Far off in the distance, a dog barked. Then another, closer. Not police dogs, McEvoy decided. Besides, if it was the police, and if it was a raid, they wouldn't knock first.

He eased closer to the door, grabbed the handle, and pulled it open. There was no one there. He slowly moved across the threshold, the gun still raised. Whoever it was, they weren't there any more. Why hadn't he heard them walk away? A black Ford Scorpio was parked where the Mondeo had been.

'Is there anybody there?' he called. The only sound was the wind whistling through the conifers at the end of the garden. McEvoy held the gun at his side as he walked towards the car. The rear of the cottage wasn't overlooked, but he didn't want to risk waving the gun around in the open. The Scorpio was a rental, and it was locked. McEvoy looked around, the wind tugging at his unkempt black hair. He shivered. He was wearing only a thin denim shirt and cotton trousers and he had no shoes on his feet.

He padded back to the cottage and locked the kitchen door. As he went through to the sitting room, something hard was rammed against the side of his neck. 'Surprise!'

'Fuck,' said McEvoy. 'How the hell did you get in?'

The gun was taken away from his neck. 'That's for me to know,' said Egan, tucking the gun back into the waistband of his jeans.

'You couldn't have got in through the back door,' said McEvoy, flicking the safety catch of the .38 into place. 'You were lucky I didn't blow your fucking head off.'

Egan raised a disbelieving eyebrow and McEvoy felt his cheeks flush with embarrassment. He knew that if it had been for real it would have been his brains and not Egan's that were splattered across the carpet. 'Canning's at the airport?' asked Egan. He zipped up his leather bomber jacket and looked around the room. There was a half-empty bottle of Bushmills on the coffee table and dirty plates left over from the previous night's meal, a cardboard box on the floor, and a video camera and a stack of videotapes on the sofa. Egan picked up the camera and checked it. He was wearing black leather gloves.

McEvoy nodded. 'Should be back in an hour or so.'

'How are you getting on with him?'

McEvoy shrugged indifferently. 'He'll do.'

'And the girl?'

'No problems.' He jerked a thumb at the basement door. 'Quiet as a lamb.'

Egan put the camera down. 'Good job, George. Couldn't have done it better myself.' He reached into the inside pocket of his bomber jacket and took out an envelope. He handed it to McEvoy. 'Bonus for you.'

McEvoy took the envelope and slid it unopened into his back pocket. 'Cheers.'

'Split it with Canning if you want, but I'll leave it up to you.' He nodded at the video camera and the cassettes. 'Get them done as soon as you can, yeah? Then get Canning to take them over to McCracken.'

They walked outside together. 'Make sure you torch the cottage afterwards,' said Egan. 'Burn it to the ground. Forensic scientists these days, all they need is one hair. The car, too.'

'And the rest of the money?' McEvoy had been paid twenty thousand pounds in advance and had been promised a further eighty thousand pounds, not counting the bonus in his pocket.

Egan patted him on the back. 'It'll be in the account within ten days,' he said. He climbed into the Scorpio and McEvoy watched him drive away.

McEvoy went back into the cottage and locked the kitchen door. He took out the envelope and riffled through the notes. Five thousand pounds. New notes. McEvoy stuffed the envelope back into his pocket. Egan was a true professional. When he had first approached him, McEvoy had been suspicious. Kidnapping, especially kidnapping a child, wasn't something that could be done lightly. Egan seemed to know everything about McEvoy, from the state of his bank account to his record with the Provisional Irish Republican Army. He seemed to know where all McEvoy's bodies were buried, figuratively and literally. Some of the information Egan had could only have come from the IRA's Army Council. Other details had obviously been obtained from government computers. McEvoy, however, knew next to nothing about Egan. He was an American, that was clear from his accent, and he had a military bearing that suggested he'd been in the armed forces, but he remained tight-lipped about his background. He was equally reticent about what he was up to, and would only give McEvoy and Canning the information they needed to carry out the kidnapping. It was for their own protection, he insisted. The less they knew, the less they could tell the authorities in the event of them being captured. Egan had assured McEvoy and Canning that the same level of secrecy applied over in England. If anything went wrong there, the two men wouldn't be implicated.

McEvoy went through to the sitting room and poured himself a measure of Bushmills. He sat down and put his feet up on the coffee table. It wasn't the first kidnapping that McEvoy had been involved in, but this was the first time he was doing it purely for financial reasons. It was the first time he'd been involved with the kidnapping of a child, too. Not that the fact that the victim was a seven-year-old girl worried McEvoy. The victim was meat, nothing more. A means to an end. He sipped his whiskey and brooded.

Martin's company was based on an industrial estate twenty miles north of Dublin. The offices were in an H-shaped brick building with a flat roof, with a storage yard for heavy equipment behind and car parking spaces in front. When business was slow the yard would be full of earth movers, trucks and cement mixers, but for the past two years the company had been busier than ever and the yard was virtually empty. He parked and walked through reception to the management offices. His secretary looked up from her word-processor. 'Coffee?' Jill Gannon had been with the company for more than a decade. She was in her fifties, with a matronly figure that defeated all dieting and a kindly face that always seemed to be smiling. Martin had never seen her depressed, or without a chocolate bar on her desk.

'No thanks, Jill. And don't put any calls through for the next half an hour or so.' He went inside his office and closed the door. He telephoned his bank and asked for the balance of his accounts. There was a little over ten thousand in his current account, another thirty thousand in a deposit account. Martin wrote the numbers down and then called a building society in the Channel Islands. He had a further ninety thousand pounds there, out of the reach of the Irish taxman. He arranged to have it transferred to his current account in Dublin, though he was told that they wouldn't be able to carry out the transfer until they received written confirmation. Martin promised to send a letter by courier.

His next call was to his stockbroker, Jamie O'Connor. Jamie was an old friend – they'd been at school together and lived less than a mile from each other. According to Jamie, Martin's stock portfolio was worth just under a quarter of a million pounds.

'How long would it take to turn it into cash?' Martin asked.

'Cash? You want to sell them all? Jesus, Martin, I wouldn't recommend that. The market here might be getting a bit toppy, but you've got a worldwide portfolio, and besides, you're taking a long-term view, right?'

'Things change, Jamie.' The shares and bonds had been

acquired over a ten-year period and had been intended as Martin's pension fund. It would be easier to liquidate the portfolio than to arrange an overdraft or remortgage the house. He could always buy more shares. The company was flourishing, and if they went public as planned the shares he'd be placing would be worth millions. 'Could you sell everything by close of business today?'

'I could, sure. But I wouldn't recommend it. The Irish shares, okay, but your Far Eastern exposure has taken a bit of a tumble recently. I'd suggest you hang on to them. And there's a couple of your holdings that are due to pay their annual dividends next month – you'd be better off keeping them until they've gone ex-dividend.'

'Everything, Jamie.'

'Martin, are you okay? Has something happened?'

'Everything's fine. I just need some cash, that's all. Andy's got her heart set on a villa in Portugal and like a fool I agreed to buy it for her. We can afford it, what with the flotation and all.'

'Well, it's your decision, of course. All I can do is offer my professional advice, and I wouldn't recommend liquidating a perfectly decent portfolio of shares to buy a villa in Portugal.'

'Advice noted, Jamie. Close of business today, right?'

There was a slight hesitation from the broker, as if he was about to argue but then decided not to press the point. 'Consider it done.'

'And put the money straight into my current account with Allied Irish, will you?'

'Oh, now that's just being silly, Martin. You'll be throwing away the interest.'

'I'm going to need it in a hurry. Do you need written confirmation?'

'No need. All the firm's conversations are recorded. Look, are you sure about this?'

'Dead sure, Jamie. Look, I've got another call. I'll talk to you again soon.'

Martin put down the phone. A quarter of a million pounds, plus the money already in the bank, gave him a total of three hundred and eighty thousand pounds. Surely that would be enough? He sat at his desk with his head in his hands. What if it wasn't? What if they wanted more? What would he do then?

'Something to drink?' asked the stewardess.

The voice jolted Andy out of her daydream. 'Sorry?'

The plastic smile was a little less friendly, as if the stewardess resented having to ask twice. 'Would you like a drink?'

Andy shook her head. The stewardess served the elderly couple who were sitting next to Andy and pushed her trolley down the aisle. Andy closed her eyes. Images of Katie filled her mind. Katie laughing at cartoons on the television, Katie smiling in her sleep, Katie holding her arms out to be lifted up and hugged. Andy breathed in through her nose. She could almost imagine that she was inhaling the fragrance of her daughter's hair, sweet and clean. She wondered how Katie was feeling. Would she be scared? Crying for her mother? Would the men holding her be taking good care of her? Andy pictured her crouching tearfully in the corner of a dark room, with a menacing figure standing over her. She shivered and opened her eyes. It wasn't fair. It just wasn't fair. What had Katie ever done to deserve this? Katie, who'd never harmed anyone, never shown anything but love to everyone around her, to strangers even. Katie, who was forever asking her parents to give money to the beggars in St Stephen's Green, to adopt stray cats and to send money to each and every charitable appeal featured on television. Katie was a little angel, and whoever was putting her through this ordeal would burn in hell. Andy promised herself that whatever happened she would get her revenge on the men who'd kidnapped Katie. If it took her for ever, she'd make them pay.

She looked out of the window. Through the wispy clouds below she could make out the English coastline. It had been six months since she'd last been in London, a surprise weekend trip to celebrate her birthday. Martin had arranged everything – tickets for *Cats*, two nights in the Savoy and a rose on her pillow. Her parents had looked after Katie, but Andy had phoned every night. She'd always hated to be away from her daughter.

The captain announced that they were starting their descent and that they'd be landing within twenty minutes. Andy checked her seat belt. At the rear of the plane, the woman with dyed blond hair and unnaturally green eyes slid her burgundy briefcase under the seat in front of her.

Martin looked up as the quick double knock was followed almost immediately by the office door opening. It was his partner, Padraig, his coat on and carrying his briefcase. 'Are you up for a drink?' he asked. Padraig was red-haired with a sprinkling of freckles across his nose, broad-shouldered from long sessions in the gym.

'Nah, I want to get back,' said Martin.

'What about you and Andy coming around for dinner tomorrow? Louise wants to try out her fondue set. Up-market cheese dip.'

'Tomorrow's not good, mate. Maybe next week. I'll check with Andy and let you know, okay?'

Padraig gave him a thumbs-up. 'Okay, I'm off, then. I'm sure I'll find somebody to drink with at the golf club.'

The telephone rang as Padraig closed the door. It was Jamie O'Connor, confirming that the entire portfolio had been sold. A total of two hundred and sixty-eight thousand pounds, which had been wired to Martin's current account in Dublin.

Martin thanked him and put the phone down. He had the money, but why hadn't he heard from the kidnappers? He'd checked with Jill several times but there had been no calls that she hadn't put through. Maybe they were going to phone him at home. Maybe they'd already phoned Andy in London.

Martin had called directory enquiries and asked for the telephone number of the Strand Palace Hotel. He hadn't called, though several times he'd started to dial the number. He was supposed to behave as normal, but did that mean that it was okay to telephone his wife?

The intercom on his desk buzzed, startling him. It was Jill, telling him that she was going home. He said goodnight. It was six o'clock. What was he supposed to do now? He was normally in the office until seven, but did the kidnappers know that the switchboard closed when Jill went home? Would they try to phone the office number? What would they do if they couldn't get through?

He stood up and paced around the office. It was the not knowing that was driving him crazy. Not knowing the timescale, not knowing how much they wanted, not knowing how they intended to collect the money. And worst of all, not knowing what they had done to his dear, darling daughter. He kicked the door to his office and then punched it, so hard that he bruised his knuckles. He licked the bleeding flesh as tears pricked his eyes.

Andy sat on the hotel bed, staring at the telephone. All she had to do was to pick it up and within seconds she could be talking to her husband. Or the police. She shook her head. What could the police do?

She heard a whispering sound at the door and she went over to it. There was a white envelope on the floor. She picked it up and reached for the door handle, then hesitated. What would happen if she opened the door and saw whoever had delivered the envelope? What if she saw his face? She felt helpless – she didn't know how she was supposed to react or what she was supposed to do. All control had been taken from her. She went back to the bed and sat down again. The envelope had been sealed and she used a fingernail to slit it open. Her mind was whirling. Forensic evidence, she thought. Fingerprints. Saliva. DNA. She had to keep the envelope – the police would be able to get information about the kidnappers from it.

There was a single sheet of paper inside. Andy unfolded it. It was hotel notepaper and the letter was typed. Capital letters again. Andy read it with shaking hands.

YOUR DAUGHTER IS QUITE SAFE AND SO LONG AS YOU FOLLOW OUR INSTRUCTIONS SHE WILL NOT BE HARMED.

AT NINE O'CLOCK TOMORROW MORNING YOU ARE TO CHECK OUT. TAKE ALL YOUR THINGS WITH YOU.

TURN RIGHT OUT OF THE HOTEL AND WALK DOWN THE STRAND. TURN RIGHT INTO BEDFORD STREET, AND LEFT INTO BEDFORD COURT. YOU WILL SEE A MULTI-STOREY CARPARK ON YOUR LEFT.

GO INSIDE THE CARPARK. GO UP TO THE THIRD FLOOR. THERE YOU WILL SEE A DARK BLUE TRANSIT VAN. ON THE SIDE OF THE VAN IS THE NAME OF A LANDSCAPING FIRM.

MAKE SURE NO ONE IS WATCHING YOU. OPEN THE REAR DOOR OF THE VAN AND GET IN. CLOSE THE DOOR BEHIND YOU. INSIDE

*THE VAN YOU WILL FIND A BLACK HOOD.
PUT IT OVER YOUR HEAD AND WAIT.*

   *WE DO NOT INTEND TO CAUSE YOU ANY
HARM. BUT MAKE NO MISTAKE. IF YOU DIS-
OBEY OR IF YOU MAKE ANY ATTEMPT TO
CONTACT THE POLICE, YOUR DAUGHTER
WILL DIE.*

Andy reread the letter several times. A van? A hood? What did these people want from her? She looked at her watch. It was six o'clock in the evening. Fifteen hours before she was supposed to check out. What was she supposed to do for fifteen hours? She read the letter again. It didn't say. Why the delay? Was it because they were watching her, checking that she wasn't being followed?

She stood up and began pacing up and down the room. Was she allowed to contact Martin? The letter said only that she wasn't to talk to the police. Would they consider a phone call to Martin a breach of the conditions? Had they tapped the phone in Dublin? Could she risk it?

She stopped at the window and looked out on to the busy street below. Who was doing this to her? Who had turned her life upside down? And why?

Martin Hayes lay staring up at the ceiling. There was no way he'd be able to sleep, but he knew he had to make the effort. It wouldn't help anyone if he collapsed from exhaustion.

He'd got back home just after seven and had sat next to the telephone for most of the evening, willing it to ring. It had, once, but it was only Padraig checking that Martin had seen a letter from one of their suppliers, raising prices by twenty per cent and blaming the strong pound. They'd chatted for a while, but Martin had been fairly abrupt with his partner, not wanting to tie up the phone line. He had the 'call waiting' facility, but he didn't want to do anything that might spook the kidnappers.

He rolled over and curled up into a ball. His stomach ached, but it wasn't hunger. He'd forced himself to eat a ham sandwich in the office, and he'd eaten a can of soup when he got home, though he hadn't tasted anything. What he really wanted was a drink, but the way he felt he doubted that he'd be able to stop at one. It would be so easy to use alcohol to take the edge off his panic, but he knew it'd be a big mistake. He had to keep a clear head, he had to remain totally focused on what he had to do.

The telephone rang and Martin sat bolt upright. He grabbed for the receiver. 'Yes?'

'Martin?' It was Andy, her voice little more than a whisper.

'Hiya, love. Are you okay?'

'Can't sleep. I'm just lying here. Martin . . .'

Martin could hear the despair in her voice. 'I'm still here, love.'

'Have they called you?'

'No. Nothing. I've spoken to the bank, and I've sold our shares and stuff. The money's in the bank and there's no problem in raising more. All we need now is to know how much they want.'

'Martin . . .'

She was close to crying, and Martin wished with all his heart that she was in the bed with him and that he could reach over and cuddle her.

'Martin . . . I'm not sure if this is about money.'

'What do you mean?'

'They want me to go somewhere tomorrow.'

'Where?'

'A van. I have to go to a van in a carpark around the corner. I guess they're going to take me somewhere.' There was a long pause, and Martin thought they'd lost the connection until he heard her breathe. 'I'm not sure if we should even be talking,' she said. 'Maybe they're listening.'

'If they're listening, love, they know that we haven't gone to the police. They know that we're doing everything they've asked. They know that there's no reason not to give Katie back to us. Okay?'

'I suppose so,' she said, but he could tell from her tone that she wasn't convinced.

'It's going to be all right, love,' said Martin. 'Do you know where they want to take you?'

'They didn't say. It was a note, like before. They haven't called you?'

'No.'

'Martin, if it was money they wanted, they'd have called by now, wouldn't they?'

'I don't know what they're playing at, love.'

There was another long silence. 'It couldn't be to do with the business, could it?' she said eventually.

'In what way?'

'You haven't been doing business with anybody you shouldn't have? Have you?'

'Jesus, Andy, what a thing to say.' Martin was stunned. It was as if she were trying to find some way of blaming him for what had happened. 'What would make you think that?'

'Well, why else could this be happening? Why would anyone take Katie and then make me do this? Check into a hotel. Get into a van. It's as if they want you on your own. Isolated. That's why I thought maybe it wasn't about money.' There was another pause.

'We don't have any choice, Andy. We have to do what they say. They've obviously got something planned.'

'I know that. Look, are you sure it's not connected to the business, Martin? You haven't crossed somebody? Do you owe somebody money?'

'The company's never been better,' said Martin. 'Our

overdraft is well under control, orders are coming in, we've a few problems with suppliers, but we're well ahead of where we were this time last year.'

'I know you've always kept problems from me,' said Andy. 'The times the business was going through a rough patch, you never let on. I knew, but you never told me. I just thought . . .'

'It's late at night and the demons are out, that's all. You're thinking too much. I'm the same. I've been lying here imagining all sorts of things, but that's all it is. Imagination. And if it was to do with the business, there'd have been some lead-up to it. They wouldn't just snatch Katie. There'd be threats, there'd be other pressures they'd apply. And Andy, love, the sort of people I do business with wouldn't dream of hurting a child. Or a wife. They're men and they behave like men.' There was no answer from his wife. 'Andy, did you hear what I said?'

'Yes.' There was a tearful sniff. 'I'm sorry, Martin. I just feel . . . alone, you know.'

'I know exactly what you mean, love. This bed has never felt so bloody big. What's your room like there?'

'It's okay. I wish I was there with you.'

'Mutual. Times a million.'

'I just wish it was over.'

'I know,' said Martin. 'It won't be much longer, I'm sure. They must want to get this over with as quickly as we do.'

'Oh God, I hope so.'

'Try to get some sleep, okay?'

'I'll try.' She sniffed again. 'I wonder how they're treating Katie. She'll be so scared.'

'I'm sure they'll be taking good care of her. They won't hurt her. Everything they're doing depends on us getting her back safely. Try not to worry. I know that's an impossible thing to ask, but try.'

'I'll try. I have to check out at nine. I'll try to call you later in the day.'

Martin said goodbye and replaced the receiver. A van? What the hell did they want her to get into a van for? Martin had been doing his best to keep his wife's spirits up, but he knew that she was right. This was about more than money. But what?

Egan replayed the tape of the conversation between Andrea Hayes and her husband. He frowned as he listened, but by the time he had played it through to the end he was smiling to himself. Andrea had said nothing that could jeopardise the operation. If anything, the conversation would make the Hayes woman more compliant. Her husband had been reassuring. Soothing, even.

Egan had half expected the Hayes woman to call her husband. At this stage, he wanted their full co-operation, and that meant keeping their stress levels as low as possible. If the notes had insisted that there be no contact, there was a chance that one or the other might panic and call in the police. The phone call also gave Egan an insight into how they were thinking. They were scared for their daughter, but it was clear that they were going to do everything that was asked of them. They still believed that the kidnapping was money-motivated. By the time they realised what was really going on, it would be too late.

DAY THREE

Andy stood in the middle of the hotel room, looking around. She had to do something. She had to let Martin know what was happening. She'd wanted to say more to him on the phone the previous night, but couldn't take the risk that someone had been listening in. But now she was preparing to check out of the hotel, and she realised that it might be the last opportunity she had to get a message to her husband. She had to let him know where she was going, because if anything went wrong it might be the only way he could find out where Katie was. She thought of leaving a message in the room, but even if she addressed it to Martin the chambermaid might open it, and if she realised its significance she'd probably pass it on to the police. And there was a possibility that the people who had kidnapped Katie might be preparing to search her room after she checked out. If they found a letter, there was no saying what they might do to Katie.

Above the writing desk was a framed watercolour of a gondola on a canal, the colours all hazy as if viewed through a mist. Andy stared at the picture. There had to be something she could do to let Martin know where she was going. Suddenly she knew exactly what she had to do. She sat down at the desk and opened the leather writing folder that was embossed with the hotel's name. There were several sheets of writing paper, and a ballpoint pen. She began to write furiously.

47

It was just after nine when she walked up to the cashier's desk. A blonde receptionist with shocking-pink lipstick and matching nail varnish took her credit card and printed out a copy of the bill. 'Anything from the mini-bar?' she asked, and Andy shook her head. She pretended to check the print-out while she had a quick look around to see if anyone was looking at her. An old couple were sitting on a sofa close to the door, and half a dozen Japanese tourists were pulling brochures off a rack. A businessman in a dark blue suit was checking in, his briefcase at his feet like an attentive Labrador, and a woman in a fur coat was using one of the house phones. No one appeared to be paying Andy any attention. She slid an envelope from inside her jacket, put it on top of the print-out and slid them both across the counter to the receptionist.

'Could you do me a favour?' asked Andy. 'If my husband should pop by in the next few days, could you give this to him?'

The receptionist looked at the envelope. Andy had written 'MARTIN HAYES' in capital letters. 'I could post it, if you like?'

Andy shook her head. 'He's not at home. He's travelling. He had hoped to meet me here but I've got to go up to my parents'. She nodded at the envelope. 'It's not really that important. If he doesn't call for it, you can throw it away.'

'No problem,' said the receptionist. She gave Andy a credit card slip to sign and put the envelope in a drawer. Andy left the hotel. She followed the instructions she'd been given the previous evening and carried her suitcase into the multi storey carpark. The blue Transit van was on the third floor. There was a sign on the side that said 'CITY LAND-SCAPING', and underneath it an 0181 telephone number. Andy put her suitcase on the floor by the rear doors. A man in a blue suit and a red tie drove by in a BMW. Andy wondered if she was being watched, if someone had followed her from the hotel. She'd looked around a couple of times but the streets were too crowded for her to have picked anyone out.

Another car drove by, a grey Volvo hatchback. Then there was silence. Andy reached out and turned the door handle. She'd half expected, hoped maybe, that it would be locked, but it turned easily and she pulled open the door and threw her suitcase in. She took a last look around the carpark and then climbed in after the suitcase.

She sat down and scanned the metal floor of the van. There was no sign of a hood. She took the typed letter out of her jacket pocket and reread it. A black hood. There should be a black hood. She got down on her hands and knees and checked the corners, right up to the seats at the front. There was no hood. Had she got the wrong van? No, of course not. It was blue, it was a Transit, and it was on the third floor. And it had the name of a landscaping firm on the side. It had to be the right van. She crawled over to the suitcase and lifted it up. The hood was underneath it. She felt a sudden surge of relief. So long as everything went as planned, then she'd get her daughter back. It was like a long line of dominoes, standing on end – they all had to be in the right place so that when they were pushed, they'd all fall down. The hood was one of the dominoes, and the fact that it was there reassured her. It was going to be all right. Katie was safe.

She pulled the door closed behind her and locked it. The hood was made of some sort of woollen material with a drawstring around the open end, like a bag that might be used to hold shoes. She held it to her nose and sniffed. It smelt like a new cardigan. It didn't feel particularly thick, but even so she was worried about how easy it would be to breathe through. The kidnappers had planned everything down to the last detail, but she doubted that they'd have put the bag over their own heads to try it out. She slowly pulled it on, then put her hands on the drawstring. She couldn't bring herself to tighten the bag around the neck. After taking a few deep breaths to steady her nerves, she sat back against the side of the van and drew her knees up to her chest.

Time seemed to crawl by. Andy tried counting off the seconds, then the minutes, but after a while her mind began to wander. She started counting again, but soon lost interest. It didn't matter whether they made her sit in the van for minutes, hours or days, she had no alternative but to wait. She was in their hands. She tried to think of happier times. Birthdays. Christmasses. Just lying on the bed, Martin next to her, Katie curled up between them, smiling in her sleep. Martin giving Katie horsey rides, prowling around the sitting room on his hands and knees, Katie lying on his back, her arms around his neck.

Andy stiffened at the sound of a key being inserted into the driver's side door, then a double click as the door locks opened. There was a pause, then the driver's door opened.

'Have you got the hood on?' A man's voice. Deep. Guttural, as if he were trying to disguise it.

'Yes,' said Andy, hesitantly.

'Lie down on the floor, face down.'

Andy did as she was told, folding her arms and resting her chin on her hands. She felt the van lurch as the man climbed in. The passenger side door opened and another man got in. Two clunks as the doors closed, then the engine started.

They drove out of the carpark and made a series of turns in quick succession. Andy had no idea in which direction they were heading. More turns. Lots of traffic, the loud hiss of air brakes, a far-off siren. They stopped. A minute later and they were off again. More turns, then a sudden acceleration. They drove in a straight line for a long time, so Andy figured they were on a motorway. They seemed to be travelling for hours, but as she didn't know how fast they were going she had no way of knowing how far from London they were. She wanted to go to the toilet and cursed herself for not using the lavatory before she left the hotel.

The hood made it difficult to breathe, but she found that by turning her head to the side and pushing her cheek along the floor, she could create enough space around her chin to suck in fresher air.

Eventually she heard the sound of the indicator, and they turned off the motorway. More turns, a curve that felt like a right turn at a roundabout, then a series of further turns. The driver changed down through the gears. Third. Second. First. Then a sharp turn to the left and the tyres were crunching over a rough surface. She jumped as the driver sounded the horn, then there was a loud metallic rattling noise from somewhere in front of the van. They edged forward and the rattling noise was repeated, this time from behind them. A gate maybe? Andy lay still, not daring to move. She didn't know if the men were looking at her or not.

The van doors opened and the two men got out, and a few seconds later they opened the rear doors. 'Out you come,' said one. Andy didn't think it was the driver who'd spoken earlier.

She crawled towards the sound of his voice and then hands reached for her, holding her arms and pulling her out. Her knees banged against the ground, making her wince, and she scrambled to her feet. The men gave her no time to regain her balance and frogmarched her away from the van. Their footsteps echoed, making Andy think that they might be inside a large building.

The two men holding her came to a sudden stop and they both tightened their grip on her arms. They turned her to the side, then forced her down. She thought they were pushing her to the floor, but then she felt something on the back of her legs and realised that they were making her sit on a chair. They let go of her arms and she heard them move a few steps away from her. She strained to hear through the hood. Two men, breathing heavily. But she was sure there was someone else near by. It wasn't so much that she could hear the third person, it was more as if she could sense his presence. Andy waited, her hands in her lap, her head down, her eyes closed, breathing steadily. She had to stay calm.

She tilted her head as she heard one of the men move, then she felt a tug at the hood. She blinked as the bag was ripped off her head. A man sat in front of her, a man wearing a ski mask and baggy blue overalls. In front of him, were a notepad and a cheap plastic Biro. Andy already had her speech rehearsed – she'd been going over it in her mind all the time she'd been in the van.

'Look, please don't harm Katie. We'll give you whatever you want. Just let her go and we'll do exactly as you say. You have me now, my husband will give you just as much for me as he will for Katie, so you might as well let her go.'

The man in the ski mask stared at her with unblinking green eyes, saying nothing.

'He will, you know. He's already told me that he's got the money ready, and he'll pay. However much you want. So you might as well let Katie go. You can keep me here for as long as you want. Okay?' Andy heard the words tumbling out of her mouth as if they belonged to somebody else.

The green eyes stared back at her. Andy suddenly realised that there was mascara on the lashes. It wasn't a man, it was a woman. She heard a chuckling over her shoulder and she looked around. A large man with a wrestler's build was laughing at her. Like the woman, he had on a black ski mask that revealed nothing other than his eyes and part of his mouth, and was wearing similar blue overalls which were strained tight against his barrel-like chest. Next to the burly man was a taller, gangly man, also in a black ski mask and overalls. He was wearing pristine white Nike training shoes.

'Have you finished?' asked Green-eyes.

Andy whirled around to face her. 'What?'

'Have you said all you want to say?' said the woman. A Scottish accent, but there was a hint of Northern Irish, too. 'Are you ready to listen?'

Andy swallowed and nodded.

'You're free to go if you want, Andrea. We're armed but we're not going to hurt you. The guns are in case . . . well, let's just say they're insurance. If you stay, it's going to be your choice. But if you go, you'll never see your daughter again.'

'Katie's okay?'

'Katie's just fine. And so long as you do as we say, she'll stay that way. If everything goes to plan, you'll be back with her and your husband within a week or so.' Her voice was soft and persuasive, as if she were selling life insurance and not threatening the life of Andy's only child.

'How much do you want?' asked Katie.

Green-eyes shook her head slowly. 'Hasn't the penny dropped yet, Andrea? Haven't you figured it out?'

Andy looked at her, not understanding. 'What is you want? If it's not money, what do you want?'

Green-eyes put her gloved hands flat on the table, either side of the notepad and pen. 'Why, Andrea, we want you to do what you do best. We want you to build us a bomb. A very large bomb.'

Martin sat at his desk, staring at his computer screen. He barely noticed the spreadsheet in front of him. All he could think about was his wife and daughter. He'd arrived at the office at eight o'clock, thinking that Andy might telephone him before she checked out of the hotel. She didn't. The kidnappers hadn't called either. His phone rang and he picked it up. It was Jill, his secretary. 'Martin, it's a Mrs O'Mara,' she said. 'She's from Katie's school.'

'Okay, Jill, put her through.' There was a click, then the

woman was on the line. She was the headmistress's secretary, calling to see why Katie wasn't at school.

Martin thought quickly. If he said Katie was sick, the woman might ask for a doctor's note. An unexpected holiday wouldn't be an acceptable excuse. Besides, it would be very unlikely that Andy and Katie would have gone on holiday without him. 'It's my wife's mother, Mrs O'Mara. I'm afraid she's had a bit of a fall and my wife has had to go up to Belfast and see her. We didn't have anyone to take care of Katie because I'm up to my eyes in work here. We thought it best if Katie went with my wife. It'll only be for a few days.'

He regretted the lie immediately. It was just about possible that the school had Andy's mother's name and address on file, and all it would take would be one phone call to prove him a liar.

'It's very irregular, Mr Hayes,' said the woman frostily.

'I know, and I apologise for that,' said Martin. 'I should have called you yesterday.'

'Do you know when we can expect to see Katie again?'

Martin wished that he did know. 'I would think three days. Maybe four. If it's any longer, I'll be sure to let you know, Mrs O'Mara.'

'And your mother-in-law, how is she?'

'Poorly. She's in her seventies, so any sort of fall is dangerous.' Martin was surprised at how easily the lies were coming.

'Well, I hope she gets better soon,' said Mrs O'Mara.

'We all do,' agreed Martin.

When he put the receiver down, his hand was shaking.

'You're crazy,' said Andy. 'Why would you think . . .'

Green-eyes silenced her by holding up a gloved hand. Then she wagged her finger at Andy, side to side, like a parent warning a child not to misbehave. 'You're wasting your time, Andrea. We know everything. We know who you are and we know what you are. We're not asking you to do something you haven't done a hundred times before.'

Andy slumped back in her chair and stared at the masked woman. It felt as if all the blood had drained from her head. She tried to speak but no words would come.

Green-eyes bent down and pulled a briefcase out from under the table. She placed it on top, her eyes never leaving Andy's face as she clicked open the two locks. Click-clack, like the sound of a bullet being chambered. She opened the case, took out a large manila envelope, and tossed it casually in front of Andy.

'What's this?' asked Andy.

Green-eyes nodded at the envelope. Andy opened it and took out a dozen or so sheets of paper. They were photocopies of newspaper cuttings. Andy flicked through them. They were a mixture of Irish and English newspapers – tabloids and broadsheets. Andy scanned the headlines. BEL-FAST STORE DESTROYED. BOMB ON MAIN LINE, TRAINS DELAYED. BOMB DISPOSAL EXPERT KILLED. FIRE IN DEPARTMENT STORE, IRA BLAMED. TWO SOLDIERS DIE IN BOMB BLAST.

'Great reviews, huh?' said the lanky man. He chuckled and looked across at Green-eyes. Even through the ski mask he could see the warning look she threw at him and his laughter dried up. Green-eyes waited until he was silent and fidgeting with his gloves before turning back to Andy.

Andy stared at the photocopied cuttings. 'If you know everything, then you know why I can't do what you want.'

Green-eyes reached into her briefcase again and took out a piece of newspaper. She unfolded it. It was the front page of the *Belfast Telegraph*, ripped along one edge as if it had been torn in a hurry. There were four black-and-white photographs of small boys in school uniforms, smiling at the camera. Just heads and shoulders, the type that might have been stored in a school's files. The headline was brutal in its simplicity. IRA BOMB KILLS FOUR SCHOOL-BOYS.

Andy turned her head away.

'Squeamish?' said Green-eyes. 'I wouldn't have thought of you as the squeamish type.' She put the page down in front of Andy. 'Read it, Andrea.'

Andy shook her head. 'I don't have to.' She knew every word, almost by heart, and the four young faces were burnt into her memory, seared there for all time. Four boys. Three aged ten, one just weeks away from his tenth birthday. His mother had already paid for the bicycle he was getting as his main present. Four boys killed, another one in intensive care who would later lose a leg and the sight of one eye. For weeks his life had hung in the balance, and Andy had followed his recovery in the paper and on the television. She'd never understood why she'd prayed so hard for the boy to live. Four dead. Five dead. There was no difference morally, not really. But Andy had seen the crying mother on television, condemning the IRA and anyone who helped them and appealing for information. Four dead. One maimed. Innocents. And Andy was to blame. She'd carry the guilt with her to the grave.

Green-eyes pushed the page towards her. 'We're not asking you to do something you haven't already done, Andrea.'

Andy closed her eyes and shook her head. 'That was a mistake. A terrible mistake.'

'Casualties of war, the IRA High Command called it. But they never apologised, did they? Even though they were all good Catholic children. Two of them were altar boys, weren't they?'

Andy put her hands over her face and slumped forward so that her elbows were resting on the table. 'Is that what this is, revenge for what happened ten years ago? Who are you?'

'It doesn't matter who we are. All that matters is that we have your daughter. That's all you need to think about. We have Katie. We have the power of life and death over her, Andrea. But the decision as to what happens next is totally in your hands. Do as we say and you'll soon have her back home. Refuse, and you'll never see her again. We're not holding a gun to your head, we're not going to torture you or hurt you, all . . .'

'You don't think this is hurting?' hissed Andy.

Green-eyes tapped the newspaper page. 'I can promise you something else, Andrea,' she said quietly. 'We won't be hurting children this time. There won't be any mistake, no innocents killed. A lot of thought, a lot of planning, has gone into this. We won't be leaving a holdall in a railway tunnel for children to find.'

Andy shook her head again. 'I can't.'

'Yes, you can,' said Green-eyes firmly. 'You can, and if you want Katie back, you will.' She took a small padded envelope from the briefcase and handed it to Andy.

Andy took it, frowning. It felt empty, but it had been sealed.

'Open it,' said Green-eyes.

Andy slid a nail under the flap and ripped it open. She pushed the sides together to open the mouth of the envelope and peered inside. 'Oh no,' she whispered. She tipped the envelope up and shook out the contents. Blond curls. A handful. Andy could tell from the length that they'd been cut close to the scalp. 'Not her hair,' she said. 'She's so proud of her hair.' She looked at Green-eyes, tears trickling down her cheeks. 'How could you do that to a little girl? How could you cut her hair?'

Green-eyes leaned forward slowly until her masked face was only inches away from Andy. 'It could have been an ear, Andrea. Or a finger. Think about that.' She stared at Andy for several seconds, then visibly relaxed. She motioned at her two companions, and they stepped forward and seized Andy by the arms. The hair and envelope tumbled from Andy's grasp.

'No!' she shouted. She pointed at the blond curls. 'Please,' she said.

Green-eyes walked around the table, scooped up the hair clippings and put them back in the envelope, which she then slotted into the back pocket of Andy's jeans before the two men hustled her away from the table. The men took her over to the far corner of the factory where there was a cluster of offices, large white plasterboard cubes with cheap wooden doors that looked as if they'd been brought in as an afterthought. The men spun Andy around so that her back was to one of the plasterboard walls. Green-eyes appeared in front of her with a Polaroid camera in her gloved hands.

'Smile, Andrea,' she said.

Andy stared at her in disbelief. 'Smile?'

'For the camera.'

Andy forced a thin smile and blinked as the camera flashed and whirred. The two men hustled her away down a narrow corridor that ran between the two lines of offices.

Egan used a Stanley knife to slit the black garbage bags along the sides, then he pulled them open into single sheets of plastic. It took five to line the boot of the Scorpio, and he used thick strips of waterproof tape to seal them together. He slit open another three bags and taped them together into a single sheet, then put it and the tape into the boot.

Back in the apartment he checked the action of his Browning, slotted in a clipful of cartridges and gave the silencer a thorough cleaning.

He had taken a risk planting the listening device in Martin Hayes's office. He'd gone in at night, having disabled the burglar alarm system, and it had taken a full six hours from start to finish. It had proved to be time well spent, though. If it hadn't been for the office device, he'd never have known about Mrs O'Mara's phone call.

Egan could tell from the recording that the school secretary wasn't the sort to be deterred by Hayes's clumsy explanation of his daughter's absence. He'd have to do something to silence the meddlesome woman. And quickly.

It had taken just one telephone call to the school's personnel office, pretending to be an official of the Revenue Commissioners wanting to check her employment details, and Egan had all the information he needed.

Katie was sitting at the Formica-covered table when she heard the bolts slide back. She looked up apprehensively, wondering which of her captors it was. It was the man who'd been nice to her, the one who'd given her Garfield. He was carrying a tray.

'Are you hungry?' he asked as he carefully made his way down the stairs.

Katie wasn't, but she said that she was. He placed the tray on the table in front of her. It was scrambled eggs on a paper plate and a paper cup of milk. She smiled up at him. 'Thank you,' she said.

'I wasn't sure how you liked your eggs,' he said. 'I'm sorry if they're too runny.'

'They're fine,' said Katie. They weren't, they looked horrible, pale yellow and watery, but she wanted to be nice to him. If she was nice to him then maybe he'd be nice to her. She picked up the plastic fork and took a small bite of the eggs. 'Delicious,' she said.

The Nice Man headed for the stairs, but then turned and looked across at her. 'Is there anything you like to eat? I'll try to get it for you.'

'Heinz tomato soup. And fish fingers.'

'Same as my kids.'

'You've got children?'

The Nice Man went stiff, as if she'd said the wrong thing. Then he turned around and went up the stairs without saying anything else. Katie looked down at the eggs in disgust. They tasted horrible.

She wondered what the Nice Man looked like underneath his mask. She was sure of one thing – he'd be better-looking than the other man, the man who'd cut her hair. He'd been really rough with her as if he'd wanted to hurt her. He was ugly. Really ugly. Katie hoped with all her heart that the Ugly Man wouldn't come down the stairs again.

Andy sat on the floor with her back to the wall. The padded envelope was in her lap. In her hands, she held the locks of Katie's hair. There was a lot of hair. Clumps of it. Big clumps. Someone had savaged Katie's head. There'd probably be bald patches. Poor, poor Katie. She had always been so proud of her hair. Every night, before she went to sleep, she would sit in front of her dressing-table mirror, brushing her blond locks a hundred times. She'd loved it when Andy had brushed it for her. Katie would count the strokes, and wouldn't let Andy get away with even one less than the hundred.

They'd left her in a disused office. Bare white walls, faded blue carpet tiles on the floor, polystyrene tiles on the ceiling. Two fluorescent tubes filled the office with a clinical white light. They hadn't locked the door. There was no need. She couldn't run because if she ran she'd never see her daughter again. She was as trapped as if they'd chained her to the floor.

Andy lifted the hair to her face and gently sniffed it, inhaling Katie's fragrance. She closed her eyes and imagined that her face was up against her daughter's neck. God, had it been just thirty-six hours ago? Less than two days? Two days in which her life had been turned upside down.

Who were they, these people? Terrorists? Why else would they want a bomb? Could they be Irish? The only one who'd said anything at length was the woman, and the more Andy listened to her, the more she was sure there was an Irish accent mixed with Scottish. But that didn't mean anything. They could be Provisional Irish Republican Army. Or INLA. Or any of the Republican splinter groups like Real IRA or Continuity IRA. But then why would they need her? The IRA had their own explosives experts, experts who were far more up to date than Andy was. And if it was the IRA, why the kidnapping? She knew most of the members of the Army Council by name, and they knew her. They could have summoned her before them at any time over the past decade and she would have gone. Maybe not willingly, but she would have gone. So if not the IRA, then who? The Protestants? The Ulster Defence Volunteers? The Ulster Volunteer Force? The Ulster Freedom Fighters? Or maybe one of the fringe terrorist groups, the Orange Volunteers or the Red Hand Defenders. The Protestant groups were less able to mount major bombing campaigns because they didn't have the IRA's technical expertise or access to equipment. Was that what this was all about? Did the Protestants want her to build a bomb for them? Or was someone else behind the kidnapping? Someone else who wanted a bomb built in England. A very big bomb, Green-eyes had said. Andy wondered how big. As big as the bomb the IRA had used at Canary Wharf in 1995, the bomb that had caused almost a billion pounds of damage? Is that what they wanted from her? And if it was, could Andy do it? Could she give them a bomb in exchange for Katie?

Andy lost all track of time as she sat on the floor, holding Katie's curls next to her cheek. Eventually the door to the office opened and the two men walked across to where she was sitting and grabbed an arm each. The bigger one she thought of as the Wrestler, while the thinner man with the gleaming white Nike trainers was the Runner. Both were still wearing the blue overalls and black ski masks. The Wrestler had put on a black nylon shoulder holster from which protruded the butt of a large automatic.

'Okay, okay,' said Andy. 'You don't have to be so rough.'

Her captors said nothing, though the Runner dug his gloved fingers even deeper into her flesh. Andy pulled her arm away and shoved the handful of hair into the pocket of her jacket. The men pulled her through the doorway and along the corridor to the main factory area. The woman was already sitting at the far side of the table, her arms at rest, her gloved fingers interlinked. She watched with unblinking green eyes as the two men pushed Andy down on to the chair then stood behind her, arms folded.

There was a notepad and pen in front of the woman. Next to the pad was a pistol, the barrel of which was pointing towards Andy. The woman picked up the pen and began to tap it on the pad. 'So, Andrea, have you had enough time to think it over?'

'You're crazy,' said Andy. 'You're asking for the impossible.'

The green eyes seemed to harden fractionally. 'Let me be quite clear about this, Andrea. You are not the only option. If you don't want to co-operate, we'll use someone else.' She paused for effect. 'But you'll never see Katie again.'

Andy said nothing. The woman sighed, then pushed back her chair and began to stand up. 'No . . .' said Andy. The woman sat down again. She waited for Andy to speak, the pen poised in her gloved hand.

'Look, it's not as easy as you seem to think,' said Andy eventually. 'It's not just a question of mixing a few chemicals. There's specialised equipment . . .'

'We can get everything you need,' said the woman.

'But even if you were to make the explosives, you still have to detonate the bomb. It's not like setting off a firework – you don't just light the blue touch-paper.'

'Don't patronise me,' said the woman, coldly. 'I've set bombs before.'

'Then why do you need me?' asked Andy quickly.

The woman tapped the pen on the notepad. She looked up at the Wrestler. 'Take her back to . . .'

'It's okay, it's okay,' interrupted Andy. 'I'll do it.'

The woman stared at Andy for several seconds, then nodded slowly. 'What will you need?' she asked. Her pen was poised over the notebook.

Andy swallowed. Her mouth was unbearably dry. She didn't want to do this but she had no other choice. If she didn't co-operate, if she didn't tell them what they wanted to know, then she knew without a shadow of a doubt that they'd carry out their threat. Katie would die. She swallowed again. 'What sort of bomb are you talking about? A letter bomb? A car bomb? What are you planning to do with it?'

'We want a fertiliser bomb. A big one.'

'How big?'

Green-eyes said nothing for a few seconds. She tapped her pen on her notepad. 'Four thousand pounds,' she said eventually.

'Four thousand pounds? That's almost two tons. No one's ever made a two-ton fertiliser bomb before.'

'So we'll get you into the *Guinness Book of Records*,' said Green-eyes.

'How are you going to move it?' asked Andy. 'That's a truck-load of explosive.'

'You can leave the logistics to us. All you're concerned about is the building of the device.'

Andy shook her head. 'You could blow up a small town with a bomb that big. I can't be responsible for something like that.' She leaned forward, resting her arms on the table. 'I can't.'

Green-eyes' lips tightened. 'If you can't, we'll get someone else. But you know what that means.'

Andy put her hands up to her face. 'Jesus, Mary and Joseph,' she whispered.

'Whatever,' said Green-eyes. 'The major component is ammonium nitrate fertiliser,' she said. 'Correct?'

Andy nodded.

'We already have that,' said Green-eyes. 'Fifteen hundred kilos. Do you work in kilos, or pounds?'

'Pounds,' said Andy. Ireland used the metric system but she'd been born in Belfast, in the north of the country, and most of the time she still thought in pounds and ounces, miles and gallons.

'So we have just over three thousand pounds of ammonium nitrate fertiliser. Will that be enough?'

Andy shook her head, trying to clear her thoughts. 'What?'

'Please try to focus, Andrea,' said Green-eyes. 'We don't have all day.'

'It depends.'

'On what?'

Andy shook her head again. It was all too much for her to take in. She put both hands up to her temples and massaged them. 'It's complicated.'

'I appreciate it's a complicated process, Andrea. That's why we need you.'

Andy cupped her hands around her chin. 'Where are you planning on building it?'

'That's none of your concern.'

'Yes it is. That's what I mean about it being complicated. You need pure ammonium nitrate, but you can't buy it in Northern Ireland. At least, you can buy it, but it's not pure. The government's not stupid – they know what the pure chemical can be used for, so in Ireland you can only buy it mixed with other stuff. Bonemeal, potash, the sort of stuff farmers need. The pure stuff isn't for sale to the public, and if you order it, you'll be checked out. So if you're building it in Northern Ireland, you've got to buy tons of common-or-garden fertiliser and boil off the impurities. It would take for ever to get two tons of pure ammonium nitrate.'

'What about in the UK?'

'That's different. Is that what you're planning? A bomb here in England?'

The woman ignored Andy's question. 'How much would we need? Is three thousand pounds enough?'

Andy tried to concentrate. A four-thousand-pound fertiliser bomb. The fertiliser accounted for eighty per cent of the mixture. Eighty per cent of four thousand. Three thousand two hundred. She nodded. 'That should be okay, give or take.'

The woman pointed at the far corner of the factory with her pen. Andy turned her head to look. A green tarpaulin covered a mound almost three feet tall. Next to the mound were a dozen large conifers in black plastic pots and several boxes of smaller plants. 'You can check it yourself later. What else?'

'Hang on,' said Andy. 'You can't just use it straight from the sack. It's got to be prepared.'

'And how do we do that?'

'Even if it's sold as pure, there'll still be some impurities and you've got to get rid of them first. You have to mix it with alcohol, then strain off the liquid.'

'So how much alcohol will we need?'

Andy did the calculation in her head. 'Assuming you re-use it a few times, a hundred gallons or so. The more the better. It's got to be denatured alcohol. It's used as paint thinner or antifreeze.'

'Where do we get it from?'

'Any biggish paint suppliers should have some.'

'What would happen if we didn't use the alcohol?'

'It might not go off.'

The woman nodded. 'What equipment will you need, to purify the fertiliser?'

'Large containers. Plastic or glass. Stirrers. Wooden or plastic. Then something to heat the mixture. Electric woks are good.'

'How many?'

'The more you have, the faster you can process it. Every pound of fertiliser has to be mixed with alcohol, then heated for three or four minutes. Say you do five pounds at a time. Three thousand pounds could take a full two days, working around the clock.'

'Two days?'

'It's a big job. You don't seem to understand how big a job it is.'

'So, if we can get six woks going, it'll take eight hours?'

'That's right. But it's hard work. And you have to have someone stirring all the time. It's a sort of stir-fry job, you know.'

'So, four. There'll be four of us, so four woks. What else?'

'Electric coffee grinders. I'd get four of them, too.'

'Four it is.'

Andy sat back and folded her arms. 'What are you going to do with it? The bomb?'

'That's not your concern.'

'Well, it is, sort of. There are different mixtures for different effects.'

'Whatever's most effective. Whatever'll give us the biggest bang, okay?'

Andy wanted to lie, to give her wrong information or to withhold something vital, something that would render the explosive inert, but she couldn't risk it. She didn't know how much they already knew. This could be a test, and if she failed the test it could be as dangerous as refusing to co-operate. She nodded slowly. 'Aluminium powder,' she said. 'You'll need about six hundred pounds.'

'Where would we get that from?' asked the woman.

'Paint suppliers again,' said Andy. 'The best sort to ask for is pyro grade 400 mesh.' She was surprised how easily the technical terms came to her. It had been years since she'd even thought about the components of a fertiliser bomb. The information belonged to another life, a life she had long ago walked away from.

'It's easy to get?' asked Green-eyes. 'There's not a register or anything?'

Andy shook her head. 'It's got too many uses. No one checks. But you'd be better buying it through a front company, something with decorator in the letterhead. And with that sort of amount, you might be better getting it from several different suppliers.'

'What about the alcohol?'

'It's got lots of legitimate uses, too. I'd buy it from several sources, though.'

The woman scribbled on her pad again.

'Sawdust,' said Andy.

'Sawdust?'

'As fine as possible. Two hundred pounds. Any sawmill will sell it to you. You can say it's for a pet shop. That's what we used to do. And detergent. Sodium dodecyl benzenesulphonate.' She spelled out the words slowly. 'A chemical supplies company will sell you the pure stuff. But almost any soap-based washing powder will do.' The information was all still there, she realised. It always had been, and probably always would be. A shopping list of death, imprinted somewhere in her neural pathways.

'How much will we need?'

'Thirty pounds or so.'

'And?'

'That's it,' said Andy. 'Ammonium nitrate, aluminium powder, sawdust and detergent. You can add diesel oil if you want. It's not vital, but it helps.'

'How much would we need?'

'Ten gallons or so.'

'And what equipment are you going to need?'

'Desiccators.'

'Desiccators?'

'To dry out the fertiliser. It absorbs moisture, and as soon as it's damp it's useless.'

'Are they easy to get?'

Andy shrugged. 'Depends. You might have to order one.'

'Is there anything else we could use?'

'An electric oven. And baking trays, a couple of inches deep.' Andy did a quick calculation in her head. 'One oven will dry about four hundred pounds a day. So it'll take you about eight days working around the clock to do it all.'

'And if we get four ovens – two days, is that right?'

Andy nodded.

'Okay. What else?'

'Respirators. Protective glasses. Overalls. Gloves. Plastic gloves and oven gloves, too.' She steepled her fingers under her chin and furrowed her brow as she thought. It had been a long time. A long, long time, and she wasn't sure if she'd remembered everything. She ran through the processes in her mind. 'Thermometers. Metal ones. And a tumble-drier,' she said. 'Two would be better.'

'This isn't an ideal home exhibition,' said the woman.

'It's for mixing the fertiliser and aluminium powder,' said Andy. 'It's got to be well mixed. We used to pack it in Tupperware containers then put it in a tumble-drier for half an hour or so.'

The woman nodded. 'Innovative,' she said.

'We had to be,' said Andy.

'How many?'

Andy thought for a few seconds. 'Two should do it.'

'Anything else?'

'That's all for the explosives. But the skill is in the preparation. You can't just throw it together.'

'And once we've made it, it's not unstable?'

'You could smash a train into it and it wouldn't go off. In fact, it's only good for a week or so. Maybe two weeks, but after that the fertiliser will have absorbed water again and no matter what you do to it, it won't go off. So you'll need lots of Tupperware containers, the bigger the better. And lots of black plastic rubbish bags. The more you wrap the stuff, the longer it'll take the water to penetrate. And you'll need bags to pack the finished product in. Hundreds of black bags.'

The woman made another note on her pad. Then she looked up. 'Timer?'

'Depends on when you want it to go off. Minutes, hours, days or weeks.'

'Hours.'

'Any small clock will do.'

'What do you prefer?'

'A battery-operated digital model.'

'Any particular brand?'

Andy shrugged. 'Whatever. Can I ask you something?'

'No. What do you pack it in? Oil drums?'

Andy shook her head. 'No. Like I said, we'll use black bags. You have to pack it around the initiator. If it's in barrels the initial explosion might just knock the rest of the barrels over.'

'Okay. Black bags it is. What do you need wiring-wise?'

'Bell wire. Several different colours would help. Soldering iron. Solder. Batteries – 1.5 volts. Torch bulbs and bulb-holders, for circuit testing. Wire. As many different colours as you can get. Look, what are you going to use this for?'

'That's not your concern.'

'Is it against people, or property? I have a right to know.'

The woman put her pen down and looked at Andy, her

eyes narrowing under the ski mask. 'We have your daughter, and unless you do exactly as we say, she'll die. I mean that, Andrea. I mean that as sure as I'm sitting here opposite you. The men who are looking after her are taking good care of her, but they're just as capable of putting a bullet in her pretty little head or cutting her throat. This isn't a game, it isn't a joke. You have no rights. You do as you're told or Katie's dead. Do you understand me?'

Andy stared at the woman. It was as if she were the only static thing in the vicinity – everything else was whirling and spinning around her. She tried to speak, but before any words came she felt her stomach heave and her mouth filled with vomit. She twisted around from the table and threw up with loud, gagging gasps. The Wrestler jumped to the side, away from the foul-smelling yellow flow, but it splattered over his legs.

'You stupid cow!' he yelled.

Andy fell to her knees and bent low, her head only inches from the ground as heaving spasms racked her body. Even when her stomach was empty she continued to heave and cough. A glass of water appeared before her and she took it gratefully. She swilled the water around her mouth and then spat it out before drinking deeply. She sat back on her heels and drained the glass. The woman in the ski mask was standing in front of her, her hands on her hips. Andy gave the glass back to her.

She looked around as she squatted on the dusty concrete floor. There were no windows, though there were barred skylights high overhead. Thick metal girders ran below the roof, and suspended from them were winches and lifting equipment. There were thick metal bolts in the floor, as if massive pieces of machinery had once been bolted into place. The place had obviously been used for some form of manufacturing in the past.

Up against one wall was a metal bench, and on it a

computer. It looked like an expensive system with a large VDU and a tower unit containing the disk drives. A wire led from the computer to a phone socket. A modem, Andy realised. It had a modem. The Wrestler was using a tissue to wipe his trousers and continuing to curse her under his breath. The Runner took Andy's arm and helped her back on to the chair. She wiped her mouth with the back of her hand.

Green-eyes sat down and picked up her pen again. 'Right, are you ready to go on?' she asked.

Andy nodded. She methodically went through everything else they'd need while Green-eyes took notes. When she'd finished, Green-eyes put her pen down on her notepad and nodded at her. 'We'll get most of this stuff tomorrow morning,' she said. 'We start work the day after that.'

Andy looked around the factory. 'Here?' she asked.

'No. We'll be moving somewhere else.'

'Can you tell me where?'

'Not right now, no. But you'll know soon enough. Let me show you the fertiliser.'

Green-eyes stood up and walked over to the tarpaulin-covered mound. She pulled the green sheet back. Dust billowed around her and she coughed.

Andy went over to the stack of bags and examined the labels. She recognised the brand. It was an English firm, based just outside Oxford. Under the brand name were the words AMMONIUM NITRATE, and below that, in slightly smaller type, the word FERTILISER. To the right were three numbers, separated by hyphens: 34–0–0.

'Okay?' asked Green-eyes.

'It'll do,' said Andy. She'd half hoped that they wouldn't have the correct type of fertiliser, but now she realised that they knew exactly what they were doing. Some manufacturers coated their ammonium nitrate with calcium to stop it from absorbing water. But the calcium coating rendered the fertiliser useless as an explosive base. Other fertilisers were a mixture of chemicals, perhaps containing ammonium sulphate or urea. Only pure ammonium nitrate would explode, and that was what Green-eyes was showing her. The numbers on the bag referred to the ratio of nitrogen, phosphorus and potash. Only pure ammonium nitrate had the ratio 34–0–0.

There were other sacks, too, containing compost. Andy pointed at one of the compost bags. 'What are you planning to do with that? Compost isn't explosive.'

Green-eyes ignored her.

'Why are you doing this?' Andy asked.

'Why do you care? You've done it before.'

'That was a long time ago. A lifetime ago.'

'Like riding a bike,' said Green-eyes. 'As soon as you get back in the saddle, it'll be as if you never gave it up.' She motioned to the Runner, and he came over and took Andy by the arm, leading her like a naughty child back to the office.

Mick Canning pushed the trolley down the aisle, scanning the rows of canned goods. He stopped by the soups section and took half a dozen cans of Heinz tomato soup off the shelves. He added a few cans of baked beans and spaghetti hoops to his trolley, sticking to the Heinz brand. He knew that children applied the same brand awareness to their food as they did to their clothing. Training shoes had to be Nike, Reebok or Adidas, beans had to be Heinz, fish fingers had to be Bird's Eye, cornflakes had to be Kellogg's. Anything else resulted in sneers and pushed-away plates. Canning's own children weren't much older than the Hayes girl – his son was eight and his daughter nine. He hadn't seen either for almost three months; they were living in Larne with their mother. Canning and his wife had separated, and the last letter he'd received from her solicitor made it clear that she wanted a divorce. And the house. In exchange, she was offering him unlimited access to the children, though she was insisting that they live with her. Canning knew there was no point in arguing, either with her or her solicitor. He was resigned to becoming a part-time father, but figured that being a part-time father was better than being no father at all.

Canning paid in cash and took the carrier bags out to the carpark and loaded them into the boot of the Ford Mondeo. He turned on the radio and tapped his fingers on the steering wheel as he drove. If everything went to plan, it would all be over within two weeks. The Hayes girl would be back with her parents, Canning would have the rest of the hundred thousand pounds he'd been promised for the job, and he'd be able to get his soon-to-be-ex-wife and her money-grabbing solicitor off his back.

Laura O'Mara jumped as the doorbell rang. The clock on the mantelpiece said it was a quarter past seven, and she wasn't expecting visitors. She put her knitting on the coffee table and turned down the volume of the television set, then peered through the lace curtains. An expensive car, a black saloon, was parked in the road outside her house. She didn't know anyone with a black car. She went over to the door and slid the security chain home. Since her husband had died four years earlier, she'd always taken great care not to let strangers into the house. The newspapers were full of stories about old women being mugged for their life savings. Not that Laura O'Mara considered herself old. She was fifty-nine, and her own mother was still active and living alone, and she was in her mid-eighties. Nor did Laura O'Mara keep her life savings in her two-up, two-down cottage. She was too smart an investor for that. Her savings were tucked away in tax-efficient bonds and unit trusts, and she even had several thousand pounds in a Guernsey bank account, safe from the prying eyes of the taxman. But she did have some valuable porcelain, and she knew that children these days would smash up a person's house for the thrill of it. She eased open the door, keeping a reassuring hand on the lock.

A man in a suit smiled down at her, wire-framed spectacles perched on the end of his nose. 'Mrs O'Mara?'

She frowned. The illicit bank account sprang to mind, and she felt herself blush.

The man looked at a clipboard he was carrying, then smiled again. He had even white teeth, she noticed, not a filling in his mouth. Mrs O'Mara's own teeth betrayed a childhood of sweets and adult years filled with smoking and coffee-drinking. She self-consciously put her hand up to cover her mouth as she returned his smile.

'My name's Peter Cordingly,' he said. 'I'm with Dublin City social services.'

He had an Irish accent, but it wasn't local. It was as if he'd spent some time away from Ireland, smoothing out the peaks and troughs so that his accent was somehow vague and hard to pin down. A bit like the man himself, thought Mrs O'Mara. He was a pleasant enough chap, but not particularly good-looking, with a bland, squarish face, and apart from the glasses he didn't have any distinguishing features.

'I understand you've expressed concerns about one of the children at your school.' He looked at the clipboard again, pushing the spectacles further up his nose with his index finger. 'Katie Hayes?'

'Oh, I only called her father. She was away without permission and . . .'

The man held up a hand to silence her and leaned forward conspiratorially. 'Mrs O'Mara, could I come in and have a word with you about this?' He looked left and right as if he feared being overheard. 'What I have to see is a wee bit . . . confidential.'

'Oh my,' said Mrs O'Mara. She unhooked the security chain and pulled the door open, eager to hear what it was exactly that Mr Hayes had done, all thoughts about the dangers of strangers totally forgotten.

DAY FOUR

Andy woke up as the fluorescent lights flickered into life. She squinted over at the door to the office. The Wrestler stood there with a brown paper bag in one hand and a paper cup in the other. He put them down on the floor in the centre of the room. 'Breakfast,' he said. He'd taken off his shoulder holster.

Andy sat up and rubbed her eyes. 'Thank you,' she said.

'She wants you outside in fifteen minutes.'

'Okay.'

The Wrestler went out and closed the door behind him. Andy climbed out of the sleeping bag that Green-eyes had given her the previous evening. There was no pillow – she'd had to rest her head on a rolled-up pullover, and now she had a crick in her neck. She picked up the brown paper bag and opened it. There was a croissant inside, and a bran muffin. She sat with her back against the wall and ate them both in between sips of hot coffee. She was surprised at how hungry she was, but then realised that she hadn't eaten for almost thirty-six hours.

When Green-eyes had given her the sleeping bag, she'd shown Andy where the bathroom was, at the end of the corridor farthest from the factory area. All it contained was a washbasin and toilet, but it was better than nothing, and Green-eyes had told her she could use it whenever she wanted. There was one stipulation. Andy had to shout that she wanted to leave the office, to give her captors time to put on their ski masks if they weren't already wearing them.

Andy got her washbag out of her suitcase and banged on the office door. 'I want to go to the bathroom!' she shouted.

'Okay!' shouted Green-eyes, off in the distance. Andy opened the door and went along to the bathroom, had as good a wash as was possible in a sink, and brushed her teeth.

Green-eyes was waiting for her in the factory area, still wearing the blue overalls and ski mask. The Runner was loading the bags of ammonium nitrate into the back of the blue Transit van.

'Sleep well?' asked Green-eyes.

'Do you care?' said Andy.

'If it makes you feel any better, I slept on the floor too,' said Green-eyes. She nodded over at the far corner of the factory space. There were three rolled-up sleeping bags there, along with a couple of holdalls. The woman's pistol was on a small plastic table, along with the Wrestler's gun and holster.

'It doesn't,' said Andy.

'We'll be moving tomorrow anyway,' said Green-eyes.

'Where to?'

'You'll find out soon enough, Andrea.' Green-eyes pointed at the plastic chair on Andy's side of the table. 'Sit down.'

Andy did as she was told.

The Runner started loading the conifers into the back of the van, and then packed in the boxes of smaller plants.

'I want you to go through the list again,' Green-eyes said to Andy. 'Everything we'll need for a four-thousand-pound fertiliser bomb.'

'Don't you trust me?'

The green eyes stared at Andy through the holes in the ski mask.

Andy leaned forward. 'Or are you testing me, is that it? To check that I'm consistent?'

'Maybe I just want to make sure that you didn't forget anything,' said the woman. 'Deliberately or otherwise.'

'When can I see Katie?'

'You can't. She's still in Ireland.'

'Let me talk to her.'

'I can't do that.'

'I have to know that she's okay.'

'You have my word.'

Andy snorted. 'Why the hell should I believe anything you tell me?'

'If you ever want to see Katie again, you've no choice,' said the woman.

Andy glared at her. 'At least give me some sign that she's okay. A phone call. Anything.'

'A photograph in front of today's paper?' said Green-eyes, her voice loaded with sarcasm.

'Look, what you're asking me to do is complicated. Really complicated. And I'm going to find it impossible to concentrate if I'm worrying whether or not my daughter is alive. Doesn't that make sense to you?'

Green-eyes tilted her head to one side as she looked at Andy. 'Maybe you're right at that,' she said. 'I'll see what I can do. Now, let's go through the list.'

The Runner finished loading the Transit van. 'Oy, Don!' he yelled. Green-eyes stiffened. Andy pretended not to notice. 'Ammonium nitrate fertiliser,' she said. 'Ratio 34–0–0.'

The Wrestler came out of one of the offices and headed over to the metal door. He began to pull on the chain to open it and the Runner climbed into the driver's seat of the van.

'Aluminium powder. Pyro grade 400 mesh.' Andy fought to keep her voice steady. She brushed a stray lock of hair from her eyes and smiled at the woman in the ski mask. 'Sawdust. Soap powder. Diesel oil.'

The van engine kicked into life. Green-eyes began to write on her pad. Andy forced herself to breathe. Had she managed to convince Green-eyes that she hadn't heard the Runner's slip? That she didn't know that the man built like a wrestler was called Don?

Andy kept talking. 'Three thousand two hundred pounds of fertiliser, six hundred pounds of aluminium powder.' Green-eyes pounds of sawdust and thirty pounds of soap powder.' Green-eyes continued to write as the Runner edged the van out of the factory. Andy stared at the pen as Green-eyes wrote. Did she know that Andy had heard the name? Was she pretending not to attach any significance to the slip so that Andy would think she was in the clear? Andy was trying to bluff Green-eyes; maybe Green-eyes was attempting a double bluff. One thing Andy knew for sure – if Green-eyes thought she'd caught the name, she was as good as dead. She continued to recite the list of components of the bomb, all the time staring at Green-eyes.

To her left, the metal door rattled down. She heard the Wrestler climb into the van and slam the door, then it drove away.

The woman looked up, her pen poised. Andy stared at her green eyes, wishing with all her heart that she could look inside the woman's mind and see for herself whether she was safe or whether her life had just been rendered forfeit by the mistake the Runner had made. Her mouth had gone suddenly dry, and when she swallowed she almost gagged.

O'Keefe stuffed his ski mask into the glove compartment. 'I should fucking blow your brains out here and now,' he said.

Quinn looked across at him, his mouth open in surprise. 'What?'

O'Keefe pointed a finger at Quinn's face, just inches from

the man's nose. 'You're a fucking amateur. A fucking piece of shit amateur.'

'Don, what the hell's got up your arse?' Quinn sounded genuinely confused. He braked and brought the van to a halt at the roadside.

'You used my name, you ignorant, stupid shit.'

Quinn gripped the steering wheel with both hands. 'What the fuck are you talking about?'

O'Keefe jerked his thumb back at the industrial estate behind them. 'Back there. You called me Don.'

'I fucking did not.'

'I'm not imagining it, Quinn. I'm not plucking this out of the fucking ether. I was in the bog, you were loading the van. What did you shout?'

Quinn ran a hand through his thick red hair. 'I don't know. But I know I wouldn't use your name. I'm not stupid.'

O'Keefe seized Quinn by the throat, his big, square hand gripping either side of the younger man's neck like a vice. Quinn's eyes widened and his gloved hands clawed ineffectually at O'Keefe's iron-hard fingers. His lips moved silently, white spittle dribbling down his chin. O'Keefe's other hand grabbed Quinn's hair and he yanked the man's head back so that he was staring fearfully up at the roof of the van. 'Not stupid!' O'Keefe screamed. 'Not fucking stupid! I'll give you not fucking stupid!' He tightened his grip on Quinn's throat, threatening to crush his windpipe. 'Now, think back, you little shit. Think back to what you said.'

Quinn's hands fastened around O'Keefe's wrist, but he was powerless against the bigger man's grip.

'Are you thinking?'

Quinn tried to nod but could barely move his head. O'Keefe let go of Quinn's throat and the younger man gasped for breath.

'I'm sorry. For fuck's sake, I'm sorry.'

O'Keefe let Quinn's hair slip through his fingers. 'It's coming back to you now, is it?'

Quinn nodded.

O'Keefe folded his arms and settled back in the passenger seat. 'You've got to be on your toes every second of every minute. You can't let your guard down once, because if you do it can be the death of you. This isn't a game. We get caught and they'll throw away the key.'

Quinn put the van into gear and pulled away from the kerb. His hands were shaking on the steering wheel.

They drove to London, and cut across the city towards the financial district. Quinn brought the van to a halt and nodded at the line of half a dozen cars waiting to drive into the City of London. A uniformed policeman waved through the car at the front while his colleague went to speak to the driver of the second.

'Bloody joke, isn't it?' said Quinn. 'Ring of steel, my arse. What the fuck do they expect to find, huh?'

'They're not the ones to worry about,' said O'Keefe. He jerked his chin to the side. 'It's the eye in the sky that does the damage.'

Quinn twisted around in his seat and looked in the direction that O'Keefe had indicated. High up on the office building was a wall-mounted camera pointing at the checkpoint. 'Video, yeah?' he said.

'Not just a video,' said O'Keefe. 'The camera picks out the registration number and runs it through the police computer. It's all done automatically – takes seven seconds to get a read-out on the vehicle. If it's stolen or used by anyone on the Special Branch watch list, there'd be more armed police around us than fleas on a dog.'

They edged towards the front of the queue of cars. O'Keefe reached under his seat and pulled out a metal clipboard. The uniformed policeman walked up to the window and O'Keefe wound down the window.

'Morning, sir,' said the policeman. 'Can you tell me where you're going?'

O'Keefe showed him the clipboard. There was an order form clipped to it with the landscape gardening company's letterhead on the top. 'Cathay Tower,' he said. 'We're doing a rooftop garden. Trees, bushes, the works.'

The policeman stepped back and waved them on, his eyes already on the next vehicle.

'Have a good one,' said O'Keefe as Quinn accelerated away. It was the third time they'd been into the City in the van that week, and as anticipated there hadn't been any problems. It was registered and insured in the name of the landscaping company, taxed and MoT'd and totally legitimate. Quinn's driving licence was clean, though the name and address weren't his.

The main entrance to Cathay Tower was in Queen Anne Street, close to Bank Tube station, but the entrance to the carpark was at the rear, down a narrow side street. O'Keefe showed his pass to the elderly security guard. Like the van's paperwork, it was genuine. The office had been rented some three months earlier, and included in the lease were three parking spaces. They were on the second level of the subterranean carpark, and Quinn drove down and parked.

The service lift was some fifty feet away, so O'Keefe went over to press the button while Quinn opened the rear doors of the van and began unloading the sacks of fertiliser on to the trolley they'd brought with them. Each bag weighed fifty kilos, and Quinn could get six on the trolley. As he put the last one on, the lift arrived and O'Keefe held the door open while Quinn trundled the trolley over.

They went up to the ninth floor. The lift doors opened on to a corridor which led to the main reception area where the passenger lifts were. A door led off the reception area to the lavatories; a corridor led to the main open-plan office area which ran the full length of the building. The entire floor was rented in the name of an overseas stockbroking firm, paid for through a Cayman Islands bank account.

O'Keefe walked into the main office area, which had previously been a dealing room for a major American bank, and went inside. Quinn followed with the trolley. White vertical blinds covered the ceiling-to-floor windows. The NatWest Tower was almost directly opposite. It would be all too easy for one of the thousands of office workers to look in and see what they were doing. The blinds would have to remain closed all the time they were there.

There were already eighteen sacks of fertiliser piled up in one corner. The two men unloaded the trolley, adding the sacks to the pile. O'Keefe waved at a smoke detector in the middle of the ceiling. A red light blinked in the centre of the white plastic disc.

'You think she's watching?' asked Quinn.

'Wouldn't put it past her,' said O'Keefe.

Quinn nodded at the sacks of fertiliser. 'Weird, isn't it?' he said, wiping his hands on his overalls. 'Gardeners all over the country spread this over their lawns, and we're gonna blow a building to kingdom come with it.'

The two men walked over to the window.

'What's weird about that?' asked O'Keefe. 'Give us another cigarette, will you?'

'McCracken said we weren't to smoke here.'

'Fuck McCracken.' He gestured at the smoke detector. 'Anyway, this is a blind spot.'

'You sure?'

'I fitted the thing myself. I'm sure.'

Quinn shrugged and tossed the pack of Silk Cut over to O'Keefe.

O'Keefe took a cigarette, lit it, and tossed the pack back.

Quinn lit a cigarette for himself, and looked over at the sacks of fertiliser. 'I just meant it's weird that like this it's dead safe, right? Regular fertiliser. But add other stuff to it and . . . you know . . . bang!'

'Bang?' O'Keefe pushed the blinds to one side and peered across at the NatWest Tower. Thousands of men and women going about their business. Worrying about careers, office politics, their home life. Worrying about a million things, but totally oblivious to the one thing that was going to change their lives for ever. A four-thousand-pound bomb only a few hundred metres away.

'Yeah, bang. Ka-boom!'

O'Keefe let the blinds fall back into place and turned to look at Quinn. 'You think a four-thousand-pound bomb's going to go bang? Or ka-boom? You ever heard a bomb go off? A big one?'

Quinn shook his head.

'Well, I can tell you from the horse's mouth, bang doesn't come into it. Bang's what you get when you burst a balloon. Or fire a gun. Bombs don't go bang. Not big ones.'

'What sort of noise do bombs make, then?'

O'Keefe narrowed his eyes as he took a long pull on his cigarette. He exhaled a tight plume of smoke. 'Are you taking the piss?' he said.

The Mercedes swept up the driveway and parked in front of the two-storey house. Two men in dark suits walked up to the car, nodded when they saw who was inside, then walked back to their post by the front door. Deng sat where he was until his bodyguard had climbed out of the car and opened the door for him. He stood for a moment to admire the view of Hong Kong harbour far below him. Some of the most expensive real estate in the world towered over the narrow strip of water between the island and the mainland of Kowloon. Deng turned back to the house. It had once been the home of one of the richest taipans in Hong Kong, a man whose family had made their fortune running opium into China and who had left the day before the colony was handed back to its rightful masters, vowing never to return. Now it was the property of the People's Liberation Army.

Deng climbed the stairs to the verandah and walked across it and into the house, his Bally shoes squeaking across the polished oak floors. The general was in the taipan's study, the walls still bedecked with the books he'd left behind, bought by the yard and never read. A wooden-bladed fan spun silently above the general's head as he stared out of a picture window that gave him an unobstructed view of Kowloon. In Cantonese, Kowloon was Nine Dragons, signifying the hills that surrounded the peninsula. In fact there were only eight hills – the ninth dragon represented a warlord who'd visited the area hundreds of years earlier. 'What is this place called?' he'd asked.

'Nine dragons,' he was told.

The warlord counted the hills. 'But there are only eight,' he said.

'Until you arrived, sire,' he was told. 'Now there are nine dragons.'

Flattery could be a dangerous thing, Deng knew. It was flattery that had got him into his present predicament. He'd believed everything he'd been told, and now he stood to lose millions of dollars. And more. His life was on the line. His life and the life of his family.

Behind the general's wheelchair stood a Chinese nurse in a starched white uniform, her hair hanging down to the middle of her back like a black veil. Deng walked to stand in front of the general. The old man was pressing an oxygen mask up against his face with one hand. He waved his free hand, indicating that Deng should sit down on a leather winged chair at the side of the window.

The general wheezed heavily, and the nurse stepped forward and adjusted the valve on the oxygen cylinder. The old man gulped several times, and then his breathing steadied. 'I have to go to London soon,' he croaked. 'My doctor . . .'

'I understand,' said Deng.

'The air here. It's not good at this time of year.'

Deng nodded. 'It would not be a good idea for you to be in London when . . .' He left the sentence unfinished.

The general looked at him with watery eyes. 'How long?'

'A week. Seven days.'

'And the money?'

Deng pushed his spectacles up his nose. 'We would anticipate receiving payment a month after the . . . incident.'

The general began to cough, then he cleared his throat noisily. He took the plastic mask away from his face, leaned to the side and spat noisily into a brass tureen at the side of his chair. Greenish phlegm dribbled down his trembling chin and the nurse rushed forward to dab it with a tissue. Deng averted his eyes, embarrassed by the man's infirmity.

'Will he wait?' wheezed the general eventually.

'I assume so,' said Deng. 'It is the only chance he has of getting his money back. It is the only chance any of us has.'

Deng heard footsteps behind him. A man in a dark suit, not one of the guards at the front of the house, walked across the study and emptied a sack in front of the general. Deng grimaced as a dead dog flopped out on to the floor. A spaniel, the fur on its chest matted with blood. 'My daughter's dog,' said the general.

'A warning,' said Deng.

'My daughter's dog,' repeated the old man. He gestured with his chin at the dead animal, and the bodyguard picked it up by one of its back legs and put it back in the sack. 'He is an evil man, that Michael Wong.'

Deng nodded.

'We should never have done business with him,' said the general. He began to cough again and his chest shuddered.

85

The nurse bent over him but the general waved her away impatiently.

Deng didn't react to the criticism. It had been his idea to bring in Wong as an investor, but what was done was done. It was too late for regrets – the only way out of their predicament was to get Wong's money back. And for that they needed Egan, the American. Only he could save their lives. Their lives and the lives of their families. If they failed, Michael Wong's vengeance would carry far and wide. The general's daughter's dog was just a sign of how far the ripples would spread.

McCracken's mobile rang. It was Egan. 'Everything okay?' he asked.

McCracken walked to the far end of the factory area, away from where Andrea was sitting. 'No problems,' she said.

'I'm five minutes away. Make sure she's out of the way, will you?' The line went dead. Like all of Egan's phone calls it was short, to the point, and unidentifiable. He never used names and always spoke in the vaguest terms possible.

McCracken went back over to Andrea. 'Right, you can stay in the office until the boys get back,' she said. 'Take a coffee with you if you want. And there's doughnuts over there.'

'I'm not hungry.'

'Suit yourself.'

Andrea stood up. 'Why are you doing this?'

McCracken said nothing. She pointed to the offices. 'Keep the door closed until I come and get you.'

Andrea did as she was told. McCracken took off her ski mask and rubbed her face. She made herself a cup of coffee, and as she sipped it she heard Egan's car pull up outside. He let himself in and nodded at her. 'Where is she?'

McCracken jerked a thumb at the offices. 'We've got her well trained,' she said. 'You want a coffee?'

Egan shook his head. He was wearing a black leather jacket over a grey crew-neck pullover and blue jeans and carrying his mobile phone in one hand and his car keys in the other. He looked like a used-car salesman on his day off, a short, well-built man with receding fair hair, cut short, almost army-style. McCracken studied him as he walked over to the table and picked up her notepad. One word came to mind when she thought of the man who was paying her wages. Bland. Pale blue eyes, fair hair, medium height, a squarish face with an average nose, no distinguishing features. If she closed her eyes, she could barely picture his face. Egan studied the list, nodding thoughtfully.

'It's okay?' McCracken asked, going over to join him.

'It's fine. Perfect.'

McCracken pulled off the rubber band that she used to hold her hair back when she had the ski mask on and shook it free. 'If you know what the ingredients are, why do we need her?' she asked.

Egan tapped the side of his nose with a forefinger. 'Need to know, Lydia, love. How are Quinn and O'Keefe getting on?' Egan's accent was mid-Atlantic. At times it sounded West Coast American, but generally his voice was as unremarkable as his physical appearance.

McCracken tilted her head to the side. 'O'Keefe's fine. Very professional. But Quinn . . .'

Egan put down the notepad and narrowed his eyes. 'What?'

McCracken winced under his gaze. She didn't want to badmouth Quinn, but he was the weakest member of the team and she wasn't sure how reliable he'd be under pressure. 'He's a bit . . . unfocused. Considering what we're expected to do. The next phase and all.'

'It's not too late to replace him, Lydia.' His pale blue eyes watched to see how she'd react.

McCracken knew what he meant by replaced. 'I don't know,' she said.

Egan walked up close to her and looked into her eyes. 'It's got to be your call,' he said. 'Your responsibility. I can't be here all the time.'

'I know. It's just I haven't worked with guys like him before.'

'He's not a terrorist. He's a career criminal. They have different motivations. Different behavioural patterns.'

'He's undisciplined.'

'That's a function of his background, Lydia. You were trained by the best, mentally and physically. So far as the Provisional IRA are concerned, it's just as important that their volunteers are politically educated as it is that you can fire a gun or place a bomb. Quinn's all action and reaction. A couple of years back he was involved in a bank robbery. Sawn-off shotguns, stun guns, a team of six. They were unlucky and a passing armed response vehicle piled in. Quinn was the only one to get away. Shot two cops. Drove off in their car, cool as a cucumber. Plus he's good with vehicles.' He smiled reassuringly. 'What I'm saying is that if anything does go wrong, Quinn's a good man to have in your corner. But as I said, it's your call. Has to be.'

McCracken nodded. 'He'll be okay. Besides, we're going to need everyone to do the mixing.' She gestured at the notepad. 'According to what the Hayes woman says, there's a hell of a lot of work involved.'

'She's co-operating fully?'

'Carrot and stick,' said McCracken. 'She thinks she's going to see her daughter if she helps us. And that we'll kill her if she doesn't. She keeps asking if she can call her husband. What do you think?'

'Only if it's the only way you can get her to co-operate. The husband hasn't gone to the cops, so the phones are clean. But if you do allow it, keep it short and watch what she says.' Egan jangled his keys. 'Right. I'll leave you to it. I've got to get back to Ireland.' He reached into his jacket pocket and took out an envelope. He handed it to McCracken. 'Be careful with her,' he said, nodding at the offices. 'She's not to be trusted, not for a minute.'

Katie crept up the stairs and put her ear to the door. She couldn't hear anything. 'Hello!' she shouted. 'I have to use the bathroom!' There was no answer. 'It's an emergency!' she shouted at the top of her voice. Still no answer. Katie tried the door handle. It twisted but the door wouldn't move. She didn't think it was locked because if it was locked then the handle wouldn't move. That meant it was only the bolts that kept her in. Katie pushed and pulled the handle, wondering if it would be possible to shake the bolts loose, but the door hardly moved.

Katie kicked the door, but that didn't seem to move it much – it just hurt her foot. She ran her fingers around the edge of the door. There was a gap between it and the frame where the hinges were, and she pressed her eye to it. If she moved her head to the side she could just see the kitchen door at the end of the hallway. If she pushed her head to the other side all she could see was the wall opposite.

She went back down the stairs, sat on the bed and held Garfield in her arms. Cats were always getting out of places, but they were small and could squeeze through tiny holes. There were no holes that Katie could squeeze through. She sat and frowned, her chin resting on Garfield's head. She had to find another way out.

Andy was sitting on the office floor when she heard her name being called. She got to her feet and walked through to the factory area where Green-eyes was standing at the rear of the blue Transit van, still dressed in the overalls and ski mask she'd had on the previous day. There were smaller vans parked next to the Transit. One was grey and one was black, but they both had the name of the same courier firm stencilled on the side.

'Some stuff here I want you to check out,' said Green-eyes.

Andy walked over to the Transit. The green tarpaulin that had covered the bags of fertiliser was lying on the floor. There was no sign of the bags. The Wrestler was over at the table, drinking from a bottle of water. The Runner climbed down from the driver's seat of the van and went to open the rear doors.

The back of the van was filled with dozens of cans of denatured alcohol, batches of twelve wrapped in clear plastic. Andy didn't recognise the brand name but each can was labelled 'Pure Denatured Alcohol' and carried a series of warnings that the contents were flammable, that the vapour could irritate eyes and that the contents were poisonous if swallowed.

'It's what we need?' asked Green-eyes.

'It's fine,' said Andy, checking the labels.

'The aluminium powder's in the box.'

Andy clambered over the stack of cans and pulled open the lid of a large cardboard box. Inside were cans of aluminium powder. She pulled out one of the cans and read the label. Pyro grade 400 mesh.

'We could only get two hundred pounds,' said the Runner. 'We've fixed to pick up another four hundred pounds from a supplier in Essex.'

Andy put the can back into the cardboard box and climbed out of the van, wiping her hands on her jeans.

The Wrestler put his bottle of water down and straightened his ski mask as if it were troubling him. 'It's okay?' he called over to Green-eyes.

Green-eyes waved him over. 'Yeah. Get this delivered and then pick up the electrical stuff.' She turned to Andy. 'Go back to the office, Andrea.'

Andy did as she was told. Behind her, the Runner and the Wrestler took the goods out of the Transit and began loading them into the back of the two smaller vans. She sat on the floor and waited as the metal shutters were raised and the vans drove out of the factory. The shutters rattled down again and a few minutes later Green-eyes opened the door to the office.

'I'm going to make coffee. Do you want some?'

'What I want is to talk to my husband. And my daughter.'

'Maybe tomorrow.'

'Why tomorrow?'

'Who's calling the shots here, Andrea? Me or you?'

Andy glared at the masked woman. 'I just want to know that she's okay. How could you do this? Don't you have children?'

'No, I don't. But I do have people that I love, and people that love me, and I know that I'd do anything to make sure that they didn't come to harm.'

'How would you feel if someone kidnapped somebody you loved? How would you feel if someone said they'd be killed if you didn't do what they wanted?'

'I'd feel the same as you do,' said the woman. 'I'd feel angry and bitter and fearful. But the difference between us is that I wouldn't do anything to jeopardise the lives of those that depended on me.'

Andy's brow furrowed. 'What do you mean?'

The woman reached into the pocket of her overalls and brought out an envelope. She threw it at Andy and it fell on to the floor in front of her. Andy stared at it with wide eyes. It was the letter she'd left at the Strand Palace Hotel. The letter addressed to her husband.

'That was very, very stupid, Andrea,' said the woman, her voice a low growl. 'What did you think? That we wouldn't be checking on you?'

Andy closed her eyes and banged the back of her head against the wall.

'Everything's been planned, down to the last detail. And if you do as you're told, you and your family will be back together in a few days.' She pointed an accusing finger at the envelope on the floor. 'But tricks like that could screw it up for all of us. So don't whine to me about your daughter being in danger. If anyone's putting Katie's life on the line, it's you.' Green-eyes turned on her heels and slammed the door behind her.

Mick Canning drew back the two bolts and opened the door to the basement. Katie was sitting on the bed, and she looked up at him as he walked down the stairs carrying the video camera.

'Hello, Katie,' he said.

'Hi,' she replied.

'Are you hungry?' he asked.

Katie shook her head. 'Not really.'

'It's almost teatime,' he said. 'Do you want fish fingers?'

Katie nodded. 'Okay,' she said, her voice trembling as if she were close to tears.

Canning put the video camera on the table. He waved Katie to come over. She sat down on one of the wooden chairs. 'I want to take some pictures of you,' he said. He nodded at the video camera. 'With this.'

'Why?'

'So that I can send the tape to your mum and dad. So that they know that you're okay.'

'Why don't you let me telephone them? I know my number, it's Dublin six seven nine . . .'

Canning smiled beneath his ski mask. 'I know what your telephone number is, but it's better if we do it with the video camera.'

'Why?'

'Because then they can see you as well as hear you.' He picked it up and pointed it at her. 'Now, I want you to say something like, Hello, this is Katie. I'm fine. They're taking very good care of me. You can wave, too, if you want. But this is really important, Katie. I want you to say that it's Friday, okay? Can you do that?'

Katie nodded hesitantly.

'Okay, so when I press this button, the one my finger's on, then the red light here comes on and you start talking. Okay?'

'Okay,' said Katie.

'Right. Three, two, one . . .' He pressed the record button and nodded at her.

'Hello, Mummy,' she said. 'Hello, Dad. Are you there?'

Canning made a circling motion with his finger, encouraging her to talk.

'I'm fine. There's a nice man taking care of me. He's giving me fish fingers and beefburgers and comics to read. But he won't let me come and see you.'

Canning mouthed the word 'Friday'.

'Oh yes, I nearly forgot. It's Friday today. Mummy, please come and get me. I want to go home.'

Canning pressed the button to stop the recording, then reached over and ruffled her hair. 'Good girl,' he said. He took the tape out of the recorder. 'You did that really well.' He took a second cassette out of his pocket and slotted it into the recorder. 'Now, we're going to try it again. Say what you said before, but this time I want you to say that it's Saturday, okay?'

Katie frowned. 'Why?'

'Because when your mum and dad get the tape, it might be Saturday.'

'What day is it today?'

'That doesn't matter, Katie.'

Katie lapsed into silence and nibbled on her lower lip.

'What's the matter?' asked Canning.

'I don't want to,' she said.

Canning stared at her for several seconds, then he switched off the video camera. 'Okay, maybe we'll try again later. I'll go and get your fish fingers.'

'I'm not hungry,' she said. 'Not really.'

Andy picked up the envelope and opened it. It was the piece of paper that had been slid under the door of her room in the Strand Palace Hotel. Along the bottom she'd scrawled 'Martin, this is where they want me to go. I love you. Don't let anything happen to Katie'. Now he'd never get the message. She ran her hands through her hair. She had to talk to Martin. She had to let him know that she was all right.

Her eyes were tired and gritty from crying and her throat was painfully dry, but the discomfort was nothing compared with the ache in her heart. Andy had seen news reports of the bomb that Republican terrorists had detonated in Omagh in Northern Ireland in the summer of 1998. Twenty-eight people killed, two hundred injured. The aftermath of the massacre had been captured by a tourist with a video camera and she and Martin had watched horrified as shocked and bleeding survivors had staggered along streets littered with broken glass and twisted metal. Nine of the dead were children. Andy had cried when she'd seen the pictures, cried on Martin's shoulder as he'd held her.

She screwed up the letter. Four thousand pounds was a massive bomb. Bigger than any that had ever exploded in England or Ireland. The bomb that had done a billion pounds' worth of damage to London's Docklands in 1996 was a thousand-pound mixture of fertiliser and Semtex. The bomb in Omagh had been smaller, just five hundred pounds of home-made explosives packed into a car. That bomb had devastated the centre of the market town. The damage that a bomb eight times bigger would do defied Andy's imagination. Four thousand pounds. It could kill hundreds of people. It could bring down a skyscraper.

She hated Green-eyes for the way she was making her choose. The life of her daughter, or the lives of strangers. Andy would kill to protect Katie, of that she had no doubt. And if she was ever put in the position where she had to give up her own life for the life of her daughter, she'd do it willingly. Nothing was more important, no sacrifice to great, to safeguard the life of her only child. But killing and maiming innocent strangers. That was something else. It was a diabolical choice to have to make. A choice no one should ever be faced with.

Canning put the video camera down in front of McEvoy, who was cleaning their two Makarov 9mm pistols and working his way through a bottle of Bushmills. His .38 Smith & Wesson was on the floor next to the coffee table. 'Okay?' he asked.

Canning put a single videocassette tape on the table and McEvoy scowled. 'Where's the rest?' he snapped.

'Just did the one,' said Canning. He went over to the fridge and pulled a box of fish fingers and a bag of oven chips out of the icebox.

'We were told to do seven,' said McEvoy, holding the barrel of one of the pistols to his face and squinting down it. 'One's no fucking good to anybody, is it?'

'I'll do them later.'

'You'd better. Egan wants them in London tomorrow.'

Canning switched on the oven and spread a layer of chips on a metal tray. 'The kid's a bit wary, that's all.'

'Wary? What do you mean, wary? Give her a slap and tell her to do as she's told. We're the fucking kidnappers, she's the fucking kidnappee, Mick. We tell her what to do, not the other way around, right?'

Canning put the chips in the oven and closed the door. He took off his ski mask and rubbed his face. The woollen mask always made his skin itch. 'She's a seven-year-old kid, George. She's scared shitless. She needs careful handling.'

McEvoy put the gun down and took another swig from the bottle of Bushmills. 'I'll give her careful handling,' he said.

'It'll be okay. I'll take care of it.'

McEvoy scowled at him. 'You'd better. Or you can explain to Egan why you're letting a kid run rings around you.'

Mark Quinn lit a cigarette and offered the pack to O'Keefe. O'Keefe took one and grunted his thanks. They walked out of the lift towards where they'd parked the two vans.

Quinn leaned against the van he'd been driving and pulled a small notebook from his jacket pocket. 'Sawdust, diesel oil and soap. Containers and black bags.'

'You've got the sawdust sorted, have you?' asked O'Keefe.

'Yeah. And I'll pick up the diesel from a garage on the way. Can you get the rest of the stuff?'

'Sure.' O'Keefe climbed into his van and wound down the window. 'You okay for cash?'

Quinn opened his wallet and flicked through a wad of fifty-pound notes. He nodded at O'Keefe.

'Right, see you back at the factory.' O'Keefe drove off. Quinn studied the list in his notebook. Most of the ingredients were innocuous enough and wouldn't arouse the interest of the police officers who manned the checkpoints on the roads that led into the financial district. The ones that might cause suspicion, such as the aluminium powder, the alcohol and the diesel oil, could be smuggled through in the back of the courier vans. The vans bore the registration numbers of vehicles used by a genuine courier company that did a lot of business in the City.

Egan had planned everything down to the last detail. The office had been leased months before it was needed, and the vehicles had all been in place before Quinn had arrived in London. Other than McCracken and O'Keefe, Quinn didn't know who was involved in the operation, but they were obviously all professionals. He took a long pull on his cigarette and inhaled deeply. He wondered what they had to gain from building a bomb in the City of London. When he'd first agreed to the job, Quinn had asked Egan for an explanation, but Egan had told him that the reasons weren't important, that he wasn't being paid to ask questions.

Quinn took a final drag on his cigarette and dropped it on to the ground. He stamped on it, then got into the van, switched on the ignition and drove slowly out of the carpark. He turned on the radio and pushed the tuning buttons until he found a station playing heavy metal. He nodded his head back and forth in time with the beat as he drove through the City, choosing a road out that he hadn't used for a couple of days, just to be on the safe side. He was waved through the checkpoint by a bored uniformed policeman who didn't even give him a second look.

Canning knocked on the basement door and slipped back the bolts. Katie was lying on her camp bed, curled up around her Garfield toy.

'I feel sick,' she said.

'You're just upset,' he said. 'You're worried, that's all. It's going to be okay. Just a few more days.'

'No, I feel really sick. Hot.'

Canning put his hand on her forehead. She was indeed hot and her skin was clammy with sweat.

'Sit up. Let me have a look at you.'

Katie did as he asked and looked at him with sad eyes as he felt her neck.

'Open your mouth.'

She opened her mouth wide and closed her eyes. He told her to turn her head so that the light shone into her mouth. The sides of her throat were bright red, but there were no white patches which would have indicated serious infection.

Katie opened her eyes. 'Are you going to take me to the hospital?' she said.

Canning smiled. 'You've just got a bit of flu, that's all. You've had flu before, haven't you?'

Katie nodded.

'Okay. I'll go and get you some medicine. But don't worry, you're going to be all right.' Katie saw the video camera that Canning had put on the bed and began shaking her head.

'You've got to do it for me, Katie.'

'I don't want to.'

'I'm not asking you to do anything dangerous. It's not going to hurt you.'

'But it's not Saturday. I'll be telling a lie.'

'But it might be Saturday when they get the message. If you say it's Friday and they get the message on Saturday, they might be worried. You can understand that, can't you?'

Katie nodded. 'I guess.'

'I mean, suppose we put the tape in the post. It might take two days before your mum gets it. You don't want your mum to worry, do you?'

Katie rubbed her nose with the palm of her hand. 'No.'

'So let's record a message that'll make her happy, then I'll go and get your medicine. Okay?'

'Okay. I guess.'

Canning put the camera up to his face, pressed the 'record' button and nodded.

'Mummy. Dad. This is Katie. Your daughter.' She hesitated.

Canning mouthed the words 'I'm fine' and nodded encouragingly.

'I'm fine,' said Katie. 'But I've got flu, I think. My head hurts and my throat's sore. The nice man is going to give me some medicine to make it better so I should be okay soon.'

Canning mouthed 'Saturday'.

'He said to say it's Saturday and that I'm okay. Mummy, I want to come home . . .'

She started crying and Canning switched off the video camera. He gave her a hug but her little body was racked with sobs.

'I want to go home,' she said.

'I know you do,' said Canning.

She curled up on the bed with her back to him and he went upstairs and into the kitchen. McEvoy was watching the news on a portable television set.

'How's the little princess?' he snarled.

'She's got the flu. I'll go and get her some Night Nurse or something.'

'Did she do the tape?'

'Yeah. Saturday.'

'Egan wants a week's worth. He's not going to be happy with two days.'

'The kid's sick,' said Canning.

'She's going to be a hell of a lot sicker if this thing doesn't pan out,' said McEvoy. 'Sick as in dead.'

Lydia McCracken was sitting in front of her computer when she heard the van pull up outside. On the screen was a closed-circuit television image of the reception area of the office on the ninth floor of Cathay Tower. She pressed one of the function keys and a different view appeared. The sacks of fertiliser. There were six hidden cameras in the office – three in smoke detectors, two hidden behind mirrors, and one in an air-conditioning unit. She checked all six viewpoints, satisfying herself that the office was secure. She switched off the computer as the outside door opened. It was Quinn.

'Everything okay?' she asked.

'Sure. I've got the diesel and the sawdust. Don's picking up the rest of the stuff. You want me to get the woman out? Get her to check it?'

'No need. Diesel and sawdust's straightforward enough.'

She looked at her watch. It was after seven, so there wasn't enough time to get the electrical equipment. It would have to wait until tomorrow. 'Leave the stuff in the vans. Best we use them rather than the Transit.'

'You hungry?' asked Quinn. 'I'm starving. I'll go out and get a takeaway, yeah?'

'Might as well,' said McCracken. 'But nothing close by, okay? Drive into Milton Keynes. And don't use the vans, take the Volvo or the VW.' She nodded over at the offices. 'And ask her what she wants. She hasn't eaten since breakfast.'

Quinn pulled his ski mask on and tucked it into his shirt collar. He went over to the office where they were keeping the woman. Andy was sitting with her back against the wall, her suitcase by her side.

'Room service,' he said.

Andy looked up at him, confused.

'I'm going out for food. Do you want something?'

She put a hand on her stomach and nodded her head. 'Yes. Please.'

'Any requests? Indian? Chinese? Burger King? I'm driving into town.'

'Anything.'

'You'll have to give me a clue,' said Quinn, closing the office door behind him. He tucked his thumbs into the pockets of his trousers and stood with his legs apart, his groin thrust slightly forward. 'I don't know what you like.'

'A sandwich. Anything.'

Quinn pulled a face. 'I'm not sure if I can get sandwiches. Fast food, yeah?'

Andy pushed her hair away from her face. 'A burger'll be fine, then.'

'Cheeseburger?'

'Okay.'

'Anything to drink?'

'Coffee'll be fine. Thanks.'

Quinn nodded. He looked her up and down. She had long legs, and a good, firm bust. Nice hair, too. Soft and blond. She looked good for a thirty-four-year-old. That was what O'Keefe had said, but Quinn didn't believe him. She couldn't possibly be a whole ten years older than he was. Nice mouth. Full lips and really white teeth, the sort of teeth that the models in toothpaste adverts had.

'I want to talk to my daughter,' she said.

'I bet you do,' said Quinn.

'And my husband. I want him to know that I'm all right.'

Quinn shrugged. 'It's not up to me. You'll have to ask McK . . .' He caught himself before the name slipped out. She wasn't going to catch him out as easily as that. 'You'll have to ask her outside.'

'You know her, right? Can't you persuade her? I just want to phone my husband. And talk to my daughter. That's not too much to ask, is it? I'm co-operating. I'm doing everything you ask.'

Quinn stared down at her for several seconds. His chest had gone tight and it was difficult to breathe. 'What's it worth?' he said eventually.

Andy frowned up at him. 'What?'

'You know. What's it worth?' He jutted his neck forward. 'I do something for you, you do something for me. Yeah?'

Andy drew her knees up against her chest. 'I just want to

talk to my daughter, that's all. And my husband. I want to know that they're all right.'

'Great. I can probably persuade her to let you use the phone. But you're gonna have to do something for me.' He licked his upper lip as he watched the rise and fall of her breasts. 'Just one blowjob,' said Quinn. He took a step closer to her. 'No one'll know.' He jerked his head towards the door. 'She won't know. Your husband won't know. It'll be our secret.'

Andy looked up at him for several seconds, then she slowly got to her knees, her eyes never leaving his face. Quinn put his hands down to his zipper but Andy shook her head. 'Let me,' she said, her voice a seductive whisper.

The breath caught in Quinn's throat and he closed his eyes, his legs trembling with anticipation.

The pain hit him like a hot poker in his groin and he gasped. Her right hand had grabbed his scrotum and squeezed like a vice. He opened his eyes, but before he could react her left hand had squeezed him around the throat and she had pushed him back against the wall. He tried to move to the side but she gripped him harder, crushing his testicles so hard that he could feel her fingernails digging through the denim of his jeans. His eyes watered and he tried to yell at her but her grip on his throat was as tight as her hold on his genitals.

Her face was only inches away from his. 'You don't scare me,' she hissed. 'You might have my daughter, but you don't scare me, do you understand?'

Quinn tried to nod but he couldn't move his head. A tear trickled down his cheek underneath his ski mask.

'If you come near me again, I'll hurt you like you've never been hurt before. I'll crush your balls or I'll poke my fingers in your eyes or I'll scratch your face so deep that the scars will never heal, do you understand me?'

Quinn nodded.

Andy stared into his eyes, then she released her grip on him and stood back, her hands up defensively. She glared at him, her cheeks flushed.

'You fucking bitch!' spat Quinn, rubbing his neck. 'Too good for me, is that it? You'll do it and more for me before I've fucking finished with you.'

Andy didn't say anything. She stood facing him with her hands up, fingers curled. Quinn stepped sideways, groping for the door handle, then he pulled the door open and slammed it behind him.

He went back to the factory area where McCracken was checking her mobile phone.

'She's not hungry,' he said, taking off his ski mask.

McCracken put her phone back in her briefcase and locked it. 'Don't fuck with her, Quinn. Okay?'

'What do you mean?'

'You know what I mean. We need her – the more she co-operates with us the sooner we'll be finished and the sooner you'll get your money.'

'Yeah, I know.'

'So don't fuck with her. Don't even talk to her.'

'You said ask her what she . . .'

'Yeah, well, that was my mistake. Keep away from her.'

She looked as if she wanted to say more, but she turned away when they heard O'keefe arrive in his van.

'So, what do you want to eat?' Quinn asked. 'It's on me.'

'Whatever,' said McCracken. 'I've lost my appetite.' She went out to meet O'Keefe, leaving Quinn staring sullenly after her.

Martin Hayes left the office early. He hadn't been able to get any work done so he'd told Padraig that he wasn't feeling well. He was in the house by four o'clock. He let Dermott out into the garden, and was making himself a cup of instant coffee when the doorbell rang. The noise startled him and he spilled boiling water over the counter top. He cursed and went to see who was at the front door. There were two uniformed officers of the Garda Siochana, the Irish police, standing on the doorstep, one grey and in his late forties, the other younger and taller. They were both wearing waterproof jackets, flecked with rain.

'Mr Hayes?' asked the older one. 'Mr Martin Hayes?'

'Yes?' said Martin. He had a sick feeling in the pit of his stomach. Two unsmiling policemen could only mean bad news. He held on to the door handle for support, gripping it tightly.

'Is your wife at home?'

Martin narrowed his eyes, confused. The question was totally unexpected. He'd assumed that they were there to tell him that Katie or Andy had been found. And found meant dead, because if they were okay then they'd be on the doorstep with the policemen. 'What?'

'Mrs Hayes. Mrs Andrea Hayes. Is she at home?'

'No,' said Martin, hesitantly.

'What about your daughter?'

'My daughter?'

'Katie. You only have the one child, don't you?'

'Yes,' said Martin.

'Can we see her, please?'

Martin shook his head. 'I'm sorry. What?'

'Your daughter. We'd like to see her.'

'She's not here.'

'Where is she?'

'What's this about?' asked Martin. He looked from one garda to the other. They both looked back at him like undertakers weighing up a corpse.

'Could you tell us where your wife and daughter are, Mr Hayes?'

Martin realised that he was gripping the door handle so tightly that he was losing the feeling in his hand.

'They're out.'

'Out where?'

'Look, could you tell me what this is about? Is something wrong? Has something happened?'

'That's what we're trying to find out, Mr Hayes.'

Martin could feel his legs start to shake. The more he tried to stop them shaking, the worse it got, and he was sure that the two gardai could see the effect their presence was having on him.

'My wife's out. With Katie. They'll be back tomorrow. They've gone up to Belfast.'

The older garda raised an eyebrow and waited for Martin to continue. Martin could feel his lips slide across his teeth as he widened his smile. His legs were starting to tremble again.

'To see her aunt. Her aunt's sick and Andy wanted to go and make sure that there was food in the house, stuff like that.'

'And she took your daughter with her?' said the older garda.

Martin nodded. 'I've been really busy at work. I couldn't guarantee that I'd be able to pick Katie up from school. We decided that it'd be better if she went with Andy. It's only going to be for a few days.'

'Andy?'

'My wife. Andrea. I call her Andy.'

'And you didn't think of informing the school?'

Martin suddenly realised what the visit was about. The woman in the headmistress's office, Mrs O'Mara, must have called them. He shrugged. 'She's only seven. We didn't think she'd be hurt by a few days off school.'

'I've got kids myself,' said the older garda. 'Boy of fifteen, girl of twelve. A few years back I took them to Galway, caravan holiday. I love caravans, me. Love the freedom. Thing is, I asked the school if they could be allowed to take their holidays a week early. I was having trouble getting time off. It was like pulling teeth. They wouldn't have it.'

Martin nodded. The garda was smiling ingratiatingly, trying to put him at ease. There was no warmth in the man's smile and his cold eyes continued to stare at Martin.

'So maybe that's why you didn't tell the school, eh?' the garda continued. 'Maybe you thought they wouldn't let her go?'

Martin shrugged. 'I didn't really think about it. It was my wife's idea, really. It was all short notice, you know. Her aunt called and Andy went the same day.'

The older garda nodded. 'How did she go?'

'What?'

'How did your wife go up to Belfast?'

Martin's mind whirled. Why was he asking that? The reason hit him like a blow to the stomach. There were two cars parked in the driveway. Martin's Range Rover and Andy's Renault Clio. So the gardai knew that Andy hadn't driven up to Belfast.

'She took the train. I mean, they took the train. Andy and Katie.'

'Which train?'

'The Belfast train,' said Martin.

The garda smiled as if there had been a simple misunderstanding. 'The time,' he said. 'What time did the train leave?'

Martin had no idea how often trains went from Dublin to Belfast. 'Morning. Tennish. On Wednesday.'

'Wednesday?'

Martin nodded.

'About ten?'

'That's right.'

The two gardai exchanged looks but Martin couldn't tell what they were thinking.

'And your wife's aunt. What was her name?'

'Bessie.'

'Bessie. Where exactly does she live?'

'I'm not sure of the address, exactly. But it's north Belfast.' Martin figured the best thing to do was to keep his answers as vague as possible. Specifics could be checked.

'And how was your wife going to get from the station to her aunt's house?'

'Taxi, I guess.'

'And why didn't she drive up to Belfast?'

Martin shrugged but didn't answer.

'Has she phoned? Your wife?'

Martin rubbed his nose with the back of his hand. It was unlikely in the extreme that Andy would have gone away and not telephoned him. But if he said yes, could they check? He was sure that the phone company could provide a list of numbers called from the house, but were they also able to tell who had phoned in? He had no choice, he had to lie. They wouldn't believe that his wife and daughter would have gone away for five nights and not phoned. 'Several times,' he said. 'In fact, she called last night.'

The younger garda took out a small green notebook and a pen. 'Could you give us the number, please, sir?'

'The number?'

'Your Aunt Bessie's telephone number?' said the older garda.

'She's not my aunt. She's Andy's aunt.'

'And the number?'

'I don't think she's on the phone.'

'But you said she phoned to ask your wife to go up and take care of her.'

'She must have used a phone box.'

'But you said she was ill. Needed looking after.'

Martin could feel himself being painted into a corner. The older garda didn't look particularly bright – he had a wide chin and a flattish nose and he spoke slowly, as if he had trouble putting his thoughts together, but it was clear that he wasn't missing anything.

'I'm not sure if it was her that phoned. Andy took the call. It could have been someone else, phoning for her.'

The older garda nodded thoughtfully. 'And when are you expecting your wife back?'

'I'm not sure.'

'She didn't say when she called last night?'

'No. No, she didn't. Look, what's this about? Has something happened?'

The older garda looked at Martin for several seconds before answering. 'We're not sure, Mr Hayes. In fact, it's all a bit of a mystery, really. You know a Mrs O'Mara?'

'She's a secretary at my daughter's school. She phoned yesterday, she wanted to know why Katie wasn't at school.'

'Well, now she's missing, too.'

'My daughter isn't missing,' said Martin, and the older garda held up his hand as if trying to calm him down. Martin found the gesture patronising in the extreme, but he bit his tongue.

'There's no need to get upset, Mr Hayes. You know what I mean. Mrs O'Mara had mentioned to the headmistress that she was concerned about your daughter. Now Mrs O'Mara hasn't turned up for work. We've been around to her house and she's not there.'

Martin put his hand up to his forehead, frowning. 'I don't get what you're saying. Mrs O'Mara isn't at home so you think something's happened to Katie? That makes no sense. No sense at all.'

'That's right,' said the garda. 'It's a mystery. And mysteries annoy the hell out of me. But nothing you've said so far has reassured me that your daughter is safe and sound.'

'What?' Martin didn't have to feign his reaction. 'That's fucking ridiculous!'

The younger garda stepped forward as if he was expecting

Martin to attack his colleague. Martin realised he'd bunched his hands into fists and he forced himself to relax.

'Look, my wife and daughter are out of town, that's all. They'll be back any day now.'

The older garda nodded slowly. He reached into the inside pocket of his waterproof jacket and took out a business card. 'My name's O'Brien,' he said. 'Sergeant O'Brien. Next time your wife phones, would you get her to call me? Just so's we know that she's okay.'

Martin reached for the card, but the garda didn't let go of it. 'Sure. I will,' said Martin.

The two men stood for a few seconds, both holding the card.

'Don't forget now,' said O'Brien. He let the card slip through his fingers, then stepped back from the doorstep. The two gardai walked down the path, away from the house. The younger garda twisted his head and said something into his radio and there was a burst of static.

Martin closed the door and leaned against it, his heart pounding like a jackhammer.

Egan frowned as he listened to the tape. The two gardai turning up was an unexpected development, and it meant he was going to have to revise his plans. Martin Hayes had handled it better than Egan had expected, but one of the gardai, the one who'd introduced himself as O'Brien, had been persistent in his questioning, especially about the train that Hayes claimed his wife had taken up to Belfast. By the end of the conversation he seemed to have accepted what Hayes had said, but Egan doubted that the gardai had been deceived. They'd go away and make further enquiries, but eventually they'd be back.

Egan was surprised that they'd made the connection between the O'Mara woman and the Hayes girl. Mrs O'Mara was safely buried in a wood some twenty miles south of Dublin – it was sheer bad luck that the secretary had expressed her concerns about Katie's absence to the school's headmistress.

He swivelled his chair around and hit the print button on his computer keyboard. The laser printer whirred and Egan picked up the letter and read it through carefully before signing it. He fed it into the fax machine on the desk and dialled the number of his bank in Zurich. The letter contained instructions to transfer one million dollars to another of his accounts, this one in the Cayman Islands. From there he'd move it to the Dutch Antilles. He'd only had the Zurich account for six months, and once his work for the men from Beijing was finished he'd close it. The fax machine swallowed the sheet of paper and Egan flicked the top off a bottle of Budweiser. He went over to the window and looked out over the city as the fax machine whirred behind him. The serviced apartment he was renting was little more than a hotel suite, and just as anonymous. Anonymity was something that Egan worked hard at. In public he never expressed emotion, never lost his temper. His passage through life was as smooth and unhindered as that of a razor slitting flesh. Any obstruction and he simply slid around it; any confrontation was to be avoided at all cost.

Egan had the ability to enter a room and leave without anyone remembering him. He had friends who took pride in being able to get the best table in restaurants or walk to the front of a nightclub queue, but Egan hated the idea that a maître'd or a bouncer would know who he was. He dressed casually but conservatively, wore no jewellery other than a battered Rolex on a leather strap that had once belonged to a friend of his, a Navy SEAL who'd died in Kuwait, and drove the sort of cars favoured by sales reps. Ostentation was for film stars, musicians or high-profile businessmen who wanted to see their faces in the tabloids. Egan was a professional terrorist, and the only people he wanted to acknowledge him were the people who paid his wages.

He took a swig from the bottle of Budweiser. Behind him, the fax finished transmitting and ejected the letter. One million dollars. The equivalent of twelve years' salary in his last job. Egan had worked for the Defence Intelligence Agency in a black operations department that spent most of its time attempting to destabilise anti-American governments in South America. Blackmail, bribery, assassination – it had been the best possible training for his present career. Egan had left after five years, spent six months travelling the world establishing fake identities and opening a daisy-chain of bank accounts, then set up on his own. Freelance. It had been the best move he'd ever made. A militant Islamic group funded by Osama Bin Laden had paid him a total of three million dollars for his work with Muslim terrorists in Kenya and Tanzania, and he'd been paid half a million dollars for his past in a series of bomb attacks by white supremacists in America, including the bombing of the Federal Building in Oklahoma City. Three months as an adviser with the Palestinian Liberation Organisation had netted him two million dollars, and his work for the men from Beijing would earn him a further seven million, minus expenses.

By the end of the year his account in the Dutch Antilles would contain more than twelve million dollars. The money itself was of little practical concern to Egan. He lived modestly, owned no property or cars, and virtually all his outgoings were work-related. Money was simply a way of keeping score. The more he had, the better he was doing.

He put down his beer and went over to the fax machine. He used a cheap plastic lighter to set fire to the letter, then dropped it into a metal wastepaper bin at the side of the desk.

He looked at his Rolex. Everything was on schedule, everything was going to plan. The DIA had taught Egan well. All he had to do now was to work out the best way of killing Martin Hayes.

Andy lay on her side, her head resting on a rolled-up pullover. There had been no sound from outside for more than hour, though a strip of light still seeped in under the office door. Her stomach growled, but she steadfastly refused to ask her captors for food. She'd gone to the bathroom, remembering to shout for permission first, and had come back with a paper cup of water.

She rolled over and stared at the door. It wasn't locked; nor was the metal door that led outside. All she had to do was walk out of the office, down the corridor, across the factory area and out of the main door. There was nothing stopping her, nothing physical anyway. What was the expression? Iron bars do not a prison make. Andy didn't know if it came from a poem or one of Shakespeare's plays, but it described her situation perfectly. She was powerless, totally, utterly powerless, because the moment she walked out the kidnappers would vanish and Katie, her dear, darling Katie, would be dead. If she did run away, and if she did go to the police, what could she tell them? What did she know about her captors or what they were doing?

She knew that one of them, the one built like a wrestler, was called Don. And she knew that the woman had a name that started with 'McC'. Or 'McK'. The woman had an accent that suggested she was Irish but had spent a lot of time in Scotland. Or vice versa. That was it. The sum total of her knowledge. She knew that they wanted to build a big bomb, a huge bomb, but she didn't know where they planned to use it or why. If she did walk out and her captors had disappeared by the time she got back with the police, then there was no way that they would ever be able to track them down. Green-eyes, the Wrestler and the Runner always wore their ski masks and gloves – she was totally incapable of identifying them.

And even if she could get outside and get to the police, and if they managed to get back in time to arrest her captors, then what? They hadn't tied her up, they hadn't put a gun to her head. They'd used the threat of what might happen to Katie, but how on earth could she prove that? They were putting together the ingredients for a bomb, but Andy knew from experience that until the ingredients were actually combined, all the evidence was circumstantial. And if she did bring in the police, what incentive was there for Green-eyes and her companions to confess? If they admitted it, they'd face long prison sentences for kidnapping and terrorism. Their best option was to say nothing and to get rid of the evidence. And that meant she'd never see Katie again. No, there was no way she could walk away. No way could she rely on the police. If there was a way out of the nightmare she was trapped in, it was up to her to find it. Up to her and Martin.

She closed her eyes tight and tried to imagine herself in her husband's arms. She wished with all her heart that she was back with him, back in her house in Dublin, safe and warm, with Katie asleep in the next room. It was no good. The unyielding floor beneath her was a constant reminder of where she was, and what lay ahead.

DAY FIVE

Canning was stirring a pan of scrambled eggs when Mc-Evoy banged open the kitchen door and stood in the doorway, scratching his stomach. 'What are ya cooking?' he asked.

'Eggs.'

'Eggs again? I fucking hate eggs.'

'They're not for you. They're for Katie.'

McEvoy walked across the fake marble linoleum to the cooker and stood behind Canning, so close that Canning could smell the man's stale breath. 'What's this with Katie? You'll be calling her Miss Hayes next. It's best to keep your distance, Mick. Don't let it get personal, yeah? Call her the kid. The girl. The bitch. Call her anything, but don't call her by her name. If the shit hits the fan, we might have to do her, and it's going to be a hell of a lot harder to do it if you've forged a relationship with her. Get it?'

'Got it.' Canning spooned the scrambled eggs on to a paper plate, then put the plate and a plastic fork on a tray. 'You've done this before, haven't you?'

'Not with a kid, no. But I've held guys before.'

'For ransom, like?'

'No. Not for ransom.'

'For what, then?'

McEvoy made himself a cup of instant coffee and spooned in three sugars. 'What is this, *Twenty Questions*?'

'Just want to know where I stand, that's all. Background.'

McEvoy folded his arms across his chest and leant against the fridge. 'Background it is you want, huh? Background? I used to work for a unit attached to the Civil Administration Team, how's that for background?'

Canning raised his eyebrows in surprise. He'd known that McEvoy was active in the IRA, but the Civil Administration Team was the organisation's internal security unit, composed of only the most trusted, and vicious, activists. When the IRA needed prisoners or traitors interrogated or tortured, it was the Civil Administration Team that was called in. And most of the men and women they interrogated ended up dead.

McEvoy saw the look of surprise. 'Yeah, the best of the best, the hardest of the hard.'

'Shit.'

'Yeah. If there was anyone they thought was bad, we'd go in and get them, hold them until we were sure we weren't being watched, then the heavy mob would move in. To do the business. They were hard bastards, Mick. You wouldn't want to meet them on a dark night. On any fucking night. You knew that if they were on the case, someone was gonna end up dead. That's what I mean about not getting involved. You don't use their names, you don't say please and thank you, you don't ask them how they are. Okay, you might smile and keep them chatting until you get them into the safe house, but then you tie them up and throw a blanket over their heads. You don't talk to them and you don't look at them. You treat them like meat because that's all they are. Meat. Dead meat.'

'And are you saying that's what Katie is? Dead meat?'

'She might be. She might not be.' He sipped his coffee. 'But why take the risk? Maybe her mother's going to do what Egan wants, maybe everything's going to go exactly the way Egan's planned, but if worst comes to worst, we've got to be prepared to do what's necessary.' He looked across at Canning with narrowed eyes. 'What we're being paid for.' He nodded at the tray. 'Her eggs are getting cold.'

Lydia McCracken thanked the two shop assistants and gave them each five pounds. The two teenagers had trundled two tumble-driers and four electric ovens out of the discount warehouse and loaded them into the back of the blue Peugeot van, and they were both panting and sweating. They thanked her and walked away, grinning at the unexpected tip. Mark Quinn loaded four large coffee grinders and four electric woks into the van and slammed the door shut.

McCracken got into the passenger seat and told Quinn to drive back to the industrial estate. As he drove, she checked a computer print-out that she had attached to a metal clipboard. Most of the items on the list had now been purchased, and all the chemicals had already been delivered to the office in Cathay Tower. They were ready to go on to the next stage.

It took an hour to get back to the factory unit that they were using as their base. It was on a large industrial estate on the outskirts of Milton Keynes, less than half a mile from the M1. McCracken had leased the unit almost a year earlier in the name of a metal tubing manufacturing company. There was a parking area at the rear of the unit, with spaces for more than two dozen vehicles. The blue Transit van in the landscaping company livery was there, along with the two courier vans, a grey Volvo and a black VW Passat. There was also a 250cc Yamaha motorcycle with a black back-box, and a small scooter. All the vehicles had genuine paperwork and were taxed, insured and MoT'd.

Quinn parked the Peugeot next to one of the courier vans. 'Don and I'll take the Transit to the airport,' said McCracken. 'Leave the stuff in the van for now.'

They got out of the van and went inside the factory. O'Keefe was sitting at the table, playing Patience.

'She okay?' asked McCracken.

'Not a peep,' said O'Keefe, flicking the pack of cards with his thumbnail. His gun was hanging in its holster on the back of his chair. McCracken's gun was where she'd left it, on top of her holdall.

She looked at her wristwatch. 'Right, we're going to drop the Hayes woman at Shepherds Bush at two. Mark, you'd better head off now. Careful how you park the bike.'

'No sweat,' said Quinn. He went over to a large canvas duffel bag and pulled out a black crash helmet, a leather motorcycle jacket and a pair of padded leather gloves. 'Catch you later,' he said, heading for the door.

'Mark, hold on,' said McCracken. She went over to him, brushing her dyed blond hair behind her ears. 'Remember, keep your distance. No eye contact, right? Just check she gets there, and that she doesn't talk to anyone or use the phone.'

Quinn looked pained, as if he resented being given such specific instructions. 'I'm not stupid,' he said. He pulled the crash helmet over his head and flipped down the visor.

McCracken wanted to emphasise how important it was that Hayes didn't spot Quinn following her, but she could see that he wasn't receptive to any advice. He was young and headstrong, and McCracken was starting to wonder if it had been a mistake recruiting him. Not that it was her mistake. Egan had put the team together.

She took her ski mask off the table and put it on. O'Keefe put his on, too. Outside they heard Quinn start up the motorcycle and drive away.

McCracken slipped on her leather gloves and went through to the office section, where she called out Andy's name. Andy opened the door. She'd changed into a pair of black jeans and a white shirt.

'Have you got a suit?' asked McCracken. 'Something suitable for an office?'

Andy looked down at her jeans. 'No. I've got these and what I was wearing when you brought me here.'

'What are you? A size ten?'

'On a good day.'

'You can wear one of mine. We're about the same size.'

McCracken waved at Andy to follow her, and the two women went through to the factory area. McCracken sat down at the table next to O'Keefe. She nodded at the third chair and Andy sat down.

'We're moving out of here,' said McCracken. Her brief-case was on the floor next to her chair, and she swung it on to the table and clicked open the locks. She took out an *A–Z* London street directory and passed it over to Andy. 'Page forty-two,' she said. 'I've marked the building. It's called Cathay Tower. The address is on a card at the front.'

Andy flicked to the front of the book and found a three-by-four-inch piece of white card. On it was written 'OR-VICE WILLIAMS BROKING INTERNATIONAL LIMITED' and an address.

'It's on the ninth floor,' said McCracken.

'I don't understand . . .' protested Andy, but McCracken held up a gloved hand to silence her.

'You don't have to understand,' she said. 'You just have to do as you're told.' She took a laminated identification badge from the briefcase and handed it to Andy. 'This'll get you into the building. You go there and wait for us. We'll be there first thing tomorrow morning.'

Andy looked at the badge. It had a small metal clip so that it could be attached to clothing. The name of the broking firm was on the badge. So was another name, Sally Higgs, a scrawled signature and Andy's photograph, the Polaroid picture that had been taken on her arrival at the factory unit.

McCracken stood up. 'On your way to the tower, you don't speak to anyone, you don't phone anyone. You will be watched, Andrea. Every step of the way. If you try to communicate with anyone, anyone at all, we'll simply disappear and you'll never hear from us again. Or your daughter.'

Andy stared at the badge.

'You understand?'

'Yes,' mumbled Andy. She looked around the factory area as if trying to get her bearings. 'How do I get there?'

'I'll explain that later. But first there's something I want to show you.' She stood up, and Andy followed her across to the computer.

McCracken clicked on the mouse and a view of the Cathay Tower office filled the screen. Andy stared at it, not understanding.

'This is the office we'll be using,' explained McCracken. She clicked on the mouse again. Another view of the office appeared. 'We can see every bit of the office from here,' she said. 'So when you get there, just make yourself comfortable and wait for us. You'll be there on your own tonight, but we'll be watching you.'

Andy nodded, but said nothing.

'You're doing fine, Andrea,' said McCracken. 'Just keep on doing as we ask and this will all be over soon and you'll be back with your family.'

'I want to call my husband.'

'I can't let you do that, Andrea.'

Andy lowered her voice. 'If you don't, Martin'll go to the police, I know he will.'

'He won't. He'll be too worried about what'll happen to you and Katie.'

'No, you don't know him. He'll want to do something. He'll want to react, and by not communicating with him, you're not giving him any choice. There's only one thing he can do. He'll go to the police.'

Green-eyes studied Andy without replying.

'It's been almost five days since you took Katie. He hasn't heard from me since Wednesday night, so . . .'

Green-eyes stiffened. 'You spoke to him on Wednesday night? You called him from the hotel?'

'You didn't say I wasn't to,' said Andy. 'It was the only call I made. You just said I wasn't to call the police. He needed to know that I was okay. And he needs to know that I'm still okay. Because if he doesn't . . .' She left the sentence hanging.

'He's not going to do anything that might endanger you and your daughter,' said Green-eyes.

'If he doesn't hear from me, or from Katie, he's going to think that there's nothing to lose by going to the police. Five days is a long time when you're waiting for news. He's a builder, he works with his hands, he's used to doing things, don't you understand? He'll feel that he has to do something. And if you don't let me talk to him, I think he'll go to the police. He'll want to do something, anything, and by not communicating with him you've taken away all his options.'

'I can't trust you, Andrea. Look at that business with the letter at the hotel.'

'I'm sorry. That was stupid. Look, you know I want to talk to him because I miss him – you can understand that, can't you? I want to talk to my husband. But I know what will happen if he does go to the police and you find out. I don't want that to happen. I don't know why you're doing this and I don't want to know. I just don't want anything to happen to my daughter. And if Martin knows that I'm okay, and that Katie's okay, then he'll be more likely to wait and see how it works out.'

'Let me think about it,' said Green-eyes.

'You've got a mobile phone, haven't you? A cellular?' Green-eyes didn't react.

'So let me use that. It's not in your name, is it? I mean, I'm assuming that . . .'

Andy wanted to say more but she didn't want to risk antagonising Green-eyes. Green-eyes hadn't known that Andy had phoned Martin from London. That meant the phone in Dublin wasn't tapped. There had to be a way that she could make use of that knowledge. Green-eyes looked across at her and Andy forced herself to smile.

Green-eyes went over to a table and picked up her mobile phone. 'What's the number?'

Andy gave her the number and Green-eyes tapped it in. She listened to check that it was ringing, then handed it to Andrea. 'Any tricks, any at all, and it'll be Katie who'll suffer. And I want you to ask him if he's gone to the police.'

'Okay. Okay.' Andy couldn't believe that Green-eyes was letting her use the phone. Part of her was convinced that she was going to snatch the handset away at the last moment.

Martin answered and Andy's heart pounded. 'Martin? It's me.'

'Oh, sweet Jesus, thank God. How are you? Where are you?'

'Martin, did you go to the police?'

'Where are you? Are you okay? Andy, what's happening?'

'Martin, listen to me. Did you go to the police?'

'No. No I didn't.'

Andy put her hand over the receiver. 'It's okay. He hasn't spoken to the police.' Green-eyes nodded and motioned for Andy to continue with the call.

Martin panicked. 'Andy, Andy, don't go. Talk to me, don't go . . .'

'It's okay,' said Andy. 'I'm here. But you have to listen to me, love. I'm okay, and they say that Katie's okay. I'm fine, too. They're not hurting me. Look, Martin, there's something they want me to do for them. It's not going to take long, then they say they'll let me come home. Katie, too.'

'I've got the money ready,' said Martin. 'Almost four hundred thousand pounds. Tell them I've got the money.'

'They don't want money, Martin. Listen to me, love. They don't want the money. They just want me to . . .'

Green-eyes stepped forward and tried to take the phone from Andy. Andy took a step back, trying to keep the phone away from her. 'No details,' Green-eyes hissed.

'Okay, okay,' said Andy. 'Sorry. I'm sorry.' She held the phone to her face again. 'Martin, they don't want money. That's all I can tell you. But they've assured me that so long as you don't go to the police, they won't hurt me or Katie. You have to promise me that you won't go to the police.'

'I promise,' said Martin. 'But what's happening? What do they want?'

Andy ignored his question.

'Just wait there and we'll be back with you soon. We'll all be together again, just like we were before. You can take us to Venice. Like you promised. It'll be so great to go back. You and me, and Katie. It's going to happen, Martin. Just don't do anything to rock the boat, okay?'

Andy was rambling; the words were tumbling out and running into each other as if she were scared that he might interrupt.

'Okay, love. I promise. Swear to God. I won't go to the police. Tell them, I won't go to the police.'

Green-eyes grabbed the phone and pulled it away from Andy. 'That's enough,' she said.

'Thank you,' Andy said. 'Thanks for letting me talk to him. He was frantic.'

Green-eyes switched the phone off. She went over to the table and put the phone in her briefcase and locked it. 'What did you mean about Venice?'

'That's where we went on our honeymoon. He's been promising to take Katie there for ages. She saw the honeymoon pictures and wanted to know why she wasn't there. You know how kids are.'

Green-eyes turned to look at Andy, scowling. 'You weren't trying to be clever, were you, Andrea?'

'What do you mean?'

Green-eyes didn't reply. She sat down, steepled her fingers under her chin and stared at Andy with unblinking eyes.

'He hasn't gone to the police, and now he won't,' said Andy. 'Now he knows that I'm okay.' She dropped down on to one of the chairs. 'Are you really going to use it? The bomb?'

'Does it matter?'

'Of course it matters. Are you building it as a threat, or are you going to set it off?'

'Would it make you feel better if I said we weren't going to use it?'

'Of course.'

Green-eyes smiled thinly. 'Is that what you used to do in the IRA? Build bombs and not use them?'

'Sometimes you can get the same effect by just putting a bomb in place, if disruption's your aim. That's the purpose of coded warnings. You want civilians out of the way and you want to tie up the authorities. You make your point but you don't actually kill anyone.'

'Maybe that's what we're going to do, then. Does that make you feel better?'

'Now you're humouring me.'

'What do you expect me to do, Andrea? Do you think I'm going to tell you what we're planning to do? Why would I do that?'

'Have you thought this through? Have you thought through what'll happen if you explode a four-thousand-pound bomb in the City of London? Whatever it is you think you're going to achieve, the backlash will destroy you.

Look at what happened when the bomb went off in Omagh. It finished the Real IRA. Everyone turned against them.'

Green-eyes picked up her briefcase. 'We've got work to do. Come on.'

Martin absent-mindedly patted Dermott's chest and the dog panted happily. 'She's okay,' Martin said, and the dog's grin widened as if he understood and was as overjoyed as his owner. 'She's okay and Katie's okay.'

Martin felt light-headed, almost drunk. Part of him wanted to jump around and shout with relief. Andy was alive. So was his Katie. Over the past few days his imagination had run riot, and he'd come close to convincing himself that his wife and daughter were dead, that the only option he had left was to go to the police. He thanked God that he hadn't. He'd done the right thing by waiting. Andy was safe. And if what she'd said was true, she and Katie would be back home soon. They'd be a family again. His heart had almost stopped when she'd asked him if he'd spoken to the police. He realised that the kidnappers were monitoring the conversation, and he'd decided on the spur of the moment that he had to lie. If he'd told Andy that the police had turned up on his doorstep the kidnappers might think that he'd called them. Best not to mention it and hope that Sergeant O'Brien believed his story.

Martin's sense of relief was tempered by the realisation that he still didn't know what the kidnappers wanted. She'd made it clear that they didn't want money. So what did they want? What was so important that they needed Andy? It didn't make any sense at all. Andy was a housewife. A homemaker. She took care of him and she raised Katie and she did occasional freelance work for the *Irish Independent* and some Dublin magazines. She had been a journalist for a couple of years before Katie was born, a feature writer with a growing reputation, before she'd decided that she didn't want to miss out on Katie's childhood. Once Katie had been old enough to go to school, she'd tried to restart her career, but only in a half-hearted way. Her family was her main concern, and it wasn't as if they needed the money.

So what was it that the kidnappers wanted from her? It couldn't have been her journalistic skills. So what else did she have that they wanted? It was a mystery, and it was driving Martin crazy.

He stopped patting Dermott and lay back on the bed, staring up at the ceiling. And what had Andy meant by taking her to Venice? They'd never discussed going there. He'd never been to Venice. Neither had she. Hell, they'd never even been to Italy.

McEvoy looked up from the portable television set. 'It's almost noon,' he said. 'The flight's at two-thirty.'

'Yeah, I know,' said Canning.

'So we'll need the fucking tapes. All seven of them.'

'For fuck's sake, George, I'll take care of it.'

'So take care of it.'

'Look, the wee girl's sick. Her throat's swollen up like I don't know what.'

'She's got flu, you said.'

'It looks like flu. But her throat's bad. She can barely talk.'

McEvoy looked at his wristwatch, then pushed himself up out of his armchair. 'Let's see if I can't get the little bird to sing.' He reached for the video camera and a stack of tapes on the table next to where Canning was filling in the crossword in the *Irish Independent*.

'I'll do it,' said Canning.

McEvoy patted him on the shoulder, then gripped it tightly, his fingers biting into Canning's flesh. 'You stay where you are, Mick. I'd hate to tear you away from your crossword.'

McEvoy grinned wolfishly and put on his ski mask. He went down into the basement. The girl was curled up on her bed. She looked over her shoulder as he went up to her.

'Sit the fuck up,' he said.

'What?' she said sleepily. She rubbed her eyes.

'Sit the fuck up and do as you're told. I don't have time to piss around.'

'I don't feel well,' said Katie.

'Yeah, me neither.' He pulled the wooden chair away from the table and sat on it, facing the bed. 'Right, when I press this button, I want you to tell you mum and dad that you're all right. Tell them that you miss them, tell them anything you want. Then I want you to say that it's Sunday.'

'But it isn't. It's Saturday.'

McEvoy grabbed her by the hair. 'I don't give a flying fuck what day it is. I want you to say it's Sunday, okay?'

Tears sprang into Katie's eyes. 'I don't feel well.'

'You're going to feel a lot fucking worse if you don't do as you're told,' hissed McEvoy. 'Remember how I cut your hair? How would you like it if I cut off one of your ears? You wouldn't like that, would you?'

Katie shook her head. 'No,' she said.

McEvoy released his grip on her hair and she rubbed her head, glaring at him reproachfully. 'And if you don't wipe that fucking sour look off your face, I'll smack you good and proper.'

Katie forced a smile.

'That's better,' said McEvoy. 'Right. Now let's record this message. Then we'll do one for the rest of the days of the week. And if you give me any more trouble, any trouble at all, I'm going to cut off your ear, okay?'

Katie stared at him with wide eyes. She nodded slowly.

Andy lay in the back of the Transit van, the sound of the engine muffled by the hood she'd been made to wear.

Green-eyes was in the front passenger seat and the Wrestler was driving.

Next to her on the floor was a black briefcase that Green-eyes had given her. That and the dark blue suit and raincoat she'd been supplied with would give credence to her story that she was an office worker having to work a weekend shift. Green-eyes had said that the rest of Andy's belongings would be delivered the next day.

Outside the van she heard blaring horns and motorcycle engines, and in the distance the siren of an ambulance. They'd turned off the motorway some twenty minutes or so earlier.

'Nearly there, Andrea,' said Green-eyes. 'Are you okay?'

'No, I'm not okay,' said Andy. 'I'm hot and uncomfortable and I can hardly breathe.'

'Just a few minutes.'

The van braked and Andy slid along the metal floor, her knee banging against the briefcase. The van made a series of turns, then came to a halt.

'Now then, Andrea, listen to me carefully. I want you to sit up with your back to us, then take off the hood. Open the doors, close them, then walk away from the van. The Tube station is right ahead of you. Don't look back. Just keep walking into the station. And remember, you're going to be watched every step of the way. Do you understand?'

'Yes.'

'Go on, then.'

Andy followed the instructions and climbed out of the back of the van with the briefcase. She slammed the doors shut and walked straight to the station, keeping her head down. She knew they'd be watching her in the mirrors and didn't want to give them any reason to suspect that she was trying to sneak a look at them.

She went over to the ticket machines and bought a single ticket to Bank station with the change that Green-eyes had given her, then went through the barrier and took the escalator down to the eastbound Central Line platform.

The platform was crowded. The overhead indicator said that the next train would be along in two minutes. She walked along the platform, weaving in and out of the waiting passengers. She passed a chocolate vending machine and a public telephone. The phone was of the kind that took pre-paid phone cards and not cash, but even if she had a card there was no way she could risk making a call. There were almost a hundred people on the eastbound platform and any of them could have been tailing her. She walked by the phone and stood at the edge of the platform, staring down at the rails. A mouse scuttled along the sleepers, seeking the sanctuary of the tunnel.

Andy looked back along the platform. A businessman in a pin-stripe suit was looking at her. He smiled but she ignored him. A tall man in his twenties walked by nodding his head in time with the music he was playing through a Sony Walkman. He was wearing a denim jacket with a Harley Davidson emblem on the back, and had the volume up so high that other passengers were giving him dirty looks. A woman in a sheepskin jacket looked up from the copy of the *Evening Standard* she was reading and glared at the guy in the denim jacket. Could she be Green-eyes? wondered Andy. Had she got out of the van as soon as Andy had gone into the station? She had no way of knowing. The only means she had of identifying her was from her eyes, and she was too far away to see what colour they were.

A teenager in a black leather motorcycle jacket was leaning against the vending machine, picking his teeth with a match. He looked away. Could he be one of them? She'd heard a motorcycle drive away from the factory about half an hour before Green-eyes had given her the suit and told her to get into the back of the Transit. She looked away, then stole another quick glance at him. He seemed shorter than the Runner, and he was certainly thinner than the Wrestler, but there could be other members of the gang that she hadn't seen.

A breeze on her left cheek signalled the imminent arrival of the eastbound train, and Andy took a step back from the platform. The train pulled into the station and Andy stepped into a carriage. There were several empty seats but she was too tense to sit down. She held on to one of the overhead bars and braced herself as the doors closed and the train roared off into the tunnel. She looked around. The man in the motorcycle jacket was sitting at the far end of the carriage, picking his nose. Was he the one? Andy looked away, not wanting to establish eye contact with him.

The journey to Bank station seemed interminable. People got off. People got on. The man in the leather jacket stayed put, his arms folded across his chest.

Eventually Andy reached her destination. As she rode up the escalator to the surface, she looked over her shoulder. There was no sign of the man in the leather jacket.

After she'd passed through the ticket barrier, she took the A–Z street directory out of her raincoat pocket and used it to find her way to Cathay Tower.

There was a grey-haired security man with a drinker's nose sitting at a reception desk. He barely glanced at Andy's name badge. She walked past him to the lifts.

From the entrance to a building on the opposite side of the street, Quinn watched Andy go into Cathay Tower. He switched off his Walkman and pulled his headphones down around his neck. From the inside pocket of his denim jacket he took out a mobile phone and tapped out McCracken's number. She answered on the fifth ring. 'She's home and dry,' he said.

'Okay. Get back to the bike and head up to the factory,' she said. 'Keep an eye on the computer until we get back.'

She cut the connection. Quinn put the phone back into his pocket and put the headphones back on, then headed back to Bank station. He'd parked his motorcycle in a multistorey carpark in Shepherds Bush, his helmet and leather jacket locked in the back-box.

Canning looked up as McEvoy came out of the basement and bolted the door. 'Easy peasy,' said McEvoy, tossing the videocassettes on to the kitchen table. 'I've always had a way with kids and small animals.'

Canning gathered up the cassettes and put them into a plastic carrier bag together with the two he'd recorded.

'Is she okay?'

McEvoy reached for a bottle of Bushmills and poured himself a glassful. 'She's fine and dandy, Mick, my boy. Don't you worry your pretty little head about her.' He looked at his wristwatch. 'You'd best be going.'

Canning looked across at the bolted door. He didn't like the idea of leaving McEvoy alone with the little girl, but didn't see that he had any choice. McCracken had said that he was to deliver the tapes, and he doubted that he'd be able to persuade McEvoy to go in his place. He put the carrier bag into his holdall and got his British Midland ticket from a drawer in the sitting room. When he got back to the kitchen, McEvoy was draining his glass. He held up the bottle. 'Get some more whiskey, will you?'

Canning nodded and went outside to the Mondeo. He drove to the airport, parked the car in a short-term carpark, and checked in an hour before his flight to Heathrow.

McCracken was waiting for him in the buffet on the arrivals floor of Terminal One, sitting at a table with a cup of coffee in front of her. Canning bought himself a coffee and a sandwich and sat at a neighbouring table with his back to her.

'Everything okay?' McCracken asked, her voice little more than a whisper.

'Everything's fine,' said Canning, not looking around. He took the carrier bag from his holdall. A middle-aged couple with three unruly children sat at a nearby table. Two of the children started arguing about where they were going to sit on the plane, and the mother slapped the bigger of the two. Canning flinched. He'd never hit either of his own children – never had, never would. He put the carrier bag down on the floor and gently pushed it back under his seat.

He heard McCracken bend down and pull the carrier bag between her legs, then heard her open and close her briefcase. A few minutes later she stood up and walked away, her high heels clicking on the tiled floor. Canning stayed where he was, finishing his coffee. He listened to the three children squabbling and arguing and wished that he was with his own kids. His soon-to-be ex-wife he could live without, but his children were the most important things in his life.

McCracken opened the door to the Transit and slid into the passenger seat, placing her briefcase on her lap. O'Keefe started the van and edged away from the terminal, squeezing in front of an Avis coach. McCracken wound down the window.

They drove in silence for a while, the slipstream tugging at McCracken's dyed blond hair. She took a pair of sunglasses from the glove compartment and put them on. O'Keefe broke the silence first. 'What are we going to do with the Hayes woman?' he asked.

'What do you mean?'

'When it's over.'

McCracken tapped her red-painted fingernails on her briefcase but didn't reply.

'She did hear, didn't she?'

McCracken turned to look at him. 'I'm not sure. If she did, she hid it well.'

'She must have heard. She knows my name.'

'Maybe.'

'Maybe? That twat Quinn yelled it across the factory, right enough. She must have heard.'

McCracken screwed up her face as if she had a sour taste in her mouth. 'She might have heard, but that's not to say that she realised the significance.'

'Significance my arse,' hissed O'Keefe. 'He used my name. She heard it. If she tells the cops, I'm fucked. How long do you think it'd take to track me down?'

'All she heard – all she might have heard – was Don. Maybe she'll think you're a Mafia boss.'

'This isn't fucking funny, McCracken. This is my life we're talking about. I'll put a bullet in her myself rather than go down for this.'

McCracken turned away and stared out of the windscreen.

'She's got to be dealt with, McCracken. If I go down, we all go down. There's going to be no Marquis of Queensberry rules after this – it'll be a rubber-lined room with a drain in the floor, and they'll beat the fuck out of me until they get what they want.'

'No one's going down,' said McCracken quietly.

'So when it's over, she's dead.' O'Keefe banged on the horn as a minibus cut him up. He accelerated and overtook the minibus, flashing the driver a dirty look.

McCracken opened her briefcase and took out the carrier bag. She counted the tapes. Seven.

Mick Canning parked the Mondeo by the wooden garage and let himself in through the back door. McEvoy was watching the portable television in the sitting room, his feet propped up on a low coffee table. The Smith & Wesson was in his lap, and he had a glass of Bushmills resting on his stomach.

Canning asked McEvoy if he wanted a coffee but McEvoy just lifted his whiskey glass and shook his head, his eyes never leaving the television screen.

'How's the girl?' asked Canning.

'No idea,' said McEvoy. 'How was McCracken?'

'She was there. I gave her the stuff and got the next plane back.'

'She say there were any problems?'

'Didn't say a word. Just took the tapes and left.'

McEvoy pulled a face. 'Must be going okay, then. I guess if it wasn't, she'd have told us to off the kid.' He grinned at Canning. 'Only messing with you, Mick.'

Canning nodded at the gun. 'You expecting trouble, George?'

'You can never have your gun too close,' said McEvoy. 'Didn't they teach you that in the INLA?' He noticed that Canning was holding a white plastic carrier bag. 'What's in the bag?'

'Comics. For Katie. Picked them up at the airport.'

McEvoy shook his head in disgust. 'You'll spoil the little brat.'

Canning held the bag to his chest as if he feared that McEvoy would try to take it away from him. 'The happier she is, the easier she'll be to handle.'

'Bribe her, you mean? Is that how you control your own kids?' He took a swig of his whiskey. 'Never got anything from my da, other than a clip around the ear when he'd had too much of the amber fluid.'

'Yeah, well, that probably accounts for your well-balanced personality and your easy-going nature,' said Canning.

'Never did me any harm,' said McEvoy.

'You an only child?' asked Canning.

'Nah. One of eight. Seven sisters. That's probably why me da used to knock me around. He'd never lift a finger against a woman.'

Canning leaned against the door. 'What about you, George?'

McEvoy balanced his glass on his stomach and stretched his arms above his head as he yawned. 'What do you mean?' he growled.

Canning gestured with his thumb at the door to the basement. 'Suppose McCracken had said that the mother wasn't co-operating. Suppose she said that we had to, you know . . .' He pointed with his first and second fingers, forming his hand into the shape of a gun and cocking his thumb. 'Would you?'

'Like a shot,' said McEvoy. He laughed at the unintentional pun. 'Like a fucking shot.' His belly rippled as he laughed and the glass tumbled to the floor. 'Fuck. Now look at what you've made me do,' he said. He sat up, retrieved the glass and poured himself a refill.

Canning headed towards the basement door.

'Where the fuck are you going?' said McEvoy.

'I'm going to give her the magazines.'

'She'll be asleep. Leave it until tomorrow.'

Canning stopped in the hallway. McEvoy was right – it was almost eleven o'clock. He'd give them to her tomorrow.

'Are you gonna cook?' asked McEvoy, lounging back in his chair and sipping his fresh glass of whiskey. He grinned when he saw the look of annoyance on Canning's face. He put down his whiskey and held up his hands in mock surrender. 'Okay, okay, I'll cook if you want. But you know it'll taste like shit.'

Canning walked back to the kitchen. McEvoy had only cooked once since they'd moved into the cottage, and it had been a disaster. Sausages fried to a crisp, mashed potatoes with half the peel still on them, and lukewarm peas. It had taken the best part of an hour to clean the frying pan afterwards. 'What do you feel like?' he asked.

'I feel like going out and getting my end away,' said McEvoy, kicking off his shoes. 'That's what I fucking feel like.' He took another swig from his glass. 'But I'll settle for beans on toast.'

Mark Quinn clicked on the mouse and the picture on the VDU changed to a view of the bathroom. He leaned back in his chair and watched as the Hayes woman brushed her teeth. She held her blond hair in a ponytail as she spat into the sink and rinsed her mouth.

Her hair looked genuinely blond, soft and golden, not at all like McCracken's dyed hair which was dark brown, almost black, at the roots. She came out of the bathroom and Quinn clicked the mouse again. He found her in the giant trading room, walking across to one of the half-dozen desks that were still in place. There was a telephone on the desk and she reached out a hand to it.

'Naughty, naughty,' said Quinn. 'You've been told not to use the phone.'

The woman looked around furtively, squinting up at the ceiling.

'You'll never find it,' said Quinn. 'It's too well hidden.'

The woman looked at the phone again, her hand only inches away from it. Quinn grinned, wondering how she was going to resolve her dilemma. She'd been told not to use the phone, but she obviously wanted to talk to her husband.

There was a squeal of brakes outside and Quinn stiffened. A door opened and then slammed shut. Quinn relaxed. It was the Transit van. On the monitor, the Hayes woman was still frozen, hand outstretched. The second van door open and closed and Quinn heard McCracken say something to O'Keefe.

The side door opened and McCracken and O'Keefe came

in. McCracken called across the factory floor, 'What's she doing?'

'Struggling with her conscience,' said Quinn.

McCracken walked up behind Quinn and looked at the monitor. On the screen, Andrea turned away from the phone and wrapped her arms tightly around herself.

'No balls,' said Quinn.

'Well, that's the thing about women, Mark,' said McCracken. 'As I'm sure you'll learn one day.'

Quinn scowled at her. 'It would have been easier just to tell her that all the phones have been disconnected,' he said. McCracken had already walked off to the offices and didn't hear him. 'Bitch,' he added, under his breath.

Egan had thought long and hard about what to do with Martin Hayes. Not that he had any doubts that Hayes had to die – that had been a foregone conclusion once the Garda Siochana had turned up on his doorstep. What concerned Egan was the method; he wanted to cause as few ripples as possible, and his first thought had been to kill Hayes the same way he'd disposed of the headmistress' secretary – talk his way into the house, hold a gun to his head, make him stand on the plastic sheeting, then put a bullet in his skull. It was relatively mess-free – the body could be wrapped up in the sheet of plastic, placed in the plastic-lined boot of the car, and then buried in some out-of-the-way place. The big drawback was that if Hayes disappeared, the police would start looking for him. And they'd start searching for his wife and daughter. They might turn to the media, and the last thing Egan wanted was to have Andrea Hayes's face splashed across the evening news.

The police would need a body, but if they knew it was murder they'd start a full-scale investigation, and that meant more publicity. They'd be looking for a killer, some-one who had a reason for wanting Hayes dead, and that would start them looking into his background, and eventually that would lead them to his wife's past. Egan would have to give them a body, but in such a way that there wouldn't be a murder investigation, and that meant that Martin Hayes would have to kill himself.

On the passenger seat of the Scorpio was a length of rope, already knotted, in a white plastic carrier bag. Under his jacket, snug in its leather shoulder holster, was the Browning. There'd be no need to use the gun, no need even to threaten violence against Hayes. Egan would give the man a simple choice: Hayes could write a farewell note saying that he couldn't live without his wife and daughter, and then hang himself with the rope. If he refused, Egan would simply tell Hayes that he was going to kill him anyway, make it look like suicide, and then he would torture and kill his wife and child. Egan knew without a shadow of a doubt that Hayes would do anything if he thought it would save the lives of his wife and child. Even if it meant taking his own life.

Egan guided the Scorpio down a tree-lined road, his gloved hands light on the steering wheel. Ahead of him was Martin's redbrick house, its slated roof glistening wetly from a recent shower of rain. Egan checked his rear-view mirror. There was a police car behind him. No blue light, no siren, just two uniformed officers going about their duties, not suspecting that a few yards in front of them was a man with a gun who would shortly be forcing another human being to take his own life. Egan smiled to himself as he drove. It was going to be so easy, but then the best plans always were.

Martin Hayes was lying on the sofa watching the late-night news when the doorbell rang. Dermott started barking and ran into the hall. Martin shouted at the dog to be quiet and went to open the door. It was the two gardai who'd called the previous day. The older one, O'Brien, tapped the peak of his cap with a gloved hand. 'Evening, Mr Hayes.'

'What's wrong?' asked Martin.

O'Brien smiled without warmth. 'Why should anything be wrong, Mr Hayes?'

'It's ten o'clock at night and there are two officers of the Garda Siochana on my doorstep. I don't suppose you're here to sell me tickets to your Christmas ball.'

O'Brien chuckled, but his younger colleague stared at Hayes with hard, unsmiling eyes. Martin wondered if they'd rehearsed the 'good cop, bad cop' routine before pressing his doorbell, O'Brien playing the relaxed, matey garda you could trust, the younger one staring with barely concealed hostility, hoping to put Martin off balance.

He looked over O'Brien's shoulder, wondering if the kidnappers were watching the house, and if they were, what they'd make of a second visit by uniformed gardai within twenty-four hours. He knew there was no point in worrying – if the house was under surveillance, then the damage had already been done.

'Could we come in, Mr Hayes?' asked O'Brien.

Martin held the door open for them and sighed in resignation. O'Brien smiled and nodded as he walked by. 'It's a miserable night out,' he said.

Martin didn't reply. He closed the door and followed them into the sitting room. The gardai didn't sit down and Martin didn't ask them to. All three men stood in the middle of the room. O'Brien took off his cap. 'We were wondering if Mrs Hayes was back,' he said.

'No,' said Martin. 'Not yet.'

'But yesterday you said that she'd be back today, right?'

'That's what she said.'

'And she hasn't phoned?' he asked.

'Not since you were last here,' said Martin. The younger garda was looking around the room.

O'Brien pulled a face. 'Pity,' he said. 'We were hoping to have a word with her.'

'As soon as she calls, I'll have her phone you,' said Martin. 'I'm as keen as you are to put your minds at rest.'

'The thing is,' said O'Brien, 'we've spoken to your wife's Aunt Bessie.'

Martin caught his breath. He forced himself to smile. 'Really?'

'Took us a while to track her down, what with the limited information you had. Aunt Bessie. North Belfast. But we had a word with the local police and they were very co-operative.' He scratched his chin. 'Very co-operative,' he repeated.

Martin felt his hands begin to shake and folded his arms across his chest defensively. 'And?' he said.

'Oh, I think you know what the "and" is, Mr Hayes.'

Martin stared at O'Brien in silence. There was nothing he could say. If O'Brien really had spoken to the woman, then he'd already been caught in a lie.

'Where is your wife, Mr Hayes?' O'Brien asked.

'Belfast.'

O'Brien shook his head slowly, but he was still smiling avuncularly, as if the worst he was going to do was cut off Martin's allowance.

The younger garda looked at the door to the hall. 'Do you have a bathroom I can use?'

Martin knew that the garda wanted to look around the house, and while he didn't like the idea of him prowling around, he couldn't refuse without appearing to have something to hide. 'Go ahead,' he said. 'Upstairs. Second on the right.'

O'Brien tapped his cap against his leg. 'Did you and your wife have an argument, maybe?'

Martin swallowed. If he said he'd had a fight with Andy, then maybe they'd be more willing to accept that she'd left without warning. And if she was angry with him, that would explain why she'd taken Katie. He'd have to admit to lying, but it was an understandable lie. O'Brien was offering him a way out, but that didn't make any sense, not after all the questions. It was a trap, it had to be. Martin licked his lips. His mouth was painfully dry. All he had to do was admit to an argument and the pressure would be off him. He was just about to speak when he realised where the garda was leading him. Andy's car was in the drive. If she'd stormed off after a fight, she wouldn't have walked away, she'd have taken the car. The garda knew that, and he was hoping to catch Martin out in another lie. A lie that could imply he'd done something to harm his family. He looked O'Brien in the eye. 'No,' he said firmly. 'There was no argument.'

The garda nodded. 'All husbands and wives argue,' he said.

'I'm not disputing that,' said Martin. 'But Andy and I didn't have a fight on Wednesday.'

'Sarge!' called the younger garda from upstairs. 'There's something here you should look at.'

O'Brien sighed and smiled at Martin. 'Ah, the enthusiasm of youth,' he said. 'Why don't you come with me, Mr Hayes. Let's see what's got the boy all fired up.'

Martin and O'Brien went through into the hallway. The younger garda was standing at the top of the stairs, staring at the banister.

'What is it, Eamonn?' asked O'Brien.

'Have a look at this, Sarge.'

O'Brien climbed the stairs. He peered at the section of banister that his colleague was pointing at. It was the spot where Andy had fainted, Martin realised. Where she'd fainted and hit her head. 'It looks like blood,' said the younger garda.

O'Brien straightened up. 'I think you'd better come down to Pearse Street with us, Mr Hayes.'

They drove into the city centre in silence. Martin sat in the back of the patrol car, with O'Brien in the front passenger seat. They pulled up in front of the grey stone Garda station and O'Brien took Martin in. They walked through a reception area where a uniformed garda buzzed them through into a corridor. O'Brien led Martin to the far end of the corridor and showed him into a small room, barely three paces square. Martin turned to ask O'Brien how long he was going to be kept at the station, but before he could say anything the garda had closed the door.

There was a table which had been screwed to the concrete floor, and four plastic chairs, two each side. The walls were painted a mustard yellow which glistened under the fluorescent lights. Martin sat with his back to the door. The table was up against the wall to his right, and above it, on a thin chipboard shelf, was a black tape recorder with two cassette decks. Martin rested his elbows on the table and cupped his eyes with the palms of his hands. He had no idea what he could do or say to get himself out of his predicament.

He tried to get his thoughts straight. The gardai obviously thought that Andy and Katie were missing. And they suspected that he had something to do with their disappearance, suspicions heightened by the discovery of the blood on the banister. They hadn't asked Martin for an explanation of the bloodstain, but he was sure that they'd test it and establish that it was Andy's. Then what? They'd assume that he'd hurt her, and the only way he'd be able to convince them otherwise would be to tell them about Katie's kidnapping.

Egan settled back in the black Ford Scorpio and listened to the engine click as it cooled. He patted his left armpit and felt the reassuring hardness of his Browning Hi-Power pistol. The length of rope was under the front seat. Ahead of him he could see the grey granite frontage of Pearse

Street police station. The two gardai had driven around to the back of the building and presumably taken Hayes inside through the rear entrance. From where he sat, Egan could see the front entrance and the way in to the carpark.

He had been just about to stop in front of Martin Hayes's house when a sixth sense had told him to keep on driving. He'd checked in his rear-view mirror and grinned to himself as the police car had pulled up at the kerb. Egan had driven on a few hundred yards past the house and waited. He'd seen the two gardai speak to Hayes on his doorstep, go inside, and then the three of them walk to the car several minutes later. Hayes looked pale, and he kept putting his hand up to his forehead as if trying to stave off a headache.

The two gardai were coldly efficient. One opened the back door for Hayes and got in next to him; the other, the younger one, waited until Hayes was in the back before climbing into the driving seat. The body language was enough to tell Egan that Hayes wasn't going willingly.

Egan doubted that Hayes would tell the police anything. Nothing he'd done so far suggested that he'd cave in under questioning. He'd stick to his story that his wife and daughter were out of town visiting a sick relative. But the police were suspicious, and they wouldn't be satisfied until they found out where his wife and daughter were. The more they probed, the more likely they were to discover what had happened.

They'd probably keep him in for a few hours, then release him. They'd have to let him go because they had nothing in the way of evidence against him. And once Hayes was back at home, Egan would pay him a visit. With the rope.

Apart from the arrival of the gardai, Egan was pleased with the way things were going. Following her phone call to her husband, the Hayes woman had been working hard on the bomb, and it looked as if it would be ready within three or four days. Well on schedule. Egan was looking forward to seeing the effects the massive bomb would have on the City of London. And to reaping the benefits. Seven million dollars.

Once the bomb had been detonated and the money had been transferred from Zurich to the Dutch Antilles, Egan would be able to start work on his next commission. He'd already been approached by a fanatical Muslim group in the Lebanon who wanted to blow up an El-Al flight. The Israeli airline was recognised as one of the safest in the world and had never been the victim of a successful terrorist attack. Egan was about to change all that. For a fee of two million dollars. But first things first. He had to take care of Martin Hayes.

The door behind Martin opened but he didn't turn around. He sat where he was, his hands together on the table, fingers interlinked. Two men came into the room and sat opposite him. Not the gardai who'd brought him to the station – these were men in suits. Detectives. The man who sat directly opposite was in his late thirties, a thickset man with a comb-over and a sandy moustache. He looked at Martin over the top of spectacles with thick black frames, the sort Michael Caine used to wear in sixties spy films. He was wearing a grey suit with stains on the lapels and a brightly coloured Bugs Bunny tie. 'How are you doing, Mr Hayes?' he said jovially. 'My name is Detective Inspector James Fitz-Gerald. My colleague here is Detective Sergeant John Power.'

The other man nodded. He was younger, in his late twenties maybe, and considerably better dressed. He had on an expensive blue pin-stripe suit, a crisp white shirt and a tie with a crest on it, and gold cuff links peeped out from his sleeves. He had a sharp, almost pointed nose, and inquisitive eyes that watched Martin's every move.

'Am I under arrest?' Martin asked.

'No, you're not,' said FitzGerald. He took off his spectacles and wiped them with the end of his tie. He looked up and saw Martin staring at the cartoon rabbit. 'Birthday present from my son, so I figured I had to wear it, you know? The wife bought it, obviously. My boy's only eight. I think she just enjoys embarrassing me.'

Martin said nothing. FitzGerald finished cleaning his lenses and put his spectacles back on, pushing them up his nose with his forefinger.

'So,' he said. 'Tell me about your wife, Mr Hayes.'

'What do you mean?'

'Does she embarrass you? Does she sometimes get on your nerves?'

'What the hell are you talking about?'

'Your wife is missing, Mr Hayes. So is your daughter.'

'And you're saying I did something to them, is that it?' He jerked a thumb at the tape recorder. 'Shouldn't this be switched on? Shouldn't you be recording this?'

FitzGerald exhaled slowly through pursed lips. 'All we're doing at the moment is having a wee chat, Mr Hayes. If you want to make it official, we can do that. But then I'd have to caution you and then a whole process would start that once started can be difficult to stop. So if it's all right with you, I'd like to keep this low-key just at the moment.'

Martin nodded slowly. 'Okay.'

'So, where is Mrs Hayes?'

'She told me that she was going to Belfast. To see her aunt. Her Aunt Bessie. But I've just been told by your Sergeant O'Brien that she's not with Bessie.'

'But you told the school that she'd gone to see her mother. Your mother-in-law.'

Martin shook his head. 'No. She must have misheard. It's her aunt. That's what Andy told me. But now I don't know what to think.'

'And you told the gardai that you don't have this Aunt Bessie's telephone number or address.'

'That's right.'

'So you can see why we're a little concerned, Mr Hayes. What with there being blood in the upstairs hallway and all.'

'Andy tripped. She tripped and banged her head.'

'Recently?'

'Last week.'

'Did she go to hospital?'

'There was no need. It was a small knock, that's all.'

'The thing of it is, Mr Hayes, we'd like to reassure ourselves that your wife isn't in any trouble,' said FitzGerald.

'I wish I could help,' said Hayes. 'Look, last time I spoke to my wife, she said she'd be back soon. As soon as she calls again, I'll have her telephone you. How's that?'

'Where did she call from?' asked Power. It was the first time he'd spoken since walking into the interview room.

'Belfast. Well, I assumed Belfast. Now I'm just plain confused.'

FitzGerald leaned forward. 'Are you sure there isn't something you want to tell us, Mr Hayes? Something you want to get off your chest?'

Martin folded his arms and sat back in his chair. 'This is a complete waste of time. My time and yours. When Andy turns up you're going to look pretty stupid.'

'I'm quite happy to look stupid if it means we find your wife and daughter, Mr Hayes,' said FitzGerald.

'It's not a question of finding them,' said Martin. 'They're not lost.'

FitzGerald and Power exchanged looks. Power shook his head. Martin had the feeling that they'd run out of questions.

'Can I go now?' he asked.

FitzGerald grimaced. 'To be honest, we'd rather you stayed here for a while yet, Mr Hayes. We're continuing with our enquiries, and it'd be a big help to us if you were here to answer any questions that might arise.'

'Enquiries? What sort of enquiries?'

'We're checking the blood on the banister, obviously. We'd like a Scene of Crime Officer to call round. With your permission, of course.'

'I've already explained about the blood. My wife tripped.'

'We'd still like to check. And have the SOCO take a look at the rest of the house. And the garden.'

'The garden?' Martin's jaw dropped. 'What the hell are you suggesting? That I've buried my wife and daughter in the garden?'

FitzGerald put his hands up. 'We're not suggesting anything, Mr Hayes. We're just working our way through a standard set of procedures, that's all.'

Martin shook his head. 'No, that's not all. You're suggesting I murdered my family.'

'Please, don't get upset,' said FitzGerald, in a soft, low voice that a parent might use to try to calm a petulant child. 'If everything happened as you've told us, you've nothing to worry about.'

Martin glared at the two detectives. He wanted to lash out, verbally and physically, but he knew that such a show of raw emotion would only be counterproductive. The only way he was going to walk out of Pearse Street was if he co-operated. Or at least, appeared to co-operate. He forced himself to smile. 'Okay,' he said. 'Do whatever you have to do.'

Power held out his hand. 'Can we borrow your keys?'

'Sure,' said Martin. He handed then over. 'Be careful of Dermott, will you?'

'Dermott?'

'Our dog. He might run off.'

'We'll be careful,' said Power.

'And what happens to me while your people are checking the house?'

FitzGerald and Power stood up. 'This room's free, so you're welcome to wait here,' said FitzGerald. 'I'll send a garda in with coffee. Maybe a sandwich.'

The two detectives left. They closed the door but Martin didn't hear a lock turning or a bolt being pushed across. He put his head in his hands, wondering what he should do, whether he should tell them what had really happened to Andy and Katie or continue to lie to them.

DAY SIX

———————◆———————

Canning switched on the light and unbolted the door to the basement. Katie was sitting up in bed, rubbing her eyes, when he put the tray down on the table. 'Scrambled eggs and beans,' he said. 'Come and eat it before it gets cold.'

'What time is it?' she asked.

'Eight o'clock.'

'And it's Sunday today, isn't it?' Her voice sounded stuffy as if her nose was blocked.

'That's right.' He had three comics under one arm and he waved them at the little girl. 'I got these for you. Come and eat your eggs.'

Katie slid out of bed and padded across to the table. She picked up a glass of orange juice and drank half of it in one gulp.

'How's your throat?'

Katie shrugged and took another gulp of orange juice. 'It hurts a little bit.'

'Let me have a look,' said Canning. Katie tilted her head back and opened her mouth. Canning peered down her throat. It was still red, and when he gently touched the sides of her neck she winced.

Canning sat down at the table. He removed the glove from his right hand and touched her forehead. She still had a temperature.

149

'You didn't bring any clothes with me.' She pointed at her nightdress. 'This is smelly.'

Canning smiled. 'It's not smelly.' He put his glove back on, then took a pack of Day Nurse from his pocket, popped out a tablet and put it on the table. 'Eat your eggs and then swallow this,' he said.

Katie started to eat and Canning put his elbows on the table as he watched her.

'Mummy says that's bad manners,' she said.

Canning raised his eyebrows. 'What is?'

'Putting your elbows on the table while people are eating.'

Canning sat up straight. Katie put a forkful of egg in her mouth and chewed thoughtfully, then put down her plastic fork and leaned over her paper plate. 'If you let me go, I won't say anything. I promise.' She smiled. 'You won't get into trouble.' She waited to see what he'd say, smiling and nodding. Canning smiled behind his ski mask. Even aged seven, children, especially girls, could be so damn manipulative. His own daughter was the same. He could imagine Katie twisting her father around her little finger. Daddy, buy me this. Daddy, do this for me. Daddy, lift me up, carry me, love me.

Katie made the sign of the cross on her chest. 'Cross my heart and swear to die,' she said solemnly.

Canning shook his head. 'I can't let you go, Katie. Not yet. I'm sorry.'

Andy lay on a sofa in the reception area, a big, sprawling sofa with huge cushions that seemed to fold around her like clouds. It had been just over four days since Katie had been kidnapped, and during those four days Andy's life had been turned upside down. Her daughter had been taken from her, she'd been forced to fly to London, she'd been kidnapped herself by three masked terrorists and told that she was to build a massive bomb in the City of London. Now here she was, sleeping on a sofa nine storeys up in an office block, under surveillance from hidden cameras, awaiting the arrival of the components of a bomb that, if successfully detonated, could lay waste to several city blocks. As she drifted in and out of sleep, it felt as if it was all happening to someone else, as if it was a weird, surreal dream.

She half heard the lift doors open and close, but she didn't sit up until the doors to the outside corridor were flung open. It was the Wrestler, pushing a boxed spin-drier on a trolley. He was wearing dark blue overalls with the name of a kitchen-fitting firm emblazoned on the back in fiery red letters. 'Rise and shine,' he said. He wheeled the box by her sofa and into the office. He was followed by the Runner, who was also wearing overalls and pushing another loaded trolley. Even through the ski mask he was wearing, Andy could see that he was leering at her.

Green-eyes came in last, carrying several assorted boxes. Like the men, she was wearing overalls and training shoes. There wasn't a gun in sight, but that didn't mean anything because it wasn't the threat of being shot that was keeping Andy in the office.

'In here,' Green-eyes said to Andy, and Andy followed her through to the main office area. The Wrestler was manoeuvring the spin-drier off its trolley next to the wall farthest from the windows. Green-eyes put the boxes she was carrying down on the floor and pointed at the spin-drier. 'Andrea, you start taking them out of their boxes while we bring the rest of the stuff up.'

Andy tried opening the box with her bare hands but the cardboard was too tough. The Wrestler gave her a small penknife, and she hacked away at the box with it while her three captors went back outside.

It took them more than an hour to carry in all the equipment, and another half an hour until all the boxes were opened. The Wrestler had several extension cords, and he plugged in the spin-driers, ovens, electric woks and coffee grinders and checked that they were all functioning.

The Runner brought in a filter coffee-maker and took it along to the suite of offices at one end of the open-plan area, and a few minutes later he returned with mugs of steaming coffee. Green-eyes showed Andy her clipboard. On it was a computer print-out listing all the chemicals and equipment she had purchased. 'Am I missing anything?' she asked.

Andy scanned the list and shook her head. 'I don't think so.'

'I don't think so isn't good enough, Andrea. Check it carefully. Am I missing anything?'

Andy ran her finger down the list. Everything seemed to be there. Except for one thing. 'Detonators,' she said. 'You haven't got detonators.'

'That's in hand,' said Green-eyes. 'For the next couple of days, your only concern is the explosive, okay?'

Andy handed back the clipboard. 'In that case, it's all here.'

Green-eyes put the clipboard down on top of one of the spin-driers. 'Come this way,' she said, and she led Andy to a suite of offices, each with a floor-to-ceiling glass panel next to the door so that the interiors were visible from the corridor. One of the offices had been used as a meeting room and contained a long cherry-wood table with a dozen high-backed leather chairs around it. In one corner of the room was a large-screen Sony television and a video recorder. 'Sit down, Andrea,' said Green-eyes.

Andy did as she was told. The blinds were drawn, but the slats were a white opaque material and enough light seeped in to make the overhead fluorescent lights unnecessary. The coffee machine had been put on a sideboard along with several cartons of long-life milk, a bag of sugar and a box of Jaffa Cakes.

Green-eyes unlocked her burgundy briefcase and took

out a small cassette tape. She slotted it into a larger cassette and fed it into the video recorder. 'You wanted to know that Katie's safe,' she said.

Andy leaned forward with anticipation. Green-eyes pressed the 'play' button. There were a few seconds of static, then Katie was there, smiling at the camera.

'Mummy, Dad, this is Katie. Your daughter,' said Katie. She sounded far away, as if she were at the end of a long, long tunnel. There was a short pause as if she were gathering her thoughts, then she continued. 'I'm fine. But I've got flu, I think.' She put her hand up to her throat, and Andy copied the gesture. 'My head hurts and my throat's sore. The nice man is going to give me some medicine to make it better so I should be okay soon.'

Katie paused and looked past the lens. Andy had the feeling that someone was prompting her to continue.

'He said to say it's Saturday and that I'm okay. Mummy, I want to come home . . .' The recording ended abruptly and Andy knew it was because her daughter had burst into tears.

Green-eyes clicked the video recorder off. 'She's safe, Andrea, and she'll stay that way so long as you do as we ask.'

'She's sick. I have to go to her,' said Andy.

'Don't be ridiculous!' snapped Green-eyes. She ejected the cassette and put it back in the briefcase. 'She's got flu,' she said. 'Kids get flu. She'll be fine.'

'She needs me.'

'What she needs is for you to do what you have to do. Then you can get back to Dublin and be with her. We're taking good care of her, Andrea. I promise you.'

'I want to talk to her.'

'That's not possible. Not now. Maybe later on in the week. We'll see how you get on.' She stood up. 'First things first. I need you to show the lads what to do. Step by step.'

She took her mobile phone out of her overall pocket and put it in the briefcase, then took out her pistol and flicked the combination locks closed.

Andy followed Green-eyes into the corridor. Green-eyes put the briefcase in the office opposite the meeting room, then took Andy back into the open-plan office area. The Wrestler and the Runner had lined up the four ovens next to each other and were unpacking dozens of clear plastic Tupperware containers. The Wrestler was wearing his shoulder holster and gun again. 'Can we open the windows?' Andy asked. 'It's going to get hot in here.'

Green-eyes looked over at the Wrestler and he shook his head. 'They're sealed,' he said. 'Double-glazed and sealed.'

'Is there a thermostat? If there is, set it to the lowest level.'

The Wrestler pointed to a thermostat on one of the walls and the Runner went to turn it down. Andy looked around the huge office area. 'Right, we're going to need a line of desks here. Close to the ovens.'

The four of them carried half a dozen desks over and lined them up. Green-eyes, the Wrestler and the Runner waited expectantly as Andy gathered her thoughts. Then, like an officer mustering her troops, she explained what they had to do.

Mick Canning dropped the carrier bags on to the back seat of the Ford Mondeo and drove away from the shopping centre. It had been a long time since he'd bought clothes for a child and he'd found the experience somewhat daunting. He knew Katie's size, but he had no idea what she liked. Jeans, skirts, dresses – Canning had been over-whelmed by the choice on offer. He'd settled on a pair of blue Wrangler jeans, three different shirts in assorted colours, and two pairs of white socks. He'd decided against buying her any shoes because she wasn't going to be leaving the house, and anyway he wasn't sure of her size, but he'd found a pair of Garfield slippers that he figured would make her smile.

He thought of his own daughter as he drove back to the cottage. Mary was two years older than Katie. Mary's eyes were the same shade of green, though her hair was auburn, thick and curly, the same as her mother's. It had been almost three months since he'd last seen Mary. And his son, Luke. They were both with their mother in Larne, presumably being poisoned with stories about what a cruel, selfish bastard their father was. Canning looked at his watch, wondering what his children were doing.

He drove past a telephone box and pulled the car over. He sat for a few minutes, tapping his fingers on the steering wheel. Egan had been insistent that once the operation was under way there had to be no contact with family or friends. No letters. No phone calls. An ambulance went by, its blue light flashing but its siren off. Canning couldn't see what harm one phone call could do. His wife and children were hundreds of miles away, and they had no idea where he was. He climbed out of the Mondeo and walked back to the phone box, sorting through his pockets for change. It was starting to drizzle, and he jogged the final few yards. He had to pause and recollect his wife's number. It had been more than six weeks since he'd spoken to her, and that had ended in an argument over money. He slotted in half a dozen coins and tapped out the number, then closed his eyes as it began to ring, wondering if he was doing the right thing.

'Hello?' It was her. Canning thanked God it wasn't her mother.

'Maggie? It's Mick.'

'I know who it is.' Her voice was cold. Impersonal.

'How are you doing?'

'What do you want, Mick?' If anything her voice was even colder.

'I just wanted to call and see if the kids are all right.'

'They're fine.'

He waited for her to say something else, but the silence stretched on and on. It was as if she was challenging him to speak first.

'Can I have a word with them?'

'What about?'

'Just to say hello, you know. Come on now, Maggie, it's been weeks since I've spoken to them.'

'Well, whose fault is that?'

Canning took a deep breath. He didn't want to fight with his wife, but it seemed that every conversation he had with her ended in an argument. 'I just want a word. That's all.'

'Mary's in the bath. Luke's out.'

'Out where?'

'What business is it of yours, Michael Canning? You call once in a blue moon and you expect the whole world to be at your beck and call, is that it?'

'No, it's not that. Could you just tell them that I called to say hello? Give them my love.'

'Anything else?'

Canning could tell from her tone that she had no intention of passing on any message. 'No. I guess not.' The line went dead. Canning replaced the receiver and walked slowly back to his car.

Andy wiped her forehead with the back of her arm. Sweat was pouring off her, and she could feel beads of it trickling down the small of her back. She'd changed out of the suit that Green-eyes had given her and was wearing a blue checked shirt and loose-fitting denim jeans, but it was still uncomfortably hot in the office. She went over and looked at the thermostat. It was set to the minimum, but the temperature read-out showed that it was in the mid-nineties.

Green-eyes was at the water-cooler, helping herself to a cupful of water. Andy joined her. 'The air-conditioning isn't coping,' she said. 'We're going to need dehumidifiers.'

'It's not too bad,' said Green-eyes. She'd unzipped the overalls almost down to her waist, and Andy could see her white bra underneath. Sweat was dripping down her neck, and Andy figured the ski mask must have been annoyingly uncomfortable. The woman's neck was reddening and bathed in sweat.

Andy poured herself a paper cup of water and sipped it. All four ovens were working, their doors ajar. In each of the ovens were metal baking trays full of the ammonium nitrate fertiliser, four trays per oven. Other trays were lined up on the desks, waiting to be filled. The Wrestler was on his knees in front of one of the ovens, testing the temperature with a metal thermometer.

The Runner was taking trays out of the middle oven and tipping the heated fertiliser into Tupperware containers, which he was then sealing in black rubbish bags. At the far end of the office was a pile of black bags that had already been filled with fertiliser.

The doors of the ovens had to be left ajar so that the water could escape, and the temperature had to be constantly monitored because the fertiliser would liquefy at 170 degrees Fahrenheit. It would actually explode at 400 degrees, but it would start to bubble and smoke long before it reached that temperature. Andy had told the two men to make sure it didn't get above 150 degrees.

She drained her paper cup and tossed it into a basket at the base of the cooler, then rolled up her shirtsleeves. 'I want to show you something,' she said. She took Green-eyes over to the window and pulled back the vertical blinds to show her the window. It was blurry from condensation, and water was pooling at the bottom of the pane. Andy ran her finger down the glass and showed Green-eyes how wet it was. 'This is after four hours,' she said. 'It's going to get a lot worse. It's getting too humid.'

'So?'

Andy nodded at the electric ovens. 'So the point of this is to dry out the fertiliser. But if the atmosphere's this moist, the ammonium nitrate is going to soak the water right back up. Even when it's in the containers and bags. You've got to get the water out of the air. The best way would be to open the windows, but they're sealed. So the only thing you can do is to bring in dehumidifiers.'

Green-eyes put her hands on her hips. 'It'll have to be tomorrow,' she said.

'Whatever,' said Andy. 'And another thing. We're going to need fans, because when we start to use the alcohol, we're going to have to keep the air moving. If we don't . . . it'll explode. You won't even need a detonator. The fumes will be explosive enough.'

Mick Canning knocked on the basement door before slipping back the two bolts. 'What the fuck are you knocking for?' McEvoy shouted from the sitting room. 'This isn't a fucking hotel.'

Canning ignored him and went down the stairs. Katie was sitting at the table, reading one of the comics he'd given her. 'Hiya, kiddo,' he said.

She put her chin on her hands and pouted. 'I want to go home.'

'I know you do.'

'When can I go?'

'I don't know. Not long.'

'How long's not long?'

'I don't know.'

'You can't keep me here for ever,' she said.

'We don't intend to.'

She looked up at him. 'Are you going to kill me?' she asked.

The matter-of-fact way she asked the question took

Canning's breath away. He sat down next to her. 'Of course not. We don't hurt little girls. You have to believe me, we're not going to hurt you. I promise.'

'Cross your heart?'

Canning made the sign of the cross on his chest. 'Cross my heart,' he said. 'Look, we've already sent the videotapes to your mummy so that she knows you're all right. And we've told her that you'll be home soon.' He crossed himself again. 'Swear to die.'

Katie smiled and nodded. 'Okay,' she said. 'I believe you.'

Canning showed her the carrier bags. 'I got you some clothes. And Garfield slippers.' He pushed the carrier bags towards her and she pulled out the clothes and looked at them.

'Are you hungry?'

'A bit.'

'I'll go and get you something. Beefburgers? With chips?'

Katie nodded. 'Can I use the bathroom first?'

'Of course you can.'

He held out his hand. Katie hesitated for a couple of seconds, then took it. Her hand felt tiny in his as he helped her up the stairs.

James FitzGerald knocked on the door to the Chief Inspector's office and pushed it open as his boss gruffly told him to come in. Garda Chief Inspector Eamonn Hogan looked up from a stack of files that he'd been working his way through, fountain pen in hand. 'Morning, Jim, how's it going?' Hogan had turned fifty the previous week, though he looked almost a decade older, virtually bald with thick jowls that lay in folds against his shirt collar. There was a bag full of golf clubs leaning against one wall. Hogan rarely worked on Sundays, but they'd had two successful murder investigations completed during the previous week and the paperwork had mounted up. Like FitzGerald he wore spectacles, though his had wire frames. Hogan grinned at FitzGerald's Bugs Bunny tie. 'You know, in some parts of the country you could be arrested for wearing that.'

'It was a present,' said FitzGerald. He leaned against the door jamb. 'It's about this guy Martin Hayes.'

'The missing wife? Is he still in custody?'

'Helping us with our enquiries,' said FitzGerald. 'We put him in one of the cells overnight, but he's here of his own volition.'

'What's your take on it, Jim?'

FitzGerald shrugged and ran a hand through his thinning sandy hair, as if to reassure himself that it was still in place. 'He's hiding something, there's no doubt about that. But he's not a wife-killer. We've given the house and garden a going-over, and there's nothing to suggest foul play. We've spoken to neighbours and relatives and there've been no arguments. No rows. Just your average suburban family.'

Hogan sat back in his chair and put his pen down on top of his stack of files. 'You know as well as I do, Jim, your average suburban family pretty much accounts for half of our murder cases. All that suppressed anger. Crying babies. Kitchens full of knives.'

'Their daughter's seven, hardly a baby,' said FitzGerald, humouring his boss. 'No money problems, so far as we can see. And when we accuse him of doing something to his wife and child, he gets upset. Really upset. If it's an act, it's a bloody good one.'

'So she's left him. She's walked out on him.'

'So why doesn't he just say that? The thing of it is, there was blood on the banister upstairs, so there's something going on. But there are no signs of a struggle, and she's taken some clothes with her.'

'So she went away, took the daughter with her?'

'That's the way it looks.'

'Without telling him?' Hogan pulled a face as if he had a sour taste in his mouth. 'Bit unlikely, don't you think? No note?'

'He says not.'

'And you've checked with her relatives?'

'Sure. With her mother and an aunt. The aunt that Hayes said she'd gone to stay with. She's not with either of them. I've had both addresses checked by the RUC.'

Hogan took off his spectacles and polished them with a large blue handkerchief. 'So what's your feeling, Jim?'

'I don't think he's done anything to her. Or the daughter. He's not the type. Things like that don't happen out of the blue, and there's no history. Plus, if he had done anything, he wouldn't have left the blood on the banister. One thing he's not is stupid. No, he's not done away with them. But I think he knows where she's gone.'

'Why do you say that?'

'Because if he didn't, he'd have been on to us, right? Wife and kid vanished. He'd have called us, for sure.'

'Unless he really believed that she'd gone to stay with the aunt.'

FitzGerald shook his head. 'He didn't have a phone number, she didn't take the car, he didn't know what train she was on. No, she didn't go to Belfast. She went somewhere else, and I think he knows where.'

'So why won't he tell you where she is?' Hogan put his spectacles back on.

'Maybe he's embarrassed. Maybe she went off with someone he knows.'

'He's lying to the police to save himself from embarrassment?' Hogan pulled another face, screwing up his nose and wrinkling his eyes.

'Yeah, I know. It doesn't make much sense to me, either. But I figure that if he knows she's alive and well, he knows he's not going to be convicted of hurting her. He probably figures that if he just keeps on denying that he knows what's happened to her, eventually we'll just go away.' FitzGerald shrugged. 'Hell, maybe he figures she'll come back.' He scratched his chin. 'The O'Mara woman is a strange one, too. There's no sign of her. Spoken to her relatives – they haven't seen her. She hasn't withdrawn any money recently, didn't buy a ticket anywhere, car's still parked in front of her house. She's just disappeared into thin air.'

'But the only connection is that she worked at the school, right?'

'Well, it's a bit more than that. She spoke to Hayes the day she disappeared. Or the day before. Frankly, we're not quite sure when she went. She was last seen driving away from the school at five o'clock in the evening. The school rang us the following lunch-time when she didn't turn up at work.'

Hogan removed his wire-framed spectacles, took a small yellow cloth from his desk drawer and began polishing them again. 'You're not suggesting Hayes has had anything to do with her disappearance, are you?'

FitzGerald shrugged. 'I honestly don't know. There's no evidence he ever met her.'

'So it could just be a coincidence.' Hogan sighed and put his glasses back on. 'God, I hate coincidences,' he said. 'Bane of our lives, coincidences.'

'And another thing,' said FitzGerald. 'He's not asked for a solicitor. Keeps asking if we've finished and wants to go home, but he's not asked to call a solicitor. If he'd done something, he'd know that his best bet would be to be legally represented.'

'Unless he thinks he's smarter than we are.'

FitzGerald shook his head. 'No, he's not playing mind games with us. I think he knows he hasn't done anything wrong and that we're going to have to let him go eventually.'

Hogan put the yellow cloth back in his drawer and picked up his fountain pen. 'So you're going to treat it as a domestic?'

'I think so. Until I can prove otherwise. I thought John and I would have another go at him after lunch, and if he doesn't budge we'll let him go later this afternoon.'

'What about keeping an eye on him?'

'Yeah, are you okay with that? Overtime considerations and all.'

Hogan grinned. 'Ah, so you don't want to sit outside his house yourself, is that it?'

FitzGerald smiled ruefully. A night in a car wasn't his idea of a good time. He put his hands up in mock surrender.

'Go ahead, Jim. But have a word with uniforms first. See if they've got a couple of men spare. Just for a day or two, mind.'

Andy twisted the metal tie around the black rubbish bag, then eased it into a second bag and sealed that as well. Even sealed inside two plastic bags, the fertiliser in the Tupperware containers would absorb moisture from the air to the extent that it would be uselessly damp within two weeks. She had explained the chemistry to Green-eyes, but Green-eyes had said that it wouldn't be a problem. That meant that whatever Green-eyes was planning, it would be over within a fortnight.

Sweat was beading on Andy's forehead and she wiped it with a towel. Early that morning, Green-eyes had sent the Wrestler and the Runner to buy dehumidifiers and electric fans, and they'd gone some way to lowering the humidity, but it was still in the mid-eighties in the open-plan office. It was somewhat cooler in the smaller individual offices and meetings room, so they all took frequent breaks to cool down.

They'd spent most of the day processing the fertiliser

through the ovens and then sealing it in the Tupperware containers and black bags, but by midnight the offices had become so humid and hot that Andy had told Green-eyes it was pointless continuing. They'd have to let the air-conditioning recover. Green-eyes had given Andy a sleeping bag and told her to sleep in one of the offices and not to open the door until morning. Andy figured it was so they could take off their ski masks. The discomfort of wearing them for twelve hours while they worked the ovens must have been almost unbearable.

Now that the dehumidifiers had been brought in, they'd be able to work throughout the night, but it was still uncomfortably hot.

'I'm going to take a break,' Andy said to Green-eyes, who was checking the thermometer in one of the ovens.

'Are you hungry?' Green-eyes asked. 'There are some sandwiches in the coffee room.'

Andy went along to the meeting room. There was a Marks and Spencer carrier bag next to the coffee machine, containing a dozen packs of sandwiches. Chicken salad, sausage and mustard, bacon, lettuce and tomato, cheese and pickle, smoked salmon. And there was an assortment of canned drinks. Andy popped open a Diet Coke and drank, and then took a smoked salmon sandwich and sat down at the long table.

She looked through the glass panel by the door at the office opposite. Green-eyes had a camp bed there, and it was where she kept her clothes. It was also where she'd left the briefcase. The mobile phone was in the briefcase, but the case had combination locks. Each lock had three dials. Zero to nine hundred and ninety-nine. If it took two seconds to try each combination, she could do all one thousand in just over half an hour. An hour to do both locks. Maximum. In all probability it would take a lot less than an hour. But what then? She'd have access to the phone, but who would she call? The police? She was no further on than when she was being held on the industrial estate. Sure, she knew where the bomb was, and the police would be able to arrest her three captors, but what would happen to Katie? Could she be sure that Green-eyes would confess all and tell the police where Katie was being held?

Andy chewed slowly, barely tasting the sandwich. First things first. The briefcase was in the office on the other side of the corridor. She put down her half-eaten sandwich and went to the door, easing it open carefully. She could hear her three captors working in the main office area. There was no way they could see her unless they were standing in the corridor itself.

Andy took a deep breath, then tiptoed across the corridor and opened the door to the second office, her heart in her mouth. The briefcase was on a teak desk. She set the first combination to zero, zero, zero. She tried the lock. It wouldn't move. She flicked the end dial. Zero, zero, one. Still locked. She looked at her watch. She'd try for five minutes, then she'd have to get back to the main office.

The door to the interview room opened and Martin Hayes looked up. It was the inspector. FitzGerald. 'Now what?' said Martin. 'Back to the cell?'

FitzGerald shook his head. 'You can go, Mr Hayes. I think we've taken up enough of your time.'

Martin ran his hand over the stubble across his chin. He'd been in the Pearse Street station for almost eighteen hours and hadn't been given the chance to shave or clean his teeth, though he'd managed to wash his face in a sink in the men's room. He felt dirty and his shirt was sticking to his back. 'You're letting me go?'

'It's not a question of letting you go, Mr Hayes. You're not under arrest. You've just been helping us with our enquiries. You've been free to leave at any time.'

Martin stood up. 'So you believe me?'

'Let's just say we've no evidence that you've had anything to do with the disappearance of your wife and daughter,' said FitzGerald, holding the door open wide. 'But we might want another word with you again soon. So don't leave town, as they say.'

'They've not disappeared,' said Martin, but he knew that the detective wasn't interested in his denials.

He walked away from the grey stone Garda station and caught a taxi near Trinity College. They'd let him go, but it was as clear as day that FitzGerald didn't believe him, and Martin didn't blame him. He had never been a good liar, and authority figures always made him nervous, even when he hadn't done anything wrong.

He stared out of the taxi with unseeing eyes, wondering what he should do next. They'd presumably taken him out of the house so that they could check the bloodstain on the banister, and they'd probably searched through the house, too. He'd already admitted that it was Andy's blood, so hopefully it wouldn't be an issue any more. But they'd keep digging, and if they were to speak to his financial advisers, they'd discover that he'd been liquidating his assets and transferring money into his current account. What would they make of that? Martin wondered. They'd assume that he was about to withdraw the money. That he'd killed his wife and daughter and was about to disappear himself.

If nothing else, he'd be hauled into Pearse Street again for more questioning, and the more often that happened the more likely it was that Katie's kidnappers would discover that he was in contact with the police.

The taxi dropped him outside his house and he went inside, where he was practically bowled over by Dermott. He went straight to his answering machine. There were no messages. He let the dog out into the back garden, then made himself a cup of instant coffee and took it upstairs.

Dermott came running up the stairs after him, tail wagging like a metronome.

Martin went into Katie's bedroom and sat down on the bed. Dermott dropped down and rolled over on to his back, begging for his stomach to be rubbed. Martin patted the dog and sipped his coffee. He leaned over to put his cup on Katie's bedside table, and froze. There was a car outside his house. A Garda patrol car. Not exactly outside – they'd parked about a hundred feet away from the driveway, but they had a clear view of the house. Martin cursed under his breath. He hadn't put the light on so he didn't think they'd be able to see inside, but he slowly backed away from the window and went downstairs.

He paced around the kitchen, clenching and unclenching his fists. They were giving him no choice. He'd have to leave Dublin. If the kidnappers saw the Garda car, they'd think they were there because he'd called them in. Even worse, there was a good chance that the detectives would haul him in again for more questioning. They surely suspected him – why else the overt surveillance?

It was late, probably too late to get a flight out of Dublin that night. Besides, there was an outside chance that Fitz-Gerald had men at the airport watching for him. He'd be safer flying through Belfast.

He took a briefcase from his study and emptied out the papers it contained. He put in an unopened flight kit he'd been given on a business trip he and Padraig had made to Copenhagen a few months earlier, together with two clean shirts, underwear and socks. He put his mobile phone in his suit pocket. It was a GSM model and would work in the UK. He closed the briefcase. What else? Money. He'd need money. He had Visa cards that he could use to withdraw cash from money machines in the UK, but he also had some Irish money in his desk drawer. He took the money out and put the notes into his wallet.

He put his briefcase by the back door and then went out into the hallway and looked at the answering machine. What if Andy called again? Or if the kidnappers tried to get in touch? He recorded a fresh message, asking callers to telephone his mobile number, then checked it. He could hear the tension in his voice, the sound of a man about to go over the edge. He took a deep breath and recorded a second version. This time he sounded more relaxed.

In a cupboard under the hall were several electrical timers that he and Andy used to set lights to go on and off while they were on holiday. He went upstairs and fitted one to the plug of a lamp on the dressing table, timed to go off later that night. Then he drew the curtains and went downstairs. He fitted timers to lamps in the sitting room and the kitchen, overlapping the on and off times.

He took a last look around the house. Now what? Both cars were parked in the drive at the front. He'd have to go through the back garden and over the wall, maybe catch a taxi. He shook his head. No, a taxi driver might remember him. But he couldn't walk to the station. In fact, catching a train wasn't a good idea, either.

He went back into the kitchen and finished his coffee, then washed his mug. As he put it on the draining board, he realised what he'd have to do. He called Padraig on his mobile.

'Padraig. It's me, Martin.'

'What's up, Mart?'

'I need a favour. Big time.'

'Sure.'

'Can you pick me up on Morehampton Road? Opposite Bloomfield Hospital?' Martin went into the hallway and locked and bolted the front door, still talking on the mobile phone.

'No sweat. What's up? Car broken down, yeah?'

'Something like that. I'll explain when I see you. About ten minutes, okay?'

Martin thanked his partner and cut the connection. He looked down at Dermott, who was sitting with his head on one side, clearly wondering what was going on. 'What the hell am I going to do with you?' he said, and the dog woofed softly. He didn't want to leave Dermott locked in the house because he didn't know when he'd be back. But if he left the Labrador in the garden, he might bark and attract the attention of the watching garda. He decided he'd leave him inside.

Martin walked through to the kitchen, picked up his briefcase and let himself out of the back door. He locked it and slipped the key into his pocket. The sun was just about to dip below the horizon, smearing the grey sky with an orange glow. He jogged to the end of the garden and clambered over the brick wall that bordered a narrow path leading to the local golf course. He headed down the path, skirted the golf course and then walked through a carpark to the main road. Only then did he start to relax.

Egan slid the Browning Hi-Power out of its brown leather shoulder holster and checked that the safety was off. He had followed the taxi from the Pearse Street Garda station, but he'd abandoned the tail as soon he realised that a Garda patrol car was also following Hayes. Hayes had been released, but it was clear that the police still suspected him and were planning to keep him under observation. When Egan had driven past the Hayes' house, the patrol car had been parked in the road outside. He had stopped his Ford Scorpio in a road that led to a housing estate bordering a golf course, well away from any streetlights.

In his left ear was a small earphone connected to a receiver that allowed him to listen in to the five bugs planted in the house. He'd missed the first few seconds of the conversation that Hayes had had with his partner, but he'd picked up the rest via the device in the hall. Hayes was going to run, and Egan had only minutes in which to stop him. There was no time for a suicide note, no time to coerce Hayes into using the knotted rope.

He leaned over and took a street map out of the glove compartment and flicked through it. He found the page where Bloomfield Hospital was, and traced a gloved finger from Morehampton Road to the house. Assuming he left through the back garden, Hayes would have to walk close to the golf course. He put the map back in the glove compartment, along with the receiver and earpiece, then got out of the car and walked towards the golf course, putting the collar of his leather jacket up against the wind.

There seemed to be no one around, so Egan jogged, his breath feathering in the evening air. The lights were on in the clubhouse and several golfers were still out on the course, though there were only minutes to go before the sun went down. He reached the golf club's carpark and stopped jogging, not wanting to draw attention to himself.

There was a path running around the edge of the course, and beyond it a line of three bunkers. To Egan's left was a clump of trees, to the right were the fringes of an up-market housing estate. Egan kept his face turned away from the carpark, and waited until he was past before taking out his handgun and screwing in a bulbous silencer.

He reached the path and headed towards the trees. There were voices off to his right, two men arguing over a missed shot. Egan kept the Browning pressed against his stomach inside his jacket, his finger inside the trigger guard. He scanned the path ahead of him. In the distance was Hayes, walking towards him, his head down, a coat flapping behind him. Egan took a quick look over his shoulder. There was no one behind him and the voices of the two arguing golfers had already faded into the distance. Egan picked up the pace. The silencer was efficient, but even so the farther away he was from the clubhouse, the better. An owl hooted above his head but he barely registered the sound; all his senses were totally focused on the man walking towards him.

Egan could feel sweat dribbling down his back. He was breathing shallowly, his chest barely moving, the gun tight against his stomach. Hayes had his head down as he walked, and there was something in his right hand, something that he was swinging back and forth. He was about fifty feet away. Midway between them was a broad-trunked beech tree, perfect cover for what Egan was about to do. Egan moved over to the right-hand side of the path so that Hayes would have to pass on the side closest to the tree. One shot to the side of the head, maybe a second to the heart if he had time. He'd drag the body behind the tree and then head back to the car. By the time the body was discovered, Egan would be in London. Thirty feet. Egan began to pull the gun out, his finger already tightening on the trigger.

Hayes stopped. He peered out across the golf course as if looking for someone. Then suddenly he whistled, a piercing shriek that stopped Egan in his tracks. A dog ran across the grass. It was a German Shepherd. It wasn't Hayes, Egan realised. He'd come within seconds of shooting the wrong man. It was just a guy out walking his dog. The object in his right hand was a dog lead.

Egan started walking again. The man was bending down, patting his dog, as Egan went by. There was no one else on the path, and Egan could see all the way up to the wall at the end of the Hayes' garden. Somehow Egan had missed him. He turned and went back the way he'd come, walking quickly, his head turned to the side as he went by the man with the German Shepherd.

Martin looked at his watch and slowed down. He didn't want to have to hang around outside the hospital, just in case the Garda car was only making periodic visits to his house. He had no need to worry. Padraig arrived just as he was walking by the hospital's stone gateposts.

Padraig flashed the headlights of his BMW and Martin waved. He looked around as the car pulled up. A man in a leather jacket and jeans was walking along the pavement, his shoulders hunched against the cold. The passenger window slid down. 'Where's your car, Mart? I'll have a look at it.'

Martin heard rapid footsteps and turned to see who it was. The man in the leather jacket was running towards the car. As he ran he pulled his hand from under his jacket. Something glinted in the BMW's headlights. Something metallic. Martin pulled open the passenger door and climbed into the car. 'Drive!' he shouted.

Padraig sat stunned, his mouth open in surprise.

'Padraig! For fuck's sake, drive!'

The passenger window shattered, spraying Martin with cubes of glass. Martin ducked and held his briefcase over his face as Padraig put the car in gear and stamped on the accelerator. The seat seemed to punch Martin in the small of his back as they roared away from the kerb. A second bullet thudded into the door, and then Martin caught a glimpse of the man in the leather jacket standing with his feet apart, the gun held in both hands, arms outstretched, his face totally relaxed.

Padraig looked anxiously in his mirror as they drove away. 'Christ, who was that?' he said, his voice shaking.

Martin twisted around in his seat. The man in the leather jacket was walking away from the hospital, his head down and his hands in his jacket pockets.

'I don't know,' said Martin.

'You don't know? What do you mean, you don't know?' Padraig already had the car in fourth gear and they were doing almost eighty.

'Slow down, Padraig. You'll kill us.'

Padraig frowned, and then began to laugh. Despite his pounding heart and shaking hands, Martin laughed too, but it was an ugly, disjointed sound, and both men were soon silent again.

Padraig slowed slowed to just under the speed limit. 'What the fuck's going on, Mart?'

'I don't know. I really don't know.'

'Where do you want to go?' asked Padraig.

'North. Belfast.'

Padraig frowned. 'What?'

Martin pointed down the road. 'Belfast. I've got to get out of Ireland, and the police have probably got Dublin airport covered.'

'The police? The police are after you?'

Martin didn't say anything. He picked pieces of glass from his jacket and dropped them on to the floor of the car. Padraig drove, flashing Martin anxious looks as he headed north. Martin kept checking his mirror, wanting to reassure himself that no one was following him.

'Martin, what the hell's going on?' asked Padraig again eventually.

Martin hugged the briefcase to his chest. 'I can't tell you, Padraig. I really can't. I'm going to London for a few days. My mobile is going to be on, so if it's an emergency you'll be able to get me on that.'

'An emergency? What the hell do you call what just happened?'

Martin nodded. He tensed as he saw a police car in his mirror, but it streaked by them.

'The guy who shot at you. He wasn't a cop,' said Padraig.

'No,' said Martin.

'So who was he? For God's sake, Martin, I could have been killed back there. You owe me an explanation.'

Martin sighed. His partner was right. He'd put Padraig's life on the line – he had a right to know why.

'Katie's been kidnapped. They took her last week. The kidnappers wanted Andy to go to London. Now the cops have found out that Andy and Katie are missing and they think I've got something to do with it. I figure London's the best place for me. If Andy's left any sort of message for me, it'll be there. I know it sounds crazy, but that's the situation.'

'And who was the guy with the gun?'

'I don't know. One of the kidnappers maybe. They must have seen the Garda take me away. Or maybe they saw the car outside the house.' Martin put his head in his hands. 'If they think I'm co-operating with the cops, they're going to kill Katie. Oh, God.'

He explained about being taken to Pearse Street, and the patrol car parked outside his house.

'Jesus, Mart.' Padraig pushed down the accelerator and the BMW powered to ninety miles per hour. 'What are you going to do? You have to go to the police. You have to.'

'No. Not yet. I need time to think. Just take care of the company and don't tell the cops anything.'

'Mart, you can't just run away like this.'

'I can't stay in Dublin,' said Martin. He gestured at the smashed window. 'There's no saying he won't try again, whoever he was.'

Padraig looked anxiously in his rear-view mirror, but he was driving so fast there was no way anyone could be following them.

'So you go to London. What then?'

'I don't know,' said Martin flatly. 'I really don't know.'

Egan walked back to his Ford Scorpio and climbed in. With hindsight, shooting at Martin Hayes had been a mistake. He'd missed him by inches but it had still been a mistake. Egan started the car and drove off, checking to see if anyone was watching him. No one was. And no one had seen him firing at the BMW. Egan knew he'd been lucky and he hated himself for depending on luck. Anyone could have driven by while he had the gun out; anyone could have seen him shooting at the car. He should have let Hayes go and followed at a distance, choosing his moment with more care. Now Hayes would be spooked, and Egan could only hope that he wouldn't be spooked enough to go to the police and tell them everything. So long as he was running scared, he wasn't a threat.

Hayes was running, but he had nowhere to run to. He clearly wasn't co-operating with the police, and there was no one else he could turn to. He'd probably lie low with his partner, the guy driving the BMW. Egan had intercepted the letter that his wife had left for him at the hotel, so that was a dead end. And there were only three days left before the bomb would be ready. Even if Hayes told the police that his daughter had been kidnapped and that his wife had disappeared in London, there was nothing they could do to prevent the bomb going off. Egan smiled to himself as he drove. Shooting at Hayes had been a mistake, but not a fatal one.

The sky outside was beginning to darken, so Green-eyes switched on the banks of fluorescent lights in the main office area. She had to walk practically the full length of the office, almost a hundred and fifty feet, to get to all the switches. Andy put on a pair of oven gloves and began taking trays out of one of the ovens. The Wrestler was unclipping the lids of a dozen large Tupperware containers, and Andy carefully tipped fertiliser into them, scooping out the last few pounds with a wooden spoon. She put the metal tray on a pile of other used trays, then went over to the stack of fertiliser bags. She dragged one of the bags across to the table, then used one of the empty Tupperware containers as a scoop to refill the trays. They were down to the last ten sacks. By morning all the fertiliser would have been through the ovens and they'd be ready for the next step.

Green-eyes finished switching on the lights and then headed towards the meeting room. Andy watched her go as she levelled the fertiliser with her hands into a layer two inches thick. Any deeper and the fertiliser wouldn't dry all the way through to the bottom. She filled four trays and slotted them into the oven.

The Runner was checking the temperature of one of the other ovens. He looked across at her and loosened the bottom of his ski mask. 'This mask is a bitch,' he said. He reached up and grabbed the top of it. 'How about if I take it off, here and now.' He pulled at it gently and it moved up half an inch. 'How about that? Would you like to see what I look like?'

'No!' said Andy quickly.

'Why not?'

'You know why not.'

The Wrestler was standing over by the pile of sacks of fertiliser, watching them. Andy stared in horror as the Runner pulled the mask up another inch.

'Don't!' said Andy, holding out her hands, fingers splayed.

'Why not?'

'Because if I see your face . . .'

The Runner nodded and gave his mask another tug. Andy could see most of his neck, almost up to his chin. 'That's right,' he said. He laughed, a high-pitched whinny like that of a nervous horse.

Green-eyes came out of the meeting room, a mug of coffee in one hand. The two men stopped laughing as soon as they saw her. The Runner let go of his ski mask and bent down to check the thermometer again, and the Wrestler picked up a sack of fertiliser.

'Andrea, do you want anything?' Green-eyes asked.

'No, I'm okay.' What she really wanted was to be alone in the office so that she could continue working on the brief-case. She'd got up to the mid-three-hundreds before nipping back across the corridor to the meeting room. Another twenty minutes at most and she'd have one of the locks open. She still hadn't decided what she'd do if and when she got her hands on the mobile phone, but at least she was doing something.

The girl was stunning, just short of six feet tall in her high heels, with glossy black hair that reached to just above her hips. She wore a skin-tight cheongsam, scarlet with a gold dragon entwined around it, its head breathing fire across her ample breasts. She said she was nineteen years old and that her name was May. Deng waved at the seat next to him and asked her to sit with him.

She bent forward and swiped a plastic card through a reader in the centre of the table. Customers in the nightclub were billed by the minute for the company of the hostesses. A bottle of champagne arrived. Deng hadn't asked for the champagne, but he knew the score. Girls like May didn't come cheap. She spoke Mandarin with a Hong Kong accent. Cantonese was her first language, but with an ever-growing number of mainland Chinese businessmen and financiers visiting the former British colony, Mandarin was a necessity in her line of work.

She sat with a delicate hand on his thigh, her red-painted fingernails gently scratching the material of his Armani suit as she made small talk. Her skin was like porcelain, smooth and unblemished, and she smelt of flowers. After fifteen minutes of banal chatter she asked if a friend of hers could join them. Deng readily agreed. Her friend was just as tall as May, with longer hair and larger breasts. She wore a bright yellow evening dress cut low at the front to emphasise her cleavage. Her name was Summer, and she spoke better

Mandarin than May, and almost perfect English. She swiped her card through the reader and a second bottle of champagne arrived.

After half an hour May whispered into Deng's ear that a regular customer of hers had arrived and did he mind if she left his table. He kissed her on the lips and told that he was more than happy with Summer. May swiped her card through the reader and went over to another table.

An hour later and Deng was in bed with Summer in a Kowloon Tong love hotel. It was one of Deng's favourite places to take girls – every room had a different theme. There was an Arabian Nights room, a Wild West room, a Parisian Brothel room, and each came with a set of costumes which could be worn if desired. Deng had been more than a dozen times and had never been in the same fantasy twice. He and Summer were in a room made up to look like a Swiss cottage, lined with wood, a big cuckoo clock on one wall and a mural of an Alpine scene framed in a mock window.

Deng lay on his back as Summer rode him, her mouth slightly open, showing perfect white teeth, her head thrown back so that her hair brushed against his thighs every time she ground against him. She was good, she was very good, and Deng had to fight to stop himself from coming too soon. His hands moved up her soft, compliant body and he caressed her breasts. She put her hands on top of his, squeezing him, moaning softly. She'd told him that she wanted to be an actress, that she was taking acting lessons and had a producer friend who'd promised her a part in his next kung-fu film. Deng could see that she had talent.

He could feel himself passing the point of no return and he pounded into her, half disappointed that he hadn't managed to last longer. He came inside her and she fell down on top of him, kissing his neck and whispering his name. That was a nice touch, he thought. Almost as if she cared. She squeezed him inside her, draining every last drop from him. Deng smiled and stroked her hair. Another nice touch. He'd be back to see Summer again, he decided. Maybe even offer to set her up in a flat. A small one, mind – there was no reason to be extravagant, not when Hong Kong was so full of pretty young girls.

Deng heard a noise at the door. The sound of a key being turned. 'We've not finished yet,' he shouted in Cantonese. He'd paid for two hours and he still had thirty minutes left. There was silence, and muffled voices, then the door burst open. Summer rolled off him and pulled the sheet around her. Deng sat up. What little remained of his erection shrank to nothing. It was Michael Wong. And three of his Red Poles. Triad heavies. One of the Red Poles closed the door and stood with his back against it. The other two men had handguns. Big ones.

Wong grinned, showing a gold tooth at the back of his mouth. 'Good, was she?' he asked in guttural Mandarin.

Deng pushed himself back against the headboard. 'What's this about, Michael?'

Wong walked over to Summer. She looked up at him fearfully, forcing a smile. 'Hello, Summer,' he said, in Cantonese. 'Long time no see.'

Summer was shaking, and her smile was little more than a baring of teeth, the smile of a frightened dog. 'Hello, Mr Wong,' she said. She wasn't such a good actress after all, Deng realised.

Wong grinned at Deng again. 'Did she go down on you? Great mouth, Summer has. She's got this trick of taking it all, you know? All the way in.' He looked across at the frightened girl. 'Don't you, Summer?'

She nodded, her eyes wide with fear. Wong beckoned for her to come closer. She crawled over to him, letting the sheet slip from her body. Her skin was still glossy with sweat. Wong unzipped his fly and took his penis out. Without being asked, Summer slipped off the bed and knelt down in front of him. He gripped her hair tightly with one hand as he worked himself in and out of her mouth, barely giving her a chance to breathe. Deng turned his head away in disgust.

'Don't you look away, you piece of shit,' said Wong. Summer was moaning softly, caressing the back of Wong's thighs, her head moving back and forth, matching his rhythm. Wong came quickly, holding Summer's head tightly until he was sure that she'd swallowed, then he grunted and pushed her away. She crawled back to the bed and wrapped the sheet around herself. She bent almost double, as if trying to make herself as small as possible, and scampered towards the bathroom. Wong pulled a silenced automatic from inside his jacket and pointed it at her. She froze. He pointed the gun at one of the armchairs and she went over to it and sat down, wrapping her arms tightly around her knees.

'There's no need for this, Michael,' said Deng.

'Where's my fucking money?'

'You'll have it soon.'

'That's not what I've heard.' He nodded at the frightened girl. 'The thing I can't work out is why you're in a short-time hotel fucking hookers when what you should be doing is getting back my twenty million dollars.'

'It's in hand,' said Deng. 'One more week and our problems are solved, I promise.'

'I've heard your promises before, Deng.'

Summer began to whimper. She begged Wong to let her go, and he glared at her with contempt. 'Shut up, whore,' he said in Cantonese.

Summer fell silent and pulled the sheet tighter around her neck. Tears began to run down her cheeks.

'The triad entrusted you with twenty million dollars,' Wong said, walking to the foot of the bed and staring down at Deng. 'Twenty million US dollars. Then you come and tell us that we're at risk of losing that investment.'

Deng held his hands up defensively in front of his face. 'We're all in the same boat, Michael,' he said. 'The bank invested more than a hundred million dollars of its own money. We've investors in Singapore and Thailand. We've all . . .'

The gun kicked in Wong's hand. The only noise it made was a slight coughing sound. A bullet buried itself in the pillow by Deng's side and a few small white feathers fluttered into the air. 'I don't care about your bank. I don't care about the other investors. You lied to us. You took the Triad's twenty million dollars and you fucking lied to us.' Wong looked at Deng dispassionately, tapping the barrel of his silenced gun against his lips. 'How can I convince you how serious I am?' he asked. He slowly pointed the weapon at Deng's left foot. 'Perhaps if I gave you a limp. Do you think then you'd realise how important this is to me and my associates?'

Deng drew his foot back. Wong grinned malevolently and pointed the gun at Deng's groin.

'Or maybe I should blow something else off? Something a little closer to home? Do you have children?'

Deng nodded. 'Two.'

'Boys or girls?'

'Two boys.'

Wong nodded thoughtfully. 'Two sons? You are a lucky man. It's good to see how flexible the motherland is regarding the one family, one child policy.' He tightened his finger on the trigger. Deng's hands went across his groin in a reflex action. 'There's no flexibility here in Hong Kong, Deng. We want our money. All of it.'

'I told you, you'll have it. Every last penny.'

'That's good. Because if we don't, I'll kill you, your wife, your two precious sons, and every other member of your family I can find. That goes for you and the rest of the members of the board. I want you to tell them that, Deng. Tell them from me.'

Deng nodded furiously. 'I will. Of course I will.'

Wong shook his head. 'But I have to do something to show you how serious I am.'

Deng shook his head even faster, his breath coming in ragged gasps. 'Please don't,' he whimpered.

Wong grinned scornfully. He pointed the gun at Deng's chest, then quickly moved his gun arm in a smooth motion around to his right and shot Summer in the face. Blood and bone fragments splattered across the wall behind her, a smear of red across the Alpine snow scene, and she fell backwards without a sound, what was left of her face staring up at the ceiling.

Deng put his hands up to his mouth, horrified at what the Triad leader had done, but relieved, too, that it had been the prostitute who had died. It could so easily have been him.

'I'll leave the mess for you to clean up,' said Wong, putting his gun back inside his jacket. 'I'm sure you know the right sort of people.'

DAY SEVEN

———◆———

Andy woke up to the sound of someone knocking on the office door. It was Green-eyes, with a mug of coffee and a croissant. Andy had spent the night on a leather sofa with one of her pullovers as a pillow. She sat up and took the coffee and pastry.

'We finished the drying a few hours ago,' said Green-eyes.

'You haven't slept?'

'I'll catch a few hours once we've started on the next stage.'

Andy put her coffee mug down and ran a hand through her hair. 'I could do with a shower.'

'You and me both. But the washrooms are all we have. A full washbasin is the best we can do. Sorry.' Green-eyes looked at her wristwatch. 'Ready in ten minutes, right? The troops are waiting.'

Green-eyes went back to the office floor. Andy drank her coffee and ate half the croissant, then went to the washroom to clean her teeth and wipe herself over with a damp flannel.

Green-eyes and the two men were waiting for her in the office area. The temperature had dropped to a more bearable high seventies now that the ovens were switched off. The four electric woks had been taken out of their cardboard boxes and were lined up on the desks. Andy went over and examined them. They were Teflon-coated, with dials that controlled the heat settings.

'Right,' said Green-eyes. 'What do we do?'

Andy picked up one of the five-gallon cans of alcohol. 'We use this to wash the ammonium nitrate. It gets the impurities out of it.'

She went over to the pile of black garbage bags and dragged one of them over to the woks. 'You need a container. The Tupperware'll do. Half fill it with the ammonium nitrate, then pour in just enough alcohol to cover it. Stir it well for about three minutes, then pour off the alcohol. It should go a dirty brown. You can use it a few times. Okay?'

Green-eyes and her colleagues nodded.

'Okay, so then we have to evaporate off the alcohol. Pour the wet ammonium nitrate into the wok and sort of stir-fry it. You've got to keep it moving, at a low heat. The same applies as when we were drying it in the ovens – try to keep the temperature around one hundred and fifty degrees. You've got to keep watching it. If it gets to four hundred degrees, it'll blow.' She looked around the office. 'The fumes can be fierce. I'd suggest we spread out, and use the fans.'

'What about the respirators?' asked Green-eyes.

'No use. The respirators are for particles, not fumes. The best thing would be to open the windows, but that's not possible, so we'll have to make do with the fans. I warn you now, it'll give you a headache.'

'How long do we heat it for?'

'Three or four minutes should do. It's just like when you stir-fry food – keep it hot and keep it moving.'

Green-eyes grinned. 'You might have to give the boys a demonstration. I don't think they're particularly at home in the kitchen.'

She laughed, and Andy started to laugh along with her. She stopped suddenly when she realised what she was doing. She was laughing with the woman responsible for kidnapping her daughter, the woman who was forcing her to build a four-thousand-pound bomb in the City of London. Green-eyes stopped laughing too. She stood looking at Andy, as if sensing her confusion. 'Go on, Andrea,' she said. 'What then?'

Andy clenched and unclenched her hands, bunching them into fists and then relaxing them. What could she be thinking of? These weren't her friends, she shouldn't be enjoying herself, she shouldn't be letting her guard down. How dare she laugh with them? It was a betrayal – she was betraying Katie and she was betraying Martin. They both deserved better.

'What then, Andrea?' Green-eyes repeated.

'You have to grind it up into a fine powder,' said Andy, her voice shaking. 'In the coffee grinders. A couple of minutes should do it. Then seal it back in the Tupperware containers as quickly as possible. Every second it's exposed to the air, it absorbs water.'

The Wrestler held up a hand, pointing a finger at her. 'Wait one fucking minute,' he said. 'We've already treated all three thousand and odd pounds of it. Pound by pound. Are you saying we have to do it again?'

'That's right. It all has to be treated. It has to be uniformly pure, uniformly fine. If there are wet spots, or rough spots, the detonation velocity won't be consistent.'

'It's going to take for ever,' moaned the Runner. The Wrestler and the Runner stood looking at each other, clearly unhappy at the prospect of the work that lay ahead.

Green-eyes went over to Andy. 'Why don't you get yourself a coffee, Andrea. I want to have a word with the boys.'

Andrea went off to the meeting room, knowing that Green-eyes was going to give the men a talking-to. She closed the door behind her, poured herself a mug of coffee and set it down on the table. She looked through the glass panel at the office opposite. She had just about plucked up the courage to open the door and tiptoe across the corridor when she heard footsteps. She rushed back to the table and picked up her mug of coffee just as the door opened. It was Green-eyes. 'Right. Come on,' she said to Andy. 'Let's get started.'

Martin Hayes telephoned the Strand Palace Hotel from a call-box at Belfast airport ten minutes before he was due to board his flight to London and asked to speak to someone on reception. A girl answered, and Martin explained that his wife had stayed there the previous Wednesday night and asked if she'd left a message for him. The girl checked and said that no, there was no message. Martin thanked her and cut the connection. He called Padraig's mobile and his partner answered. Martin thanked him again for driving him up to Belfast and for waiting with him in the airport carpark until dawn broke. He reminded his partner to check on his dog, thanked him again, then hung up and went to catch his flight.

He arrived at Heathrow at nine o'clock in the morning and caught a black cab to the Strand. He figured that whoever had answered the phone would have been at the end of the night shift and had probably gone home. To make absolutely sure that he didn't speak to the same person, he went up to a young man in a black suit. Martin wasn't sure why he was in the hotel – he just knew that it was the only link he had to Andy. She'd have known that too, so if she'd left any sort of trail it had to have been at the hotel. He leaned forward over the reception counter and smiled at the man. 'My wife lost an earring when she was staying here last week. Can you tell me if anything was handed in after she checked out?'

The man tapped away on his computer and shook his head. 'Nope, nothing was handed in,' he said. 'And House-keeping haven't reported finding anything.'

Martin sighed. 'Damn. It was hellish expensive. Diamond. Cost me an arm and a leg. Look, I don't suppose I could have a quick look around, could I? Just to check?'

The man consulted his computer again. 'The room's empty. I don't see why not.' He look around. 'I'll get someone to go up with you.'

'That's okay, I don't want to trouble anybody.'

'Security, sir,' said the man. He waved over a teenage bell-boy in a beige uniform and handed him a key before explaining the situation.

The bell-boy took Martin up to the fifth floor and opened the door for him. 'An earring, huh?' he said, bending down and looking under the bed.

'Yeah. Gold with a diamond.' Martin went into the bathroom and looked around. If he'd been Andy, where would he have hidden a message? The toilet cistern was boxed in and there was no way he could see of removing the base of the bath or shower. There was a small ventilation grille close to the ceiling but the screws holding it in place had been painted over and there was no sign of it having been moved.

He went back into the bedroom and put his briefcase on the dressing table. The bell-boy was still on his hands and knees, peering under the bed. Martin took his wallet out and gave the teenager a twenty-pound note. 'There's no point in me holding you up, lad,' said Martin. 'I'll have a look around myself, yeah?'

'Are you sure, sir?' said the teenager as the note smoothly disappeared into his pocket. 'I don't mind helping.'

'Nah, you go on down. I won't be long.'

The bell-boy left, closing the door behind him. Martin stood in the middle of the bedroom. 'Come on, Andy,' he whispered. 'You must have left me something. You must have.'

He looked at the bed. She couldn't have left anything

there – the bedding would be changed after every guest. He went over to the desk and checked the drawers. There was a wallet of hotel stationery and Martin went through it piece by piece. Nothing. He flicked through the pages of the Gideon Bible. Nothing. Most of the drawers were empty. There was a picture above the writing desk. A banal water-colour, probably reproduced in its hundreds specifically to hang in hotel bedrooms. Martin reckoned he could prob-ably have done a better job himself. It was a gondola with a young couple cuddling in front, a bored gondolier in a large black hat standing at the rear. The perspective was wrong – the buildings at the far side of the canal seemed to be leaning to the right, and the shadows weren't consistent. It didn't even look like Venice. Martin's breath caught in his throat. Venice? What had Andy said when she phoned? Going back to Venice. A place she'd never been to. He ran his hands around the frame. It wouldn't move. It was screwed to the wall. There were four screws, two on the right, two on the left.

With trembling hands, Martin searched through his pockets for a penny. He found one, and used it to take out the screws. He pulled the painting away from the wall and a sheet of paper fluttered to the floor. Martin tossed the painting on to the bed and picked up the sheet of paper. As he straightened up, he was startled by an angry voice behind him.

'What the hell do you think you're doing?'

The receptionist in the black suit was standing in the doorway, the key to the room in his hand.

'I'm sorry,' said Martin. He folded the piece of paper and thrust it into his jacket pocket.

The receptionist looked at the picture, and at the space on the wall where it had been hanging.

'I'll pay for the damage,' said Martin, taking out his wallet.

'You'll stay right where you are,' said the man, holding his hands up as if warding off an attack. 'I'm calling Security.'

'There's no need for that. All I did was take the painting down.' He pointed at the desk. 'Look, the screws are there. Hell, man, I'll even put it back for you.'

The man went over to the phone by the bed and picked it up. 'Don't touch anything,' he said.

Martin tossed two twenty-pound notes on to the bed, picked up his briefcase and headed for the door.

'No you don't,' said the receptionist, grabbing for Martin's arm.

Martin hit the man across the head with his briefcase and he fell to the floor. He kicked the door shut, then pulled the bed cover over the man and roughly tied him up with the phone cord before running out of the room. He dashed down the emergency stairs, knowing that the man wouldn't stay tied up for long.

He reached the ground floor and burst through into the reception area. Heads turned as he dashed over to the main doors and out into the Strand. He kept running as hard as he could, the briefcase banging against his leg, his chest heaving with the effort. He didn't know whether or not he was being pursued, but he didn't care – he just wanted to put as much distance between himself and the hotel as he could.

He barged through a group of tourists and sprinted down a side road. He ran in front of a black cab and the driver slammed on his brakes, cursing him through the side window.

Martin looked over his shoulder as he ran. There was no one following him, and he slowed to a jog, then a walk. He was sweating and his heart was pounding. He took deep breaths, trying to calm himself down. He looked over his shoulder again. Nothing. He began to relax.

He walked across the main plaza in Covent Garden, where a clown was walking along a broom handle suspended across a pair of stepladders. A dwarf in a clown suit was walking around a crowd of onlookers, collecting money in a red plastic bucket. Martin threaded his way through the crowds and went into a large café. There were plenty of empty tables outside, bordering the plaza, but Martin chose a table inside, close to the toilets. He ordered a cappuccino from a pretty blonde Australian waitress, then took the sheet of paper out and carefully unfolded it. It was a piece of hotel notepaper. The writing was Andy's.

Dear Martin

My love. If you've found this it can only mean something's gone terribly wrong and that you've called in the police. Dear God, my hands are shaking so much as I write this. Please, just know that I love you, I love you with all my heart. If it has gone wrong, you must never stop looking for Katie.

They've told me to go to a carpark in Bedford Court and to get into a van. A dark blue Transit van. They say it's got the name of a landscaping company on the side. I don't know where they're going to take me or what they plan to do. I'll do whatever it takes to get Katie back, I promise.

Martin, if the worst has happened, if you've had to go to the police or if I'm dead (God, it feels so strange writing that), then there's someone I want you to call. Someone who might be able to find out where Katie is. His name is Detective Chief Inspector Liam Denham. He works for Special Branch in Belfast. Tell him it's about Trevor. Tell him what's happened. He'll help, if anyone can.

Please, my love, never, ever forget that I love you.

At the bottom of the letter was a Belfast telephone number.

Martin reread the letter several times, his mind in a whirl. A Special Branch detective? Trevor? What in God's name was Andy talking about?

The waitress returned with his coffee. Martin left it untouched as he sat staring at the letter. Who was this Liam Denham? And who was Trevor? In the ten years he'd known Andy, she'd never mentioned either name. Special Branch? They dealt with terrorists. They were the élite of the Northern Ireland police. Why on earth would Andy have been involved with them?

Martin folded the letter up and put it back in his jacket pocket. Andy had obviously assumed that it would be found after her death. So far as Martin knew, she was still alive, but the fact that the police were now involved meant that she was in danger. Her life was on the line. The kidnappers wouldn't know that the police had been called in by Katie's school – they'd assume that it was Martin who'd gone to them. And if they assumed that, what was to stop them killing Katie and Andy? Martin had to do something, and he had to act quickly. But what could he do? Alone, he was powerless. He had a partial description of the van that had taken Andy away, but he had no way of finding out who it belonged to. He couldn't speak to the Irish police, not now that he'd run away from them. They'd regard everything he said with suspicion. Besides, Andy wasn't in Ireland, she was in England, and the Irish police had no jurisdiction over the water. Martin dropped a couple of pound coins on the table and left the café. He had only one option, the option that Andy had given him.

He walked through Covent Garden, sidestepping a juggler who was tossing flaming torches high into the air, and found a call-box in King Street. He popped a pound coin into the slot and tapped out the Belfast number that Andy had given him. It was answered on the third ring. 'Yeah?' It was a man's voice. Hard and guttural.

'I'd like to speak to Liam Denham.'

'Who's calling?'

'Is he there? It's urgent.'

'Who's calling?'

'Look, this is an emergency. I need to speak to Detective Chief Inspector Liam Denham. This is Special Branch, isn't it?'

The line went quiet for a few seconds, then a second man spoke, his voice softer. 'Who am I speaking to?' asked the second man.

'That's not important,' said Martin. He looked at the digital read-out on the phone. Half his money had already gone. He slotted in a fifty-pence coin. 'Just tell Liam Denham that I have to speak with him.'

'I'm afraid that's not possible,' said the man. 'How did you get this number?'

Martin slammed his hand against the wall of the call-box. Not possible? What did he mean, not possible? 'Look, is this Special Branch or not?'

'Where did you get this number from?' the man repeated.

Martin wanted to shout at the man, but he clamped his jaws together and fought to stay calm. Denham could help, Andy had said. He was the only lifeline that Martin had, and he had to hang on to it. 'My wife gave me the number,' said Martin slowly. 'My wife gave me the number and said that I was to ask for Chief Inspector Liam Denham. Now is he there or not?'

'And you wife's name would be what?'

'Andy. Andrea. Andrea Hayes.'

Martin heard a clicking sound and realised that the man was typing on a computer keyboard.

'I'm not familiar with that name,' said the man.

'I don't give a shit whether you're familiar with her name

or not. She told me to ask Denham for help. That's what I'm doing. Get him on the line, now.'

'You're Mr Hayes, is that right?'

'Yes, damn you.'

'What's your wife's maiden name?'

'What?'

'Her maiden name. Before she married you.'

'Sheridan.'

More typing on the keyboard. 'No. I'm not familiar with that name either.'

Martin wanted to scream. His wife and daughter were missing, maybe they were dead already, and the voice on the end of the line was being as cold and impersonal as a telephone answering machine. It was like speaking to a robot. The phone read-out showed that he had only thirty pence left. 'Look, you have to help me,' Martin pleaded. 'You have to put Denham on the line.'

'I've already said that I can't do that.'

'What the hell is wrong with you? My wife said that I was to call this number and to ask for Denham. To tell him that it was about some guy called Trevor. Shit, I don't know . . . what more can I do?'

Martin heard the clickety-click of the keyboard. Then a sudden intake of breath. 'Mr Hayes?'

'Yes. I'm here.'

'Where are you calling from?'

'London. Covent Garden. I'm in a call-box, and I'm running out of money.'

'Give me the number.'

Martin gave the man the number of the call-box. The man repeated it back to him. 'Mr Hayes, please stay by the phone. Someone will call you back shortly.'

Martin was midway through thanking the man when the line went dead. It was only then that he remembered the mobile phone in his briefcase. He should have given that number to the man, but it was too late now. He waited in the call-box. An elderly man in a blue blazer and yellow cravat rapped on the door with a walking stick. Martin pointed at the phone and shrugged apologetically. 'I'm waiting for a call,' he mouthed. The man glared at him. Martin turned around. He could feel the man's eyes burning into his back. The seconds ticked by. The man knocked on the door again. Martin tried to ignore the noise, but he was embarrassed at having to behave so badly.

The phone rang and he grabbed the receiver. 'Denham?' he said.

'I'm afraid Mr Denham isn't available at the moment,' said a woman. She sounded middle-aged, certainly over thirty, and there was the vague hint of a West Country accent.

'Where the hell is he?'

'Please try to stay calm, Mr Hayes. I'm trying to help you. Okay?'

'Okay. I'm sorry.'

The man in the blazer walked around the call-box and continued to glare at Martin. He had tufts of white hair protruding from his ears and nostrils and deep wrinkles at the edges of his eyes. He rapped on the glass and tapped his wristwatch. Martin turned his back on him again.

'Right. Good. Now, my name is Patsy, Mr Hayes. I want you to tell me exactly what's happened to your wife.'

Martin told her about Katie's kidnapping and Andy's disappearance in London. Patsy listened without interrupting. He told her about the gardai coming around to his house, and how he'd fled to London. He told them about going to the hotel, and finding the note.

'How did you know to look behind the painting?' Patsy asked.

Martin told her about the brief phone conversation he'd had with Andy on Sunday night.

'Did she tell you anything else? Anything that might suggest where she'd been taken?'

'No. She was only on the line for about twenty seconds. She just said she was okay, and that she was doing what they asked her.'

'She didn't say who "they" were?'

'No. No, she didn't.'

'Okay, Mr Hayes, you're doing just fine. Now, it's important that you do exactly as I tell you.'

'What about this man Denham? Andy said I should speak to him.'

'Chief Inspector Denham retired some time ago, Mr Hayes. We're trying to contact him now.'

'What's all this about? Why does my wife know him?'

'There'll be time for explanations later, Mr Hayes. First, we want you to go along to a police station in London so that someone can talk to you face to face. I'm going to arrange for you to be met at Paddington Green . . .'

'No way am I talking to the police,' interrupted Martin. 'They think I did something to Andy and Katie. And I hit a guy, in the hotel.'

'You don't have to talk to them, Mr Hayes. This is far too important to be handled by the police. But I need you to be somewhere safe until we can meet.'

'I'm not going into a police station,' Martin insisted. The man in the blazer appeared in front of him, his cheeks flaring red, his upper lip curled back in a snarl. Martin stared at the man, but barely saw him. His mind was a million miles away. He closed his eyes and rubbed the bridge of his nose. He had to think. He had to work out what to do.

'Mr Hayes?'

'I'm still here. I'm confused.'

'I understand that. But if we're to get your wife and daughter back, we have to stay calm. Do you understand, Mr Hayes? We have to act professionally.'

'Who the hell are you?' hissed Martin.

'You know who we are, Mr Hayes. You called us. Now, will you just do as I ask, go along to Paddington Green police . . .'

'No,' said Martin. 'We'll meet somewhere else.'

'Where, then?'

'I'll book into a hotel. You can come and see me there.'

'Fine. Which hotel?'

Martin tried to think of a hotel. The Savoy flashed into his mind. He'd stayed there with Andy six months earlier. But the Savoy wouldn't do because there was an outside chance that he might be recognised. He wouldn't be able to use his own name because he'd told the receptionist at the Strand Palace that he was Andy's husband and they'd have been sure to have called in the police by now. He remembered a hotel he'd stayed at during a business trip to London a few years previously, a big hotel close to the City with hundreds of rooms. A big hotel guaranteed anonymity. 'The Tower,' he said. 'It's near the Thames. Near Tower Bridge.'

'Okay,' said Patsy. 'Check in and stay in your room. We're trying to track down Chief Inspector Denham now. But someone will contact you later this afternoon. You shouldn't check in under your own name, Mr Hayes, you realise that?'

'Of course. I'll use Sheridan. Martin Sheridan. Okay?'

'Fine. Please go to the hotel immediately, Mr Hayes.'

The line went dead. Martin replaced the receiver and left the call-box. The man in the blazer had gone. Martin went off in search of a cab.

Andy used a wooden spatula to scrape the hot ammonium nitrate from the wok into a coffee grinder. She had a blinding headache, the result of breathing in the alcohol fumes for several hours. It was repetitive and backbreaking work, and she was thankful that she didn't have to wear a ski mask like Green-eyes and the two men. She put the glass cap on top of the coffee grinder and pressed down on it. It whirred loudly, the vibrations travelling up her arm as it reduced the fertiliser to a fine powder.

The Wrestler was doing the same about thirty feet away, using both his hands on the cap of the grinder. Green-eyes had taken a break, and the Runner was by the water-cooler, his back to Andy, splashing water on to his face, the ski mask pushed up on his head. Andy hurriedly looked away and turned her back to him. She didn't want to take the risk of seeing his face.

It was taking the best part of seven minutes to wash, dry and grind a four-pound portion of fertiliser. If all four of them worked flat out, it would take them almost twenty-four hours to process it all. And that wasn't taking into account breaks for sleep and food. Andy figured it would take at least two full days to get it all done. Then there was the mixing of the other ingredients. Say another day. Three days, then the explosive would be ready.

Did Green-eyes actually plan to use the bomb? Andy was still clinging to the hope that she had something else in mind, that the construction of the device was part of some political strategy that wasn't going to end in an explosion and death. Green-eyes still hadn't explained what she was going to use as a detonator. The ammonium nitrate mixture was a powerful explosive, but it needed an equally powerful detonator, components that the IRA were able to acquire through their worldwide terrorist connections but which weren't the sort that could easily be purchased in England. The fact that she hadn't mentioned the detonation system meant that perhaps, just perhaps, she had no intention of using the bomb. It was a slim hope, but one that Andy clung to as she sweated over the electric wok and the coffee grinder.

The Wrestler's shoulder holster was fastened over the top of his overalls, and Andy found her gaze constantly returning to the butt of the pistol nestling under the man's left armpit. It was held in place by a thin strap across the trigger which had to be unclipped before the weapon could be slid out. If she caught him unawares, Andy could probably pull the gun out before he realised what was happening. But what then? She could threaten to shoot him unless he told her where Katie was being held, but what if he refused? Could she shoot him? And what if she did and she killed him? Then she'd never know where Katie was. There had to be another way, but no matter how hard Andy racked her brains, she couldn't think of one.

Liam Denham looked up from the fishing fly he was tying and scowled in annoyance at the rattling window. He pushed up his magnifying visor and put his tweezers down on the mahogany desktop. The window overlooked his sprawling garden, the best part of five acres which he and his wife had transformed from a cow pasture into a manicured lawn, a Japanese rock garden, several large curving rockeries, and a rose garden which produced blooms that had twice won first prize at the local agricultural shows. Not to mention an orchard and vegetable garden that meant they hadn't had to visit a greengrocer's for years.

Something flashed above the house, clattering and roaring, then just as quickly it had gone. Denham stood up and peered upwards. Seconds later, the helicopter appeared again and the windows shook even more violently than before. The helicopter was a Wessex, dark green. Army colours. Denham took his visor off and put it down next to the vice that held the brightly coloured fly that he'd been working on. He turned around to find his wife standing at the door to the study, her arms folded across her chest.

'That'll be for you, then,' she said. Like Denham, she was in her early sixties, though she looked a few years younger, with hair that had kept its auburn lustre and skin still tanned from their winter cruise.

'Aye. I suppose so,' said Denham. He ran a hand over his bald patch and down to the back of his neck. He could feel the tendons tightening already.

'Did you know they'd be coming?'

Denham tutted. 'If I knew they'd be coming, I'd have told them to keep their infernal machine away from the roses.' He nodded at the window. 'I'd best be seeing what they want.'

He walked out of the study, past the line of framed hunting prints in the hallway, and through the kitchen into the back garden. His two King Charles spaniels were standing by the kitchen door, tails between their legs, shaking. 'It's okay, boys, it's only a helicopter,' he said.

He kept to the crazy-paving path, every stone of which he'd carefully laid the previous summer.

The door of the helicopter rattled to the side and a figure climbed out in a green flying suit and a black helmet. The figure ducked its head as it walked briskly away from the machine and its still-turning rotors. Denham knew who it was even before the helmet was removed. Even the bulky flight suit couldn't hide her figure. The down-draught from the rotors tugged at her glossy black hair and she shook her head to clear it from her eyes.

'Retirement suits you, Liam,' she shouted above the roar of the helicopter's turbines.

'Hello, Patsy,' he said. He held out his hand and she shook it. She had a soft grip. Deceptively soft, he knew. A lot of men had come to grief underestimating Patsy Ellis. 'Long time no see.'

'Too long, Liam.' She looked past him to the house. 'Nice place you have here.'

The rotors kept turning. The pilot was talking into his radio mike.

'We need you, Liam.' Her hazel eyes studied him levelly, gauging his reaction.

Denham tugged at his lower lip but said nothing.

'It's Trevor. She's gone missing.'

'Missing?'

Patsy gestured at the helicopter with her thumb. 'We can talk about it on the way.'

'On the way to where?'

'London.'

'Oh, come on, Patsy. I'm retired. And not by choice, either.'

'There's no one else, Liam. No one else knows her.'

'You've cleared this? With the Branch?'

'It's nothing to do with the Branch. It's my ball park now. And I need you on my team.'

'I've got . . .'

'You've got too much time on your hands, that's what you've got,' she said.

Denham looked around his garden. At the neatly manicured lawn. The carefully tended rose bushes. The neat rockeries. 'Aye, Patsy. You might be right at that. Let me get my things.'

He walked back to the house. His wife was waiting for him in the kitchen, the two spaniels at her feet, a black leather holdall in her arms. She held it out to him. 'I've packed you two shirts. And don't go above twenty a day while you're away.'

He reached over and gently cuffed her under the chin. She'd nagged him down to a packet of cigarettes a day and was determined that he'd give up by his sixty-fifth birthday. 'The dogs need their walk,' said Denham.

'And they'll get it.' She kissed him softly on the cheek. 'Go on with you,' she said. 'That helicopter's ripping the roses to shreds.'

Denham took his fawn raincoat from the hook on the back of the kitchen door and walked briskly to the helicopter. Patsy had already climbed in and was talking to the pilot. The rotors picked up speed as Denham hauled himself inside and sat down next to her.

Martin went to a cash machine before checking into the Tower Hotel, withdrawing two hundred pounds on each of his two Visa cards. He booked in for one night, under the name of Martin Sheridan. The receptionist, a young Chinese girl who spoke with a perfect Essex accent, saw that he had only his briefcase with him and asked if he had any luggage. Martin told her he'd left it in the boot of his car. When he said that he'd be settling his bill with cash she asked if he'd leave a deposit. The Tower was mainly used by businessmen on expense accounts with company credit cards, so Martin didn't blame her for being suspicious.

He went straight up to the room to wait for the Special Branch detectives. He called up room service and ordered a club sandwich and a pot of coffee and then showered. The doorbell rang as he was getting dressed. When he opened the door, four heavily built uniformed policemen burst in. One of them grappled Martin to the floor, face down. His hands were wrestled behind his back and he felt handcuffs snap around his wrist. 'What the hell's going on?' he shouted.

Hands gripped his shoulders and he was hauled to his feet.

'I'm doing what I was told to. What the hell's this about?'

A blanket was thrown over his head and he was bundled out of the door.

'Would somebody tell me what's going on?'

Martin was ignored. He was half carried, half dragged through a door and down several flights of stairs in a stampede of boots, then through another door. He could hear traffic and realised he was outside. Within seconds he was thrown into the back of a van. His shins banged against the floor and he yelped but no one paid any attention to him. The van roared off. Someone gripped Martin's arms and helped him on to a hard bench seat. He knew it was pointless to say anything, so he just sat where he was, covered in the blanket. She'd lied to him. The Special Branch woman had lied to him.

The van drove for half an hour or so, then came to a halt, and the policemen hauled Martin to his feet and into a building which he presumed was a police station. He heard voices, and the crackling of a two-way radio, then he was frogmarched down a corridor and pushed into a room. Hands clutched at his belt and he felt it being pulled away from his trousers, then his shoes were torn off his feet one by one. The handcuffs were roughly removed and he was pushed to the side. A metal door slammed shut and there was the double click of a key being turned in a lock. Martin listened, his chest heaving. He slowly slid the sheet off his head and let it drop to the floor. He was alone in a police cell. There was a low bed, nothing more than a concrete podium with a thin plastic mattress on top, a toilet bowl cemented to the floor, and, several feet above his head, a window made of thick glass blocks.

Martin sat down on the bed. He couldn't work out what had happened. He hadn't been arrested because they were supposed to caution him and give him the chance to speak to his lawyer. And he knew enough about the legal system to know that he should have been processed before being thrown into a cell. They hadn't asked his name, they hadn't charged him, they hadn't taken away his wallet or even searched him. Whatever had happened to him, it wasn't a straightforward arrest. He settled back against the wall. He had no choice other than to wait.

*　　*　　*

Mark Quinn was dying for a cigarette, but McCracken had forbidden smoking in the offices. He was standing over his electric wok, pushing the ammonium nitrate fertiliser around so that it didn't overheat. On the table next to the wok was a metal thermometer, and he pushed it into the mixture as he continued to stir. His arms ached and his head was throbbing from the fumes. The thermometer rose to one hundred and sixty and he turned down the heat. He really wanted a cigarette now, but the last time he'd asked McCracken for a break she'd given him a withering look and told him to stick at it.

Sweat was pouring down his face and the ski mask was making him itch furiously. He looked across at the pile of black rubbish sacks containing the treated fertiliser. They'd only done about a fifth. He looked over at O'Keefe, who was clearly as unhappy as he was. This was going to take for ever. It was all right for the Hayes woman, she didn't have to wear a mask, and McCracken didn't seem to mind how many breaks she took. She was forever going to get a coffee or a sandwich. Quinn figured she was deliberately dragging her feet, trying to postpone the moment when the bomb would be finished. If it had been up to Quinn, he'd have given her a good slapping and told her to get stuck in.

He rolled up the sleeves of his overalls and grinned at O'Keefe. O'Keefe had a large tattoo on his left forearm, a lion leaping over a flag of St George, and McCracken had told him to keep it covered while the Hayes woman was around.

Quinn looked over to where she was sealing the powdered fertiliser in a Tupperware container. Her shirt was damp with sweat and it clung to her breasts. She'd rolled her sleeves up above her elbows and had tied the bottom of her shirt in a loose knot, exposing her stomach, which glistened with sweat. With her hair tied back in a ponytail she looked more like a teenager than a thirtysomething mother. She rubbed her forehead against her upper arm, trying to brush a stray lock of blond hair out of her eyes. The movement allowed Quinn to look down her cleavage. He stopped stirring and stared at her breasts, the fertiliser hissing in his wok.

She stopped what she was doing and slowly turned to look at him. Their eyes locked and Quinn grinned. She stiffened, her face an expressionless mask. Quinn stuck out his tongue and licked his lips suggestively. The Hayes woman stared back at him. He could feel the hatred pouring out of her eyes.

'Hey!' O'Keefe's yell startled Quinn and he flinched as if he'd been stung.

'What?'

O'Keefe pointed at Quinn's wok with short, stabbing movements. Quinn looked down. The fertiliser was starting to bubble and smoke. Quinn cursed and frantically scraped it out of the wok and on to the table.

O'Keefe was laughing, his hands on his hips. 'You soft bastard,' he said.

McCracken looked up from her wok. 'What's going on over there?'

'Shit-for-brains nearly let his fertiliser overheat.'

'The wok was too hot,' said Quinn. 'That's all.'

'For God's sake be careful,' said McCracken. 'The place is full of fumes. Any sort of flame and the whole place'll go up.'

'I thought that was the fucking idea,' laughed O'Keefe. His laughter echoed around the office, and McCracken shook her head contemptuously. Quinn's cheeks reddened beneath his ski mask. It was the Hayes woman's fault. He glared over at her and made a silent promise to himself that he'd get his own back before this was over.

* * *

Martin Hayes sat up as he heard the jingle of the custody sergeant's key chain. He was on his feet when the door opened. The sergeant stood aside and Martin found himself looking at a middle-aged couple who looked as if they had just walked out of a church service.

The man was in his sixties, balding and slightly overweight. He was wearing a fawn raincoat over a greenish tweed suit and was carrying a battered tweed hat in one hand.

The woman was younger, in her mid-forties, with skin so white that she must have conscientiously avoided exposing it to the sun. Her hair was cut short with a fringe, its blackness emphasising the paleness of her face. She had bright, inquisitive hazel eyes, and a smile that could have concealed the darkest thoughts. Her right hand was outstretched. 'Mr Hayes? I'm Patsy. We spoke on the phone.'

Martin found himself shaking hands before her words had sunk in. He withdrew his hand and glared at her. 'You had me thrown in here?' he said angrily. 'You lied to me.'

Her smile grew even wider and she nodded comfortingly, like a nurse breaking bad news. 'I'm sorry about that, Mr Hayes, but I had to be sure that you wouldn't go running off.' She had a small gold crucifix on a chain around her neck, and she fingered it with her left hand as she spoke. Around her wrist was a gold Cartier watch.

'Are you with Special Branch?' he asked.

She didn't answer his question, but turned to her companion. 'This is Chief Inspector Liam Denham.'

Denham held out his hand. The first and second fingers were stained brownish yellow with nicotine. 'Ex-Chief Inspector,' he said, his harsh accent betraying his Belfast origins. 'Why don't we go and get a cup of tea?'

'What the hell's going on?' asked Martin.

Denham pulled an apologetic face. 'Not here,' he said.

Martin looked down at his socks. 'They took my shoes. And my belt.'

'I do apologise for that,' said Patsy. The custody sergeant handed Martin his belongings. The two Special Branch officers waited while Martin sat down on his bunk and slipped on his shoes and belt, then they escorted him from the cell block, through the custody reception area and up a flight of stairs to a white-tiled canteen, where a group of uniformed officers were drinking coffee.

'Tea?' asked Denham.

'Coffee. White. One sugar.'

'Let me get them, Liam,' said Patsy. She went over to the counter while Martin and Denham sat at a corner table.

Denham dropped his tweed hat on to the table. There was a small red fishing fly close to the brim. 'You don't fish, do you?' he asked as he sat down.

'No. No, I don't. Sorry.' Martin felt suddenly ridiculous apologising for not being an angler. 'Look, what the hell's this all about?'

'Let's wait for Patsy, shall we?' said Denham. 'Save us going over the same ground twice.'

Patsy came over with three mugs on a tray. She nodded at one. 'That's yours, Mr Hayes. I put the sugar in for you.' Martin took his mug. Patsy put the tray down and passed one of the mugs over to Denham. He sipped his tea, then nodded his appreciation at Patsy as she sat down.

'How long have you known your wife, Mr Hayes?' asked Denham.

'Ten years.'

'And you met where?'

'Trinity. She was studying English literature.'

'And do you know what she did before that?'

Martin stared at the man for several seconds. Denham returned his stare with no trace of embarrassment, waiting for him to speak. 'No, not really,' said Martin eventually.

'What we're going to tell you is going to be something of

a surprise, I'm afraid,' said Denham. 'A revelation. Please, bear in mind that we're here to help you.'

'We're on your side,' added Patsy.

They nodded in unison. Martin felt as if he were a child being humoured by two adults, and he resented the way they were treating him. He had a sudden urge to bang his hands on the table, to scream at them to stop patronising him and to find his wife and daughter. He forced himself to stay calm. He couldn't afford to lose his temper, not in a canteen full of policemen. 'Just tell me what the hell is going on,' he said.

Denham and Patsy looked at each other. There was an almost imperceptible nod from Patsy, as if she were giving Denham permission to go ahead. Martin wondered what role she played in Special Branch. Denham had retired, so maybe she'd taken over his job. Or perhaps she'd been his superior.

'Your wife, Mr Hayes, was once an IRA bombmaker.'

Martin's head swam. The walls of the canteen seemed to bulge in and out, and for a moment he felt as if he was going to faint. His eyelids fluttered and he tried to speak but no words would come. A feeble 'What?' was all he could manage.

'She manufactured explosive devices for the Provisional Irish Republican Army.'

'No,' said Martin flatly. 'You're not talking about my wife.'

'It was before she was your wife,' said Denham. 'When she was in her early twenties. Before she met you.'

'You're telling me that my wife is a terrorist?'

'Oh no,' said Denham quickly. 'Oh no, that's not the situation at all.'

'But you said she was an IRA bombmaker?'

'She was recruited by the IRA during her final year of university.'

'At Trinity?'

Denham shook his head. 'Queen's University. Belfast. She got a first in electrical engineering.'

Martin laughed out loud. 'Andy can't change a plug,' he said.

Denham took a packet of cigarettes and a silver lighter from the pocket of his raincoat. 'She was recruited by her boyfriend at the time, and was trained by one of their most experienced bombmakers. He was killed a year after she graduated.'

'The boyfriend?'

Denham smiled thinly. 'The bombmaker. Her mentor. She took his place. But by that time, she was working for us.' Denham put a cigarette between his lips but Patsy pointed at a sign on the wall. NO SMOKING. Denham groaned and put the cigarette back into the packet.

'Hang on a minute,' interrupted Martin. 'First you tell me she's an IRA terrorist, now you're saying she works for Special Branch?'

'Worked,' said Patsy. 'Past tense. This is all past tense, Mr Hayes.'

'She'd never really been political,' continued Denham. 'I think she got talked into it by the boyfriend.' Patsy flashed Denham a warning look and he smiled at Martin. 'Ex-boyfriend,' he said. 'They were only together for six months or so. He probably only got close to recruit her.'

Patsy was smiling at Martin again, as if trying to let him know that Andy's love for him wasn't in dispute.

'We'd had her under surveillance, almost from the moment she was recruited, but she got wind of it. Smart girl, she was. Took the wind out of our sails by approaching us. We persuaded her to stay with them. Did a hell of a job, for nigh on three years. Until the accident.'

'Accident?'

Denham scratched at a small wine-coloured birthmark

on his neck. 'She'd let us know where her bombs were going to be used, and what sort they were. Our bomb disposal boys always had the edge. They knew which ones were booby-trapped, and how. Some we'd let explode, providing there was no risk of loss of life. We'd release stories to the media that soldiers had been killed, or that a bomb disposal officer had died. Others we'd pretend to stumble on. Get the army to send a patrol through the area, maybe have a guy out walking his dog pretend to find it. There were a million and one ways to make it look as if the IRA had just been unlucky.'

There was a peal of laughter from the uniformed policemen at the neighbouring table, and Denham waited for the noise to die down before continuing.

'Your wife saved many, many lives, Mr Hayes. She deserved a medal. She played a most dangerous game – not a day went by when her own life wasn't on the line.' He paused, tapping his fingers on the packet of cigarettes. 'What happened was a terrible, terrible accident. A small bomb, a few pounds of Semtex. Set to go off with a timer. It had been placed on the Belfast-to-Dublin rail line, under a bridge. There were two booby traps – a mercury tilt switch, and a photoelectric cell. Nothing major – the bomb disposal boys were dealing with half a dozen similar bombs every week. Your wife had tipped us off that the bomb was being set, but she didn't know where on the line it was going to be placed. We were waiting for the coded call.'

Patsy sipped her tea, her eyes never leaving Martin's face, as if she were assessing his reactions to what Denham was telling him.

'The call came, but before we could react to it, a group of schoolchildren found the bomb.'

'Jesus Christ,' whispered Martin as he realised where the story was heading.

Denham nodded. He moved his face closer to Martin's

and kept his voice barely above a whisper. 'Four boys died. One crippled for life. It wasn't her fault. It wasn't anybody's fault. It was just one of those things.'

'Jesus Christ,' said Martin again. He slumped back in his seat.

'Drink your tea,' said Patsy.

Martin lifted his mug to his lips, barely conscious of what he was doing or where he was. The Andy he knew, the woman he'd married, the woman he'd shared a bed with for almost a decade, had nothing in common with the woman that Denham was talking about. An IRA bombmaker? A Special Branch informer?

'She walked away,' said Denham. 'Told her IRA bosses that she'd built her last bomb. Told us the same. They tried to talk her out of it, and so did we. But she was adamant.'

Martin remembered how Andy had always hated to see reports of bombings on television. How she'd sat with tears streaming down her face on the day that the bomb went off in Omagh in Northern Ireland, killing twenty-eight people. He'd sat on the sofa next to her, holding her but powerless to stop her tears. At the time he thought he understood why she was so upset. Everyone in Ireland was shocked to the core by the horror of the bombing, but now he knew that there was another reason for Andy's grief. She'd had to live with the deaths of four innocents on her conscience, and knowing what a loving, caring, sensitive person she was, he realised that the strain must have been unbearable.

'She moved to Dublin. Started a new life.'

Martin shook his head, trying to clear his thoughts. 'They let her? They let her walk away from the IRA?'

'They understood why she wanted to leave. She was a woman, and children had died. What else could they do, Mr Hayes? They're not animals, despite what you might read in the papers. What choice did they have?'

'So they never found out that she was working for you?'

Denham toyed with his cigarette lighter. He looked across at the 'NO SMOKING' sign as if checking that it was still there. 'No. She cut all ties with us.'

'And Trevor? Who was Trevor?'

'Trevor was her code-name.'

There was another burst of laughter from the neighbouring table, then the uniformed policemen stood up and filed out of the canteen.

'This is unbelievable,' said Martin.

'I'm afraid it's all too real,' said Patsy.

Martin held his mug in both hands and stared at the remains of his tea. The milk had curdled slightly and oily white bubbles floated on the surface. 'That's what this has all been about, isn't it? Her bomb-making skills?'

Patsy reached out and gently touched Martin's wrist. 'That's why we're here, Mr Hayes. The fact that your daughter's kidnappers wanted her to fly to London suggests that . . .'

'. . . they want her to build them a bomb. Here.'

Patsy nodded. 'Exactly.'

'Can she do it?'

'Oh yes,' said Denham. 'She can. There's absolutely no doubt about that.'

Andy wiped the perspiration from the back of her neck with a cloth. Her shirt was damp with sweat and stray locks of her hair were matted to her face. Green-eyes was at the table next to her, scraping hot fertiliser into a Tupperware container. 'Nearly done,' she said.

'A couple of hours, I reckon,' said Andy. She nodded towards the offices. 'Okay if I get a sandwich? I'm starving.'

'Can't you wait? Best to get this stage finished, then we'll take a break.'

Andy tried to hide her disappointment. She wanted

another go at the briefcase locks. 'I could do with a coffee. I'm flagging.'

Green-eyes sealed the lid on the container and straightened up. She looked across at the Runner and the Wrestler, who were both bent over their woks. Despite the air-conditioning being full on, the air was full of alcohol fumes and the stench of the fertiliser. 'I guess the boys can hold the fort,' she said. 'Okay, let's take a break.'

Andy forced a smile. 'I'll get one for you.'

Green-eyes looked suspiciously at Andy. 'Are you up to something, Andrea?'

Andy shrugged carelessly. 'I don't know what you mean.'

'You're not deliberately dragging your feet, are you? Trying to slow us down?'

'I just want a coffee, that's all. If it's too much trouble, forget it.'

Green-eyes looked at Andy for a few seconds, her lips pressed tightly together. It was an eerie feeling, being scrutinised by someone in a ski mask, and Andy forced herself to smile as naturally as possible. Eventually Green-eyes nodded. 'Come on.'

Andy followed her down the corridor and into the office. Green-eyes poured two mugs of coffee and they sat down at the long table. Green-eyes clicked sweetener into her mug. 'You always drink your coffee without sugar?' she asked Andy.

'Since I was at university,' said Andy.

'Worried about your weight?'

Andy sipped her coffee. 'Not really. I gave up salt, too. And cigarettes.'

'Some sort of penance?'

'Maybe. I don't know.' She put her mug down. 'Why are you doing this?'

Green-eyes didn't answer. She stirred her coffee and stared at the ripples on its surface.

'People are going to die if this thing goes off. A lot of people.'

'You're a fine one to talk,' said Green-eyes. 'I could ask you the same question. You made bombs for the Provos.'

'But not like this.'

'Your bombs killed people, Andrea. Is it the numbers that worry you? Is killing a hundred worse than killing four?'

'That was an accident. The children were in the wrong place at the wrong time.'

'There were others, though, Andrea. Soldiers. Bomb disposal guys. Police. What you did hasn't stopped you from living a normal life. So why are you concerned about this bomb?'

'You're going to kill innocent people, that's why. The war's over. It's finished.'

Green-eyes sneered at Andy and tossed the teaspoon on to the table-top. 'Did the Brits murder any of your family, Andrea? How many funerals have you been to, eh?'

Andy said nothing. The woman's eyes were burning with hatred, and flecks of spittle peppered across the table.

'Well, how many?'

'None,' said Andy quietly.

'Well, I have. I buried my brother and two cousins. The SAS murdered my brother and British paratroopers shot my cousins. My family's been drenched in blood, and you think I should just forgive and forget because the weaklings at the top want to sit in an Irish Parliament?'

'Revenge?' said Andy. 'Is that what this is about? Revenge?'

'You think there's something wrong with revenge? You think politics is a better motive? That it's okay to kill for power but not okay to kill because they murdered my brother? I don't give a fuck about a united Ireland. I don't give a fuck whether or not Protestants and Catholics live together in peace and harmony. I want revenge, pure and simple.'

'For God's sake, you're going to kill hundreds of people, hundreds of innocent people. Jesus Christ, woman, that's not going to bring your brother back.'

'I don't want him back. I want the people here to know what it's like to suffer. Anyway, I don't know why you're so concerned. You've made bombs before. You've killed people. I'm just doing what you should have done ten years ago.'

Andy shook her head. 'That was different.' Part of her wanted to tell Green-eyes that she'd never been a terrorist, that all the time she'd been part of the active service unit she'd also been a Special Branch informer. But she had no way of knowing how Green-eyes would react to the news. She was in enough danger already.

'Different? Why? Because what we're doing now is on a bigger scale?'

'Because at least then there was a political dimension. It was a means to an end. The war's over. Can't you see that?'

Green-eyes stood up. 'Come on. We've got work to do.'

Andy gestured at her mug. 'I haven't finished.'

Green-eyes picked up the mug and poured the contents on to the floor. 'Yes you have.'

Martin stared down at the table, his mind in turmoil. None of what he'd been told made any sense to him. It had been hard enough to cope with the kidnapping of his daughter and the disappearance of his wife, but being told that his wife was an IRA bombmaker turned Special Branch informant was more than he could cope with.

'Mr Hayes?' It was the woman. Patsy. Her first name. That was all he knew about her.

'You're going to have to give me time to get my head around this,' he said.

'We don't have time, Mr Hayes. We have to act now. And we need your co-operation.'

Martin frowned. 'Co-operation?'

Patsy had a notebook in front of her, and she was holding a slim gold pen. It looked expensive. Everything about the woman seemed expensive. 'Who the hell are you?' Martin asked her. 'You're no policewoman.'

'No, you're right. I'm not. All you need to know at the moment is that Chief Inspector Denham and I are the only hope you've got of seeing your daughter and wife again. Now, who else knows what's happened to your family?'

Martin glared at the woman, then slowly nodded. She was right. It wasn't her he was angry at, it was the situation he was in, and it wasn't a situation of her making. 'The Gardai. In Dublin. Inspector James FitzGerald. And a sergeant. Power, his name was, I think.'

Patsy wrote the names down in her notebook.

'Two uniformed gardai called at the house. They're the ones who took me to the Garda station.'

'Do you know their names?'

Martin shook his head. 'The secretary at Katie's school got in touch with them. Mrs O'Mara, her name is. She's disappeared. That's what the police say, anyway.'

'Disappeared?'

'They said she hadn't turned up for work and there was no sign of her at her house. That's why they came to see me in the first place. She'd telephoned me to see why Katie wasn't at school, and I guess she'd spoken to the head-mistress.'

Patsy looked across at Denham and raised an eyebrow. Denham nodded. Martin had the feeling that each knew what the other was thinking.

Patsy looked back at Martin. 'Anyone else?'

'I told my partner what had happened. Padraig. Padraig Martin.'

Patsy wrote down the names. 'So your first name's Martin, and so's his surname?'

'Yeah. That's how we became friends at school.' He shrugged. 'It's a long story. We ended up as business partners. We called the firm Martin and Martin. Sort of a joke.'

'What exactly did you tell your partner?' asked Denham.

Martin massaged his temples as he tried to remember the conversation he'd had with Padraig while he was driving him up to Belfast. 'I think I pretty much told him everything. I told him that Katie had been kidnapped. And that the kidnappers told Andy to go to London.'

'That's just wonderful,' said Denham under his breath. Patsy gave him a cold look and he held up his palms apologetically.

'I had to tell him something,' said Martin. 'He's my partner. He was nearly killed.'

'Killed? What do you mean, killed?' asked Patsy.

Martin realised he hadn't told them about the man with the gun, the man who'd shot at the BMW outside the hospital. He quickly explained what had happened.

'This man, what did he look like?' asked Patsy.

'I didn't see his face, not really,' said Martin. 'He was average height. Medium build. He was wearing a leather jacket. Black or brown. And jeans, maybe.' He shook his head. 'It all happened really quickly. He shot twice, I think. Hit the window and the door. I didn't hear the shots, just the window going and then a thud against the door. I had my head down most of the time.'

'What colour hair did he have?' asked Denham.

Martin shrugged. He didn't know.

'Moustache? Facial hair? A scar? Anything that made him stick out?'

Martin shook his head. 'I'm sorry,' he said. 'It was dark, and I just wanted to get away.'

Patsy and Denham exchanged looks of frustration but said nothing.

'That's okay, Mr Hayes,' said Patsy.

'What do you think they'll do to Katie?' asked Martin. 'The guy who shot at me was presumably one of the kidnappers – he must know I've spoken to the Dublin police. What if they . . .' He couldn't bring himself to finish the sentence.

'I don't think they'll do anything to hurt your daughter,' said Patsy. 'Not so long as they need your wife's co-operation. Katie is the leverage they need to get your wife to do what they want.'

'God, I hope you're right.'

Patsy smiled reassuringly at Martin. 'We know what we're doing, Mr Hayes. Trust us. Or at least, have faith in us.'

Martin closed his eyes and nodded. 'It doesn't look as if I've any alternative.'

Denham toyed with his packet of cigarettes. He tapped one side against the table. Then turned it through ninety degrees and tapped it again. Turn. Tap. Turn. Tap. 'The note that the kidnappers left,' he said. 'Do you still have it?'

'No. Andy took it with her.' He reached into his trouser pocket and took out the sheet of paper he'd found behind the hotel painting. 'This is the note she left for me in the Strand Palace.' He gave it to Denham, who read it and passed it over to Patsy.

'The phone conversation you told me about,' said Patsy. 'When your wife told you about this. Where were you?'

'At home. In Dublin.'

'And she called on the land line? Or your mobile?'

'The land line.'

'And she only made one call?'

Martin nodded.

'When she called you, did it sound like she was using a call-box?'

Martin shrugged. 'It sounded like a regular phone. I think there was somebody listening, checking that she didn't say the wrong thing.'

'But could you hear any traffic? People walking by? Any sounds that might suggest she was outside? Or in a public place?'

Martin rubbed his face with both hands. 'I don't remember any,' he said.

'Did you get any sense that she was calling from a land line? Or a mobile?'

Martin shook his head. 'I'm sorry.'

Patsy smiled reassuringly, the smile of a parent consoling a child who'd just come second. 'You're doing just fine, Mr Hayes. Now, can you run through everything your wife said to you when she called.'

'She was only on the line for a few seconds. She made me promise not to go to the police. And she said they didn't want money. That they wouldn't hurt Katie so long as I didn't go to the police. Then she said that after it was all over, we'd go back to Venice. I didn't know what she meant – it was only when I saw the picture that I realised what she was trying to say. And that was it.'

'You're sure?'

'Yes, damn it, I'm sure.'

Patsy looked across at Denham. He raised an eyebrow. Martin had no idea what the gesture meant.

'Did I do something wrong?'

Patsy put down her gold pen. 'No, you didn't, Mr Hayes. But they might have done. We're going to need your help. If she calls again.'

'You think she might?'

'It was obviously your wife who initiated the call,' said Patsy. 'It was unstructured. Unrehearsed. And the only information imparted was that which your wife wanted to give you. It wasn't a message from the kidnappers. If she managed to get them to allow her one phone call, she might be able to persuade them to let her make another. And the closer she gets to completion, the more leverage she'll have.'

'But if she calls, I won't be there.' Martin stood up. 'God, I've got to get back.'

Patsy gestured for him to sit down. 'We can handle that from here.' She looked across at Denham. 'I'll get the number transferred to Thames House.'

'You can do that?' asked Martin.

Patsy nodded. 'It's not a problem.'

'Where's this Thames House?'

'It's an office. Near Whitehall. We can use it as a base.'

'And if they call, they'll think I'm still in the house?'

'That's the idea.'

Martin scratched his chin. 'The machine's on. The answering machine. I left a message saying that anyone who calls should try me on my mobile.'

'You still have the mobile?'

Martin shook his head. 'It was in my hotel room. In my case. I don't know if your goons brought it with me.'

Patsy looked pained. 'I'll get it for you. But it's best she doesn't call the mobile. I'll get the answering machine turned off.' She looked at her watch. 'No time like the present.' She stood up. 'I'll make a couple of calls.'

Martin fished his house keys out and slid them across the table.

Patsy smiled and shook her head. 'The people I'll be using won't be needing keys, Mr Hayes.'

Andy stole glances at Green-eyes as she packed Tupperware containers into a black rubbish bag. It was hard to judge her age because she'd never seen her without her ski mask, but she guessed the woman was in her early thirties, probably about the same age as herself. They were pretty much the same height and build, and seemed to have the same taste in clothes. Under different circumstances it was perfectly possible that they could have been friends.

The conversation they'd had in the office had disturbed Andy. She hadn't realised before that Green-eyes was driven by revenge, that her motives were personal rather than political. Andy had been clinging to the hope that the bomb she was helping to build wasn't intended to be used, but after speaking to Green-eyes she was certain that the woman intended to detonate the device once it was finished.

She was equally certain that Green-eyes wasn't the prime mover in the building of the bomb. She was working for someone else, someone who was funding the operation and organising it from a distance. But who? Whoever had recruited Green-eyes must have known how fanatical she was, and how determined she'd be to see the bomb explode. That presumably meant that whoever was backing her also wanted to see the bomb go off. Andy had meant what she'd said about the war being over. The IRA was set to achieve virtually all its aims without compromising its stance on decommissioning; they had nothing to gain by restarting the conflict. Andy doubted that Green-eyes would allow herself to be used by a Protestant terrorist organisation, so who did that leave? Terrorists from outside the United Kingdom? Arabs maybe? The Serbs? Iraq? Iran? Syria? Libya? Someone with the resources to pay for the equipment, the office rental, the manpower. Someone who knew about Andy's past.

Andy fastened the metal tie around the top of the black plastic bag and carried it over to the pile of other bags containing treated fertiliser. She threw it on top. The ammonium nitrate was totally inert at this stage. Even when it was mixed with the rest of the ingredients, it could still be handled in total safety. It was a powerful explosive, about half the strength of commercial dynamite, but it required a very heavy charge to detonate it. That was what Andy was clinging to, her last hope that the bomb wouldn't go off. Without the necessary detonator, the pressure wave wouldn't be powerful enough to detonate all the explosive. It might explode, but only partially, with the energy from the initial detonation scattering the fertiliser mixture. The building would be damaged, but not destroyed. There'd be flying glass and debris but it would be nothing in comparison to a successful detonation. So far Green-eyes hadn't mentioned a detonator, and Andy was praying that the woman didn't fully appreciate how critical it was to have the right type.

Green-eyes turned around and rubbed her knuckles into the small of her back. 'Is that the lot?' she asked Andy.

'That's it,' said Andy.

The Wrestler and the Runner were standing by the water-cooler, large, damp patches of sweat under the armpits of their overalls. It was in the high eighties, even with the thermostat set to its lowest level and the fans full on. As Andy watched, the Wrestler took off his shoulder holster and draped it on top of the cooler.

Andy went over to the line of ovens and switched them off.

'Now what?' asked Green-eyes.

Andy gestured at the cans of diesel oil. 'We mix the fertiliser with the aluminium powder and the diesel oil. But you don't want to do that until the last moment. Until you're ready for the last phase.'

'Why?' asked Green-eyes suspiciously.

'It starts to break down. Gives off hydrogen as a by-product. It's a slow process, but the hydrogen is explosive, so you don't want it hanging around too long.'

Green-eyes looked at her watch.

'Okay. We start mixing tomorrow.'

*　　*　　*

Egan kept the Ford Scorpio below seventy as he drove towards London. The ferry crossing from Dun Laoghaire had been uneventful, if a little choppy, but Egan was a seasoned sailor and had managed a hearty meal in one of the restaurants before they'd docked at Holyhead.

He hadn't expected any problems – checks on travellers between Ireland and the United Kingdom were perfunctory at best – but he hadn't even glimpsed a Customs officer or policeman as he drove off the ferry. Not that Egan would have been worried if he had been pulled in for a random check – the Semtex explosive and detonators were well hidden within a secret compartment inside the petrol tank. The only way they could be discovered was if the tank were dismantled, and that was unlikely in the extreme. Any smuggling, be it drugs or arms, was generally into Ireland, not out of it.

Egan had taken the explosive from a farmer in Dundalk who had been put in charge of an IRA arms cache back in the early eighties. It was part of a consignment sent from Libya, and had been buried in a plastic dustbin swathed in black polythene. The farmer and his wife had dug up the dustbin as Egan had stood over them with his Browning. He'd taken only as much as he needed – six kilograms. And a pack of Mark 4 detonators. The rest had gone back in the bin and into the ground, along with the bodies of the farmer and his wife.

Liam Denham looked around the office and nodded appreciatively. 'They certainly look after you, Patsy.'

Patsy sat down in the high-backed leather chair and folded her arms across the blotter on the rosewood desk. Her back was to a large window with an impressive view over the river, looking east towards Waterloo station. There were several oil paintings on the walls, portraits of old men in wigs, resplendent in massive gilt frames, and the carpet was a rich blue and so thick that it threatened to engulf Denham's battered Hush Puppies. 'Don't be ridiculous, Liam. This isn't mine.'

'Even so . . .' said Denham, settling into one of two wing-backed armchairs that faced the desk. 'It's a damn sight more impressive than my old shoe box.' Patsy gave him a severe look and he held up his hands to placate her. 'I'm just happy that you're doing so well. It must be satisfying to be given the necessary resources to do the job.' He gestured at one of the paintings. 'That there would probably have paid my staff's overtime bill for a year.'

'Special Branch, I seem to recall, was never kept wanting,' said Patsy. 'How's Hayes?'

'He's in the canteen with Ramsey. Good lad, Ramsey. One of the new breed, I suppose?'

'He's not Oxbridge, if that's what you mean. But then, Liam, neither was I. Anyway, let's keep to the business at hand, shall we? The phone divert's in place, and if she calls again, GCHQ will track it. I reckon it'll turn out to be a mobile, so we're not going to be able to get an accurate fix, but it should narrow it down for us.'

'We're assuming London?'

Patsy sighed and ran her fingers around the blotter. 'I don't think we can, Liam. My gut feeling is yes, it'll be the capital, but we'll both have egg on our faces if they blow up Manchester, won't we?' Denham took his packet of cigar-ettes out and showed it to Patsy. 'They're not my lungs, and it's not my office,' she said. Denham lit up and inhaled gratefully. It had been three hours since he'd last had a cigarette. Patsy picked up a mobile phone and passed it over to Denham. 'It's a digital GSM,' she said. 'But it's not secure, so . . .'

'Mum's the word?'

Patsy smiled. 'Exactly.' Denham slipped the phone into his jacket pocket.

'Do you think the husband is up to it?' Patsy asked.

'I think so. They're going to expect him to be nervous, anyway. All he has to do is to keep her talking.' He looked around for an ashtray and Patsy pushed a crystal dish towards him. He flicked ash into it, and waited for her to continue.

'Has he asked you what we're doing to find his daughter?'

'Not yet. No.'

'That's something.'

'What are you going to tell him when he does?'

'That we're doing everything we can.'

Denham blow smoke up towards the ceiling. There were elaborate plaster carvings of fruit around the central light fitting. The only decoration in Denham's old office had been a smoke alarm missing a battery. 'And if he realises that we're not?'

'Liam, our first priority is to prevent them exploding whatever device it is that Andrea Hayes is building for them. If we make any attempt to locate the girl, they'll know we're on to them.'

'So we do nothing to find the girl?'

'There's nothing we can do, not without showing our hand.'

Denham took a long pull on his cigarette and looked at the ceiling again.

'We find them here first, then they'll tell us where the girl is,' said Patsy. 'But the converse isn't true. In fact, I'd bet money that the kidnappers in Ireland don't know the full details of what's going on here.'

Denham nodded. She was right. But he didn't think that Martin Hayes would see it her way. 'And what exactly is it you want from me?' he asked. 'Why've I been brought in from the cold?'

'Hardly the cold, Liam. You've a very nice pension, from what I hear. Certainly more than I'll be getting when I retire. The government has always been more than generous to its employees in the North.'

'I was sacked, Patsy.'

'You retired.'

Denham gave her a tight smile.

'You were the only one who dealt with Trevor. You're the only one who knows how she'll react.'

'I've not seen or spoken to her in ten years.'

'You're all we have. You and her husband. But even her husband doesn't know her the way you do.'

Denham tapped ash into the ashtray. 'People change.'

'Of course they do. But you were with her when she was under the most pressure. When her life was on the line. She knew what they'd do to her if they ever found out she was betraying them. And you were the only one she could confide in.' She paused for a while. The only sound in the room was the ticking of a clock on the mantelpiece, a big polished oak monstrosity, around a tiled fireplace in which stood a vase of dried flowers. To the side of the fireplace was a large brass scuttle filled with chunks of wood. Denham could imagine the fire burning cheerfully on winter days. His own office, in a fortified concrete bunker in north Belfast, had had a single-bar electric fire that didn't even take the edge off the winter days. 'Liam, I have to know. Given the choice between the life of her daughter and the hundreds of lives that could be lost if a device went off in a mainland city – what would she do?'

Denham shrugged. He took another long pull on his cigarette and drew the smoke deep into his lungs. He exhaled slowly. 'You know why she walked away?'

'Because four children died.'

'Four died and one mutilated. It damn near destroyed her. It didn't matter to her how many lives she'd saved. She came close to killing herself. She had the tablets and everything.' He stubbed the cigarette out in the ashtray. 'She didn't turn up for a meeting we'd arranged so I broke all the rules and went looking for her. Found her sitting on her bed with the tablets out and a bottle of vodka.'

'I read the file. It wasn't her fault.'

'I knew that. I think she knew that, too. Deep down. But it was children, Patsy. That's what pushed her over the edge. So think what her own daughter means to her. She'll do anything. Whatever it takes. She'd die for her.'

Patsy reached for the cross around her neck and stroked it as she studied Denham with unblinking eyes. 'But we're not talking about her giving up her life for her daughter's, are we? Would she kill others? Would she allow others to be killed? If it meant saving her own daughter?'

Denham stared at one of the oil paintings. A cruel face. A pinched mouth. White cheeks with smears of rouge. Watery eyes. 'She's an intelligent girl, is Andrea. Smart as a whip. Got a first at Queen's, you know? Top of her year. By far. I never won an argument with her, not in all the time I ran her. You'd never know, not to look at her, because she was so damn pretty. The softest blond hair you ever saw. Blue eyes that you felt you could just dive into. And her figure. Jesus, Mary and Joseph, the heads she turned.'

'And you a married man,' said Patsy, shaking her head and smiling. 'What's your point, Liam? That pretty girls aren't expected to be intelligent?'

'The point is, she's going to work out what we both know already. That if they are forcing her to build a bomb, they're not going to want her around after it goes off. They're going to want her dead. And if they're going to kill Andrea, they've really nothing to lose by killing the little girl, too.'

He looked at Patsy. She looked back at him, her face giving nothing away.

'She'll know that,' Denham continued. 'She'll know that

if she doesn't do what they want, the girl will die. And she'll know that if she does do what they want, the girl will die.'

'Which leaves her where?'

'Looking for a third way.'

'Which is?'

Denham's mouth twisted as if he had a bad taste in his mouth. 'She's the one with the first, Patsy.'

'But she'll be building the bomb?'

'Definitely. Because so long as she's in the process of constructing it, they won't hurt the girl.'

'Which gives us how long?'

'Oh, come on now, Patsy. How long's a piece of string?'

'Assuming it's a big one. A spectacular?'

'A week. Give or take.'

'That's what I figured. So we've got a couple of days. Maybe three.'

Denham nodded. He stretched his legs out and crossed them at the ankles. His Hush Puppies had seen better days – the suede was stained and the laces were fraying.

'There's something else I need you to do, Liam.'

Denham nodded slowly. 'I was wondering when you'd get around to it.'

'Somebody's going to have to ask him. And I think it'd be better coming from you.'

Denham lit another cigarette. At the height of the Troubles he'd smoked eighty a day, and he could feel the old cravings returning.

'There's a plane waiting. A bit rough-and-ready, I'm afraid. And a car outside. I'll have transport arranged for you in Belfast.'

'You know where he is?'

Patsy smiled. 'Every minute of every day,' she said. 'I'm going to address the troops.'

She walked down the office to the briefing room. Twenty expectant faces looked up at her as she went over to where two whiteboards were mounted on the wall. The blinds were drawn and the overhead fluorescent lights were on. 'Right, let's get straight to it, shall we?' she said.

Just over half the operatives in the room were female, and almost all were under thirty, a reflection of the changing face of the Security Service. Young, enthusiastic, and not necessarily educated at Oxford or Cambridge. It was a change that Patsy approved of, and had herself benefited from. Most of them were sitting around a long light oak table, notepads in front of them. Two of the younger men stood by the double doors, and they closed them as she stood in front of one of the whiteboards. There were four photographs stuck to it. Three of them were of Andrea Hayes, one was of Katie.

Patsy pointed at one of the photographs of Andrea, a head-and-shoulders shot that had been in an album retrieved from the Hayes house when the answering machine had been turned off. 'Andrea Hayes. Housewife, thirty-four years old.' She tapped the photograph next to it. Another head-and-shoulders shot, this one a blow-up of a passport photograph taken twelve years earlier. 'In a previous life, Andrea Sheridan. Top IRA bombmaker and Special Branch informer. She is presently in the UK, and active. Not by choice.' She tapped the photograph of Katie. 'Her daughter, Katie. Seven years old. Kidnapped from their home in Dublin.'

She tapped the first photograph of Andy. 'Someone wants her to build a bomb. Presumably a big one. At this stage, I don't really care why. Why we can work out later. As to when, we think the bomb's likely to be completed within the next few days. Assuming it's a massive fertiliser bomb, which was Andrea Sheridan's speciality, once the ingredients are mixed, their shelf life is limited. A week at most. So we're looking at a timeframe of between two days and ten. So, these are our priorities. We need to know who's building the bomb, and we need to know where the bomb is. As regards who, we have video of a vehicle leaving a carpark in Covent Garden.'

She moved across to the second whiteboard. There were six photographs stuck to it. One was a grainy black-and-white print that had been blown up from a still taken from the closed-circuit television video at the carpark in Covent Garden. She tapped it with her marker pen. 'This van has the name of a garden landscaping firm on the side, though you can't see it on the video. Andrea Sheridan is in the back. We've run a check on the registration number. The van is owned by a company in the Midlands. It's being checked out as we speak, but I don't recommend anyone holding their breath. This has been too well planned for it to be as easy as that.' She pointed to the portion of the photograph showing the van's windscreen. 'Two occupants. Male. They're sitting well back but we can just about make out the bottom of the passenger's face and three-quarters of the driver's. Our technical boys are working on the video now. We've also got all the tickets handed in that day and we're looking for the one that corresponds to their exit time. If we get it, we get the driver's prints.'

She folded her arms and moved away from the white-board. 'Whoever they are, the two men in the van aren't working alone. So what are the possibilities? We think it unlikely it's the IRA, or anyone else in the Republican movement. Let me rephrase that. We think it unlikely that they're acting for the Republican movement. If it was in any way official, there'd be no need for the kidnapping. In fact, there'd be no need for them to use Andrea Sheridan. Her expertise is a decade out of date. What we believe is happening is that someone wants it to appear that there is an IRA involvement. Now, that leads to two lines of enquiry. First, someone within the IRA must have offered up Andrea Sheridan. Her role as a bombmaker was known to less than a dozen people. Only one man within RUC Special Branch knew what her position was. Chief Inspector Liam Denham. Ex-Chief Inspector. He's working with us on this. Chief Inspector Denham is hoping to obtain a list of those members of the IRA who knew of Andrea Sheridan. We have some names already. She was recruited while still at university by one Denis Fisher. Fisher was killed in London in 1992.'

There were five photographs underneath the surveillance shot of the van. All head-and-shoulder pictures that had been blown up. Patsy waved at them. 'These are the five members of her active service unit during the time she was active.' She tapped the photographs one by one.

'James Nolan. The late James Nolan. Scored an own goal in Hammersmith in '93 and blew himself out of a third-floor bedsit in a couple of dozen pieces.'

Several of the agents laughed, but they stopped when she gave them a frosty look. 'Thomas Kennedy. Last heard of in Kilburn, north London. Michael and Gordon, he's yours.' Michael Jenner and Gordon Harris, who were sitting at the far end of the table in almost identical dark blue suits, nodded in acknowledgment.

'Eugene Walsh. Managed to win the green card lottery a couple of years back and is now working for a diving company in the Florida Keys. Our Miami office is looking for him.'

The fourth face was the youngest of the group, still in his twenties. Patsy pointed at it. 'Shay Purcell. The ASU's runner. He was barely eighteen when he was active. He's in Mountjoy Prison in Dublin, midway through a life sentence. Killed his girlfriend with a bread knife so he's not regarded as political and won't be getting early release. We'll be speaking to him there.'

She tapped the final picture. 'Brendan Tighe. Still in Belfast. He turned informer about four years back. He's still in the IRA, deep cover, and we know he's sound.'

She turned back to the whiteboard and with a blue marker pen wrote the word 'TREVOR' in capital letters.

'Her code-name within Special Branch was Trevor. As of now, that's how she's to be referred to. I don't want to hear the names Andrea Sheridan or Andrea Hayes referred to outside this room. Once we have the list, we'll be bringing them in, one and all.'

She put the cap back on her marker. 'So, who is behind this if it's not the IRA?' She held up her hand and raised her index finger. 'One. A Protestant group wanting to implicate the IRA in a terrorist outrage.' She counted off a second finger. 'Two. A terrorist group within the United Kingdom. Muslims. Right-wing groups. Animal activists. You name it.' She held up a third finger. 'Three. A terrorist group from outside the United Kingdom. Iraq. Iran. Libya. You know the possibilities as well as I do.' Several of the agents nodded. Patsy held up a fourth finger. 'Four. Some other group. Some other reason. If anyone here has any thoughts, I'd like to hear them.'

No one in the room had any suggestions. Patsy hadn't expected any, not at such an early stage in the investigation. 'So, we trawl through all the intelligence we have, looking for possibilities. Anyone who isn't where they should be. Anyone recently arrived in this country who might be behind something like this. Anyone who's suddenly gone underground. Speak to all your contacts. But tactfully. We don't want to make waves.'

One of the men by the door raised a hand. It was Tim Fanning, a relatively recent recruit from a City stockbroking firm where he'd worked as an analyst. 'Yes, Tim?'

'What about the Americans?'

'I'll be contacting the CIA officially for details of American terrorist activity,' said Patsy.

'I meant as possible targets,' said Fanning. 'Their embassies have been hit worldwide.' He grinned. 'They're even blowing up Planet Hollywood outlets these days.'

'Good point, and one that brings us to the question of where. Tim's right – the target could be an American institution here in the UK. Or it could be any one of a hundred targets. Downing Street. The City. The Houses of Parliament. It doesn't even have to be in London. It could, quite literally, be anywhere. So, how do we narrow down the location?' She tapped the photograph of the van. 'First, we chase down this vehicle. Parking tickets. Police reports. CCTVs. Has it been to Ireland? Been involved in any accidents? It's four years old, so who used to own it?' She pointed to three women sitting at the far end of the table. 'Lisa, Anna, Julia, that's your priority. You know Peter Elfman?' All three nodded. 'He's checking up on the landscaping company. Liaise with him.'

Patsy nodded at the oldest man in the room, David Bingham. He was in his mid-forties but his hair had gone prematurely grey while at university and his skin was weathered and peppered with broken veins from years pursuing his love of dinghy sailing. He had worked in Dublin for eighteen months prior to the 1994 IRA ceasefire, and had only just returned to Thames House after a two-year posting to MI5's Belfast office, where he'd been Patsy's number two. He was hard-working and totally trustworthy, and more than once she'd been grateful for his safe pair of hands. He also did the best impersonation of Gerry Adams that she'd ever heard.

'David, if and when we locate the men in the van, we're going to want to know where they've been. I'd like you and Jonathan to handle that. Keep on top of the technical boys.' David nodded at her and then flashed a smile across at Jonathan Clare. Clare was ten years younger than Bingham, but they'd worked together briefly in Belfast. 'I'd also like the two of you to liaise with Chief Inspector Denham when he gets back from Northern Ireland. If he does manage to obtain a list of IRA members who knew about Trevor's role as a bombmaker, other than those names we already have, it has to be our first priority. Any resources you need, you only have to ask.'

There was a stack of folders on a table against the window, and at Patsy's signal Lisa Davies and Anna Wallace began distributing them. 'The folders contain full briefing notes and copies of the photographs. They're not to leave this room. There's to be no contact with the police, at any level, without prior clearance from me. No phone calls to pals in Special Branch or Anti-Terrorism. I don't want to see this on the front page of the *Daily Mail*, okay?'

Nodding heads responded.

'Good. That's the state of play. This room is our operations centre. If I'm not here I'll be in Jason Hetherington's office down the corridor. Tim, would you come with me? You too, Barbara.'

Fanning opened the door for her and walked with her to Hetherington's office. Behind them followed Barbara Carter, a twenty-six-year-old psychology graduate who Patsy knew was originally from Dublin. Patsy closed the office door behind them and waved them over to the two armchairs in front of her desk. 'I've got something special for the two of you,' she said, sitting down. 'Martin Hayes is going to need his hand held through this, and I'm not going to be able to be with him all the time. Until this is resolved I want one of you to be with him at all times, and ideally I'd like you both there for as much of the time as is humanly possible. No going home, no popping into the gym. If one of you wants to use the loo, the other sticks with Hayes. When he sleeps, one of you stays in the room with him. Every minute of every hour of every day.'

The two agents nodded. They were both single and had no regular partners, so Patsy knew it wouldn't be too much of an inconvenience for them. In fact, they made a good-looking couple. He was tall with a runner's build and a crop of thick, blond hair. Carter was a few inches shorter with high cheekbones and long chestnut hair that she normally had tied back in a ponytail. They were both stylish dressers – he favoured dark Boss double-breasted suits and she generally wore well-fitting suits in pastel shades, usually cut just above the knee. There was clearly no attraction between the two of them, however. No sideways looks, no cute smiles when they thought no one was watching. Patsy had a keen eye for intra-office relationships and there was no sign of one developing, which was one of the reasons she'd given them the job of baby-sitting Martin Hayes.

She could see from the look on Fanning's face that he wasn't happy about the assignment as he slowly folded his arms across his chest. He was keen to be part of the team chasing the bombmaker and obviously regarded looking after the husband as being sidelined. If Carter was disappointed, she hid it well, smiling amiably with her Mont Blanc pen poised over a small leather-bound notebook that Patsy thought might have a Chanel logo on the front.

'There's something I didn't mention at the briefing, and I want it to remain between us, for the time being at least.'

Patsy had to resist the urge to smile as she saw Fanning's reaction. His whole body language changed. He uncrossed his legs and leaned forward expectantly, eager to hear what she had to say.

'They allowed her to phone her husband. On Sunday.'

Fanning and Carter both raised their eyebrows in surprise.

'Little was said, just that she was okay. And that there was something she had to do for them. She was obviously being closely monitored during the call, but our feeling is that if she managed to convince them to allow her to make one call, she should be able to do it again the closer she gets to completion.'

'Hell of an error,' said Fanning. 'Considering our technical capabilities.'

'Most of which isn't public knowledge,' said Patsy. 'Besides, the husband had been told not to contact the police. That if he did, his daughter would be killed. I think that under the circumstances they'd be justified in thinking that a tap would be unlikely in the extreme. Whatever, they allowed the call, and if they allowed one, they might allow another. Or, a more likely scenario in my opinion, she'll find a way of getting to a phone without them knowing. Either way, we've arranged with British Telecom and Telecom Eireann to have all calls to the Hayes house to be routed to an office here.' She nodded at the door to an adjoining room. 'In there, in fact. So far as the caller's concerned, they'll be through to the house. We'll be running a trace, but I doubt they'll be on long enough. Still, nothing ventured . . .'

'There is the possibility that she'll ask to speak to her daughter, of course,' said Carter.

Patsy nodded. 'That's where it gets complicated,' she said. 'We'll be monitoring all England–Ireland phone traffic, looking for key words. But that's going to be done through GCHQ. I've already been in touch with our liaison officer at Cheltenham. But even if we do locate the daughter, she's not our prime concern. Though Mr Hayes must absolutely not be aware of that. Are we clear?'

Fanning and Carter nodded. Patsy put her hands flat on the desk blotter and pushed herself up. 'Right,' she said, 'let's get to it.'

They said barely half a dozen words during the drive from the airport. They were both tall, wearing Barbour jackets over suits, and Denham figured that their combined ages just about equalled his own sixty-five years. Denham sat in the back of the Rover and stared at the back of their heads. They were both balding. The driver had a bare patch the size of a fifty-pence piece! the other hadn't done so well in the genetics lottery and had a bald spot as big as a saucer. Denham wondered if it was stress-related. In his early days with the RUC he'd had a thick crop of black hair that required a handful of gel to keep it in place; it was only when he'd transferred to Special Branch that he'd started to lose it.

They'd been waiting for him on the tarmac, the rear door of the Rover already open for him as he walked off the RAF Hercules transporter and down the metal stairway. He hadn't asked where they were going. It didn't matter. All that mattered was the man he was going to see.

They drove north towards Antrim, and Denham felt a touch of sadness as they passed within five miles of his own house. Under any normal circumstances he'd have asked the men to make a quick detour, but the mission he was on was too important. His wife would have to wait.

He lit another cigarette, his third since he'd got into the Rover. When he'd lit the first one the driver had coughed pointedly, but Denham had ignored him. He looked around the back of the car for an ashtray but there wasn't one, so he was reduced to flicking his ash out of a gap in the window, though more often than not the slipstream blew it back into the car.

They joined the M22 and headed west with the vast expanse of Lough Neagh to their left, until the motorway merged into the A6. Just past Castledawson they turned right and started driving along smaller country roads. The driver was good, Denham had to admit. He drove quickly but safely, and wasn't averse to switching lanes and driving on the wrong side of the road if it meant he had a better view of what lay ahead. He was constantly checking the mirrors, but Denham doubted that anyone would have been able to keep up with them. The speedometer rarely fell below seventy as they sped between the fields.

The car eventually came to a halt by a stone bridge. The driver turned around to look at Denham and nodded, just once. 'You boys stay with the car,' Denham said. He climbed out of the Rover, dropped the remains of his cigarette on to the damp grass and trod it into the soil. The sun was a hand's width from the horizon and reddening, and Denham buttoned up his raincoat. He walked down towards the fast-flowing stream, holding his arms out for balance as his Hush Puppies skidded and slipped along the muddy gravel path.

The man standing in the stream must have heard Denham coming, but he didn't turn his head. He flicked the rod in his hand and a fly whisked through the air and plopped almost silently on to a quiet stretch of water close to the far bank.

'You always did have a hell of a smooth cast, Mr McCormack,' said Denham. Only then did Thomas McCormack turn to acknowledge his presence.

'I'm told you're no mean fisherman yourself, Chief Inspector Denham.'

McCormack turned his back on Denham and wound in his line. He was wearing bright green waders, a quilted waistcoat over a thick green pullover, and on his head was a shapeless tweed hat that could have been a close cousin to the one Denham was wearing.

'It's Mr Denham now. Retired almost ten years now.'

'Oh, I know that, Chief Inspector.'

'Same as you know I'm a fisherman?'

McCormack flicked his rod again and sent the fly high into the air, nodding with satisfaction as it dropped on to the same stretch of water as before. 'We knew about the little stream you used to favour, up by Ballymena. Lovely spot, with the beech trees right up to the water's edge.' He turned to look at Denham as he wound in his line. 'Could have got you any time, Chief Inspector. Before or after your retirement.' He grinned mischievously. 'But that's all water under the bridge now, isn't it?'

Denham tapped a cigarette out and lit it.

'Still on eighty a day?' asked McCormack.

'Down to twenty,' said Denham.

'The wife?'

'Yes, the wife,' sighed Denham.

'Where would we be without them, huh?'

'Indeed.' Denham tilted his head back and blew smoke up into the darkening sky.

'So, would this be a social call, Chief Inspector?'

'I'm afraid not.'

'You won't mind if I carry on casting, will you? There's a beautiful trout, five pounds if it's an ounce, lurking under those leaves over there.'

'You go for it, Mr McCormack.' There was a tree trunk on its side a few steps away from Denham and he went over and sat on it. McCormack made three more casts, and each time the fly dropped into the same part of the stream.

'What do you think? Too big?'

'Maybe something brighter?' suggested Denham. 'The light's going.'

'Aye, you could be right,' said McCormack. He wound in the line and replaced his fly with a slightly bigger one that had a splash of yellow in its tail.

'Andrea Sheridan,' said Denham. 'Remember her?'

McCormack's eyes narrowed. He looked at Denham for several seconds without speaking. 'That's a name from the past, right enough. Retired, like yourself.'

Denham nodded and took a long pull on his cigarette. Thomas McCormack was an old adversary, and peace process or no peace process, he was a man to be handled with care. With his horn-rimmed spectacles and grey hair, he looked like an elderly schoolmaster, but for many years he'd been a hardline member of the IRA's Army Executive.

'Maybe. Maybe not.'

'No doubt about it, Chief Inspector. She retired about the same time you did.' McCormack's head tilted to the side like that of an inquisitive bird. He looked as if he was going to say something, but instead he turned his back on Denham again and flicked the new fly out over the water. It fell short by more than four feet and he tutted to himself.

'We think that there's a chance she's active again.'

'Impossible,' said McCormack.

'Perhaps against her will.'

McCormack wound in his line and cast again. Just as the fly plopped on to the water, a big speckled trout seemed to leap from the depths, its mouth agape. It engulfed the fly and disappeared back under the surface. McCormack hauled in the fish and carefully extracted the fly before holding it up to show Denham. 'Six pounds, I'll bet,' he said.

'Hell of a catch,' agreed Denham.

McCormack bent down and lowered the trout into the stream. He let the fish swim free and then straightened up. He waded over to the bank. Denham stood up and offered him his hand and helped him climb out of the water. McCormack nodded his thanks and the two men sat together on the tree trunk. McCormack took a small pewter flask from his waistcoat pocket and offered it to Denham. Denham shook his head and gestured at the cigarette in his hand. 'One vice is enough,' he said.

McCormack chuckled as he unscrewed the top of his flask and took a swig. He smacked his lips appreciatively. 'What do you mean, against her will?' he asked.

'She has a child. A daughter. Katie. The child's been kidnapped. No ransom, but the kidnappers told Andrea to fly to London. Now she's disappeared.'

McCormack took another swig from his flask, then replaced its top and put it back in his waistcoat pocket.

'And you're suggesting what, Chief Inspector?'

'I'm not suggesting anything. I'm looking for guidance.'

McCormack wound in his line and began to disassemble his rod.

'I figure that your people wouldn't need to kidnap the little girl to get the mother to do what you wanted. Presumably you've always known where she was.'

'As have you, it seems.'

Denham blew smoke towards the setting sun. 'So, I'm ruling out an official operation. An official IRA operation.'

'I'm glad to hear that,' said McCormack, slipping the sections of his rod into a canvas bag.

'I was thinking perhaps a splinter group?'

'Very doubtful,' said McCormack. 'Gerry and Martin wouldn't stand for it.'

'Real IRA? Continuity?'

'Spent forces,' said McCormack, tying up the bag.

'Anyone new? The Dundalk boys getting restless?'

'Not that I've heard. It's all about the ballot box these days.' McCormack propped the bag against the tree trunk and stretched out his legs. 'It's not Republican, Chief Inspector. You should be looking at the other side of the fence.'

'Maybe. But how would they know about her?'

McCormack looked across at Denham, his eyes narrowing. 'I might be asking you the same question.'

Denham stared into the distance.

'Jesus Christ,' said McCormack, his voice little more than a whisper. 'She was working for you.'

It wasn't a question, and Denham knew there was no point in denying it. He'd known that the moment he asked McCormack about Andrea Sheridan he'd be showing his hand. And that if he expected to get McCormack's help, he'd have to tell him everything.

'For how long?' asked McCormack.

'From day one. Pretty much.'

McCormack shook his head slowly. 'My God. She must have iced water for blood.' He pushed his spectacles higher up his nose. 'Every bomb, every one she made, you knew about it?'

Denham shrugged but didn't say anything.

'But the people that died? The soldiers? The bomb disposal . . .' His voice tailed off as realisation dawned. 'You faked it. You faked them all. You cunning old fox . . .' He took out his hip flask and took a long drink from it, then wiped his mouth with the back of his hand. 'Except for the kids. Something went wrong. The kids died, and she walked away. And you. You got the push.'

'Somebody had to carry the can. And she was my agent.'

McCormack put the top back on his flask. 'Funny old world, huh? You think you know someone . . . You think you can trust someone . . .'

The bottom of the sun was touching the horizon. Denham turned up the collar of his raincoat. 'It's history, Thomas. Ancient history.' It was the first time he'd ever called McCormack by his first name.

'Aye. Maybe you're right.'

'But about the matter in hand. You realise what'll happen if it goes off? Her fingerprints will be all over it. Her signature.'

'Which is presumably why they're using her. You don't have to paint a picture for me, Liam. We've as much to lose as you do if they succeed.'

'So you'll help?'

'I don't see that I've any choice.' He smiled thinly. 'It's a turn-up for the books, isn't it?'

Denham flicked the end of his cigarette into the stream. 'Aye. It's an ever-changing world, right enough. So, who knew about her? Apart from the two of us.'

* * *

Martin paced up and down, staring at the floor. It was six paces from one side of the office to the other. Six paces. Turn. Six paces. Turn. He had his arms crossed and the tips of his fingers were digging into his sides, hard enough to hurt, except that Martin was beyond feeling any physical discomfort.

'Mr Hayes, please. Try to relax.' Martin looked up, his mind a million miles away. He frowned at Carter, his eyes blank.

'Can I get you something? Tea? Coffee?'

Martin blinked several times like a hypnotist's subject coming out of a trance. 'What? Sorry?'

'A drink? Do you want tea or something?'

'Coffee, maybe. Yes. Coffee. Thanks.' He started pacing again.

Carter and Fanning exchanged worried looks. Carter shrugged, not sure what to say or do to put Martin at ease. She stood up, and raised an enquiring eyebrow at Fanning. He shook his head. He rarely touched tea or coffee. On the table in front of them, next to two telephones and a digital tape recorder, were two bottles of water and two glasses. It was all they'd touched since starting their vigil with Martin. It had been four hours and neither of the phones had rung.

When Carter went out to get the coffee, Fanning suggested that Martin sit down. There were two sofas in the office, large enough to sleep on, and there was a small bathroom off to the side, so that there was no need for Martin to leave the room. Patsy Ellis had made it clear that Martin was to remain confined to the office, but that hadn't been a problem – he'd shown no desire to leave. All he'd done was to pace up and down and from time to time to stare at the silent phones.

The black phone was the line that had been diverted from the Hayes home in Dublin. The white phone was a direct line to Patsy Ellis's mobile. At least half a dozen times

Martin had asked if they were sure the phones were working. Fanning had assured him that they were.

'I can't sit,' said Martin.

'There's nothing you can do,' said Fanning, loosening his tie a little. 'The ball's in your wife's court. We just have to wait.'

'But what if she doesn't ring? What if they don't let her use the phone?'

Fanning winced. He was an only child, he'd never been married and his parents were fit and healthy – he'd never had to deal with the death of a relative or a friend, never mind a wife or child. He could only imagine the torment that Martin was going through, and while he wanted to put the man's mind at rest, he didn't want to lie to him.

'Tim, what if she's dead already? What if they're both dead? Oh, God.' Martin dropped down on to one of the sofas and sat with his head in his hands.

Fanning stood up and went over to him. He put a tentative hand on his shoulder. 'Everyone here's doing everything they can, Mr Hayes. I can promise you that.'

Martin closed his eyes and shook his head. 'I don't think it's going to be enough.' He bunched his hands into fists and banged them down on his knees. Fanning took his hand off Martin's shoulder and sat down next to him.

'Patsy's right,' said Fanning. 'The closer your wife is to completing the device, the more leverage she has. She'll know that. There'll come a point where she'll be able to put pressure on them. She'll call.'

'But the guy that shot at me? He must have been one of them, right? He'll know that I'm not at home. Why would he let Andy call me if he knows I'm not at home?'

'We don't know,' admitted Fanning. 'Patsy said that maybe your wife would be able to get to a phone herself, without them knowing.'

Martin grimaced. 'That's hardly likely, is it?'

'It's a possibility. And just because you were attacked doesn't mean they know you've left the country, does it? They've no way of knowing where you are. For all they know, you could have returned home.'

'So she calls, then what? I know phone traces aren't infallible. Things go wrong.'

'You're going by what you see in the movies, Mr Hayes. It's not like that. With a digital exchange, we can get the number almost immediately. And a trace within seconds. Even with a mobile. If she's in the City, we'll know to within a hundred feet where she is.'

Martin leaned back so that his head rested on the back of the sofa. 'And Katie? What about my daughter?'

'If we get the terrorists making the bomb, we'll find her.'

Martin wiped his hands over his face as if he were wiping away tears, though his cheeks were dry. 'There's too many "ifs", Tim. Too many fucking "ifs". Are the Gardai looking for her?'

'Patsy thinks it best not to call in the local police,' said Fanning, choosing his words with care. 'We're looking, but we're using our own people. And we're monitoring all calls to Ireland. If they make a call to the kidnappers, we'll know. And we'll have their location. We'll know where your daughter is being held.'

'Oh, come on, Tim. That's not feasible. You can't possibly monitor every single call between England and Ireland.'

Fanning sat back, wondering how much he should tell Martin. The man was at the end of his tether and needed some reassurance, but much of what MI5 did was classified. 'We can, Martin. And we do. All the time.'

'Every call?'

Fanning nodded. 'It goes on every hour of every day. All around the world.'

Martin looked at Fanning, intrigued. 'How?'

Fanning sighed. 'Can't you just accept that we can, Martin?'

The door opened and Carter came in with a mug of coffee which she handed to Martin. He thanked her, then turned back to Fanning. 'Well?'

Fanning looked up at Carter. 'I was telling Martin not to worry. That we've got all bases covered.'

'He was telling me about tapping phones between England and Ireland so you can find out where they're keeping Katie.'

Carter pulled a face. 'Tim . . .' she said.

Fanning shrugged. 'He's not exactly an enemy of the state, Barbara.'

'I have a right to know what's going on,' said Martin quietly.

Carter held Fanning's look for a second or two, then she nodded. 'I guess it can't do any harm,' she said.

Martin nodded eagerly. 'So, what's going on?' he asked Fanning.

Fanning took a deep breath. 'I'll give you the idiot's guide,' he said. 'No offence.'

Martin smiled tightly. 'None taken.'

'The system is called Echelon. Don't ask me why. It's been around in some form or another since the seventies, but it's really come into its own in the last few years. It's the brainchild of the Americans, naturally, through their National Security Agency, but it also involves us, through GCHQ, the Government Communication Headquarters in Cheltenham, the Australians, the Canadians and New Zealand. Not through any altruistic information-sharing aspirations, but because the Americans can't physically cover the world on their own. Between the five countries, every single satellite, land line and undersea cable transmission is monitored. Every single one, Martin. Every phone call, fax, telex and e-mail in the world. Nothing escapes.'

Martin shook his head in disbelief. 'There must be millions every day. Tens of millions.'

'Billions, Martin. But Echelon can handle it. And more. It has the capacity to monitor individual transmissions, or it can search through all transmissions looking for a particular word, or combination of words. It can go back through several weeks, worth of transmissions, too. And there's more. It can even search out voiceprints, so we can be on the lookout for a particular individual making a call anywhere in the world. It gets flagged in one of the five Echelon HQs and Robert's your father's brother.'

'It sounds impossible,' said Martin. 'It's too big.'

'It's big, but computing power is now enormous compared with what it was just twenty years ago. And it's increasing by an order of magnitude every three years or so. You use the Internet, right?'

'Sure. Who doesn't?'

'And you've used a search engine? Yahoo or Altavista or one of the others, where you scan the Net looking for specific subjects. Words or combination of words?' Martin nodded. 'So you know how it works. If you get the search engine to look for a word like "heroin", in a couple of seconds it might tell you that there are some fifty thousand hits, places on the Net where the word occurs. Now, have you ever thought what that means? In the space of seconds, that search engine has looked at every site it has access to and found which ones refer to heroin. And if you want to call up a particular reference, it's on your screen in seconds.'

'I guess so,' said Martin.

'Then consider this, Martin. The Internet is old technology. Echelon is several generations ahead. It works at a speed you could never hope to comprehend. We ask it to keep a lookout for the word "Katie" or 'Mummy' and it'll flag any phone conversation that takes place in which both words are used. Immediately. Real-time. Within seconds we'll know which number is being called, and from where.'

'But I thought you could block your number from showing?' said Martin. He sipped his coffee.

Fanning smiled and shook his head. 'There's no way of hiding from Echelon,' he said.

Martin leaned forward, cupping the mug of coffee between his hands. The signs of stress were starting to diminish. He seemed much more relaxed now that he understood what was involved. 'The thing I don't get is if this system is so efficient, why doesn't it catch more terrorists?'

Fanning grinned. 'What makes you think it doesn't? The NSA keeps a very low profile. So does GCHQ. Neither shouts about its results. Other agencies, ourselves included, usually end up taking the credit.'

'But you'd be able to locate anyone. Anyone in the world. Terrorists, drug dealers, criminals. People who've gone missing. Lord Lucan. Anyone.'

Carter leaned against the table, her hands behind her for support. 'Tim's telling you what's possible technically, but generally there isn't enough manpower to go after just one person, unless they're someone like Saddam Hussein or terrorists like Osama Bin Laden. There's a constant watching brief for top-ranking bad guys like that, but for run-of-the-mill criminals, it's just not worth the effort.'

Martin opened his mouth to speak but Carter silenced him with a wave of a neatly manicured hand, the nails the colour of dried blood. 'I'll give you an example. Say a plane was bombed, flying over the Atlantic. We could search for every conversation in which the words plane and bomb were used. But think how often the incident would be referred to in general conversation by members of the public. Say it was just a hundred thousand, and believe me, that'd be a massive underestimate, Echelon will pick out the words, then include five seconds either side, so that analysts can listen to the snippet of conversation to decide if it's worth following up. That's a million seconds of conversation, Martin. More than two hundred and fifty hours. Every second has to be listened to and analysed. And I can guarantee that it'll all be time wasted, because terrorists would never use words like bomb or explosive over the phone. They'd use codes, because they know how the system works. It's the same with drug dealers. They're not going to say "heroin" or "cocaine" – they wouldn't even say "gear" or other commonly used slang. They'll say "the consignment arrives next week" or something equally vague. So Echelon isn't used for general trawling of domestic phone conversations – there just aren't enough people, even within the NSA, to listen to all the stuff that's recorded. Most of it stays on disk and is stored, never listened to.'

'So now you're saying it's a waste of time?' said Martin bitterly.

Carter held up her hand again. 'Absolutely not,' she said. 'Where Echelon is invaluable is in targeting specific conversations, in specific areas of the world. It's used to listen in on diplomatic transmissions, military transmissions, specific people and organisations. Or the way that we're using it. For a specific word that isn't going to be in general use. How often do you think the word Katie is going to be used in calls from England to Ireland? A dozen? A hundred? Those sorts of numbers we can deal with, Martin. We'll pick up the call within seconds, and almost immediately we'll have a location. The NSA and GCHQ have more computing power between them than any other organisation on the planet.'

'I hope you're right, Barbara,' Martin said.

'She is. We are,' said Fanning. He looked up at Carter and they shared a smile. Patsy Ellis might not approve of how much of GCHQ's work they'd revealed to Martin, but he was definitely a lot more relaxed having heard it.

All three jumped as the black telephone rang. The mug fell from Martin's hands and coffee splashed across the beige wool carpet.

The two men in Barbour jackets drove Denham back to Belfast in silence. Denham sat in the back of the Rover, chain-smoking and staring out of the window. They took him to a nondescript office building on the outskirts of the city, and the one who'd been in the passenger seat escorted him inside. A uniformed security guard asked him for identification, but all he had on him was his driving licence. The guard noted down the details and Denham and the man with him went up in an elevator to the third floor. The man had a swipe card which he ran through a reader at the side of a glass door, and it clicked open. They walked down a white-painted corridor past a series of identical grey doors. The man opened one of the doors and nodded at Denham. 'I'll wait for you here, sir.'

Inside the windowless room was a soundproofed booth, and inside the booth was a metal desk, a plastic chair and a telephone without a dial or keypad. The walls of the room were lined with pale green foam rubber that had been moulded into an egg-box design. Denham went into the booth and closed the door behind him. He picked up the phone and almost immediately a man's voice asked him who he wished to speak to. He asked for Patsy Ellis. She was on the line within seconds.

'Liam, how did it go?'

'Better than I expected, to be honest. Things have changed since the Good Friday agreement, more than I'd ever have guessed.'

'Men like McCormack have, sure. But there are other leopards whose spots'll never change. So what did he have to say?'

'He gave me the five who were in Trevor's ASU, but he

obviously knew that we had them anyway. And he was open about Denis Fisher, but Fisher's dead. The active service unit was under the control of Hugh McGrath, and that we didn't know because he dealt only with Nolan.'

'McGrath?'

'He's dead, too. At least McCormack reckons he's dead. He disappeared back in '92. McGrath was on the Army Council but his main function was to liaise with the Libyans during the eighties. McCormack was a bit sketchy on the details, but it seems that McGrath set up his own splinter group responsible for a bombing campaign in '92. Fisher was running the group.' Denham took out a packet of cigarettes and fumbled one out. 'They were all killed when the SAS stormed their flat in Wapping. McGrath disappeared just before the SAS went in.' He lit the cigarette and inhaled deeply.

'He could just have got wind of what was happening and gone underground.'

'There's more to it than that, but McCormack's not letting on. I got the impression that it was the IRA that did for him, you know? That they found out what he was up to and took matters into their own hands.'

'But this McGrath knew about Trevor?'

'Oh, yes. Quite definitely. And another volunteer. Micky Geraghty. Have you heard of him?'

'Doesn't ring a bell.'

'Aye, probably before your time. Bit of a legend was Micky Geraghty. He was a sniper, and a bloody good one, but he lost heart when his wife died of cancer. Long and painful, and by all accounts he was a broken man afterwards. Walked away.'

'Still alive?'

'McCormack said he wasn't sure. He hasn't heard from him for a while. Geraghty went to live near Thurso, up in Scotland.'

'I'll get him checked out. What was his involvement with Trevor?'

'He never met her, but knew of her. The ASU was setting bombs in Belfast, small ones, booby-trapped so they'd be hard to deal with, and Geraghty would be somewhere up high with his rifle. The plan was to shoot the bomb-disposal guys. Trevor let us know what was happening so we had saturation coverage plus helicopters all over the place. Geraghty didn't get a chance to stick his head up. They moved him to the border and that was that. But according to McCormack, on at least one occasion he heard McGrath telling Geraghty about Fisher and Trevor. Geraghty had a daughter about the same age, name of Kerry.'

'But no one else on the Army Council knew about Trevor?'

'Not according to McCormack.'

'And the other thing? Is he willing to help?'

'He said he'd make enquiries. But that it wouldn't be easy.' Denham looked around for an ashtray but couldn't see one. He pulled a face and flicked ash on to the floor.

'Do you think he'll do it, though?'

'I think so. But without putting himself at risk. It's a hell of a thing to be asking him to do, Patsy. If word got out that he was helping us . . . even under the circumstances, the hardliners wouldn't think twice about making an example of him.'

'How long before he gets back to us?'

'He didn't say. Couldn't say. He'll put out feelers, ask around, but softly-softly. If he does come across anyone who's gone missing, he'll get back to me.'

'That's great, Liam. Job well done. Now I'd like you back here as soon as possible. The plane's waiting for you.'

'I was thinking it might be an idea if I return via Scotland. I could pop in on Micky Geraghty.'

'Do you know him?'

Denham stubbed his cigarette out on the underside of the desk. 'Never met him. I know it's not exactly on the way, but until McCormack gets back to me, I'm not going to be much use.'

Patsy was silent for a few seconds, thinking it over. 'You're right, it makes sense. You go ahead and see if you can find Geraghty. I'll speak to our transport people, ascertain where we can get you flown into, and I'll have you met there.'

'I'm a big boy, Patsy. I don't need minders.'

'It'll save time, Liam. Just think of them as drivers.'

'Aye. Okay.'

'You be careful, you hear. And Liam?'

'Yes?'

'You're not supposed to smoke in the secure communications booth. It screws up the electronics.'

Denham was still chuckling as he left the room.

Martin's hand was trembling as he picked up the phone. He took a deep breath and put it to his ear as Carter and Fanning encouraged him with nods and urgent smiles. The counter on the digital tape recorder had already started to click off the seconds. 'Yes?' he said, his throat so dry that he could barely get the word out. Carter picked up a light-weight headset and put in on so that she could listen in on the conversation.

'Mart?' It was a man's voice. An Irish accent. 'Mart, is that you?'

It was Padraig. The strength went from Martin's legs and he sat down. He put the receiver down on the table and looked at the two MI5 agents, then shook his head.

'Shit,' said Fanning. He picked up a glass of water and drank, then walked away to look out of the window, cursing under his breath.

Martin stared down at the handset. Padraig was still

speaking but Martin couldn't make out what he was saying. He put the phone to his ear. 'Jesus, Mart, say something.'

'Hiya, Padraig. Sorry. I dropped the phone.'

'Are you at home, Mart? I've been trying your mobile but it's off.'

'I haven't had time to charge it,' Martin lied. Patsy had told him to leave the mobile phone switched off so that the kidnappers couldn't use it. They'd used the home phone the first time and Patsy wanted them to use it again.

'I was calling to leave a message. I thought you were still in England.' There was a second or two of silence as Martin's partner gathered his thoughts. 'What the hell's going on, Mart? Where are you?'

Carter shook her head firmly.

'I can't tell you, Mart. I'm sorry.'

'You're still in England, yeah?'

Another shake of the head from Carter.

'I can't tell you that either, Padraig.'

'But Katie and Andy are okay, yeah?'

Martin sighed. He hated being evasive, and he hated lying, but Carter was standing over him, one hand up to her headset. 'It's complicated, Padraig.'

'Mart, I had a visit from the Garda today. Two detectives. A guy called FitzGerald and his partner.'

'Power?'

'Yeah. Power, that was it. Right Laurel and Hardy, they were. They seemed mightily pissed off at something but I had trouble following what they wanted.'

'What do you mean?'

'It was the weirdest thing, Mart. I thought they were going to give me grief for driving you up to Belfast, but they didn't even mention it. I tell you, I was worried they were going to ask to look at my car because I've still not got the window replaced and there's glass all over the seat. They said that you were going to be away from the office for a while, and that I wasn't to worry. They said if anyone asked I was to say that you were at home, off sick. And they said I wasn't to try to get in touch with you.'

'And I can see that you took their advice, Padraig.'

Padraig chuckled. 'Yeah, fucking cops. What are you going to do, eh?'

Martin laughed along with his partner.

'Seriously, Mart. What's going on?'

'I can't tell you, Padraig.'

'They're the cops that hauled you into Pearse Street, aren't they?'

'Yeah. But they've been warned off.'

'Warned off? By who?'

Carter shook her head fiercely and wagged her finger in front of Martin's face. He glared at her and put his hand over the mouthpiece. 'He's my best friend,' he said, a hard edge in his voice. 'I trust him more than anyone.'

'You're risking your daughter's life, Mr Hayes.'

'Don't you fucking patronise me,' Martin hissed. 'I've known Padraig for almost thirty years. I've known you for five minutes. I'm damn sure I know which of you I trust.'

Carter's cheeks flushed and she straightened up. Fanning looked over at them, sipping his water. He flashed her a sympathetic look but she turned away, embarrassed that he'd heard Martin's outburst.

Martin swivelled his chair around so that his back was to them. He took his hand away from the mouthpiece. 'Padraig, the gardai have been told to lay off. It's being handled in London now.'

'That's where you are, yeah?'

'That's right. Any calls to the house are being transferred here. But no one must know, right? If the kidnappers call, they've got to think I'm still in Dublin.'

'Mum's the word, Mart.'

'Anyone asks, do as the gardai said. Just say I'm at home sick and you don't know when I'll be back.'

'Can I do anything to help?'

'No, mate, but thanks for offering.'

'If you need anything, I'm here, yeah?'

Martin thanked his partner and hung up. Carter was standing at the window, looking out at the river. As Fanning went over to the tape recorder, Martin went and stood next to her. 'I'm sorry,' he said.

Carter shrugged. 'It doesn't matter.'

'I didn't mean to snap. It's been a shitty few days.'

'I understand, Martin. But we are trying to help. We're on your side.'

Martin nodded. He felt genuinely bad about lashing out at her. 'Padraig won't do anything to rock the boat,' he said. 'He loves Andy and Katie almost as much as I do.'

She forced a smile. 'I'm sure he won't let you down.' She gestured at the spilt coffee. 'I'll get that cleaned up,' she said.

Lydia McCracken sat on the wooden bench and looked around the garden square. She was wearing a pale blue suit and was carrying a small handbag which she held in her lap. An old woman was feeding pigeons hunks of bread from a Hovis wrapper and muttering to them. Or to herself – McCracken was too far away to hear clearly. The old woman looked homeless, with a thick wool coat tied around the waist with a length of rope, and black wellington boots with the tops turned over. She had greasy grey hair and blotchy skin, and she kept wiping her nose with the back of her hand. McCracken shuddered and looked away. Several dozen office workers were strolling around the square, getting a breath of fresh air before heading back to their VDUs and keyboards. Three men in their twenties walked by, laughing. Neat suits, polished shoes and starched shirts

– only the ties offered any variety. Nothing to distinguish them from the hundreds of thousands of office workers who poured into the City every day. And nothing to distinguish them from the hundreds who'd die when the four-thousand-pound fertiliser bomb went off just a half a mile away from where she was sitting.

McCracken had helped plant bombs before, though she'd never been involved in the building of one. She'd been assigned to the IRA's England Department, but always in a support role, establishing identities and safe houses, arranging transport and, on one occasion, making a coded call to the authorities. She'd always believed in what she was doing – that the only way to drive the British out of Ireland was by force – and she'd felt betrayed by the so-called peace process and the ceasefire that followed. Her younger brother had been killed in a gun battle with SAS troopers in the early eighties, and two cousins were shot by British paratroopers when they tried to drive through an army roadblock close to the border. She wanted revenge against the British for the suffering they'd brought to her country and to her family, and Egan had offered her a way to get that revenge. He'd offered her a lot of money, but that wasn't why she jumped at the chance of working with him. A bomb in the City would derail the peace process, of that she had no doubt. There'd be a backlash, politically and militarily, and it would make the whole world sit up and take notice. But more than that, it would be retribution. Retribution for her dead brother and murdered cousins, and for the hundreds of other Catholics maimed and murdered over the years. The IRA hierarchy might have been able to put that all behind them, but McCracken couldn't and wouldn't.

'Nice day,' said a man in a dark blue pin-stripe suit as he sat down on the bench a few feet from her. He placed a black briefcase on the ground midway between them. It was

Egan. He was holding a Marks and Spencer carrier bag and he handed it to her. 'Sandwich?'

McCracken peered inside the bag. It contained two baguettes.

'Thank you.'

'How's everything going?'

'On schedule. Quinn's being a pain in the arse, though. Keeps pestering Andrea. Got a hard-on for her like a baseball bat, he has.'

'Can you handle it?'

'Sure. But he's not reliable. I know what you said about him being useful in a crisis, but he makes her nervous, and at this stage in the operation that's the last thing we need.'

Egan nodded thoughtfully. 'I'll sort it,' he said. He nodded down at the briefcase. 'Take good care of that, huh?'

McCracken smiled tightly. 'I know what I'm doing.'

'I know you do.' Egan stood up and adjusted his tie. 'That's why I hired you for this. Trial run tomorrow, okay?'

'That's the plan.'

'Bring Quinn, will you?'

McCracken picked up the briefcase and put it carefully on her lap. 'I think that's best. I wouldn't want to leave him alone with Andrea.'

Egan walked away. McCracken watched him go. He moved out of the garden square, quickly blending with the other suits and disappearing around the corner. McCracken stood up and walked in the opposite direction. She moved the briefcase as little as possible, all too conscious of the fact that it contained enough Semtex explosive to blow a crater fifty feet wide. She'd transported high explosive before, but that didn't mean she wasn't scared. She'd known too many IRA volunteers who'd been killed in premature explosions.

She thought about the man she knew as Egan as she walked back to Cathay Tower. It was almost certainly not his real name – he was far too professional to reveal his identity to her, because the bottom line was that she was a hired hand. The planning, the details, the money, they all came from Egan. So had the rest of the team. They had all been recruited by him: Quinn and O'Keefe in London, McEvoy and Canning in Dublin, and probably others that she didn't know about. She knew nothing about his background, but he seemed to know everything about her. She hadn't known the others, either, and Egan had said that was an advantage because it would be that much harder for them to betray each other if anything went wrong. It was the philosophy followed by the IRA, dividing its members into small cells which were kept isolated from each other.

When Egan had told McCracken that one of the men she was working with was a Protestant, and a member of the UDA, she had protested, but Egan had explained that she'd have to put her tribal loyalties behind her, that what they were doing was far more important than religion or politics. He'd convinced her, and with hindsight she knew that he was right. O'Keefe was in it for the money, as was Quinn. McCracken despised them for that, though she'd never show them her true feelings. All that mattered was that the bomb went off and that people died.

The Wrestler looked over Andy's shoulder at the electronic equipment spread out on the table. 'Where did you learn about electronics?' he asked.

Andy shrugged but didn't say anything. She using a magnifying glass to examine the inside of a small digital alarm clock.

'Cat got your tongue?' asked the Wrestler.

Andy looked up from the magnifying glass. 'You wouldn't want me to make a mistake with this, would you?' she said. 'If I connect the wrong wires, we could all find ourselves splattered over the building opposite.'

The Runner was sitting on the floor, his back to the wall, drinking a can of Coke. 'Stuck-up bitch,' he muttered.

The Wrestler reached over and picked up a soldering iron and held it close to his face, sniffing the end.

'That's hot,' said Andy.

'I know it's hot.' He put it back on the table. As he reached across her the sleeve of his overalls rode up and Andy caught a quick glimpse of a tattoo. It was the English flag. The cross of St George, a red cross on a white background. She pretended not to notice and concentrated on the chip at the back of the clock. Green-eyes had gone out a couple of hours earlier. She'd told Andy to check the timers and wiring, though there'd still been no mention of detonators.

Andy checked the alarm. She'd set it to go off in two minutes' time. A blue wire ran from the chip to the negative terminal of a nine-volt battery. A red wire linked the chip to one terminal of a white plastic bulb-holder into which was screwed a small flashlight bulb. A third wire, also red, connected the second terminal of the bulb-holder to the positive terminal of the battery. She could feel the Wrestler watching her over her shoulder, but she forced herself to ignore him. She pressed the switch to activate the alarm. The bulb glowed brightly. Andy cursed and sat back in her chair.

'What's wrong?' asked the Wrestler.

'Oh, nothing,' said Andy. 'It's just that if that had been connected to the device, we'd all be in a million pieces right now.'

The Wrestler peered at the circuit that Andy had put together.

'The light's in place of the detonator,' said Andy. 'It shows if the circuit's live.'

'And it is,' said the Wrestler. 'So what's the problem?' He scratched his stomach and moved his head closer to the bulb, frowning beneath his ski mask.

Andy pointed at the digital read-out on the clock face. 'The problem is it's set to go off in two minutes. I must have connected the wrong chip output.' She pulled the wires out of the clock and picked up the magnifying glass again. Everything looked okay. She put the clock face down on the table and began running the prods of a circuit tester across the chip, trying to find out where she'd gone wrong.

The Hercules landed at an airport outside Wick, in the far north-west corner of Scotland. There was only one man waiting for Denham this time, standing by a battered old Volvo. He was in his fifties with a high forehead and wind-blown black hair, and he was wearing a sheepskin jacket with the collar turned up against a bitter wind that was blowing in from the North Sea. 'Welcome to Wick!' he shouted above the noise of the Hercules, and he shook Denham's hand firmly. 'Harry McKechnie. Sorry about the transport. The office car's in for a service so I've got to use my own wheels.'

Denham climbed into the front passenger seat. He took out his cigarettes as McKechnie drove away from the airfield. 'You don't mind if I smoke, do you?' he asked.

'Not if you'll light one for me too,' said McKechnie. Denham lit two cigarettes and gave one to McKechnie. McKechnie inhaled gratefully, then turned up the heater. 'Nights are getting bloody cold up here,' he said. There was no trace of a Scottish accent, despite his name.

It was a twenty-five-mile drive to Thurso, and McKechnie spent much of his time complaining about his posting north of the border. He was from Southampton originally, and had joined the Security Service straight from Oxford. He told Denham that he thought his bosses were hoping he'd take early retirement. 'Face doesn't fit,' he said. 'New regime. Bloody kids these days. Half of them don't even drink.' He held up his lit cigarette. 'And they'd rather you farted than lit up one of these.'

Denham grinned and settled back in his seat.

'Okay, to the matter in hand,' said McKechnie. 'Michael Geraghty, Micky to his friends, lives about four miles west of Thurso. Place called Garryowen Farm. He runs executive training courses, Outward Bound for the middle-aged. Takes them rock climbing, canoeing, gives them team-building exercises, that sort of thing.'

'Keeping his nose clean?'

'By all accounts, yes.'

'And he never did time, is that right?'

'Nothing could ever be proved.'

'Bastard.'

'Yeah. His daughter helps him run it. Kerry. She's thirty-two.'

'Any IRA involvement?'

'Periphery, so far as we know.'

Denham shrugged his shoulders. He was tired and could have done with a few hours' sleep, but there was no time. He closed his eyes.

'Sir?' McKechnie's voice jarred him awake.

'Huh?'

McKechnie grinned across at him. 'Your cigarette, sir.'

Denham looked at his right hand. The cigarette had almost burned down to his fingers and he realised that he must have fallen asleep. 'Wasn't snoring, was I?' he asked. McKechnie shook his head but didn't say anything. Denham stubbed his cigarette butt into an ashtray that was already filled to overflowing.

The drive to Thurso took the best part of half an hour, then McKechnie turned off the A882 and headed east. After another ten minutes he turned on to a single-track road and slowed the Volvo down to a walking pace. 'That's it, up ahead,' he said. Denham was impressed by McKechnie. He appeared casual, dishevelled even, but he was well briefed on Geraghty, and though there was a map open on the back seat he hadn't had to look at it.

The headlights illuminated Garryowen Farm, a two-storey grey stone building with a steeply sloping slate roof. There were no lights on. McKechnie stopped the car and tapped his fingers on the steering wheel. 'Shit,' he said.

'Let's have a look around the back,' said Denham.

McKechnie drove slowly past the farmhouse. Behind it was a large stone barn which had been converted into flats with individual entrances, and a short row of cottages. They were all in darkness.

The two men climbed out of the Volvo and walked towards the rear of the farmhouse. McKechnie had left the headlights on, and they cast giant shadows as they approached a black-painted wooden door. Denham knocked on it several times. McKechnie stood back to check if a light went on upstairs, but he shook his head. Next to the door was a large sash window. Denham put his hand against the glass and peered inside. It was the kitchen, and there were no signs of life. No dirty dishes in the sink, nothing on the draining board, and a potted plant on the windowsill was wilting and clearly hadn't been watered for days.

McKechnie bent down and examined the lock on the kitchen door. 'Mortice,' he said.

'Part of your training, I thought,' said Denham, walking up behind him.

'It is,' said McKechnie, straightening up. He looked around the garden. 'But mortice locks are buggers without the right equipment.'

'And you haven't . . .'

'Afraid not. I wasn't planning on any breaking and entering.'

Denham looked up at the top floor of the building. 'I didn't see any alarm at the front, did you?'

'No point, this far away from the neighbours. And the nearest cops must be in Thurso.' He went over to a tool-shed and examined the padlock on its door. 'This is more like it,' he said. He knelt down, took a small leather wallet from the pocket of his sheepskin jacket and worked on the lock with two small strips of metal. He had it open within thirty seconds and pulled open the door. He went inside and reappeared with a large spade. He grinned at Denham as he went over to the sash window and inserted the end of the blade into the gap between the window and the frame. He pushed down on the handle of the spade with all his weight and the window lock splintered.

'You learnt that with Five?' asked Denham wryly.

'Misspent youth,' said McKechnie, leaning the spade against the wall and pushing the window open. 'Boarding school mainly.' He put a foot against the spade handle and heaved himself into the kitchen, head first. Denham was just about to follow when McKechnie called out that the key was on the inside of the door. A few seconds later the kitchen light flickered on, the door opened and McKechnie waved Denham inside. They went through to a wood-panelled hallway. There was an untidy pile of mail in front of the letterbox.

'You check the bedrooms,' said Denham. He pushed open a door as McKechnie went upstairs and flicked on the light. It was a study – floor-to-ceiling bookshelves lined one wall; the others were wood-panelled with several framed prints of hunting dogs. The furniture was sturdy and worn, comfortable leather chairs with sagging cushions and a large desk with a brass reading lamp. Denham sat down at the desk and pulled open the top drawer. It was filled with papers and Denham took them out. He flicked through them. The most recent was three months ago, a letter from a bank to Geraghty, asking him to telephone the manager about his overdraft. There were several bank statements, three different banks in all, and they were all in the red. Several thousand pounds in the red.

He found a brochure advertising Geraghty's company complete with glossy photographs of smiling executives climbing, abseiling, canoeing and sailing. There was a photograph of a man in his fifties, grey-haired and tough-looking with a nose that had obviously been broken several times. It was Micky Geraghty. Denham pulled the drawer all the way out. At the back was an Irish passport. Inside was a photograph of a slightly younger Geraghty. Denham riffled through the pages of the passport and found two entry stamps for the United States, both from the early nineties. There was a visa for Australia for the previous year. According to the stamps on the opposite page, Geraghty had spent three months there.

He found a diary in the second drawer of the desk, a big leather-bound volume, with each week running across two pages. Geraghty had used it to record the courses he ran. The last entry was for five months earlier. Two entries before that had been crossed out. From the looks of the diary, business hadn't been good for a long time. Underneath the diary were several letters from companies cancelling their courses, most of them blaming the recession.

Denham could hear McKechnie moving around from room to room upstairs. He pulled open the third drawer. It was full of letters and photographs. Letters from Geraghty's daughter, and photographs of a young woman with a man and two small children. Denham flicked through the letters. Kerry Geraghty had moved to Australia and was now living in Brisbane with her husband. She was pretty, with long chestnut hair and laughing blue eyes.

McKechnie came downstairs and Denham heard him picking up the mail by the front door. Denham twisted around in the chair to look at him as he walked into the study.

'I thought you said the daughter helped him run this place?'

'That's what the file says.'

'She emigrated. A couple of years back by the look of it.'

McKechnie looked pained. 'What can I say? The file's obviously out of date. I guess the Geraghtys weren't considered a high priority.' He dropped the letters on the desk. 'Mail's been piling up for three months,' he said. 'No empty hangers in the wardrobes, toothbrush is in the bathroom, and there's an empty suitcase in the boxroom.'

Denham held up the passport. McKechnie exhaled through pursed lips. 'What do you think?'

'I think we should give the house a good going over. Just in case. Top to bottom. The works.' He pushed himself up out of the chair. At the kitchen end of the hall was a door under the stairs, and Denham tried to open it. It was locked. He turned to look at McKechnie. 'Think your misspent youth can deal with this?'

McKechnie grinned and knelt down by the lock. 'Piece of cake,' he said. He went back outside and returned with the spade, inserted it into the side of the door and pushed against the handle with all his weight. The wood splintered and McKechnie pulled back the door and leant the spade against the wall.

Denham wrinkled his nose. A sickly-sweet smell wafted up from the basement below. He took a handkerchief from his trouser pocket and held it to his face as he groped along the wall for a light switch. He found it and flicked it on. The smell hit McKechnie and he grunted. He went through to the kitchen, took a towel and held it under a running tap for a few seconds before holding it over his mouth and nose and following Denham down into the basement.

It had a concrete floor and white plastered walls. Along the wall opposite the stairs were shelves lined with climbing equipment, boating gear and camping supplies. A canoe lay upturned on two wooden blocks, a jagged hole in its bottom. In the far corner was a metal trunk. The two men looked at the trunk. Denham went over to it and opened it. The smell was a hundred times worse, and Denham turned his head away, gagging. McKechnie joined him and looked down into the trunk. The body had been wrapped in black garbage bags and had been bent at the waist so that it would fit. A bare foot protruded from one end of the bundle, black and putrescent, the yellowed nails barely hanging on to the flesh.

'Shit,' said McKechnie, his voice muffled by the wet towel.

'Yeah,' said Denham.

McKechnie went over to the shelving, rummaged through a pile of climbing gear and came back with a piton. He stuck the pointed end into the plastic and ripped a jagged hole in it. He stepped back and pressed the towel harder against his face. 'Jesus Christ,' he said.

Denham took a couple of steps back. The stench was overpowering, like meat that had gone bad but much, much worse. It had been a long time since he had been confronted by a corpse, but the smell of rotting flesh was something he'd never forget. He moved towards the trunk again, holding his breath. McKechnie pushed the plastic to the side with the piton, revealing what was left of the face. The flesh had blown up to the size of a football, the skin bluish-green and split in places, the eyes milky and staring. The hair was grey and spiky, the only feature that had anything in common with the photographs he'd seen of Micky Geraghty.

'What do you think?' asked McKechnie.

'Hard to tell,' said Denham. 'But yes, I'd say it's him.' He motioned at the body. 'Take the rest off. Let's see what killed him.'

McKechnie used the piton to tear away the black plastic.

The corpse was wearing a denim shirt and corduroy trousers. No shoes or socks. There were two holes in the shirt, and the material was stained with dried blood. McKechnie tore the plastic away from the corpse's left hand. The little finger and the one next to it had been chopped off. McKechnie grimaced.

'So now we know,' said Denham. He reached over and closed the trunk. 'You tidy up here, Harry. I'll phone Patsy with the bad news.'

Andy was pouring herself a cup of water from the cooler when Green-eyes called her name from the door to the meeting room. She took the paper cup with her. Green-eyes was wearing a white sweat-shirt with the sleeves pulled up above her elbows, black ski pants and the ever-present ski mask. On the long table was a black briefcase and a Marks and Spencer carrier bag that Green-eyes had brought with her earlier in the day, when she'd been wearing a pale blue suit. She was holding a videocassette. 'This arrived,' she said, slotting it into the video recorder and switching on the television.

The picture flickered with static, then steadied. It was Katie. It was a short message, barely twenty seconds long, just saying that she was okay and that she wanted to be back home with her mummy and dad. She looked close to tears, and Andy put her hand up to her mouth as she watched. Katie looked much more scared than she'd appeared in the previous video. Her lower lip was quivering and her voice was shaking. 'It's Monday and I want to go home,' she said. The recording ended and the screen was filled with grey static again.

'She's terrified,' said Andy, staring at the static. 'How can you do that to a seven-year-old girl?'

'She's fine,' said Green-eyes. 'That's all you've got to worry about.' She pulled the black briefcase towards her and clicked the locks open.

Andy was still staring at the blank television screen. 'I want to speak to her.'

'You've just seen that she's okay,' said Green-eyes.

Andy turned to face her. 'She said it was Monday. Yesterday. But how do I know it was filmed then? You could have done it last week.'

'For Christ's sake, Andrea. Next time we'll have a copy of that day's paper in the shot, okay? Now come over here.' She turned the open briefcase so that Andy could see the contents. There were four oblong slabs of what looked like bright yellow marzipan, covered in thick, clear plastic. Under the plastic on each block was a white paper label with a black border containing the words EXPLOSIVE PLASTIC SEMTEX-H in capital letters.

Green-eyes took the four blocks out of the briefcase. Underneath were more blocks. Each was about nine by twelve inches, and an inch thick. In all, the briefcase contained sixteen blocks of Semtex.

'Where the hell did you get this from?'

'That's for me to know, Andrea.' She opened the Marks and Spencer carrier bag and took out two bread rolls as Andy examined the explosive. Green-eyes broke one of the rolls in half. Inside were four silver metal tubes, each about three inches long and the thickness of a pencil, with one end crimped around two white wires that had been coiled together. She laid the four tubes on the table, put the remains of the roll in the bag and then crumbled the second one apart. It contained four more tubes.

Andrea picked one of them up. It was a Mark 4 electrical detonator, the type she'd used when she made bombs for the IRA, a lifetime ago. Her hand began to shake, and she put the detonator down on the table. Up until she'd seen the Semtex and the detonators she'd half hoped that Green-eyes wasn't serious about building the bomb. Without the prop-er detonators and initiator, the fertiliser–aluminium mixture was practically inert, and Andy had been clinging to the possibility that the bomb was being built merely as a threat, in the way that she'd often set bombs in Northern Ireland to tie up the security forces rather than to kill and maim. The contents of the briefcase and the bag brought it home to her that she was building a device that was going to be used.

'They're okay?' Green-eyes asked.

Andy nodded.

'You have to build a bomb for us to use tomorrow. A small one.'

Andy's jaw dropped. 'What?'

'Tomorrow. A small bomb. A test.'

'How small?'

'Big enough to blow up a car, say.'

'Why?'

'You don't have to worry about why, Andrea.'

'Is it to kill someone?'

Green-eyes ignored the question. She went over to the video recorder and popped out the cassette. She held it under Andy's nose for a few seconds, then tossed it into the wastepaper basket.

'Tomorrow. And God help you if it doesn't work. Now get to it.'

DAY EIGHT

Patsy Ellis was sitting at the desk looking over a computer print-out when Liam Denham walked in. 'Good morning, Liam. Sleep well?'

Denham grunted. He'd arrived back in London in the early hours and had spent the rest of the night on a couch in an office on the floor above. Before catching a few hours' sleep he'd telephoned his wife and told her not to expect him home for several days. She'd accepted the news without complaint, though she'd made him promise to keep his cigarette intake to below one packet a day.

One of the three telephones on Patsy's desk rang and she picked up the receiver. She tapped her index finger against her lips as she listened. 'How do you spell that?' she said, picking up a pen and making a note on a pad in front of her. She stood up and banged down the phone. 'Briefing room,' she said. 'We've identified the driver.'

Denham heaved himself up out of his chair and followed her down the corridor. On the way she knocked on several doors and shouted that she wanted everyone in the briefing room. By the time she reached the door there were more than a dozen men and women following in her wake, like chicks in pursuit of a mother hen.

Patsy went over to the whiteboard on which were stuck the photographs of the members of Andrea's active service unit. 'Right, thanks to Chief Inspector Denham we now know who gave up Trevor. An IRA sniper, Micky Geraghty. Someone tortured and killed him several weeks ago, presumably for information about Trevor.'

She paused, then tapped the photograph taken from the video of the van leaving the Covent Garden carpark. 'Now, this where it gets really interesting. We've identified the driver of the van. One Mark Graham Quinn. An IC1 male, twenty four-year-old career criminal who has so far avoided prison but has been arrested several times on armed robbery charges. He's always walked, usually because witnesses have a habit of retracting confessions before he's due to appear in court. His prints match those on one of the parking receipts at the multistorey carpark in Covent Garden, and our technical boys have a decent match between the video pictures and photographs on file with the Met. Quinn's our boy. His police file will be with us within the hour. We still don't know who the passenger is, but computer enhancement has shown a tattoo on his left forearm. A lion leaping over a cross of St George.'

There were murmurs of surprise from her audience, and she waited for them to die down before continuing. She folded her arms across her chest. 'So what we have is a career criminal working with what we can assume is a Protestant extremist. They've kidnapped a former IRA bombmaker.' She raised an eyebrow. 'Quite a mix, I'd say. Lisa, any news about the landscaping company?'

Lisa Davies shook her head. 'Peter's spoken to them and the van isn't theirs. The details on the registration form match and the livery is the same, but it's not their van. He's been over their books and says that they're totally legit. He's working through a list of former employees, but he doesn't hold out much hope. It looks as if they've just set up an imitation. On the van itself, no parking tickets or speeding tickets. We're still checking with the ferry companies, and we're running separate checks with individual police forces to see if it's been involved in any accidents.'

'Okay, keep on top of it. And everyone start putting feelers out on Quinn. Any sniff of him and let David Bingham know immediately. But tread carefully. And if anyone has any thoughts on who might be sporting a lion and flag of St George tattoo, let David and me know straight away.'

Andy soldered the copper wire to the output from the chip in the digital alarm clock, moving her head to the side to avoid the solder fumes. Green-eyes picked up one of the detonators and began to untangle the two white wires that protruded from one end. 'I thought they'd be different colours,' she said.

Andy looked up from the clock. 'What, red and black, like in the movies?'

'I guess so, yeah.'

Andy smiled thinly. 'Doesn't make any difference which way it's connected into the circuit. So there's no need to have different colours.'

'So all that stuff about "shall I cut the black wire or the red wire" is crap?'

Andy bent over the clock again and added a touch more solder to the joint. 'I'll use different-coloured wires in the circuit, but that's purely for my benefit so that I don't make any stupid mistakes. But both wires leading to the detonator are white. Anyway, no bomb disposal man would bother cutting the wires to the detonator. There's no point – all he'd have to do is to pull the detonator out. Besides, they'd be too wary of collapsing circuits.'

'Collapsing circuits? What are they?'

'It's a live circuit with some sort of a relay in it. When the circuit is cut, the relay closes, which in turn activates another circuit, the one containing the detonator. So cutting the wire actually activates the bomb.' Green-eyes continued to unravel the wires. Andy saw what she was doing and gestured with her chin. 'Don't separate the wires,' she warned.

Green-eyes stopped what she was doing. 'What's the problem? It's not connected.'

'Yeah, but they can go off all the same if there's any electrical interference. You can get a spark jumping between the two wires and it'll go off. You'd lose a hand.'

Green-eyes winced and put the detonator back down on the table. 'It's called the Faraday effect,' said Andy, adjusting the timer and setting the alarm. 'You want this set for five minutes, you said?'

'That's right.'

'That's not long.'

'That's what he said. Five minutes.'

Andy checked the digital read-out. Three hundred seconds. She showed it to Green-eyes, then showed her which buttons to press to start the timer. She set the clock on the table and they watched it count off the seconds.

'It's the Faraday effect that's responsible for a lot of bombs going off prematurely. Anything that sends off radio frequencies can do it. Police radios, televisions being turned on and off, even household equipment like fridges and stereos.' Andy realised she was talking too quickly, but she wanted to keep Green-eyes distracted so she wouldn't realise that she'd slipped up. There was someone telling her what to do. Someone who'd told her to set the timer for five minutes.

'There was a volunteer killed a while back, in Aldwych, remember? The bomb he was carrying went off on a bus.'

Green-eyes nodded. 'I remember.'

'The papers said it was because a guy with stereo headphones sat next to him. Turned up the sound, and bang. Blew them all to bits. That's the Faraday effect.'

'Dangerous business,' said Green-eyes.

Andy wondered whether the woman was joking, but the ski mask made it impossible to tell. The Wrestler and the Runner walked into the main office area, chewing on Marks and Spencer sandwiches and laughing.

'It's okay so long as you know what you're doing,' said Andy. She realised that the soldering iron was still on, and she pulled the plug out from the wall. 'This bomb, the small one. It's just a test, right?'

'We want to make sure that the stuff will explode,' said Green-eyes.

'What, you think I'd try to trick you? You think I'd risk my daughter?'

'We just want to be sure, Andrea. A dry run. If you've done your job properly, you've nothing to worry about.'

'Where are you going to set it off?'

'Why?'

'I just wondered.'

'Wondered what? If we're going to kill someone with it?'

Andy nodded.

'We're not, Andrea. Like I said, it's a dry run.' She nodded at the circuit. The digital read-out was still ticking off the seconds. 'If someone was going to defuse this, all they'd have to do is pull the detonator out of the explosive, is that what you said?'

'Sure. If the detonator goes off, it's a relatively small bang. It'd blow your hand off, but not much more. It has to be in the high explosive to set off the bomb.'

'So they're easy to defuse?'

'In theory. But they've got to get to the fuse first. So you hide it inside the bomb. With booby traps around it. Motion detectors, mercury tilt switches, photoelectric cells. Fake circuits. That way, they can't look for the fuse. Not easily, anyway. Also, they won't know if it's on a timer or if it's going to be detonated by remote wire or radio. But an expert can always take a bomb apart. If he has enough time.'

They watched as the digital read-out counted down to zero. The flashlight bulb winked on. 'Bang!' whispered Green-eyes, her eyes burning with fanaticism.

Liam Denham wandered into the briefing room. There were two dozen agents in the room, talking into phones or tapping on computer keyboards. He smiled to himself. It was the new face of intelligence work, a face he doubted he'd ever have been able to embrace even if he'd remained in the job. Intelligence-gathering had become an office job, a job done by suits, by graduates who drank Perrier and played squash every lunch-time. But to Denham, intelligence meant people. It meant persuading people to part with information and that involved face-to-face contact. It might mean meeting them in a pub and talking over a few drinks, it might mean getting a bit physical in a locked room, or handing over an envelope packed with cash, but whatever the means, it was all down to people.

Denham took a long drag on his cigarette and blew smoke up to the ceiling, dangerously close to a smoke detector. One of the agents, a man in his twenties with red-framed spectacles and swept-back blond hair, coughed pointedly. Denham held the cigarette behind his back and walked over to where Patsy was sitting at a desk, deep in conversation with Lisa Davies. She looked up, her face flushed with excitement.

'Liam. I think we've got a lead on the van they took Andrea away in. The Transit. It's made more than half a dozen trips into the City over the past two months. The last one three days ago.'

Lisa handed Denham a computer print-out. It was a list of dates and times. The first date was about a week before

Katie had been kidnapped. At the top of the print-out was a description of the van and its registration number.

'City of London police,' said Patsy in answer to Denham's unspoken question. 'They record all vehicles entering and leaving the centre.'

'The Ring of Steel?' That was what the press had christened the security arrangements that effectively sealed off the financial district from the rest of the capital.

'I think we can assume that London's the target now,' said Patsy.

Denham handed the print-out back to Lisa. 'What next?' he asked.

'We're going to have to inform the City of London police and the Met. They can start looking for the van. But until we know exactly where the bomb is, there's not much else we can do. There're millions of square feet of office space in the City – we can hardly search it all. Not without tipping the terrorists off that we're on to them.'

Lisa's brow furrowed into deep creases. 'Shouldn't we be warning people, giving them the chance to stay out of the City?'

Patsy stood up, shaking her head. 'Absolutely not. There'd be an uncontrollable panic. The City would grind to a halt. Billions of pounds would be lost.'

'Maybe that's what they want,' mused Denham.

'What do you mean?' asked Patsy.

'Maybe that's what all this is about. Maybe it's financial and not political.'

Patsy pulled a face. 'Extortion, you mean?'

'If it was political, there are easier places to stage a spectacular.'

'That's assuming it is a spectacular, Liam.'

'Six trips? They must be using the van to transport equipment. Six trips is a lot of equipment, so I think it's fair to assume it's going to be a big one. They wouldn't go to all this trouble to build a few letter bombs, would they?'

'That's what you think? They're building the bomb on-site?'

Denham took another drag on his cigarette, ignoring the look of annoyance that flashed across Carter's face. She was less than half his age, and Denham figured he'd earned the right to smoke. 'Why else?'

'They could have been dry runs. I wouldn't want to rule anything out at this stage.'

Denham nodded at the print-out. 'They stayed in the City overnight once. They must have been parked up. Doubt they'd do that if it was a rehearsal.'

Patsy considered what Denham had said and then nodded slowly. 'So, it's a big bomb, but you think it's not political? The IRA bombed the Baltic Exchange and Bishopsgate. And remember Harrods?'

Denham looked around for an ashtray. There wasn't one within reach so he held his cigarette vertically so as not to spill ash on to the carpet. 'That was before the increased security. I don't know. Maybe you're right. At this stage we shouldn't be ruling anything out.'

Patsy looked at her wristwatch. 'Hetherington's going to be here in a few minutes. I'd better brief him.'

'One thing before you rush off,' said Denham. 'The wee girl?'

'What about her?'

'What are we doing to find her?'

Patsy looked uncomfortable, and Denham realised he'd touched a nerve. 'There's not a lot we can do from here,' she said.

'What about the Garda Siochana? Couldn't they be looking?'

Patsy put a hand on Denham's arm and guided him away from Carter's desk. She took him over to a relatively quiet corner of the room. 'Liam, we can't be making waves over there. If the kidnappers know we're on to them, first of all they might kill the girl, and secondly it'll tip off the bomb-makers that we know what they're up to.'

'Maybe not,' said Denham. 'They don't know that we know about Andrea's past. There's no reason that the Garda couldn't be investigating a straightforward kidnapping.'

'But if the men building the bomb realise we're looking for the girl, they'll hardly allow Andrea to telephone her. Or her husband.'

The cigarette in Denham's hand had burnt down to the filter. He looked around for somewhere to put it and spotted a half-empty plastic coffee cup. He dropped the butt in the cup, then turned back to Patsy. 'We've got to do something, Patsy. We can't just abandon the wee girl.'

'Priorities, Liam. We neutralise the bomb. We take the participants into custody. Then we get the girl back. It has to be done in that order.'

Denham sighed mournfully. 'Aye, you might be right.' 'How's the husband?'

'He's bearing up. God knows how, considering what he's going through.'

'And McCormack. Have you heard from McCormack?'

'Not yet. I'll give him a call.'

Patsy looked at her watch again. 'I've got to go, Liam. I'll talk to you later, okay?'

Denham watched her walk away. She was right, of course. The bomb took precedence over Katie. But knowing the decision was a logical one didn't make it any easier to accept. Denham had lost a child, a long, long time ago, and the pain was something he wouldn't wish on anyone. He lit another cigarette, then went in search of an empty office from where he could phone McCormack.

He had written McCormack's number in the small black notebook that he always carried with him, even after he'd left Special Branch. It rang out for more than a minute before the IRA man answered, and when he did he sounded out of breath. 'Ah, it's you, Liam. I might have guessed.'

'Are you okay, Thomas?'

'I was in the bath, having a soak. I'm standing here dripping water all over the hall carpet, and if my wife catches me we'll both be in trouble.'

'Do you want to dry off? I'll wait.'

'No need, this won't take long. It's names you're ringing for, I suppose.' McCormack laughed softly. 'Right turn of events this, isn't it?'

'The way of the world, Thomas. The new order. Did you come up with anyone?'

'I've one name. George McEvoy. Do you know him?'

'I know of him. Did twelve in Long Kesh, didn't he?'

'That's him. He was with the Civil Administration Team. Lives in Dundalk with his brother, but he hasn't been seen for a while.'

'How long a while?'

'A month. His brother doesn't know where he is, but George told him he'd be away for a few weeks.'

'Has he had experience in bomb-making?'

There was a long silence from McCormack, then a faint whistling sound, as if he were exhaling through clenched teeth. 'Jesus, Chief Inspector, you're not asking for much, are you?'

'I need to know, Thomas. We think they're in London. I think they're planning a spectacular.'

'Well, McEvoy wouldn't be the man for that. He was never technical.'

'Never attached to the England Department?'

'Definitely not. To the best of my knowledge, he's never even been across the water.'

'What was he doing with the CAT?'

'What do you think? He wasn't handing out brownie points, that's for sure.'

'Punishment beatings? Knee-cappings?'

'That's what CAT does.'

'Kidnappings?'

There was another pause, shorter this time. 'I see what you mean. Yes, he could be the one who's got the little girl.'

'Do you have any idea where he might be?'

'No. I'm afraid not, Liam. He's disappeared.'

'Can you give me his address? I'll run a check on his credit cards, just in case.'

McCormack gave Denham the address and he wrote it down in his notebook. 'Anyone else gone missing?' he asked.

'No one obvious. There's a limit to what I can find out, though. Some of the ASUs are still active – they're underground and impossible to check on. Not without questions being asked, questions that I'd find bloody difficult to answer.'

'Are you telling me you've got ASUs in the UK, still active?'

'And I suppose you've pulled all your agents out, have you?'

'I don't have agents any more, Thomas. I'm retired.'

'Special Branch, then. MI5. SAS. 14th Int. They're all still on the ground, North and South, so why would you expect the England Department to stand down?'

'And there's no way of accounting for them?'

'Not without going through the Army Council, no. But I can tell you that there's no way the England Department is involved in any sort of spectacular. I give you my word on that.'

'Not even in a freelance capacity?'

'That wouldn't be a possibility. Not in a million years. Did you talk to Micky Geraghty?'

This time it was Denham who hesitated. McCormack picked up on it immediately.

'What's wrong?'

'He's dead, Thomas. Murdered. Someone tortured him, presumably to get information on Andrea Sheridan.'

'Shit,' said McCormack quietly. 'He was a good 'un.'

Denham said nothing. Geraghty had been an IRA volunteer, a sniper with a good number of kills to his credit. While he took no pleasure in the man's death, he wasn't about to grieve for him.

'Who's going to be handling the arrangements?' McCormack asked.

Denham explained that they'd had to leave the body where they'd found it, in the basement of the farmhouse. 'There isn't going to be a funeral, at least not until we've got this sorted out,' he said.

'Do me a favour,' said McCormack. 'Call me when it's over. I'll take care of it.'

Denham promised that he would. The IRA would probably give Geraghty a full military funeral, a tricolour draped over the coffin and men in ski masks firing a volley of shots into the air. It would be a celebration of the man's career with the terrorist organisation, but Denham knew it would be churlish not to agree to McCormack's request. He stabbed the remains of his cigarette into a metal ashtray next to the phone, and immediately felt the craving to light up another one. He decided to call his wife instead.

The door to Jason Hetherington's office was ajar, but Patsy still knocked before entering. He was sitting behind his desk, reading a file, an antique pair of pince-nez glasses perched on the end of his nose. The glasses were an affectation, as was the ever-present white rose in his buttonhole, grown in his own Sussex garden. He looked up as Patsy walked in and gave her a broad smile. He was wearing a dark blue Savile Row suit with the faintest of pin-stripes, a crisp white shirt and a Garrick Club tie. 'Patsy, my dear, thanks for dropping by.' Hetherington was Deputy Director-General (Operational), second only to MI5's Director-General. He was responsible for all the agency's operational activities, from counter-subversion and counter-espionage to intelligence-gathering, and had been Patsy's mentor for the past ten years. It was his decision to send her to Belfast to head up the Irish Counter-Terrorism section, with the promise that in the near future she'd be brought back to Thames House as his number two. 'Any news?'

'It's definitely London,' she said, dropping into one of the chairs opposite Hetherington's desk.

Hetherington took off his spectacles and placed them carefully on top of the file he'd been studying. 'Ah, that's not good.'

Patsy smiled at the understatement. 'A van they've been using has been in and out of the City.'

'And your recommended course of action?'

'We look for the van, obviously. We'll liaise with the local police, but we won't be telling them why we want the van. And we're looking for Quinn.'

'The blagger?' The slang sounded strange in Hetherington's upper-crust accent. It was another affectation of his, as if he were keen to show that despite his Eton and Oxford background he was still one of the boys.

'Again, we'll use the local police, but without saying why he's wanted. They're being told not to approach him if he's spotted.'

'Do we have any other names in the frame?'

'Just Mark Quinn. We're assuming that the device is being constructed somewhere in the City, so we're working through all new leases taken on within the past six months, cross-referencing with company records and VAT data, looking for companies with no track record. We'll follow up with visits.'

Hetherington shifted uncomfortably in his seat. 'That could take for ever.'

'It's an outside chance considering the possible time-frame, but long shots sometimes pay off.'

'And the telephone surveillance is in place?'

'GCHQ are on-line and BT and Telecom Eireann are co-operating fully.'

'Another long shot?'

Patsy looked pained. Hetherington wasn't being critical – he was one of the most supportive bosses Patsy had ever worked for – but she was all too well aware of how little they had to go on. Two long shots and a needle in a haystack.

'She's called her husband once,' said Patsy. 'We believe she'll try again.'

'The attempt on his life worries me, Patsy. I don't see any logic in it.'

'The house was bugged,' said Patsy. 'We discovered one on the phone when our people went in to switch off the answering machine. We swept it from top to bottom and found others.'

'So even without visual surveillance, they'd know that the police were involved.'

Patsy nodded. 'They'd know that he'd been taken into the Garda station. I suppose they were moving to limit the damage.'

Hetherington nodded. 'Very well. But doesn't that make it more likely that they won't let her telephone her husband? Knowing that he's fled the house?'

'They might assume that all she'll get is the machine.'

Hethrington grimaced, as if he had a bad taste in his mouth.

'I know, shots don't come any longer. But if they think he's not at home, it'll reassure her to leave a message for him, at no risk to the kidnappers.' Hetherington still didn't look convinced, and Patsy didn't blame him. She spoke quickly, not giving him the chance to interrupt. 'A stronger possibility is that she'll be able to get to a phone of her own accord. Call her husband without them knowing. Having said that, I do feel it's more likely that it's her daughter she'll try to make contact with. And the kidnappers have no reason not to allow her to speak to her daughter.'

'Unless she's already dead.' Hetherington toyed with his wedding ring and leaned back in his chair, his brow furrowed as he considered their options. They sat in silence for a while. 'Possible targets?' he said eventually.

'If it's political, it could be anything from the Stock Exchange to the Bank of England. Mansion House. Another go at the Baltic Exchange. If it's a high profile they want, they could be targeting the NatWest Tower or Lloyd's of London.'

'So can we at least increase security there?'

'I'm reluctant to inform the local police, Jason. At the moment, possibly fifty people know of this threat, and almost all of them work for us. If we bring in the Met and the City of London police, we're talking about hundreds of people. Thousands.'

Hetherington steepled his fingers under his chin. 'They could search a lot faster.'

'Except the act of searching might well precipitate events. Plus, there'd be leakage. All it takes is one copper warning his wife to stay out of the City for a while. She mentions it to a friend, the friend gets on to the press, and we're splashed all over the front page of the *Sun*.'

'A D-notice would put paid to that.'

'Word would still get around. I'd rather keep it in-house for as long as possible. But I take your point about increasing security at the more obvious targets. Most buildings employ their own security. I can have a quiet word.'

'I'd like a list,' said Hetherington. 'What about possible American targets?'

'There are no US government buildings within the

security cordon. But there are plenty of American financial institutions.'

'Is there anything we can do there to increase security?'

Patsy nodded thoughtfully. 'I'll draw up a list,' she said.

'And we're still not issuing a formal warning to the Americans?'

'We've no reason to think that the target's American. And they do have a tendency to overreact.'

Hetherington chuckled dryly. 'Yes, I suppose they do. But if you get so much as an inkling that this venture is aimed at the Americans, I have to know *tout de suite*.'

Another affectation. Hetherington liked to throw the odd French phrase into his conversations, especially when he was under pressure.

'Are you sure that GCHQ won't inform the Americans? Echelon being under the NSA's wing, as it were.'

'We're using our own dictionary and GCHQ's K Division is handling the traffic. We should be able to keep the NSA at arm's length. For a while, at least.'

'Right,' said Hetherington, leaning forward again. 'The JIC meets tomorrow. I'm going to need a full report before last thing tonight.'

'It'll be on your desk by five,' promised Patsy.

She knew there was no point in asking her boss to hold off informing the Joint Intelligence Committee. The committee met every week in the Cabinet Office, and in theory the entire British intelligence community was answerable to it – MI5, MI6, GCHQ and the Defence Intelligence Service. The chairman reported directly to the Cabinet Secretary and therefore to the Prime Minister. The fact that GCHQ had already been asked for assistance effectively forced Hetherington's hand. He'd have to notify JIC of the bomb threat at the first available opportunity in case the committee heard it first from GCHQ.

'I think it's time to call Hereford,' said Patsy. 'When we

are ready to move we're going to have to move fast. They have a Special Projects Team on stand-by at the Regent's Park barracks, but I was thinking of requesting another sixteen-man troop from Counter Revolutionary Warfare Wing. We can have them on stand-by here.'

Hetherington nodded thoughtfully. 'Agreed. What about DII?'

'I'd rather keep Met involvement to a minimum,' said Patsy. 'CRW has sniper specialists, too. And if the troopers go in, I think they'd prefer to have their own snipers backing them up.'

'Do we inform C13?' C13 was Scotland Yard's anti-terrorist branch.

'Again, I think not. I really would prefer to keep it in-house until the last possible moment. Once we do have a location, C13 and the Yard's Technical Support Branch could be useful, but until then I think they'll just get in the way.'

Hetherington put his spectacles on again and peered over the top of them. 'If anything goes wrong and the Met were kept out of it, the Commissioner's going to do everything he can to distance himself,' he warned. 'There could be a lot of mud flying around, and it'll be heading in our direction. It won't be the SAS that gets the blame. It'll be you. And me.'

'I appreciate that, Jason. But the more they're involved, the greater the chance that something will go wrong. Horses for courses.'

Hetherington pursed his lips and nodded slowly. 'Very well,' he said. 'I'll try to get JIC approval for that. Spread the responsibility, as it were.'

He picked up the file he'd been reading and Patsy stood up. As she reached the door, Hetherington called her name and she turned expectantly. 'I don't want to be a nag,' he said, 'but has someone been smoking in here?'

'A visitor,' she said. 'Sorry.'

'Be so good as to ask them to keep it outside, would you? It's hard enough trying to give up without having temptation waved under my nose.' He pushed his spectacles further up his nose and smiled apologetically.

Andy made sure that her industrial respirator was snug against her face, then slid her plastic goggles down over her eyes. Green-eyes did the same, but as she was placing it over her ski mask she had trouble fitting the respirator. 'Why do we need these?' She asked.

'The aluminium,' said Andy. 'You've got to keep it out of your eyes and lungs.' They were standing next to a line of three desks, on which were containers of the dried ammonium nitrate, aluminium powder, soap powder, sawdust and cans of diesel oil.

Andy showed Green-eyes how to measure out the correct amounts of the different ingredients into a large Tupperware container, leaving about a third empty.

'What's the point of the aluminium powder? I mean, I can see that the oil helps it to burn, but what's the aluminium for?'

Andy explained as she mixed the ingredients with a wooden stirrer. 'That's not what the oil's for. The oil's to help the aluminium to stick to the ammonium nitrate. The better it's mixed, the more sensitive it is to the booster charge. It's the aluminium that makes it such a good explosive. When it oxidises in the initial explosion, it gives off huge amounts of heat. Aluminium burns like crazy. Remember those pictures of the aluminium ships that went up in the Falklands?'

Green-eyes nodded.

'That heat helps lengthen the detonation pulse, makes it much more powerful. You can use charcoal, but aluminium powder's better. Magnesium's even more effective but it's not as readily available.'

'And the sawdust and soap?'

'The soap enhances the detonation. So does the sawdust. They lower the detonation velocity, and keep the density down. The greater the density, the harder it is to get it to explode.'

They carried their Tupperware containers over to the tumble-driers and put one container in each drier.

'Ten minutes on the lowest setting should do it,' said Andy. 'It's just a way of mixing it efficiently.'

'How long will it take to do all four thousand pounds?'

Andy did a quick calculation in her head. Each load was about fifteen pounds, so with two driers they'd be able to mix just under two hundred pounds an hour.

'About twenty-four hours,' she said. 'But we can mix some by hand, too. It's just that the tumble-driers are more efficient.'

Green-eyes went over to a desk where Andy had been building the wiring circuit. 'This is ready?' she asked.

'I've tested it a dozen times with bulbs,' said Andy. 'I won't put the detonators in until the last minute.'

'Detonators? Plural?'

'It's always safer to use more than one. Sometimes they fail. In Belfast they used three. The last thing they wanted was for an unexploded device to fall into the hands of the army. Our signature would be all over it.'

'What do you mean, signature?'

'The style. The technique. Even the explosive mixture, the ratio of ingredients and the way they've been mixed. Every bombmaker has his or her own way of putting a device together, as distinctive as a fingerprint, or a signature.'

Andy looked across at Green-eyes, trying to gauge the woman's reaction. The ski mask made it impossible. Did she know about a bombmaker's signature? Did the person she was working for? There was no way of knowing without asking directly, and Andy didn't expect to be given a truthful answer. If they were forcing her to build the bomb so that it looked as if it were the work of the IRA, then they'd hardly be likely to admit it to her. Because the only way the deception would work was if Andy wasn't alive to contradict the evidence. If they truly wanted to make it look as if the IRA had carried out a major bomb outrage in the City of London, Andy would have to die.

Green-eyes straightened up. 'Show me again how we set the clock,' she said.

Andy went through the procedure, using flashlight bulbs where the detonators would be. The lights winked on as the tumble-driers finished their cycle.

Half an hour later they had fifty pounds of the explosive mixture in Tupperware containers on the desk in front of them. Green-eyes reached for a box of medical gloves and put on a pair. 'Did you wear gloves when you prepared the explosive?' she asked.

Andy shook her head. 'No. You need the sensitivity when you're doing the electrical work, and you have to be able to squeeze the explosive into the form you want it. It'd be like trying to make pastry with gloves on.'

Green-eyes nodded and put the box to one side. Earlier in the day she had gone out to buy a Samsonite hard-shell suitcase, and she lifted it on to another desk and opened it.

Andy pulled the lid off one of the containers. The mixture was the consistency of bread dough, grey in colour, and it still smelled strongly of fertiliser. She poured the mixture into the suitcase, using a wooden spatula to scrape it out of the corners of the container. She poured in two batches of the mixture, almost twenty pounds in all.

'You're going to take this away now?' Andy asked. 'Because if you're not, we should hold off until you're ready. You want to have it live for as little time as possible before detonation.'

Green-eyes looked at her wristwatch. 'As soon as it's ready, we're off.'

Andy nodded. 'Okay. But remember what I said about the Faraday effect. Stay away from electrical equipment. Radios. Mobile phones. Anything that gives off electrical radiation.' She gestured at the line of ovens and the two tumble-driers. 'We should unplug those before we make the circuit live. And I meant what I said about mobile phones. Have you ever held one near a radio? You can hear the buzz they give off every so often. It's the phone keeping in touch with the nearest transmitter. That buzz, under the right circumstances, can set the detonator off. Same with two-way radios.'

'But it's safe, right?'

Andy grimaced. 'It's a bomb. When all's said and done, it's a bomb.' She patted the suitcase. 'When this goes off, it'll kill anyone within a three-hundred-foot range. It could blow the front off a building. So safe isn't really an appropriate description, is it?'

Green-eyes took a step back, as if she had realised the destructive power of the device for the first time.

Andy smiled despite herself. 'You'd have to get a darn sight farther away than that,' she said. 'Besides, if it did go off and you were this close, you wouldn't feel a thing.' She wasn't sure if mobile phones would have any effect on the circuit – they'd been few and far between in Northern Ireland when she was building bombs for the IRA. But she wanted to make sure that Green-eyes left the phone in the briefcase and didn't take it with her when she went out.

When she'd emptied two of the containers into the suitcase, she flattened the mixture with her hands, then hollowed out a space about a foot square. The Semtex was on another desk, and Andy carried over one of the blocks and carefully unwrapped it. Green-eyes watched over her shoulder as she put it in the space she'd made in the fertiliser/aluminium mixture. She pressed it down with the flat of her hands, then lifted up the electric circuit and placed it on to the Semtex. She pushed the two Mark 4 detonators into the Semtex at an angle so that they were almost completely buried, just half an inch sticking out. She pressed the batteries slightly, so that they were stuck in the Semtex, then carefully moved the digital clock and the wires leading to it, resting them in the lid of the suitcase. She opened the remaining two Tupperware containers and scraped the rest of the fertiliser/aluminium mixture into the case. Again she used her hands to press the mixture down, kneading it to force out any trapped air. She put two empty garbage bags on top of the mixture, then laid the clock on top of them. She put another half-dozen empty bags on top of the clock to protect it when the lid was closed.

'That's it,' she said. 'All you have to do is set the clock.'

'It's live?'

'It's live but it won't go off until the timer's set.'

Green-eyes nodded slowly, staring at the suitcase. Andy closed the lid and snapped the catches shut.

'Keep it this way up. If you try to carry it by the handle, everything'll move inside.'

'It's going to look strange, carrying it like that, isn't it?'

Andy shrugged. 'That's not really my problem, is it? It has to be that way if you're going to carry it in the boot of a car.'

Green-eyes took off her gloves. 'Right, I'm going to get changed. As soon as we've taken the case out of here, you start preparing the rest of the stuff. We'll need it for tomorrow.'

'Tomorrow? You're going to do it tomorrow?'

'Just get the mixture ready,' said Green-eyes, walking towards the offices. 'All of it.'

Andy watched her go. Tomorrow? Twenty-four hours? She shivered. She had to do something to stop them. But what? What could she do that would prevent them blowing up the building, without endangering Katie?

A few minutes later, Green-eyes came out of the office. She'd changed out of her overalls and into a blue suit with a short skirt and high heels. It made the ski mask she was wearing all the more sinister. The Runner was with her. He'd also taken his overalls off and was wearing a denim jacket and jeans. Green-eyes showed him the suitcase. 'Make sure you don't tilt it,' she said.

He lifted it off the table, then put it down. 'No problem,' he said.

Green-eyes looked at her watch again. She nodded at the Wrestler. 'We'll be back this evening. Keep an eye on her.'

'Will do,' said the Wrestler, putting on a pair of gloves. He strapped his shoulder holster over his overalls, took out his gun and checked the action, ejecting the clip and slotting it back in.

Green-eyes nodded at the Runner. He lifted the suitcase with a grunt and headed towards the reception area. Green-eyes followed him.

'How much are they paying you to do this?' Andy asked the Wrestler.

He sneered at her from beneath his ski mask. 'More than enough,' he said. He slotted his gun back into its holster.

'For killing people?'

'There are plenty of people in the world,' he said, measuring aluminium powder into a Tupperware container. 'It can stand to lose a few.'

'You don't mean that,' she said.

'I read something once,' he said. 'It was on some charity handout. It said that every day something like forty thousand children die from hunger or preventable illnesses. That's children. Children who never harmed anyone. Hell, they don't get to live long enough to hurt anybody. Forty thousand a day, almost fifteen million a year.'

'That doesn't make any sense at all,' she said.

'Oh, it does, it's just that you don't understand.'

'You're doing this to help starving children?'

'No, I'm doing it for a quarter of a million pounds. But the world being as sick as it is, don't expect me to give a fuck if a few people get killed. Now get on with what you're doing. You talk too much.'

Jason Hetherington walked into the main briefing room, followed by a man in his twenties with short blond hair that looked as if it hadn't seen a comb for a while. The man had inquisitive eyes that flicked from side to side as he entered the room, taking everything in. He was wearing a brown leather jacket over a pale green sweatshirt, blue Wrangler jeans and Nike training shoes, and looked like a small-time drug dealer on the make.

'Ah, there she is,' murmured Hetherington as he spotted Patsy Ellis crouched over a computer terminal. 'Patsy, someone here I'd like you to meet.'

Patsy looked up from the computer and frowned at the new arrival. He looked totally out of place in the roomful of enthusiastic young agents, even more so because he was standing next to Hetherington and his Savile Row suit, made-to-measure starched shirt and club tie. It wasn't just the man's attire that made him stand out – his posture was so relaxed as to be bordering on insolence.

'Captain Payne,' said Hetherington. 'Special Projects Team. He and his men have just arrived from Hereford.'

Payne stuck out his hand. 'Stuart,' he said.

Patsy shook. He had a firm, dry grip, though he didn't try to impress by crushing her fingers. He smiled openly, and Patsy couldn't help but noticing that four of his top front teeth seemed to be capped – they were slightly whiter than the rest of his teeth. 'Patsy Ellis,' she said. 'Glad to have you on board, Stuart.'

'His team are in the gymnasium,' said Hetherington, adjusting his cuffs. 'Unpacking their equipment.'

'We weren't sure what to bring so we've got everything but the kitchen sink,' said Payne. He had a Geordie accent which he'd obviously made an attempt to tone down over the years.

'And I'm afraid we're still none the wiser,' said Patsy.

Hetherington motioned with his hand that they should go back to his office, and they walked along the corridor together.

'We're reasonably certain that they're in the City,' said Patsy. 'We've identified one as a career criminal, an armed robber.'

Payne frowned and scratched the back of his head. 'I thought this was an IRA operation.'

'The bombmaker's IRA. But she's working under coercion.'

Hetherington opened the door to his office and ushered the two of them in. 'Her child's been kidnapped,' he said, taking his place behind the desk. 'They're threatening to kill the child unless she co-operates. We're assuming she's building a bomb for them. A big bomb. We're pursuing several lines of enquiry and, not to be too melodramatic, the clock is ticking. As soon as anything breaks, we'll have to move quickly.'

Payne nodded thoughtfully. 'So the bomb is already in the City? It's not in some sort of vehicle?'

'We don't know,' said Patsy. 'They've been using a van, but we think they've been using it to transport equipment. If I were to make a guess, I'd say they were assembling it in a building. But we're not in the guessing business. We're not ruling anything out at this stage.'

'Okay. So basically we'll have to play it by ear? No rehearsals?'

'I'm afraid not,' said Patsy.

Payne smiled broadly and winked. 'That's what we do best,' he said.

McCracken and Quinn picked up Egan at a service station on the M1 outside Luton. He climbed into the back of the Volvo. 'Everything okay?' he asked.

McCracken nodded. 'We're on schedule,' she said. 'Tomorrow afternoon.'

'Excellent,' said Egan. He settled back in the seat as Quinn drove back on to the motorway and accelerated towards Milton Keynes.

On Egan's instructions, they kept to just below seventy miles an hour, but it still took them less than half an hour to drive to the industrial estate. Egan got out and unlocked the main door, and Quinn drove the Volvo into the factory and parked next to the Transit van. McCracken climbed out while Quinn pulled the lever to unlock the boot.

After he'd closed the metal door, Egan opened the boot and looked down at the suitcase. It always amazed him how something so innocuous could do so much damage. Five cubic feet of chemicals at most, a few pence worth of electrical components, and yet it had the capacity to completely destroy the building they were in. Bigger bombs didn't look any more threatening. The bomb that destroyed the Federal Building in Oklahoma, killing hundreds of US government officials, would have fitted comfortably into the back of the Transit. The one that had devastated the centre of Nairobi wasn't much bigger. Egan put on a pair of medical gloves.

McCracken opened the back of the Transit while Egan carefully lifted the suitcase out of the boot. He carried it over to the van and slid it along the metal floor. Quinn came up behind him. 'Shall I put the Volvo outside?' he asked.

Egan shook his head. 'Get the petrol and douse the offices, yeah?'

Quinn went over to a stack of red petrol cans and picked up two of them. McCracken watched as Egan opened the suitcase. He eased aside the plastic bags to expose the digital clock. 'Why the gloves?' she asked. 'It's all going to go up in flames anyway.'

Egan looked over his shoulder. 'They can get partial prints off anything these days, Lydia.'

'Even after an explosion?'

'Sure. Off the smallest fragment. DNA, too. A few skin cells or a piece of hair. That's why the authorities spend such a long time collecting all the residue after an explosion. They'll be all over the place once it goes off. The only prints I want them to find are the woman's.' He checked his Rolex and compared it to the digital read-out on the bomb's timer. Exact to the second. 'Right, show me what to do,' he said.

McCracken talked him through the setting of the alarm, then he pressed the button to activate it.

'Okay,' he said. 'Five minutes.' He could feel his heart pounding and he smiled to himself. Nothing had changed, not really. The bomb was the same as when he had lifted it out of the boot of the Volvo. Individually, the components were exactly as they had been all day. But his body recognised what his mind was trying to ignore. By pressing the alarm button he'd irrevocably changed the nature of the beast. Now it was live. Now it had the power of life and death. He shut the suitcase lid and closed the rear door of the van.

'Better get the Volvo out before the fumes get any worse,' he said. He pulled the chain to open the door for her. McCracken got into the car and reversed it out through the doorway.

Over by the offices, Quinn threw down the two petrol cans and went over to the stack for two more. The smell of petrol wafted over from the offices. 'All of it, Mark!' Egan called. 'We want the whole place to go up.'

He went over to help Quinn, and together they doused the offices with petrol, then McCracken poured more of the fuel along the sides of the factory. Egan looked at his watch again. A little over four minutes. Plenty of time, though he could feel the adrenaline pumping through his system. The fright, fight and flight response. But Egan was well used to suppressing his body's automatic reactions, and he calmly closed the rear doors of the Transit.

He walked over to where Quinn was slopping petrol around the corridor between the plasterboard offices. 'Nearly done,' said Quinn. Egan took his automatic out of his jacket pocket and slammed the butt against the back of Quinn's head. The man fell without a sound, and Egan deftly caught the petrol can before it hit the ground. He hefted the unconscious man over his shoulder and carried him and the half-empty can of petrol over to the Transit. He put Quinn in the driver's seat, then poured the rest of the petrol over him before looking at his Rolex again. Two minutes. Time to go.

He walked quickly across the factory area, pulled the chain down to close the metal shutter, then left by the pedestrian doorway, closing the door behind him.

McCracken was gunning the engine of the Volvo. 'You're cutting it close,' she said.

'Ninety seconds,' he said, pulling open the passenger door and climbing in. 'Anyway, we want to see if it goes up.'

She looked at him expectantly. 'Where's Mark?'

'Mark's not coming with us,' said Egan, taking off his gloves.

'What?'

Egan pointed ahead. 'Lydia, I think if we're going to discuss this, we should be doing it while we're on the move. Don't you?'

McCracken looked back at the factory unit as if reluctant to leave.

'Eighty seconds,' said Egan.

McCracken put the Volvo in gear and drove off. Egan looked around casually, checking to see if they were being observed, but the industrial estate's pavements were deserted. It wasn't a place where people walked around. Almost all the men and women who worked on the estate drove in. McCracken drove quickly out of the estate and on to the main road to Milton Keynes. The road curved back along the estate, giving them a clear view of the factory units.

'What happened back there?' said McCracken, her eyes flicking between the traffic and the industrial estate on her right.

'You said it yourself, Lydia. He was unreliable. It's almost over – we don't need to be carrying a liability. For the next stage we need Andrea's total concentration. What we don't need is her looking over her shoulder at Quinn every other minute.' He looked at his watch. 'Ten seconds. Nine. Eight. Seven. Six.'

There was a flash of light from the skylights at the top of the factory unit, followed almost immediately by a shower of debris erupting from the roof and the metal shutter being blown out of the side of the building. A second later there was a dull crump that they felt as much as heard.

Egan looked at his watch and frowned. 'Five seconds early.' He looked across at the burning building. It was already well ablaze and little remained of the roof.

The traffic was slowing around them as drivers craned their necks to get a better look at the inferno. People were pouring out of adjacent factory units and running away from the blaze. Thick plumes of black smoke were spiralling upwards. By the time the emergency services arrived, there'd be nothing left.

'And that was just fifty pounds?' asked McCracken, slowing to avoid a coach ahead of them that was barely travelling at walking pace. All the passengers had moved over to the right-hand side of the vehicle and were peering through the windows.

'Pretty impressive, huh? Andrea knows her stuff.' Egan looked across at her and smiled thinly. 'You're thinking of the damage that a four-thousand-pound bomb will do, aren't you?'

McCracken shrugged. She accelerated past the coach and switched over to the left-hand lane, where the traffic was moving faster.

'It's gonna be awesome, Lydia. Absolutely awesome.'

Martin reached out for the black phone, but pulled his hand back when Fanning gave a small shake of his head. 'I keep wanting to check that they're working,' said Martin.

'They're fine.' Fanning ran a hand through his thick blond hair. He tapped the digital tape recorder. 'This monitors the signal constantly. Any problems with the line and it'd show a red light. Relax.'

'Relax?' Martin stood up and paced around the office. Carter and Denham watched him from the sofa. 'What if she doesn't call? What if they don't let her use the phone?'

'There are other lines of enquiry, Martin,' said Carter. 'We're doing everything we can.'

Martin continued pacing. 'What if it's not enough? What if they kill her? What if we never find Katie?' He stopped and glared at the telephones as if he could force them to ring by effort of will.

Carter pushed herself up out of the sofa and went over to Martin. She was a couple of inches shorter than he was and had to tilt her chin up to maintain eye contact. 'Martin, you have to take it easy. Worrying isn't going to solve anything. When she calls, the kidnappers are going to be listening in. If they suspect you're with someone, they'll cut the connection immediately. You have to stay calm.'

The door opened and they all turned to look at Patsy Ellis. 'There's been an explosion,' she said.

'Is Andy all right?' asked Martin. He took a couple of steps towards Patsy. 'Is she? Is she okay?'

'We're not exactly sure what happened, Martin,' said Patsy. 'It wasn't here. It was in Milton Keynes.'

Martin bent over as if he'd been punched in the stomach. He struggled to speak but couldn't find any words. Milton Keynes? What the hell did that have to do with Andy?

'Sit down, Martin,' said Patsy. Carter took his arm and eased him down on to a chair.

'Are we talking about an own goal here?' asked Denham.

'We've no idea what happened,' said Patsy. 'Other than that there was an explosion on an industrial estate just outside Milton Keynes. It was a device of some sort. SOCO are there now, along with explosive officers from the anti-terrorist branch. Early reports are that there was a vehicle inside a factory unit and that it exploded. There was at least one person killed.'

Martin put his head in his hands and moaned. Carter patted the back of his neck and looked across at Patsy. Patsy shrugged, not sure what to say. She fingered the crucifix around her neck.

'Just one?' asked Denham.

'That's the information we have.'

Denham went over to Martin and sat down at the table next to him. 'That's good news, Martin. She wouldn't be on her own, not with the bomb.'

Martin lifted his head. Denham could see the hope in his eyes. 'Do you think?'

'I'm sure. If it was an accident, there would have been more killed.' He scratched the birthmark on his neck. 'And there's no reason for her to be in Milton Keynes. It's a wasteland. No terrorist is going to waste a bomb on Milton Keynes.'

Martin took a deep breath and closed his eyes. Denham looked over at Patsy and grimaced. He hoped he wasn't being too optimistic.

Andy took the Tupperware container out of the tumble-drier and placed it on the floor. She put in a new container, set the timer, then stood up and stretched. The Wrestler was mixing a fresh batch, measuring out the aluminium powder with a plastic cup. They'd done almost a quarter of the mixing, and had a line of black garbage bags, each containing about thirty pounds of explosive. The neck of each bag was tied with a metal fastener.

Andy went over to him. 'I'm going to take a break,' she said, her voice muffled by the respirator. 'I need something to drink.'

The Wrestler nodded. 'Bring me back a Coke, yeah?'

Andy went along to the office where Green-eyes had stockpiled the food and drink. She took a chicken salad roll out of the Marks and Spencer carrier bag and opened a bottle of iced tea. She listened at the door before easing it open, then padded across the corridor and into the office opposite. The briefcase was where she'd left it. Andy picked it up and carried it back into the meeting room. She put it on the table and started flicking through the combinations. She'd reached the high seven hundreds.

O'Keefe jumped as he felt a hand on his shoulder. He whirled around, his right hand reaching for his holstered gun, but instantly relaxed when he saw it was McCracken. She'd put her ski mask on, but he could still see that she was grinning at his reaction. He pulled his respirator down. 'Didn't hear you,' he said, pointing at his ear. 'The tumble-driers.'

'That's okay,' said McCracken. 'Where's Andrea?'

O'Keefe gestured with his thumb at the private offices.

'Getting a drink.' He looked over McCracken's shoulder. 'Where's Quinn?'

'Quinn's not with us any more.'

'What? He's buggered off?'

'Not exactly.' She frowned at the line of black bags. 'Is that all?'

'Come on, it's hard bloody work, this. There's only the two driers. I'm doing as much as I can by hand, but it's taking for ever.' He grinned. 'The IRA used to use cement mixers for this bit, you know? We should have tried to bring a cement mixer in, huh?'

'Yeah, sure. We've got to get this done by tomorrow or Egan's going to be on the warpath.'

'It'll be done. We could do with Quinn, though.'

'Quinn's dead.'

O'Keefe's jaw dropped. 'Dead? What the hell happened?'

'He went up with the van.'

O'Keefe put down his wooden spatula. 'McCracken, what the fuck happened?'

McCracken explained what Egan had done. And why. O'Keefe listened in silence, then rubbed his throat. 'He's a hard bastard, is Egan. You trust him?'

'He's come through with everything he promised. A third of our money in advance, this place, the Semtex.'

'Yeah, but he didn't say anything about blowing Quinn away, did he? What if he decides to get rid of the two of us the same way?'

'Quinn was a mistake.'

'Aye. But he was Egan's mistake. Remember that. Egan hired us all.'

'I'll be sure to tell him that,' said McCracken with a cold smile.

'You know what I mean, Lydia,' said O'Keefe. 'What do we really know about Egan, or what his agenda is?'

'He's a pro, and he pays. That's all we need to know.'

'Aye, that's as maybe. But watch your back, eh?'

'Maybe you could watch it for me, Don. And I'll watch yours.'

O'Keefe smirked. 'If it's all the same to you, I'll take care of my own back,' he said.

One of the tumble-driers reached the end of its cycle and O'Keefe went over to it. 'I'll get Andrea,' said McCracken. 'With Quinn out of the way, she's going to have to pull her finger out.'

Andy clicked the end tumbler of the combination lock and pushed the button. The lock clicked open. Eight-six-four. She stared at the lock, not quite believing that she'd done it. She swallowed and looked up at the door. She'd been in the office for almost ten minutes and wasn't sure how long she could stay without the Wrestler wondering what she was doing.

She set the second combination dial to zero-zero-zero and began working her way through the combinations. After several futile attempts, she had a sudden thought. She had a briefcase of her own, though she rarely used it. The combination was Katie's birthday. Nine-one-seven. The seventeenth of September. Andy had set both locks to the same number. She wondered if Green-eyes had done the same. She set the second dial to eight-six-four, said a silent prayer, and pushed the button with her thumb. It clicked open. Her heart pounded. Would the mobile phone be inside? And if it was, who would she call?

Just as she was about to open the briefcase, she heard footsteps outside. High heels, crunching softly along the carpet tiles.

Andy fumbled with the catches and snapped them shut. She slipped the briefcase under the table and stood up, wiping her sweaty palms on the legs of her jeans. The door was flung open. It was Green-eyes. 'What the hell's going on?' she asked angrily.

'What do you mean?' replied Andy, trying to sound as innocent as possible. She forced herself not to look down.

'I mean I want you out there working, not in here skiving.'

Andy picked up the chicken salad roll and waved it in front of Green-eyes. 'I've got to eat, haven't I?'

Green-eyes jerked her thumb at the door. 'You can eat out there.'

Andy stayed where she was. She looked at the video recorder, and then back at the woman. 'I've had a thought,' she said. 'About the timer.'

'That's another thing. That bomb went off early. Five seconds early. How could that happen?'

Andy pulled at her lower lip. 'The chip, I guess.' She went over to the video recorder and tapped the front where a digital clock was glowing blue. 'I was thinking, the timer in this might be a better bet. The electronics are easier to deal with. It'll be easier to set, too.'

'Have you used one before?'

'Sure.'

Green-eyes nodded thoughtfully. 'Okay. Whatever.'

'Andy unplugged the video recorder from the mains supply and then disconnected it from the television. Green-eyes held the door open for her as she carried it out.

Green-eyes looked around the room, shrugged, and followed her down the corridor.

DAY NINE

Martin looked up as Denham walked in. There were dark patches under his eyes and his hair was greasy and unkempt. He'd rolled his shirtsleeves up and loosened his collar. 'Any news?' he asked.

Denham shook his head. He looked at Carter and Fanning. They looked as tired as Martin. 'Why don't you get a bite to eat, or catch some sleep? I'll stay until you get back.'

'One of us has to be here all the time,' said Fanning.

'So toss for it,' said Denham. He smiled sympathetically at Martin. 'You should try to sleep, too.'

Denham sat down opposite him. 'The bomb in Milton Keynes. It was the van. The van we were looking for. The SOCO boys found part of the registration plate.'

Martin ran his hands through his hair. 'God. What if it was Andy?'

'I don't think it was,' said Denham.

A look of hope flashed across Martin's face. 'Why? Why do you think that?'

'She was too professional to make a mistake,' said Denham. 'She was very methodical. Cold as ice. It couldn't have gone off accidentally.'

'Maybe they wanted to kill her. Maybe they blew her up?'

Carter left the room. Denham lit a cigarette and blew smoke at the ceiling. 'If they wanted to kill her, they wouldn't use a bomb, and they wouldn't do it in Milton

307

Keynes. We're pretty sure that it was a deliberate explosion. A test, maybe. Or a way of getting rid of the van and any other evidence.'

'But there was a body.'

'It could have been anyone, Martin. They wouldn't have gone to all this trouble just for a small bomb in Milton Keynes. Whatever they're up to it has to be much bigger than that.'

Denham saw Martin staring at the packet of cigarettes and he offered him one. 'I don't smoke,' said Martin.

'Good for you,' said Denham.

'I gave up. Fifteen years ago.'

'I wish I had the willpower,' said Denham.

Martin continued to stare at the packet. 'Fuck it,' he said, reaching for a cigarette. Denham lit it for him. Martin inhaled and coughed, then took another drag. 'Fifteen years,' he said quietly. 'You married, Liam?'

Denham nodded. 'Almost thirty years. Thirty years next year.'

'What's the anniversary? Platinum? Sapphire?'

'Something like that.' Denham grinned and tapped ash into an ashtray. 'Bound to be expensive.'

'Children?'

Denham's jaw tightened. 'A daughter.' He took another long drag on his cigarette, held the smoke deep in his lungs for several seconds, then exhaled between clenched teeth. 'She died.'

'I'm sorry.'

Denham shrugged. 'It was a long time ago. Leukaemia.'

'Oh, God. I'm really sorry.'

'Yeah, she was twelve. She'd been sick for two years – in and out of the bloody hospital we were. Chemotherapy. Radiation. Seems like most of the memories I have of her she was wearing a baseball cap.' He blew smoke at the floor.

'Children shouldn't die before their parents,' said Martin quietly. 'That's not how it should be.'

Denham nodded, staring at the floor. Fanning stood up uneasily and went over to the window. Denham looked up and locked eyes with Martin.

'If anything happens to Katie . . .' Martin said.

'We'll find her,' Denham assured him.

Martin's eyes were as hard and unyielding as plate glass as he stared at Denham. 'You have to find them both, Liam. You have to get them both back. I'll die without them. If they die, I'll die too.'

Denham reached over and gripped Martin's wrist. 'It won't come to that,' he said.

Martin pulled his arm away, embarrassed by the contact. He looked as if he wanted to say more, but he just shook his head and put a hand up to his face, massaging the bridge of his nose and blinking away tears.

Carter reappeared with a tray containing two plates of salad and two bottles of water. Denham gestured at the food with his cigarette. 'Not on a diet are we, Barbara?'

She smiled without warmth and put the tray on a coffee table close to the sofa. Denham stood up. 'I'll take this outside,' he said, nodding at the cigarette. Martin looked at the burning cigarette in his own hand, took a final drag and then stabbed it into the ashtray. Carter's smile was fractionally warmer. She sat on the sofa and began to peck at her salad with a fork.

Denham flashed an encouraging smile at Martin, but he was staring at the carpet. Denham took the lift down to the ground floor and walked out of Thames House, putting on his tweed hat and pulling it down hard as he headed towards the river. He turned up the collar of his jacket against the cold wind that was whipping in from the east. Out of habit he checked over his shoulder several times, but he wasn't being followed. He walked past several call-boxes and chose one down a side street, pulling out a handful of change and dropping two one-pound coins into the slot before dialling the number in Dublin. He smiled with satisfaction as the number rang out. Denham took pride in his memory, which was as close to photographic as it was possible to get, especially where names and numbers where concerned. It had been more than a decade since he'd phoned Eamonn Hogan, yet he'd instantly been able to retrieve the number from wherever it was in his brain that it had been filed away. He smiled as he remembered how his wife had always teased him because his recall of names and numbers was virtually infallible but he could never remember where he'd left his car keys or the television remote control.

Hogan didn't answer the phone himself, but an efficient secretary with a clipped Cork accent took Denham's name, asked him to hold, and then put him through almost immediately. 'Liam, you old rascal, how's retirement?' asked Hogan.

'Not as quiet as I'd hoped,' said Denham. 'Still Chief Inspector, then?'

'Aye. Too many black marks on my record to climb the slippery pole,' said Hogan. 'But I know where enough bodies are buried for them not to get rid of me. We've reached a nice wee impasse, so I'll give it five more years and then I'll be able to spend all my time on the golf course. What about you? Still fishing?'

'When I can. Look, Eamonn, I just wanted a word in your ear. Can you talk?'

'Sure.'

'George McEvoy. Remember him?'

'Unfortunately, yes. Right nasty bastard. Did the dirty for the IRA's Civil Administration Team, right?'

'That's him. Can you do me a favour – see if he's on your patch at all?'

'Why would you think he'd be in Dublin, Liam?'

Denham wasn't sure how much he could tell Hogan. They'd worked together on several occasions when Denham had been serving with Special Branch in Belfast, but they weren't friends, they had no real history together.

'It's difficult to explain, Eamonn, without me dropping myself in it. And you, too.'

Hogan chuckled. 'I don't think there's much you could say that would blacken my reputation any more than it already is,' he said. 'Where are you? Belfast?'

'London.'

'So what's with the query about McEvoy? Doing a little private detective work on the side, are we? Sweetening the pension?'

'I doubt that I'm going to get paid for this,' said Denham. He fed another pound coin into the slot, and followed it with two fifty-pence pieces. 'The thing is, I think McEvoy might be involved in something in your neck of the woods.'

There was a pause lasting several seconds. 'This wouldn't be about the Katie Hayes girl, would it?'

Denham cursed silently.

'Well, Liam? Would it?'

'I can see why you're a detective, Eamonn. Putting two and two together and getting five.'

'It's not that big a leap of intuition,' said Hogan. 'Two of my boys were pulled off a case a day or two back. Little girl went missing with her mother. They pulled in the father and sweated him overnight but couldn't pin anything on them. They were coming to the view that it was a domestic and the wife had gone off. They let him go with a view to keeping an eye on him. Then he vanished. My boys had made a few enquiries with his bank and his accountant and it seems he'd been liquidating all his investments. Before they could take it any further, I got a call from the Taoiseach's office. I was told to lay off the Hayes case. No explanation, no please or thank you, just that the matter was being pursued at a higher level. So, was I right? Do two and two make five? Or is it six? Or is your call from London a total coincidence?'

Denham smiled despite himself. Hogan was a cunning old sod. 'You know I can't tell you, Eamonn. But you're following orders, aren't you?'

'Oh, yes, I'm being a good boy. Wouldn't want to do anything to jeopardise my pension.'

Denham slotted in a few more coins.

'I'd like to tell you more, but I honestly can't. Maybe when it's over we can chat about it over a few glasses of malt, but at the moment things are too frantic. But I would be grateful if you'd keep an eye out for McEvoy. Or any of his associates.'

'And if he does turn up?'

'Then I'd appreciate an unofficial call.' He gave Hogan the number of the mobile phone that Patsy had given him. 'That's a mobile and it's not secure,' he warned.

'They never are these days,' said Hogan. 'Okay, I'll put him on our watch list. I'll think of some excuse.'

'Anyone else appeared in Dublin you wouldn't expect?'

'Not that I know of, but now you've raised it I'll put out some feelers. Now you be careful, Liam. You're getting too old for cloak and dagger.'

Denham snorted back a laugh and hung up. As he left the call-box, he lit another cigarette. It was the last in his packet and the packet had been the second of the day. His wife wouldn't be best pleased if she found it. He put his hands in his pockets and went off in search of a newsagent.

Katie sat at the table, flicking through one of the comic books that the Nice Man had brought her. She had no idea what time it was or what day it was, but she was hungry, so she guessed it was almost lunch-time. She looked around the room. She had to find a way out. She had to escape. But how? There was only one way out of the basement and that was up the stairs and through the door. The last time she'd tried to run away she'd headed for the kitchen and that had been a mistake because the Ugly Man was there. She should have run the other way, to the front door. If she could get to the front door, then she could run away and shout for help. Someone would hear her. A policeman, maybe.

She looked up at the single light bulb hanging from the ceiling. If she tried to hide, they'd see her right away. They always switched the light on when they came down the stairs, no matter which of them it was. She needed to be able to hide in the dark and then run up the stairs before they saw her. She rolled up the comic and swished it through the air. If she could hit the light bulb, it would go out. But she was only little, she couldn't reach. She didn't think even her dad would be able to reach it.

She climbed on to the table and swung the comic at the bulb, but it was still too high. She frowned up at it. If she did break the bulb, it would be dark. There were no windows in the basement. She tutted, annoyed at herself for always thinking negatively. She had to get out, she had to get back to her mummy and dad, and if that meant being in the dark for an hour or so, it was a small price to pay.

She knelt down on the table and picked up the wooden chair she'd been sitting on. She hauled it up on to the table, set it down in the middle, and climbed up on it. It wobbled a bit, but not much. She swung the rolled-up comic and hit the bulb. It swung crazily back and forth, but it didn't go out. Katie waited until it had stopped swinging before lashing out again. This time the light winked out, though the glass didn't break.

She stood on the chair in darkness, suddenly afraid. She knelt down, almost lost her balance, and then clambered to the floor. It felt colder, as if the light had been keeping the basement warm, but she knew that was only her imagination. She groped around until she found her Garfield toy, then crawled to the bottom of the stairs, where she curled herself up into a tight ball and waited.

Andy looked up from the wires that she was soldering and wiped her forehead with her sleeve. She blew on the silvery lumps of still-hot solder, then tugged gently at the wire to check that it was firmly fixed to the digital timer's circuit board. She had to force herself to concentrate on what she was doing. Her mind kept wandering to the briefcase and to what would happen if Green-eyes discovered it.

The Wrestler was stacking the last of the black bags in the centre of the main office area. There was up to thirty pounds of the fertiliser/aluminium mixture in each bag, a total of one hundred and thirty bags in all.

Green-eyes watched as Andy added a drop more solder to the join, then blew on it again. 'This sort of timer's reliable, is it?' she asked.

Andy nodded. 'The big advantage is that it can be set up weeks in advance. The IRA used it to bring down the Grand Hotel in Brighton. Remember, when they almost got Thatcher?'

'I remember. But we won't be needing weeks.'

'How long?' asked Andy.

'Let's get it set up first, then we'll worry about the time.'

Green-eyes straightened up and looked at her watch. It was the third occasion she'd looked at her watch in the past ten minutes, and Andy had the feeling that she was waiting for somebody.

Andy soldered one of the wires leading from the digital timer to a nine-volt battery. She'd already soldered another wire to the battery terminal, and she'd connected that temporarily to a bulb-holder into which was screwed a small bulb. Three other wires also ran from the timer to three other bulb-holders, which were also connected to batteries. Andy was using red wires from the timer to the batteries, blue wires from the batteries to the bulb-holders, and brown wires from the bulb-holders back to the timer. She fiddled with the timer and all four bulbs lit up.

'Excellent,' said Green-eyes.

'Do you want me to show you how to set the timer?' asked Andy.

'No need,' said Green-eyes. 'You'll be setting it, not me.'

'And you want me to finish it now?'

Green-eyes nodded.

The briefcase full of Semtex slabs was on another table. Andy went over to it and unwrapped the blocks one by one, putting the plastic wrappers to the side. She began to work the blocks together like a pastry chef, squeezing out the air and forming the high explosive into one malleable roll. It was hard work, and her hands were soon aching. She flattened it out into a rough oblong, then picked it up and put it back in the briefcase, pressing it firmly into all the corners. It filled the case to a depth of almost three inches. It was, Andy knew, capable of producing a shock wave so devastating that it would virtually vaporise everything within a hundred feet. Beyond that, shrapnel would kill anything up to five hundred feet away. But the purpose of the Semtex wasn't to produce lethal shrapnel – it was to act as an initiator to set off the four thousand pounds of fertiliser explosive. If the Semtex was destructive on its own, combined with the home-made explosive it would be a hundred times more devastating.

Once she was satisfied with the Semtex, she carried the case over to the table where the electrical circuit was. She put it down and turned to Green-eyes. 'You're sure you want me to assemble it now?'

'Bit late for second thoughts, Andrea,' said Green-eyes.

'It's not that. But if you want me to put the detonators in the circuit, we should unplug all the electrical equipment. The big stuff, anyway. The ovens and the tumble-driers.'

Green-eyes nodded. She went over and pulled the plugs out of the wall as Andy methodically removed the bulb-holders. The four silver cylinders lay in a row by Andy's right hand, their white wires neatly coiled together.

'What about the timer?' asked Green-eyes. 'Won't you have to plug it into the mains?'

'What?'

'The clock? The video recorder needs a mains supply. Doesn't the clock?'

Andy shook her head as she began wiring the detonators into the circuit in the places where the bulb-holders had been. 'No. The voltage is stepped down to about twelve volts. I'm running it off batteries.'

Green-eyes studied the circuit that Andy was assembling. 'And you're going to use all four detonators?'

'That's what you wanted.' She uncoiled the wires from the last of the detonators and wired it into the circuit.

'But that's how many we need, right?'

Andy nodded. 'One would do the job.'

'But the more the merrier, you said.'

'They weren't my actual words,' said Andy. 'But you want more than one in case there's a failure. And the more you have, the stronger the original detonation pulse.'

'A bigger bang,' said Green-eyes, with evident satisfaction.

Andy looked up from what she was doing. 'Have you ever seen what a bomb does? The effect it has?'

Green-eyes gave Andy a withering look. 'Of course.'

'So you should know it's not a laughing matter. It's not funny. People get hurt. Legs get blown off. Children die.'

Green-eyes slammed a hand down on the table, rattling all the electrical components. 'I know what a fucking bomb does!' she shouted. 'And so do you!'

Andy realised she'd pushed the woman too far and she averted her eyes, not wanting to antagonise her any more.

Green-eyes grabbed a handful of Andy's hair and twisted it savagely. 'You're the one who's blown up children, you bitch!' she yelled.

The Wrestler stood watching them, his hands on his hips.

'I'm sorry,' said Andy, trying to push her away.

'Sorry? Sorry for what? For blowing up children? For killing soldiers? What the fuck are you sorry for?' Green-eyes slapped her across the face. Andy stared back at her, not flinching. Green-eyes drew back her hand to hit Andy again, but before she could slap her there was a loud knock at the reception door and Green-eyes tensed. She lowered her hand and looked at her wristwatch. 'Go to the office, now,' she hissed. 'Close the door and don't open it until I come and get you.'

Liam Denham was walking towards the office where Martin was being kept when he heard Patsy Ellis calling him. He went back along the corridor and found her sitting behind a desk in one of the offices.

'Your boss thrown you out on your ear, has he?' he joked as he removed his hat and unbuttoned his raincoat, but Patsy didn't return his smile.

'Come in and close the door, will you, Liam,' she said. Her voice was as flat and emotionless as her face, which Denham took as a bad sign. He closed the door and sat down on a chrome-and-leather chair facing her. The office was much smaller than Hetherington's down the corridor, with modern furniture and two paintings that appeared to be little more than dribbles of colour on pale blue canvases. The desk Patsy was sitting behind was glass and chrome, and Denham could see her legs through the transparent top. The only thing common to both offices was the computer terminal. Denham raised an eyebrow expectantly and waited for her to speak. 'What the hell did you think you were playing at?' she asked.

Denham raised both eyebrows and gave her a look of innocent bewilderment, but he knew that his goose was well and truly cooked. 'What do you mean?' he asked.

Patsy sneered at him contemptuously. 'You're too old to play the innocent with me, Liam,' she said, looking at him with cold contempt. 'K Division were on the hot line before you'd even hung up. What the hell did you think you were doing?'

'I thought I was helping,' he said.

'You were going behind my back. You were jeopardising an ongoing investigation. You've put hundreds of lives at risk, and if your pal Eamonn Hogan makes waves in Dublin you might well be responsible for the death of a seven-year-old girl.'

Denham reached inside his coat and took out his cigarettes and lighter, but she halted him with a stony look. 'No, not this time, Liam. I don't want you smoking around me. In fact, if it wasn't for your insight into Andrea Hayes, I wouldn't want you in this building.'

Denham put his cigarettes and lighter away. 'In my own defence, I would say that I didn't mention the kidnapping. I just asked him to keep an eye out for McEvoy.'

Patsy's fingers tapped on the keyboard, then she hit the 'enter' key with a flourish. Denham felt his cheeks redden as they listened to the conversation he'd had with Hogan, replayed through the computer's small but effective loudspeakers. Patsy made him listen to the entire exchange before tapping on the keyboard again. 'You even told him you were working for Five,' she said.

'Strictly speaking, Patsy, and I don't want to be pedantic, but if you listen carefully to what I actually said, I never talked about Five or the kidnapping.'

'Hogan said it. You didn't disagree.'

'For goodness' sake, what was I supposed to do? Lie to him?'

'What you were supposed to do was to concentrate on the job in hand, not phone your contacts in Dublin. If I wanted the Garda Siochana to be looking for the Hayes girl, I'd have made an approach through official channels.'

'And the only official action so far seems to have been to warn them off the investigation.'

Patsy narrowed her eyes. 'What are you getting at?'

Denham sighed. He hadn't wanted to pick a fight with Patsy Ellis, but he could feel himself being forced into a corner, and he'd never relished the role of human punchbag. 'I'm starting to feel that in the rush to apprehend the bombers, the little girl is being forgotten. That's all.'

'You're retired, Liam. You're here at my request. You're not here to direct the enquiry and you're certainly not here to criticise my performance.'

'I wasn't being critical, Patsy. That I wasn't. I was trying to help and I'm sorry if you think my attempt was misguided.'

'Misguided isn't the word that springs to mind,' said Patsy. 'I was considering reckless. Irresponsible, maybe.'

'I've apologised once, Patsy. I don't see what more I can do.'

'What's annoying me, Liam, is that you don't seem to appreciate the damage that your friend Hogan might do.'

'He'll be careful.'

'He's got more black marks on his record than I've had ladders in my tights, Liam. He's sailed so close to the wind that he's lucky to have a job, never mind a Chief Inspector's rank. If he was in the Met he'd have been out on his ear years ago.'

Denham wanted to defend Hogan, but he knew that to do so would only antagonise Patsy even more. He sat with his head down, holding his tweed hat with both hands and fingering the fly in the brim. 'You haven't got children, have you, Patsy?'

Patsy looked at him coldly. 'No, Liam, and at forty-three I doubt that I ever will. But I don't see what my lack of maternal instincts has to do with your irresponsible behaviour.'

'Somewhere in Ireland there's a little girl, scared out of her wits, a little girl who doesn't know why she's been taken away from her family, who doesn't know that she's a pawn in a bigger game. And down the corridor there's a father who's going out of his mind with worry. He doesn't know if he's ever going to see his daughter again. Hell, he doesn't even know if she's dead already, lying in a ditch somewhere with a plastic bag over her head or a bullet in her heart. When all this over, however it works out, Martin Hayes is going to want to know what we did to try to save his little girl. And just now, from where I'm sitting, it looks as if we're not doing a goddamned thing.' He raised his head and looked her squarely in the eyes. She stared back at him. 'I know there are hundreds of lives at stake, here in London. Hundreds of lives and millions of pounds. I know you have to consider the big picture. But I know what it's like to lose a child, Patsy. It's not something you're going to want on your conscience.'

Patsy continued to stare at Denham for several seconds. 'We're not going to agree on this, Liam,' she said eventually. 'I'm sorry.' She stood up. 'I'd rather you didn't leave the building again, until this is over.'

'So I'm under house arrest, is that it?'

'No. I just want you here if she does call.' She opened the door for him and he hauled himself out of the uncomfortable chrome-and-leather chair which had clearly been designed to be admired and not used. He massaged the small of his back with the knuckles of his left hand as he left the office.

'I suppose there is one good thing to have come out of your little escapade,' she said. 'We know that the GCHQ monitoring works. Your call was flagged immediately Hogan said "Katie".'

Denham nodded but didn't say anything. Patsy closed the door behind him as he walked down the corridor, reaching for his packet of cigarettes.

Andy put her ear to the door and screwed up her face as she tried to hear what was going on outside. Her cheek was still smarting from when Green-eyes had slapped her. She hadn't expected her to react so violently. She wondered if it was guilt, if the woman was finally realising the horror of what they were doing. Bombs in the abstract could be fascinating, exciting even, but at the end of the day they were inhumane weapons of destruction that brought nothing but sadness and grief in their wake.

She heard a man's voice, but through the door it was little more than a faint rumble, and she couldn't even tell if it was the Wrestler or the Runner. The Runner hadn't returned with Green-eyes from the dry run – maybe this was him coming back now.

She looked down at the burgundy briefcase. If she was going to do anything, she had to do it now. The bomb was ready. All that was left to do was set the timer and put it in the middle of the bags of explosive. Green-eyes was more than capable of doing that on her own. Andy had reached the stage where she was dispensable, which meant that they'd either release her or kill her.

She knelt down and pulled the briefcase from under the table. The combination locks were as she'd left them, both set to eight-six-four. She flicked the catches and pulled open the lid. The mobile phone was there. But so was something else, something that took her breath away. Five videocassettes, small ones that had been taken from a video camera.

* * *

Egan walked over to the pile of black garbage bags. 'All done?'

'All four thousand pounds of it,' said O'Keefe, pulling off his ski mask and rubbing his face. 'We should have asked for more money.'

'You're being well paid,' said Egan, lifting one of the bags to gauge its weight.

'What's going to happen to Quinn's share, now that he's . . . retired?'

'Retired?' laughed Egan. He was wearing a black leather jacket over a grey crew-neck pullover and black Levi jeans. He ran his eyes over the bags, counting quickly. When he was satisfied that the full complement was there, he turned to O'Keefe. 'Okay, Don. You and Lydia can split the money I was going to give to Quinn. Happy now?'

O'Keefe grinned and rubbed his gloved hands together. 'Suits me,' he said.

McCracken took off her ski mask and went over to the Semtex-filled briefcase. Egan joined her, and they looked down at the electric circuit that lay on top of the explosive. Egan cast his eyes over the tangle of wires. 'So everything's ready?' he said.

'All she has to do is push the detonators into the Semtex and set the timer. We don't actually need her for that.'

'No. She has to do it all.'

'So that her signature's on it?'

Egan looked across at her, frowning. 'Who told you about signatures?'

McCracken gestured with her chin to the office where she'd sent Andrea. 'She did.'

Egan's frown deepened. 'Not getting too close, are you?'

'Don't be stupid,' snapped McCracken. 'We were talking, that's all.'

Egan smiled amicably. 'Anyway, you're right. It's her signature that matters. It has to look like an IRA bomb, and even the slightest deviation will tip off the investigators. How's she been?'

'She's doing as she's told. What about her daughter?'

'Her daughter's fine. For the moment.'

O'Keefe came over and looked down at the Semtex. 'What happens to her? Afterwards?'

'The daughter?'

O'Keefe nodded.

'We'll let her go. This isn't about killing children.'

'And her?' O'Keefe nodded at the offices.

'Ah,' said Egan. 'That's a whole different ball-game. She has to go up with the bomb. It's not going to work if she's around to tell her story afterwards.'

'And us?' asked O'Keefe, watching Egan's face for any reaction. 'What about having us around afterwards?'

Egan grinned and put a hand on O'Keefe's shoulder. His leather jacket swung open and O'Keefe saw the butt of a gun in a shoulder holster. Unlike his own black nylon holster, Egan's was glossy brown leather that glistened under the overhead fluorescent lights.

'Don, you're as much a part of this as I am. You're hardly likely to go spilling your guts to the cops, are you? Plus, you don't exactly have an IRA pedigree, do you? I'm paying you to do a job, and providing you behave like a professional, I'll treat you like one. Might even have more work for you after this.' He patted O'Keefe gently on the cheek, then pulled a black ski mask from his jacket pocket. 'Right, final stretch. Let's get on with it.'

Andy rocked back on her heels, staring at the five small videocassettes in horror. She picked one up. There was a handwritten label stuck to one side. Friday. She picked up a second cassette. Wednesday. On the first cassette that Green-eyes had shown her, Katie had said it was Saturday. On the second cassette she'd been shown, Katie had said it was Monday. The five cassettes in the briefcase were for the rest of the days of the week. They weren't being sent over from Ireland. They'd all been done at the same time. Andy felt suddenly sick at the realisation of what that meant. There was no proof that her daughter was still alive. Worse, the kidnappers had probably killed her after filming the seven cassettes. She put the cassettes back in the briefcase with trembling hands and picked up the cellular phone.

If Katie was dead, if she was really dead, then she had nothing to lose by calling the police. She switched on the phone and its display glowed green. It was a Vodafone digital phone, a Nokia, the same model that Martin used. She began to tap out the emergency services number, but stopped on the second '9'. What if Katie was all right, what if she was panicking for nothing? What if they'd made the tapes on the same day just to make life easier for themselves?

Andy cancelled the call. She stood up, tapping the phone against her leg. They weren't going to let her live after the bomb was ready, she was sure of that. They wanted her fingerprints all over the device so that it looked as if it was the work of the Provisionals. The deception wouldn't work if Andy was around afterwards, so they'd have to kill her. She closed her eyes and took a deep breath. If they were going to kill her, what chance was there that they'd allow Katie to live? She opened her eyes and started to tap out '999' again. This time she stopped on the third '9'. What if she was wrong? If she called the police and Katie was still alive, what then? Green-eyes had made it clear that the kidnappers in Ireland were under orders to kill Katie if the London team were apprehended. Would the police be able to force Green-eyes to tell them where Katie was? She cancelled the call. It was a risk she couldn't take. The police's first concern would be the thousands of office workers in the City. They'd evacuate all the buildings in the area, there'd be sirens and roadblocks, and then they'd try to negotiate. Katie would be low down their list of priorities.

If she couldn't call the police, who then? Who could possibly help her? On the note she'd left behind the picture in her hotel room she'd told Martin to call her Special Branch handler, but he was in Northern Ireland. She wanted Liam Denham to explain to Martin who she really was, and why Katie had been taken from them. Martin deserved an explanation, and that was why she wanted her husband to talk to the policeman – it wasn't because she thought there was anything Denham could do to help her. Besides, even if she called Denham, what could he do? He'd probably call Special Branch in London but they were police, too. She needed experts, professionals. What she needed was the SAS, but she couldn't very well call up directory enquiries and ask for their number. She frowned. Maybe she could. Maybe she could call them and explain to someone what had happened. The SAS wouldn't bother with sirens and roadblocks – they'd storm the office and that would be the end of it. Except, of course, everyone would probably die. That was how the SAS worked. They went in with guns blazing, and their prime concern would be to stop the bomb going off, and the best way of doing that would be to kill everyone in the vicinity. And if Green-eyes and her companions were killed, who'd be able to tell them where Katie was being held?

Andy glared at the phone in her hand as if it were responsible for her predicament. She was in an impossible position. If she did nothing, she would almost certainly be killed. But if she called for help, her daughter would die. It wasn't a decision that anyone should be forced to make, and it wasn't a decision that Andy could make on her own. She tapped out the number of Martin's mobile, but it was switched off. She tapped out her home number. She had to speak to Martin. She closed her eyes and said a silent prayer as the number rang out.

All four people in the room froze as the black phone warbled. Carter grabbed for one headset, Denham picked up the other. Fanning sat down and scrutinised the tape recorder. Martin stood motionless, staring at the ringing phone. Denham motioned for him to pick up the receiver.

Martin took a deep breath and snatched it up. 'Yes?'

'Martin, thank God you're there.'

Martin felt as if he'd been punched in the solar plexus. His whole chest went numb and he couldn't breathe. He tried to speak but no words would come.

'Martin, can you hear me?'

He swallowed, though his throat was painfully dry. 'I'm here, love.'

'Martin, I don't know what to do. You've got to help me. I can't face this alone. I . . .' Her words ended in sobs.

Denham frowned and scribbled a note on a sheet of paper. He held it in front of Martin's face. 'ASK HER IF ANYONE'S LISTENING.' Carter took off her headset. 'I'll get Patsy,' she mouthed, and dashed out of the room.

'Andy, love, it's okay. It's okay.'

'It's not okay. They're making me build a bomb, a huge bomb. Hundreds of people are going to die, Martin. But if I do anything to try to stop them, they're going to kill Katie.'

'I know. I know.'

'You know? What do you mean? You can't possibly . . .'

'Andy, is anyone there with you?' Martin interrupted. 'Can anyone hear you?'

'I'm in an office, on my own, but I don't know for how much longer.'

Denham took off his headset and reached for the phone. For a second Martin tried to keep hold of the receiver, but Denham flashed him a stern look and Martin relinquished it.

'Andrea. This is Liam.'

'Liam? Liam Denham? What are you doing there?' The confusion was obvious in her voice.

'We don't have time for that, Andrea. Where are you?'

'Are you in the house, Liam? Are you in Dublin?'

'I'm in London, Andrea. So's Martin. Where's the bomb, Andrea? Where've you built the bomb?'

There was a long silence.

'Andrea, are you there?'

'Oh, sweet Jesus,' said Andy.

'It's all right. We can help you, Andrea.'

'You know what's happened? You know about Katie?'

'Yes. Martin's told us everything. Where are you, Andrea? Where are you calling from?' He scribbled on the paper as he spoke. 'ARE WE TRACING THIS?' He caught Fanning's eye and tapped the paper with his finger. Fanning read the note and gave Denham a thumbs-up and an emphatic nod.

'Please, Liam, don't do anything that'll put Katie at risk. Promise me. Swear to me, Liam, swear to me now.'

The door opened and Patsy rushed in, followed by Carter. She picked up the headset that Denham had been using and hurriedly put it on, then stood next to Denham, her head tilted slightly to one side as she listened.

'I'll do what I can, Andrea.'

'If Katie dies, I'll . . .' She didn't finish the sentence.

'I know, Andrea. We'll be careful, we won't do anything that'll put her at risk, I promise.'

Patsy's face hardened and Denham turned away from her. He knew what she was thinking. He was making promises that she wouldn't be able to keep.

'I'll hold you to that, Liam. We both know what happened last time . . .'

'It was a terrible mistake, Andrea. A mistake.'

'Children died,' said Andy.

Patsy touched Denham lightly on the shoulder. He looked at her and she made a circling motion with her finger, telling him to hurry up.

'Andrea, where are you?'

There was a slight hesitation, then Andy cleared her throat. 'Cathay Tower. It's in Queen Anne Street, close to Bank Tube station. We're on the ninth floor.'

Patsy wrote down the address and nodded at Denham.

'Good girl,' said Denham. 'The bomb, Andrea. How big is it?'

There was another hesitation, then another clearing of her throat. 'Four thousand pounds.'

Patsy's mouth opened in surprise.

'What type is it?' Denham asked.

'Ammonium nitrate, aluminium powder, sawdust and diesel.'

'Initiator?'

'They've got Semtex, Liam. Semtex and Mark 4 detonators.'

'And what stage are you at?'

Andy didn't reply.

'Andrea? How close to completion are you?'

'It's ready, Liam. All I have to do is set the timer.'

Patsy ripped off the headset and dashed across the office to the door, the piece of paper in her hand. She rushed out, leaving the door open.

'Liam, promise me you won't do anything until Katie's safe.'

'We'll do what we can,' said Denham, not wanting to lie to her.

'Liam, I want you to promise.'

Denham could hear Patsy shouting instructions down the corridor.

'Now listen to me, Andrea. If we're going to locate Katie, you're going to have to get them to let you telephone her, do you understand? If you can get her on the phone, we can trace it. No matter where she is, we can trace it. Just make sure that you use her name. You have to say "Katie", do you understand?'

'I'll try,' said Andy. 'But please, you have to promise me, don't let them storm the building, not until Katie's safe.'

Denham closed his eyes and gritted his teeth. He didn't want to lie, but he knew that the bomb was the priority, and that the life of a seven-year-old girl would come a poor second.

Patsy rushed into the briefing room, waving the sheet of paper. There were more than a dozen people there, either working on computer terminals or phoning. 'Right, everybody, stop whatever you're doing and listen. We have a location.'

Phones were slammed down and all the agents watched her as she wrote the address on the whiteboard. 'Cathay Tower, Queen Anne Street. Ninth floor. Lisa, get me a large-scale map of the area, now.'

Lisa Davies got up from her computer and dashed out of the room.

'Anna, I need an architect's plan of Cathay Tower. Every floor. And I need to know the tenants on each floor.'

Anna Wallace picked up the phone and dialled a number.

'Our information is that a four-thousand-pound fertiliser bomb has been constructed on the ninth floor. David, I need to know what effect a bomb of that size will have if it goes off. Radius of damage, direction of blast – talk to our technical boys and any contacts you've got in RAOC in Lisburn.' David Bingham nodded and picked up his phone.

'Right, everyone else, I want you to split into four groups. We need observation points around the building and we need them fast. Eyes and ears, full thermal imaging, the works. Jonathan, find a base that I and the SAS officer in charge can use. I want everyone to gather in the gymnasium in five minutes.'

Jonathan Clare nodded, then half raised his hand. She encouraged him to speak with a raised eyebrow. 'Evacuation?' he said.

'No, not at this stage. If we start pulling hundreds of people out of the area, it's going to attract attention. We don't want them spooked. So mum's the word until I say otherwise. Am I clear on that? Another thing. We don't know what effect the bomb's going to have. If we fill the streets with people, an evacuation could kill more than it saves, if the worst comes to the worst.'

The agents in the room nodded. 'Right, let's get to it,' Patsy said. She looked at her watch. It was just after eleven o'clock in the morning. The City would be at its busiest.

Andy cupped her hand around the bottom of the mobile phone. 'Liam,' she hissed. 'You mustn't let them do anything until Katie's safe. They'll kill her.'

'I'll do what I can, Andrea,' said Denham. 'But the best chance we've got of finding her is if you can persuade them to let you speak to her. Do you think you can do that?'

Andy walked over to the television. The remote control for the video recorder was on top of the TV set, and she picked it up with her free hand. She stroked it against her cheek, a faraway look in her eyes. 'I think so,' she said.

'Good girl,' said Denham. 'Now, who else is there, Andrea? How many of them are there?'

'Three. Two men, one woman. They keep their faces covered all the time they're around me. One of them's called Don. He's got a tattoo on his left forearm. A cross of St George. And I think the woman's name started with "McC". Or "McK".'

'Irish?'

'God, Liam, I don't know. Her brother was killed by the

SAS, so she's got Irish family, I'm sure, but the more I hear her speak, the more I think she's Scottish.' She tucked the video remote control into the back pocket of her jeans.

'Have they said why they're doing it?'

'No.'

'Do you get the feeling it's political?'

Before Andy could answer, she heard a noise behind her. Two figures wearing ski masks were standing at the open door. One was Green-eyes. The other man was a newcomer, short and stocky, wearing a black leather jacket and black jeans. Andy took a step back, her mouth working soundlessly. The man walked quickly towards her. His hand went inside his jacket and pulled out a gun.

Andy took another step back. She held the cellular phone in front of her in a futile attempt to keep him away, but he swept her arm away with his left hand and brought the gun crashing down against her temple. She barely felt any pain. Her vision blurred and then everything went black.

Liam Denham frowned as he looked at the phone. 'What's wrong?' asked Martin. 'Let me speak to her.'

Denham replaced the receiver. 'She's gone.'

'Gone? Just like that? Didn't she ask to speak to me?'

Denham continued to stare at the phone, a look of concern on his face. 'Maybe she was interrupted. I don't know.'

'Did you hear anything?'

Denham shrugged. 'It just went dead.' He lit a cigarette and inhaled deeply.

'Now what's going to happen?' asked Martin.

Carter took off her headset and put it down next to the tape recorder. Fanning popped the cassette out of the recorder and slotted in a fresh one.

'We'll put the building under surveillance, I suppose,' said Denham. 'It's out of my hands, though, Martin. It's Patsy's game from here on in. Patsy and the SAS.'

'The SAS?'

'They'll have to go in. There's a time element, Martin. We can't allow the bomb to go off.'

'But Katie . . .'

'Katie's one little girl. We're going to do what we can, but a four-thousand-pound bomb could destroy the centre of the city. Hundreds could die. Thousands.'

Martin's lip curled back in a snarl and he pointed an accusing finger at Denham. 'If anything happens to Katie, I'm going to hold you responsible.'

Denham looked pained. 'Martin, this is nothing to do with me. I'm retired. I'm . . .'

'You're the one who got her into this. If it wasn't for you using her as an informer, none of this would have happened. She wouldn't have built bombs for the IRA, the kids wouldn't have died, and Katie wouldn't have been kidnapped and had a fucking gun pointed at her head.'

Denham looked away, embarrassed by Martin's outburst. Embarrassed and guilty, because deep down he knew that the man was right.

The office door opened. It was Patsy Ellis. She sensed the tension immediately and motioned with her head for Carter and Fanning to leave. On the way out, Fanning handed the cassette tape to her.

'What's going on?' She asked Denham. He nodded at Martin but said nothing. Patsy turned to face Martin. 'Well?'

'He said you're going to send in the SAS,' said Martin.

'That's a possibility, Martin. I'm not going to stand here and lie to you.'

'But we don't know where Katie is. If the SAS go in, we might never find her.'

'Martin, our best hope is for the SAS to get in there and secure the building so that the explosive officers can disable the bomb. Then we can get them to tell us where they're holding Katie.'

'And what if all the kidnappers are killed? What then?'

'That won't happen. The SAS are experts at this sort of thing.'

'The SAS will do what they have to do to neutralise the threat. If the people with Andy are armed, they'll be shot. I know what the SAS have done in Ireland. They kill people. They don't shoot guns out of people's hands, they shoot to kill. Look what they did in Gibraltar. Remember that?'

Patsy nodded. 'I remember.' An SAS team had shot and killed an IRA active service unit in Gibraltar. The terrorists were planning to explode a car bomb but they were some distance from it and unarmed when the SAS moved in. They were all shot dead. She put up a hand, trying to calm Martin, but he brushed her away. 'This is a different situation, Martin,' she said.

'No it's not!' Martin shouted. 'It's the same. It's exactly the same, only this time the bomb's ten times the size so they've even more of an incentive to shoot to kill.'

Denham walked away and stood by the window with his back to the two of them. He blew a plume of smoke through tight lips.

'No one's going to shoot to kill,' said Patsy. 'We're going to monitor the situation, see what they're doing, see exactly where they are.'

'Then they'll go in?'

'Maybe. Maybe not. We'll cross that bridge when we come to it. It could be that they'll simply set the bomb and leave, in which case we could move in without a shot being fired.'

Martin put both his hands up to his face and rubbed the palms into his eyes. He sat down at the table and sighed mournfully.

Patsy put a hand on his shoulder. 'We're going to do everything we can to get your daughter back, Martin.'

'I should never have called you. I should just have let Andy do what they wanted.'

'And then what?'

Martin looked up. 'What do you mean?'

'Do you think they'd just let her walk away afterwards? You seriously believe they'd let her go?'

'That was the deal.'

Patsy looked at him with barely concealed contempt. 'You don't make deals with terrorists, Martin.'

Denham snorted softly behind her, but Patsy ignored him.

'They'll get her to do what they want, then when she's no more use to them . . .'

'You don't know that.'

'I know how terrorists operate.' She looked at her Cartier wristwatch. 'Anyway, we're wasting time arguing about this. We have to go.'

'Go where?'

'We're setting up an observation base close to the target building.' She turned to Denham. 'Liam, you'd better come with us.'

Martin stood up. 'I'm coming too.'

Patsy shook her head firmly. 'No. You'd be in the way. You'll have to stay here. I'll have Tim Fanning stay with you.'

'I don't need a fucking baby-sitter, and I'm not staying here. If you're going to send in the SAS, I want to be there when you do it.'

'Absolutely not,' said Patsy. 'Liam, let's go.'

She made to walk by Martin, but he grabbed her by the upper arm, his fingers digging into the flesh. 'I have the right to be there,' he hissed. 'It's my wife's life on the line here. My wife and my daughter.'

'You're hurting me, Mr Hayes.'

Martin let go of her. 'I'm sorry,' he said.

Patsy rubbed her arm as she looked regretfully at Martin. 'It's okay. I do understand how you feel, honestly I do.'

'Then let me come with you. I won't get in the way, I just want to be there.' He gestured around the office. 'I can't sit here, not knowing what's going on.'

Denham walked over to join them. He stubbed out his cigarette in a crystal ashtray on the table that was already overflowing with butts. 'I'll stick with him, Patsy,' he said. 'And we might need an insight into the way she thinks, the way she'll react. It's been ten years since I worked with her. Martin here could be a help to us.'

Patsy looked at the two men, then nodded curtly. Denham and Martin followed her out of the office. Martin patted Denham on the back, unable to find the words to thank him.

They walked quickly along the corridor and down two flights of stairs to the gymnasium. It was a long room with high ceilings and views of the river along one side. Treadmills, stairmasters and exercise machines had been moved to the side to give the SAS troopers space to spread out their gear. There were fifteen of them, all dressed in bomber jackets of various colours, jeans and training shoes. Several of the men had opened long, thin metal cases, revealing rifles with telescopic sights attached.

Captain Payne was bent over a map with two of his men. He looked up as Patsy came over with Denham and Martin close behind. Patsy introduced Denham and Martin and they both shook hands with the SAS captain. Payne tapped the map. 'Cathay Tower,' he said.

'That's right,' said Patsy. 'Ninth floor.'

'Evacuation?'

'I don't see we have the time,' said Patsy.

'We're going to need the tenth floor. Minimum.'

Patsy nodded. 'I'll send my people in to clear the offices on the tenth. Will your men be going in?'

Payne shook his head. 'The troop at Regent's Park is already on its way. I'm to liaise with you and we'll use my men for surveillance and long-range sniping.'

Jonathan Clare walked across the gym towards them. Patsy turned her head and he gave her a thumbs-up. 'We have an observation point,' he said. 'Solicitor's office. Hetherington knows him, apparently. The office is being cleared now. Hetherington's gone straight over there.'

More agents were filing into the gym, forming a group in front of a wall lined with climbing bars. 'Is it okay if I address your men along with my people?' Patsy asked the SAS officer, not wanting to cut across his line of command.

'Go ahead,' he said with a grin.

Patsy strode into the middle of the gym. The forty or so people gathered there fell silent.

'Okay, we're going to have to move quickly, so this is the one and only group briefing we're going to have. From here on we're going to be thinking on our feet, so the one thing we all have to keep at the forefront of our minds is that we're dealing with a four-thousand-pound fertiliser bomb. Bigger than any bomb ever used by the IRA in Britain. Bigger than any non-commercial bomb used by any terrorist group anywhere in the world. Captain Payne and I will be based in an office overlooking the tower. Jonathan has the address and numbers. We'll have radios, but no one uses a radio in the vicinity of the building.'

She looked over at the SAS captain. 'Captain Payne, that goes for your men, too. Any radio transmission could set off the bomb.'

Payne gave her a curt nod.

David Bingham slipped into the gym, a notepad in his hand.

'An SAS troop will be moving into the floor above where the bomb is located. Gordon, your team and Lisa's are to clear that floor. Subtly. It mustn't look like an evacuation.

336

Lifts two-thirds full, a mixed group in each lift. Men and women – chivalry goes out of the window on this. No hanging around outside, but no coaches, either. Everyone out moves well away from the scene. You'll be working with SAS troopers, armed and in plainclothes.' Gordon Harris and Lisa Davies nodded. Patsy looked across at Payne again. 'We can lend your men suits.'

Payne grinned and several of his troopers laughed out loud. 'Think of it as camouflage gear,' he said to them, and they laughed again.

'We'll have snipers covering the area, and we're going to want long-distance surveillance mikes and thermal imaging equipment, with all feeds sent to our surveillance HQ. Jonathan, can you take charge of that? Get as many of our technical people on board as you need. Right, let's get to it.'

Patsy went over to Captain Payne as her agents rushed out of the gymnasium. 'Do you want to come with us, Stuart?'

Payne nodded. 'Do I need a suit?' he asked with a sly grin.

Egan grabbed Andy by the hair and dragged her out of the office and along the corridor. McCracken followed him, holding the cellular phone which Andy had dropped. 'Find out who the fuck she was calling!' Egan shouted. He hauled her into the main office area, where O'Keefe was watching open-mouthed.

McCracken called up last number dialled and peered at it. 'Ireland,' she said. 'Dublin. She was calling her husband.'

Egan pulled Andy to the middle of the office and then let go of her hair. She flopped on to her side, snoring softly as if she were in a deep sleep. Egan drew back his foot and kicked her hard in the stomach. There was no reaction.

'What's happening?' asked O'Keefe.

'The bitch was on the phone,' said Egan. He turned to McCracken. 'Did she call anyone else?'

McCracken checked the mobile and shook her head. 'No. Just her husband.'

'Small mercies,' said Egan. 'What the hell was she doing with a phone anyway?'

'I don't know. It was in the briefcase. Locked.'

'Oh, that's all right, then,' said Egan, his voice loaded with sarcasm. 'I told you to watch her. I told you not to trust her.'

'I wasn't the only one here,' said McCracken. She flashed O'Keefe an angry look and he turned away, not wanting to be drawn into an argument.

'You were in charge, Lydia.' He knelt down by Andy's side and began slapping her face, trying to bring her round.

David Bingham almost had to jog to keep up with Patsy as she walked through the reception area of Thames House. Directly behind her was the SAS captain and two of his troopers carrying kit-bags, and bringing up the rear were Denham and Martin.

'There've only been three that come anywhere close to a four-thousand-pound device,' panted Bingham. 'The Baltic Exchange, Bishopsgate, and Canary Wharf. The Baltic Exchange bomb caused a third of a billion pounds of damage, Bishopsgate half a billion, and Canary Wharf a billion. The Canary Wharf bomb was one thousand pounds. All were detonated outside, so there was shrapnel damage over a wide area. If the bomb is detonated inside a building, it's confined to a smaller area but the damage will be greater. The building could come down. Depending on the direction of the blast, the building could fall vertically, which is what professional demolition firms try to do, or it could topple.'

They walked out of the building. Lined up in front of Thames House were a dozen large saloons, each with a driver. Patsy pointed to a black Rover. 'Liam, you and

Martin take this one. Wait for Barbara and Tim – they'll be right down. Barbara knows where we'll be.'

Denham nodded, and he and Martin climbed into the Rover. Patsy, Bingham, the SAS captain and one of the troopers got into another Rover. The second trooper went over to Denham's Rover.

Patsy took the front seat. Bingham sat in the middle of the rear seat between the captain and the trooper and continued his briefing as the car accelerated eastwards, towards the financial district.

'Initial damage will be the blast and ancillary shrapnel created in the explosion. The extent of that is going to depend on what's in the bomb and what's in the office. Wood, metal, glass – it'll all get thrown through the air at hundreds of miles an hour. Every building within half a mile could be affected. Then there's the damage caused by the destruction of the building itself. The people I spoke to said it will probably be damaged beyond repair. The roads around would be wrecked, and we've got the Central Line running underground fairly close. If the Underground is damaged, God alone knows how much it would cost to repair. Then we've got damage to basic services – water and sewage pipes, gas supplies, electricity, telecoms. The cost is incalculable. Billions. Plus the loss of business to the City. If a bomb that size goes off, the City will effectively close down.'

Patsy fingered her crucifix as she stared straight ahead. 'Casualties?' she said.

'The building is twenty-four storeys high. If we estimate a hundred and fifty people working on each floor, that's three and a half thousand or so. And if the building comes down, that's not a survivable scenario. Add to that anyone walking around the vicinity, anyone standing next to a window within half a mile of the bomb. Commuters on the Underground. Thousands dead. As many again injured.'

He paused for breath. He was sweating profusely, and he loosened his tie and undid the top button of his shirt.

'Of course, if it goes off at night, there'll be far fewer casualties, but we're still talking about property damage on a scale we haven't seen since the Second World War.'

Patsy twisted around in her seat to look at Bingham. 'As soon as we've arrived, you contact the Met's Explosives Office and liaise with them. We'll need a team of explosives officers ready to go in as soon as the area's secured.'

'Do I tell them why?'

'No. That'll have to be done at a higher level. Just put them on alert and refer any queries to Jason Hetherington's office.'

Patsy turned back and took her mobile phone from her bag. She tapped out Hetherington's number.

Egan stood up and sighed in exasperation. Andy lay unconscious at his feet, breathing heavily. Her blond hair was matted with blood where he'd hit her with his gun.

'Why don't we just shoot her now?' said McCracken. 'The bomb's ready. We could set the timers and she'll go up with it.' She was holding her gun at her side, her finger inside the trigger guard.

Egan nodded at the pistol. 'Be careful with that, Lydia. Let's not be hasty, yeah?' He looked at his watch. Andy had been unconscious for more than fifteen minutes. 'I want to know what she said to her husband. She might have told him to call the cops.'

'All the more reason to kill her now,' said O'Keefe.

Egan studied him with unblinking pale blue eyes. 'Who died and left you in charge, Don?'

O'Keefe stared back at Egan, unfazed. 'Security's been breached. We don't know who she spoke to or what she said. For all we know her husband could be on the phone to the police right now. We have to go.'

Egan shook his head. 'She made one call. To her husband in Dublin. We've still got her daughter – she's not going to endanger the kid.'

'She saw the videos,' said McCracken. 'Maybe she thinks her daughter's dead.'

'So let's find out,' said Egan. He went over to the water-cooler and pulled out the reservoir. He up-ended it, splashing water over his jeans, and carried it over to where Andy lay. He slowly poured the contents over her until she began to recover consciousness, coughing and spluttering and putting her hands up to try to ward off the torrent of water.

Patsy climbed out of the car and looked up at the office block. 'Tenth floor,' said Bingham. 'Donovan, Scott and Associates.' The black Rover containing Denham and Martin pulled up behind them. The SAS captain and his two troopers carried their kit-bags into the office foyer, and they all rode up in the elevator together.

Two MI5 agents were in reception, and one of them took them through to a large office where Hetherington was watching a team of half a dozen of the agency's surveillance experts unpack their equipment as he talked into a mobile phone.

The office was huge, about four times the size of Hetherington's own, wood-panelled with a massive oak desk at one end, two four-seater chesterfield sofas and an oak table with eight chairs around it. There were more than a dozen small watercolours on the walls, with small brass plates below them identifying the artist and subject, as if the occupant of the office feared that visitors wouldn't appreciate the value of the artwork.

The blinds were drawn and the lights were on.

Bingham took out his mobile phone. 'I'll call the Met boys,' he said, heading back to the corridor.

The SAS captain and his two troopers dropped their kit-bags on one of the chesterfields and went over to the window. Patsy joined them, and they pushed the slats apart. Hetherington came up behind them, putting his phone away. He pointed to a glass and steel tower directly in front of then. The base of the building was obscured by a row of granite buildings, but they could see from the fourth floor upwards.

'The blinds are drawn. White vertical ones. See them?'

'Got it,' said Patsy.

'We've got people to the north and east,' said Hether-ington.

'I'd like to put snipers on the roof here,' said Captain Payne. 'Can we have access?'

'It's being arranged,' said Hetherington. 'There's a roof garden up there but it's rarely used. I'll get someone to show you. Our people are installing long-range eavesdroppers as we speak. Patsy, a word.'

Two of the surveillance technicians were unpacking thermal imaging equipment from metal cases. Payne went over to watch as they attached the devices to tripods. They resembled huge pairs of binoculars with soda siphon car-tridges attached to the top. They were similar to the devices that the SAS used, combining ambient-light image intensi-fiers and thermal imaging. They were capable of picking up heat sources through concrete, effectively allowing the viewer to look through walls.

Hetherington took Patsy over to the far corner of the office where there was a bronze statue of a tur-baned warrior holding a spear that almost reached Hetherington's shoulder. 'The PM's been made aware of the situation,' he said. He fiddled with the tip of the spear as he spoke. 'He's in Bonn, but wants regular updates.'

Two technicians came in with more cases which they put

on top of the table. They began unpacking laptop computers. Another technician snapped open a case and took out a satellite phone.

'One thing the PM's clear on – he wants the immediate area evacuated.'

Patsy opened her mouth to speak but Hetherington silenced her with a wave of a finger.

'There's to be no argument. He's taking the view that if we know there's a bomb in that building, it would be political suicide to allow civilians to remain in the area.'

Patsy nodded. If the PM had made a decision, there was no point in arguing.

'It will have to be low-key, of course,' said Hetherington. 'The last thing we want is for us to have people streaming out of neighbouring buildings.'

'So the Met's been informed already?'

'The Director-General's spoken to the Commissioner. He's unhappy about not being told earlier, but any political in-fighting is going to have to wait until later.'

'Good. I've requested a team of their explosives officers to be on stand-by.'

'That's already in hand. Now, the evacuation. What's the position regarding the building itself?'

'We're clearing the tenth floor and the counter revolutionary team is moving in. Once they're in position, we can use our people to clear the rest of the floors. But Jason, it's going to have to be done carefully.'

'Agreed. Carefully, but quickly. Let's use the lifts and the stairways.'

'I'll have the lifts fixed so that they don't stop at the ninth.' She fingered her crucifix. 'If we're emptying the building, we're going to have to stop anyone entering or leaving the ninth floor.'

'Ah,' said Hetherington. He patted the blade of the spear. 'I see what you mean. I'll get Captain Payne to assign men to the ninth-floor stairwell. How long do you think it'll take to evacuate the building?'

'Stairs and lifts?' She did a quick calculation in her head. 'An hour, maybe. I'd recommend we take everyone down into the carpark and out through there.'

'Agreed. Now, regarding the evacuation of the surrounding buildings. The Commissioner wants to set up roadblocks to stop anyone entering the area.'

Patsy pulled a face. 'Jason, if they see what's going on . . .'

'The blinds are closed − they can't see out. We'll tell everyone there's a gas leak. We'll have gas company people all over the place. We'll put a warning on radio and television.'

'That won't fool them,' said Patsy.

'No, but it's better than nothing. We have to evacuate, Patsy. The PM won't stand for anything less.'

Four more technicians rushed in carrying monitors, followed by a fifth man who was unrolling a cable. There were now more than two dozen people in the office, hard at work.

'And what about the people on the ninth floor?' asked Patsy.

'We evacuate, we contain the area, we assess the situation, and if at all possible . . . we negotiate.'

Andy scuttled backwards, away from the man who'd been pouring water over her. She was soaked, and the side of her head ached from where he'd hit her. She had no idea how long she'd been unconscious, but with every movement of her head she felt as if she was going to pass out again.

'Who did you talk to, Andrea?' said the man. He had an American accent.

Andy put a hand up to the side of her head. When she took it away it was sticky with blood.

The man pulled a silencer out of his jacket pocket and

screwed it into the barrel of his gun, watching her all the time.

'Who did you talk to?' he repeated.

Andy looked across at Green-eyes. She was also holding a gun and aiming it at Andy's chest. She looked back at the man. There was no point in lying because they'd have been able to call up the last number dialled on the mobile. 'My husband,' she said.

The man finished attaching the silencer. He leaned against one of the desks, the gun resting against his thigh.

'I wanted to know if he'd heard from Katie.'

The man's face was hidden by the ski mask, but Andy could see his eyes harden. 'Why would he have heard from Katie?' he asked.

'I don't know. I thought maybe the kidnappers might have called him. I saw the videos. I thought . . .' Her voice tailed off. She began to shiver, the effects of being doused with cold water coupled with the terror of her situation. It wasn't the fact that he was pointing a gun at her that scared Andy. It was the fact that he'd screwed on a silencer.

The man looked across at Green-eyes. 'The videos were in the briefcase,' Green-eyes explained.

The man nodded and looked at Andy again. 'And you thought your daughter was already dead.' He tilted his head to one side as he looked at her. 'She isn't, Andrea. She's still very much alive. The videos were to put your mind at ease, that's all.'

'If Katie's alive, there'd be no point in you making the videos. You could just have let me talk to her.'

The man stared at her with unblinking eyes. 'A fair point,' he said. 'But we didn't know what was going to happen in Dublin. If anything had gone wrong, we wanted to guarantee your co-operation.'

'Wrong? What do you mean, wrong?'

'Say the police had found her. Look at it from our point

345

of view, Andrea. If something had gone wrong and we didn't have Katie, you'd hardly be likely to help us, would you? The videos were insurance against anything going wrong.'

Andy wrapped her arms around herself, still shivering uncontrollably. 'I don't believe you,' she said.

He gestured with his gun. 'I don't care if you believe me or not,' he said. 'The rules have changed. You're going to set the timer, right now.'

Andy shook her head.

The man levelled the gun at her left foot. 'I'll shoot your foot first. Then your knee. Then your thigh. Then your stomach. You'll do it eventually, Andrea, so why not save yourself the pain?'

'You're going to kill me anyway,' Andy said flatly.

'Dead is dead, that's true. But there are degrees of pain.' His finger tightened on the trigger. 'I know about pain, Andrea.'

Andy turned her head and closed her eyes, waiting for the bang, waiting for the bullet to tear into her flesh and smash through the bone.

Martin tapped the technician on the shoulder. The man took his face away from the eyepiece. 'Can I have a look?' asked Martin. 'That's my wife over there.'

The technician stood to the side so that Martin could look through the binoculars. It was like looking at a negative film. The background was dark and he could make out vague dark green shapes. Desks. Chairs. Pillars. And four light green figures that flickered as they moved. 'What am I looking at?' he asked.

'Thermal images,' said the man. He was in his forties with a small moustache and thinning brown hair. 'It picks up heat. Body heat, electrical heat, any heat sources.'

Martin put his eyes back to the binoculars. 'So I'm

looking right through the blinds? I'm looking right into the building?'

'That's right. These things can look through brick walls.'

Martin could see four figures. There was no way of telling which was male and which was female, no way of knowing which was his wife. One of the figures appeared to be sitting on the floor. Another was pointing at the seated figure. Was one of them Andy?

Anna Wallace came into the room, holding three cardboard tubes. 'I've got the floor plans,' she said to Patsy. 'All of them.'

She removed a plastic cap from one end of one of the tubes and shook out half a dozen architect's plans. 'This is the ninth,' she said, pulling out one of the drawings and laying it on the desk.

Captain Payne walked over and joined Patsy and Anna. He scratched his chin as he scrutinised the plan of the office. 'What do you think?' asked Patsy.

Payne tapped the area of the lift lobby, then ran his finger along to the reception area. 'This is a problem,' he said. 'Access here is through the main doors, but there's this left turn here to the reception. Then another turn to the open-plan area, which is where the tangos and the bomb are. It's going to take at least four seconds to take out the door and get into the main area. That's way too long.' He ran his finger across the plans to the windows on the far side of the building. 'We're going to have to go in through the windows. Here. And here.' He frowned and made a clicking noise with his tongue. 'The blinds are going to be a problem.'

'Why?' asked Patsy.

'We can't just go through the windows because our guys will get tangled up in the blinds. We're going to have blow them in. Shaped charges. And with a four-thousand-pound amfo bomb in there, that's going to be a tad . . . interesting.'

'We have visuals from Team A!' shouted one of the technicians. There was a bank of eight monitors on the table. On two of them were thermal views similar to the one that Martin had seen through the binoculars.

Captain Payne tapped out a number on his mobile phone. 'Yeah, Crosbie? We have four tangos. Repeat, four tangos.'

Martin looked at Denham and frowned. 'Tangos?' he mouthed.

'Targets,' whispered Denham. 'Tango means target.'

The picture on one of the monitors began to swing from side to side. Martin could make out more desks, a mound of something in the middle of the office area, but no more green, glowing figures.

'So far we have only four,' Payne said into his phone. 'Call me when you're in position.'

Payne clipped his phone to the belt of his jeans, then took off his leather jacket and hung it over the back of one of the chairs. He was wearing a black nylon shoulder holster; in it was a large handgun.

'Team B's on-line,' said another technician. Two more monitors flickered into life. Martin could see the same four green figures, but from a different view.

'What are we going to do about sound?' Payne asked Patsy.

'We've got laser mikes up on the roof,' she said. 'Shouldn't be long.'

'Do you want our team to try through the ceiling?' asked Payne. 'We could push fibre optics through.'

Patsy shook her head. 'Let's see how we get on with the lasers.'

Payne nodded and went over to the thermal image binoculars. One set was being connected up to a monitor.

Patsy peered at the monitors on the table. She pointed at a dark green mound in the centre of the office. Hetherington took his pince-nez spectacles out of the top pocket of his pin-striped suit and perched them on the end of his nose. 'That's it,' she said. 'A four-thousand-pound fertiliser bomb. Enough to blow the whole building to kingdom come.'

Captain Paul Crosbie dumped his kit-bag on the desk and surveyed the huge trading floor. All around him were hundreds of computers, their flickering screens full of financial information. Telephones were ringing out, but apart from Crosbie and his men, the floor was deserted.

'Right, get geared up,' he shouted. 'Full O group in five.' He picked up a phone and tapped out a number. 'Stew? Yeah, it's Crosbie. We're in. I'll have Chuckit call you for the thermal imaging feed.' Crosbie read out the telephone number of the phone he was using and hung up.

'Chuckit!'

Brian 'Chuckit' Wilson, a tall, thin Scotsman with a shock of red hair, was opening up a laptop computer. 'Yes, boss?'

'Call Stuart Payne and arrange the feed for the thermal images.' He gave Chuckit a piece of paper with Payne's number on it.

Crosbie surveyed the troop. Including Chuckit there were fifteen men, but Chuckit would be tied up with the communication links. Normal operating procedure was for the troop to operate in four four-man teams, but on this occasion Crosbie had already decided to split the men into two groups.

The troopers were emptying out their holdalls and kit-bags and laying their equipment out on the floor. Black Nomex fire-retardant suits, GPV 25 body armour, National Plastics AC100 composite helmets, black flame-retardant gloves, respirators, ankle-high boots and abseiling harnesses. One of the troopers, a burly Cornishman called Coop, was unpacking lengths of wood from a bag and leaning them against a desk.

Weapons were being assembled with practised ease and laid out next to piles of ammunition. Heckler & Koch MP5 submachine-guns, Remington 870 pump-action grenades, Browning Hi-Power pistols and Haley and Weller E180 stun grenades. It was enough fire-power to fight, and win, a small war.

The man grabbed Andy by the shirt collar and dragged her across the floor. 'Set the timer, Andrea,' he shouted. 'Finish the bomb or I'll blow your knee-cap off.'

He kicked her in the side and she grunted. She used the table leg to pull herself up and stared down at the open briefcase. The silver detonators lay on the Semtex, and around them the cluster of different-coloured wires. The timer was glowing, the digits all reading zero. Next to the timer were the batteries that she'd used to power the timer, and the four batteries she'd connected to the detonators.

'Do it,' said the man. He aimed the silenced gun at her left knee.

Andy sat down. She brushed her hair away from her eyes, then picked up an elastic band and used it to tie her hair back into a ponytail. One by one, she pushed the detonators into the Semtex.

She checked all the connections, then looked up at the man with the gun. She sniffed and rubbed her nose with the back of her hand. 'How long?' she asked. 'What do you want me to set it for?'

'One hour,' said the man. 'Sixty minutes.'

The receptionist looked up from a glossy magazine as Gordon Harris and Lisa Davies pushed open the double glass doors. 'Can I help you?' she asked in a nasal South London whine. She brushed a lock of dyed blond hair away from her eyes with a scarlet-varnished nail.

'Who's in charge?' asked Harris.

'You mean the office manager?' asked the receptionist, deep creases cleaving across her forehead as if Harris had set her an especially difficult mathematical problem to solve.

'Managing director. Whoever the top guy is.'

'She's a woman, actually,' said the receptionist. 'Miss Daley.'

Lisa grinned across at Harris but he ignored her.

'Could you tell her a Mr Harris would like to see her . . .'

'Oh, she'll be far too busy to see you,' interrupted the receptionist.

Harris held up a hand to silence her. 'Tell her it's regarding business security and if she's not in reception in thirty seconds we'll be coming in to get her.' Harris flashed her a cold smile and nodded at the telephone in front of her.

The receptionist dialled a four-digit extension number with another scarlet-painted nail.

Harris looked at his watch as the receptionist spoke to Miss Daley's secretary. It was taking up to eight minutes to clear each floor.

The receptionist put the phone down. 'She's coming out.'

'I'm so thrilled to hear that,' said Harris.

Harris and Lisa waited over by two overstuffed black leather sofas. 'You do have a way of winning friends and influencing people, don't you?' chided Lisa.

'We don't have time for niceties,' said Harris. He nodded in the receptionist's direction. 'If it was up to me, I'd let her go up with the building.'

The doors to the main office area hissed open electronically and a tall woman in a dark business suit strode out. Unlike the receptionist she had natural blond hair, tied up at the back, and she was model-pretty with high cheekbones and deep blue eyes. Her cheeks were slightly flushed and she was clearly angry at the interruption, but Harris spoke quickly and earnestly, in a low whisper so that the receptionist couldn't overhear him.

When he'd finished explaining the situation, she asked if she could call her head office, but Harris shook his head. 'No outgoing calls,' he said firmly. 'Not to your head office, friends or relatives. Everyone must leave without saying a word to anyone outside the building.'

'For how long?' she asked.

'We don't know.'

'But this is a dealing room,' she said. 'We trade in millions every minute. You can't shut us down.'

'I'm afraid we can, Miss Daley,' said Lisa.

'But at least you can allow us to move to our emergency dealing room, can't you?'

'Where is that?' asked Harris.

'On the Isle of Dogs.'

'I don't see that that's a problem,' said Harris.

'But I'll have to get permission from head office,' said Miss Daley.

Harris shook his head.

'This is outrageous,' said Miss Daley.

Harris moved his face so that it was only inches from her face. She stared back at him unflinchingly. 'What's outrageous, Miss Daley, is that we are having this conversation, when we could all end up dying here. We have only minutes to evacuate the entire building. It's not a drill, it's not a game, we're not doing this because we've nothing better to do. Now, you either do as you're told or I'll have you arrested and thrown into a vomit-stained cell somewhere while we get someone else to clear your floor. Are we clear?'

'Crystal,' said Miss Daley quietly. 'But, Mr Harris, I'd like you to be aware that I'll be making an official complaint as soon as possible detailing your behaviour and attitude. Now, what do you need?'

'I need groups of ten to be brought into reception. How many staff do you have on this floor?'

'One hundred and twenty. Do we bring the women first?'

'No. A mix of men and women. But it mustn't look as if they're carrying all their belongings. Briefcases are okay, but this mustn't look like an evacuation. I don't want you to make a general announcement – you're to quietly approach individuals. Send them into reception in batches of ten. And make it clear, no phone calls to the outside.'

Miss Daley nodded. She turned and walked back into the dealing room. Harris turned to Lisa. 'Why don't people just do as they're told?' he asked.

'You could try saying please,' said Lisa.

'Please? You heard her – she was more concerned about money than about what might happen to the building. It's like those sad bitches who insist on going back into a burning building to rescue their handbags.'

Lisa smiled thinly at him. 'If I didn't know better, Gordon, I'd suggest it was your wrong time of the month.'

Before Harris could reply the electronic doors hissed open and the first group of ten office workers began filing through into the reception area. A male MI5 agent already had one of the lift doors open and Harris shepherded them towards it, explaining that they were to go down to the carpark in the basement of the tower block and exit from there.

Patsy took her phone away from her mouth. 'Six floors clear so far,' she said to Hetherington.

Hetherington nodded his approval. He was watching the bank of monitors. There were now eight screens showing the thermal images. There were still only four figures, glowing green in the shadowy background. One of the figures was bent at the waist, obviously sitting, while the three other figures stood around it. Captain Payne stood behind Hetherington, his eyes flicking from screen to screen. Hetherington tapped the image of the seated figure on one of the screens. 'If I was a gambling man, I'd say that was Tango Four.'

Payne nodded. 'She's working on the timer.'

'Tango Four?' said Martin.

Hetherington turned, surprised at the interruption. He hadn't realised that Martin was there.

'Your wife,' said Hetherington.

'My wife has a name, Mr Hetherington,' said Martin. 'I'd be happier if you used it.'

'The tango designation makes identification easier,' said Captain Payne. 'We don't have time to memorise names.'

'My understanding is that tango means target,' said Martin. 'My wife is not a target. She's a victim. I don't want anyone referring to her as a target. She has a name. Andrea. Andrea Hayes.'

'You're quite right, Mr Hayes,' said Hetherington. 'I apologise.'

Before he could say anything else, one of the technicians shouted over at them. 'We have sound.'

The technician tapped the keys on his laptop and then started flicking switches on a console. There were small loudspeakers on either side of the bank of monitors. There was a hissing sound, then voices. The technician's fingers played across the keyboard again. The voices became clearer.

'How are you getting this?' asked Martin.

Patsy leaned across and put her mouth close to Martin's ear. 'Lasers,' she whispered. 'We bounce lasers off the windows to pick up the vibrations caused by sounds inside the building.'

The volume was increased, and suddenly Martin realised that it was Andy's voice he was listening to.

'. . . going to do? You can't go through with this.'

She sounded close to tears.

'Set it, Andrea.' A man's voice. An American accent. 'Sixty minutes.'

Patsy looked across at Hetherington. 'Sixty minutes,' she mouthed.

'Do it, Andrea. Do it or I'll put a bullet in your knee.'

Hetherington walked away from the monitors, pulling his mobile phone out of his jacket.

'We're going to have to move fast,' said Payne. 'An hour's no time at all.'

'We have to talk to the PM first,' said Patsy.

'What's happening?' asked Martin, looking over at his shoulder at Hetherington, who was whispering into his phone, a look of urgency etched into his features. 'What's going on?' He was ignored. He stared at the bank of monitors as he realised for the first time what he was looking at. The man with the American accent was pointing a gun at his wife, and if she didn't do as she was told, he was going to shoot her.

Andy sat back and closed her eyes. 'It's done,' she said. The digital display showed 01.00.

'Take it over to the bags,' said the man in the ski mask, gesturing with his handgun.

Andy stood up and lifted the briefcase. The man moved away from her as she carried it over to the pile of black garbage bags. She placed it on top of the pile and turned to face the man. The Wrestler and Green-eyes were standing by the line of ovens, watching.

'You know better than that, Andrea,' said the man. 'It has to be in the centre. Surrounded by the explosive.'

'It'll work on top.'

'I know it will. But we'll get a bigger bang if the explosive is piled around it.'

'There's four thousand pounds of explosive here. How big a bang do you want?'

'I want to bring the house down, Andrea. Stack the bags around the briefcase. And keep them tight together. We wouldn't the bags to be blown out without detonating, would we? Or was that what you were trying to do?'

'And then what? Then you kill me, right?'

The man said nothing, but Green-eyes took a step forward and pointed at Andy. 'That's right, you bitch!' she shouted. 'It goes up and you with it!'

'So I've got nothing to lose, have I?' said Andy quietly. She reached behind her with her right hand and brought out the video recorder's remote control. She slowly raised it in the air so that they could all see it, her thumb moving over the on-off button. 'If I press this, the bomb goes off.'

Captain Payne turned to Patsy. 'What is it? What the hell's she holding?' On the monitors, the green figure that was Andy had one arm held up high as if pointing at the ceiling.

Martin gripped Denham's arm so tightly that the older man winced. 'What's she doing, Liam? What's happening?'

'I don't know, Martin,' said Denham, peering at the monitors.

'Liam,' said Patsy. 'Could she have rigged the bomb?'

'It's possible. But how? What has she got there?'

Captain Payne turned to Hetherington, pushing up the sleeves of his sweat-shirt. 'If she means what she says, we have to go in now,' he said.

'Let's see what she's up to,' said Hetherington.

'We have less than an hour, whatever happens,' said Payne. 'I recommend that we go in now.'

Captain Crosbie adjusted his body armour. 'Right, orders group,' he said, and the fifteen troopers gathered for the pre-action briefing. To an outsider the men might have appeared over-relaxed as they listened to their commanding officer. Several were sitting on desks, swinging their legs.

Coop was sprawled in a chair, chewing gum noisily. The laid-back attitude was deceptive, Crosbie knew. The troopers were trained to a standard few men could ever hope to achieve and would do everything asked of them. They were used to being addressed as professionals and had earned the right to be treated as such.

'Two teams of seven,' said Crosbie. 'If we get the green light, we go in on two sides, simultaneously. Three stages. One. Lower the shaped charges. Two men on each frame. No messing – we only get one chance at it. Down and blow them. Stage two. Flash-bangs. Sandy and Coop take care of them. Throw in, minimum delay, then drop to avoid the flash. Everyone else goes in immediately afterwards. Four troopers are coming in through the front door, but they're not moving until they hear the flash-bangs.' He gestured at Chuckit, who was sitting in front of his laptop and talking on the phone. 'Hopefully we'll be getting real-time thermal images of the floor below, but we can't bank on getting them before we go in. What we do know is that we have four targets. Tango One and Tango Two are male. Tango Three and Tango Four are female. Tango Four is the bombmaker, but according to Intel she's working under duress. Having said that, all are to be regarded as hostile. We don't have time to separate the wheat from the chaff. Tangos One, Two and Three are armed. Handguns.'

Several of the troopers were cradling their Heckler & Kochs. Crosbie held up his own weapon, a Heckler & Koch MP5SD, the silenced model of the MP5. 'Down below us is a four-thousand-pound fertiliser bomb, and our first priority is to secure it. We're not sure what it looks like, but keep all fire well away from it. I'm told it's relatively stable, but no one really seems to know what effect a nine-millimetre bullet travelling at four hundred metres a second is going to have on it. I'd rather not find out, so pick your targets. Who's got MP5SDs?'

Half a dozen of the troopers raised their hands. Crosbie named the two teams, dividing the men with silenced weapons so that there were three in each team.

'MP5SDs lead the way,' he said. The silenced weapons had a much lower muzzle velocity, which Crosbie hoped would minimise the chance of a premature explosion if a stray bullet should hit the explosive. 'Coop, how are you getting on with the shaped charges?'

'One done. I'll have the other ready in ten minutes.'

Crosbie nodded. The framed charges were made of light wood which Coop had nailed into rectangles the size of the windows they intended to blow out. Around the edges of the frames was PE4 plastic explosive connected up with a continuous ring of Cordtex detonation cord, and at the top was a primer and a detonator. The charges would be detonated by wire, and if Coop had done his calculations correctly they would blow in the windows and the blinds, but with minimum damage to the interior of the office. It was a delicate balance. Too little and the blinds might still be in the way when the troopers went through the window; too much and the fertiliser bomb could be accidentally detonated.

Andy held the remote control to the side, aiming it at the briefcase, as Green-eyes and the Wrestler moved to stand behind the man in the ski mask. 'I didn't just wire up the timer,' she said, her voice cracking under the tension. 'I wired up the remote, too.'

'Could she do that?' Green-eyes asked the man in the ski mask.

'You'd better believe it!' Andy shouted.

'What do you want, Andrea?' asked the man in the ski mask.

'What do you mean, what does she want?' shouted Green-eyes. 'It doesn't matter what she wants. We've got guns. We'll fucking well shoot her!'

The man said nothing. His eyes continued to bore into Andy's as if he were trying to see into her mind. She stared back, refusing to look away, refusing even to blink.

'You can't shoot me,' said Andy. 'Because no matter how good a shot you are, no matter where you shoot me, I'm still going to be able to press the button. Even if you kill me stone dead, my hand is still going to go into spasm. The bomb'll go off. You'll all die.'

Green-eyes glared at the man. 'Is that possible?'

The man kept staring at Andy. 'If she's wired it that way, yes. The thing of it is, has she?'

Andy swallowed. 'There's only one way to find out,' she said, her voice shaking. 'I'll press the button and we'll all die.'

She raised her hand above her head.

'No!' shouted Green-eyes. 'Don't!' She lowered her gun, but the man in the ski mask kept his levelled at Andy's chest.

Captain Payne looked over at Patsy. 'I recommend we go in now. If she presses that button, everyone dies.'

Patsy bit her lower lip as she stared at the thermal images on the bank of monitors. 'Are you sure you can take them out without the bomb going off?' she asked.

Payne looked pained. 'I can't promise. But I can tell you that in hostage rescue rehearsals we get the hostage out alive ninety-six per cent of the time. So long as the woman doesn't panic and accidentally set it off, we should be okay. We'll drop down on two sides. Shaped charges to take out the windows, flash-bangs to disorientate them, then the troopers swing in. Four of my men will take out the main door. It should be over in seconds.'

Patsy exhaled through pursed lips. She looked at Hetherington and raised an eyebrow. He nodded, pulled out his mobile phone and tapped out a number. Neither of them had the ultimate authority to approve the storming of the building. Only one man could do that. Hetherington walked to the far end of the office and began talking urgently into the phone. Patsy fingered her crucifix.

Martin turned to Denham. 'They can't go in now,' he said.

'They can, if that's what they decide is the best option,' said Denham.

'But what about Katie?'

'Katie's pretty low down their list of priorities right now,' said Denham. 'I'm sorry, Martin.'

Martin looked around the office frantically, as if searching for someone he could appeal to. No one was looking at him. Hetherington was still whispering into his mobile phone; Patsy, Barbara Carter and Tim Fanning were watching the bank of thermal image monitors; the SAS captain and two of his troopers were at the window, peering out at Cathay Tower between the slats of the blinds. Half a dozen technicians were gathered around laptop computers, their hands playing over the keyboards.

'Patsy, you have to hold off,' urged Martin. 'See what they do. If he lets her talk to Katie, we can find out where she is.'

'It's not my decision any more,' she said, avoiding his gaze.

Captain Payne had his mobile phone to his face. 'Stand by, stand by,' he said.

'What if Andy accidentally presses the button?' asked Martin. 'What if she panics? Flash-bangs are like grenades, aren't they?'

Patsy didn't reply. Martin looked at Denham. 'They're going to shoot her as well, aren't they? That's the only way to stop her pressing the button, isn't it?'

Denham averted his eyes. Martin held his arms out and

waved them like a chick trying to fly for the first time. 'For God's sake, will somebody talk to me!' he shouted.

Patsy motioned with her chin at Fanning. 'Tim, take Mr Hayes outside, will you.'

Martin put his hands up in surrender. 'Okay, okay,' he said quietly. 'I'll be quiet.' He walked over to the window and stood next to the SAS captain.

Fanning looked at Patsy for guidance and she gave him a small shrug.

Hetherington clicked his mobile phone off and walked over to Patsy. 'The PM says to go in,' he said.

The SAS captain looked over his shoulder. 'That's a green light?' he asked Hetherington.

'Affirmative,' said Hetherington. 'And may God help us all.' He turned to Patsy. 'I think we should all move out of the room. Just to be on the safe side. Flying glass and such.'

Captain Payne put his phone to his mouth. Martin moved quickly, pushing the phone away with his left hand and grabbing for the man's gun with his right. He gripped the butt of the weapon and pulled it from its nylon holster. It came out smoothly, and before he realised it he was pointing the gun at Payne's head. Martin had never fired a gun in his life, but he knew enough to realise that there was a safety catch and he fumbled it into the off position with his thumb as he took a step backwards.

'Don't be stupid,' said Payne, holding his hands up, fingers splayed.

'Martin, for God's sake, what are you doing?' shouted Denham.

Martin kept the gun pointed at the captain's head. 'Tell your men to keep their hands where they are,' he warned. 'If either of them makes a move towards their weapons, I'll shoot you.'

'You're not going to shoot anyone,' said the captain.

'Martin, come on, calm down,' said Patsy soothingly.

Martin stepped to the side so that he could see everyone in the room, though he kept the gun levelled at the captain. Hetherington watched in amazement, his mouth open wide, his phone at his side. The two troopers were looking at their officer, waiting to see how he'd react.

'Martin, I know you're under a lot of strain at the moment,' said Patsy. 'But this isn't helping anyone.' She took a step closer to him.

'Stay where you are!' Martin shouted. 'If you come any closer, I'll shoot him.'

'That wouldn't be very smart, Martin,' she said.

Martin ignored her. 'Tim, push that desk against the door. Do anything else, anything at all, and I'll shoot him.'

The two troopers were moving away from the captain, one going to the left, one to the right. Martin waved the gun at Payne. 'Tell them to stay where they are,' he hissed. 'I'll try to shoot you in the leg, but I've never fired a gun before so I might hit you somewhere fatal.'

'That'd be murder,' said the SAS captain. 'Cold-blooded murder. Are you up to that, Martin? Are you up to shooting an unarmed man?'

'You've just been discussing killing my wife,' said Martin. His arms were beginning to tremble and he fought to keep them steady. 'You don't seem to have any problems with that.'

Fanning finished pushing the desk up against the door.

'Sit on the desk, Tim. On your hands.' Fanning did as he was told. Martin looked at the SAS officer, and waggled the gun at him. 'If anyone tries to come in through that door, they're going to have to come through Tim,' he said.

'I gathered that,' said Payne.

'Now, tell your men to take their guns out of their holsters. Tell them to use their thumbs and one finger. Then I want them to eject the thing that holds the bullets.'

'The clip?'

'The clip. Drop the clip on the floor, then the gun. Then they're to kick the guns across the floor to me.'

'You can tell them yourself,' said Payne.

'They're soldiers, and you're their officer,' said Martin. 'And if they don't do what you say, you're the one who's going to get the bullet.'

The captain nodded at his men. They slowly followed Martin's instructions. He kicked the guns under the desk, out of reach.

'Martin, have you thought this through?' said Patsy. 'Have you thought what's going to happen when this is over? You'll be in court for this. You'll go to prison.'

'Maybe,' said Martin. 'But you haven't given me any choice, have you? If the SAS go in, my wife and daughter are going to be killed. If that happens, I don't think I care much either way what happens to me.' He gestured with the gun. 'I might even end up using this on myself.'

'Now you're being stupid,' she said.

'We'll see.' He moved to the side so that he could see the thermal image screens. 'Turn up the sound, will you?'

Patsy turned up the volume. Everyone turned to look at the monitors.

Andy held the remote control above her head, her thumb resting on the on-off button. 'I will do it,' she said. 'You're going to kill me anyway, so I've nothing to lose.'

'Yes you have,' said the man in the ski mask. 'There's Katie.'

'Katie's dead already.'

The man lowered his gun. 'No. She's not.'

Andy shook her head, blinking away the tears that were stinging her eyes. 'I don't believe you.'

The man stretched out a hand as if he were trying to calm a barking dog. 'She is, Andrea. I promise you. She's fine. The men she's with were told to look after her.'

Andy sniffed. Her arm was starting to ache and she wanted to change hands, but she didn't want to give the man in the ski mask an opportunity to shoot her.

The Wrestler cursed and Green-eyes turned to look at him. 'I'm going,' he said. 'You don't need me any more.'

'No,' said the man in the ski mask. 'We all stay until it's finished.'

'Fuck you,' said the Wrestler. 'You've got your bomb. I'm sure as hell not going to be here when it goes off. Just make sure you transfer my money into the bank. If you don't, I'll come looking for you, Egan.' He turned and walked towards the door, muttering darkly to himself.

Patsy looked at Denham. 'You hear that? "Egan", he said.' She turned to Carter. 'Barbara, get on to records. Anything we have on a man called Egan. Aliases, everything. Notify GCHQ, too. And get them to liaise with the NSA. Search for any calls mentioning Egan. Then contact the FBI, cross-check with them.' Carter nodded and picked up the phone.

'Wait!' said Martin.

'Martin, she's only going to make a phone call. We have to know who this Egan is.'

Martin hesitated, then nodded. Carter dialled a number and began to whisper urgently into the mouthpiece, a look of fierce concentration on her face.

There was a coughing sound from the loudspeaker. On the two screens, one of the flickering green figures slumped to the floor. 'They've shot someone!' said Captain Payne.

'Who?' shouted Martin. 'Who's been shot?'

'I don't know,' said the captain, striding towards the monitors.

'For God's sake, is it Andy?' He kept the gun aimed at Payne's back.

Martin stared in horror at the monitor closest to him. One of the green figures was standing over the figure on the floor, pointing down. There was a coughing sound again. The sound of a silenced gun.

'It's not her,' said Payne. 'He's shot the man. Shot him twice.' The SAS captain slammed a fist into the palm of his other hand. 'Now,' he said. 'We have to move now. They're all distracted – we'll be in there before they know it.'

'No,' said Martin. 'We wait until they've made the call. Then we'll know where Katie is.'

'They're not going to let her speak to your daughter,' said Payne. One of the SAS troopers, the one on the captain's left, moved slightly so that he was at the edge of Martin's vision.

'Stay where you are!' shouted Martin.

'They're going to trick her, Martin,' said the captain. 'It's a distraction – she'll be so focused on the phone. He's killed one of his own people – he's not going to think twice about killing your wife. Think, man. They're not going to let her live, not after this.'

'No!' shouted Martin.

'You've got to let us go in, now.'

'He's right, Martin,' said Patsy. 'The SAS are professionals – they train for situations like this.'

'We can do it, Martin,' said the captain, his voice soft and persuasive.

Martin put a hand up to his forehead. 'You're confusing me,' he mumbled.

The SAS trooper lunged towards Martin, his hands outstretched, going for the gun in Martin's hand. Martin turned, his mouth open in surprise, but too slowly to get his gun around. Denham was quicker – he threw his tweed hat at the trooper's face and stuck out his foot, tripping the man up. The trooper tried to regain his balance, his arms flailing in front of him, but he pitched forward on to his knees. Martin jumped back, covering the man with his gun, both hands on the butt, his finger tight on the trigger.

Everyone froze. Martin's eyes were wide and staring and he was breathing heavily. His arms were shaking, and he had to force himself to relax the pressure on the trigger. 'Easy, Martin,' said Patsy. 'Take it easy.'

Captain Payne moved away from Martin, his hands up in surrender. 'It's okay. We're all cool, Martin. No one's going to hurt you.'

'Sorry,' said Denham, picking up his hat. 'I must have slipped.'

The SAS trooper glared up at him, then got to his feet. 'Damn you, Liam,' hissed Patsy.

Denham smiled in a cold imitation of an apology. 'What are you going to do to me, Patsy? Have me sacked?' He nodded at the green screens. 'Let the girl have her chance. She deserves it.'

'Thanks, Liam,' said Martin, covering Payne with the gun.

'Don't thank me,' said Denham. 'We're both up to our necks in shit now.'

The office went silent as everyone strained to hear what was being said over in Cathay Tower.

Andy stared in horror at the pool of blood that was slowly spreading around the Wrestler's head in a gruesome parody of a halo. The man in the ski mask had shot him twice. Once in the back as he walked away, once in the side of the head as he lay twitching on the floor, face down. After the second shot the Wrestler had stopped moving.

Andy tried to speak, but no words would come.

Green-eyes was also stunned. The two women looked at each other, then at the man in the ski mask. 'Why?' asked Green-eyes.

'First rule of this business, always obey orders. Second rule, never use names. He broke both.'

Green-eyes glared at the man. She raised her gun so that

it was aiming at his chest. 'How do I know you won't kill me? When it's all over. How do I know you don't want me to go up with the bomb?'

The man pointed his gun at her, smiling. 'Would you prefer that? How about we have a quick draw here and now. First one to pull the trigger wins. Are you up for that?' He straightened his arm and aimed at the centre of her face. Green-eyes flinched and the man laughed sharply. 'Look at you. You don't have the balls to shoot me, and you know it. Pull yourself together. Can't you take a joke?'

Green-eyes gestured at the body on the floor with her gun. 'That's not funny. That's not even close to funny.'

'He was walking out on us. I paid you all for your unswerving loyalty. To carry out your tasks without question. Without disobedience.' He levelled the gun at Andy once more. 'Anyway, we're wasting time.'

In her terror at witnessing the killing, Andy had forgotten the remote control in her hand. She waved it in front of her face, her thumb poised over the on-off button. 'If you shoot me, I'll still have time to press this. Then we all die.'

'I understand that, Andrea. But I know you don't want to die. No one does. Who'll look after Katie if you're not around? Who'll grow old with your husband?' He took a step closer to her.

'No!' she screamed. 'I mean it! I will! I'll do it!'

The man took a step back. 'Okay, take it easy,' he said, his tone conciliatory but firm. 'What is it you want?'

'I want to go home to my family.'

'You can do that. We can all walk out of here.' He looked at his watch. The bomb had been active for almost ten minutes. 'We walk out of here and once the bomb has gone off, you can leave.'

'And my daughter?'

'We've no interest in hurting children, Andrea. We just want this building blown up.'

'Why?'

The man shook his head. 'You don't need to know.'

'Once the bomb goes off, you're going to kill me anyway. I know you are.'

The man shook his head. 'No, we're not. I swear it.'

Andy's mouth was so dry that she could barely speak. She rubbed her mouth with the back of her left hand. 'You want it to look like an IRA bomb. If I go up with it, that's what everyone will think, that the IRA used me to build it. If I'm alive, your deception isn't going to work.'

Green-eyes and the man looked at each other. Andy knew that she was right. That had been their plan, right from the start.

'So maybe it's better if we all die,' she said. 'Together.' She pointed the remote control at the man as if it were a gun and she was about to fire.

'Wait!' he said. For the first time there was a hint of uncertainty in his voice, as if he finally believed that she might do it.

'I want to know why,' said Andy. 'I want to know why you've done all this. Kidnapped Katie. Forced me to build the bomb for you. Is it because you want to blame the IRA? You want to derail the peace process?'

The man in the ski mask snorted dismissively. 'You think we'd go to all this trouble over politics?' He laughed sharply. 'I tell you, the IRA would have been a hell of a lot more effective if they'd hired me.'

'So why, then? If it's not politics, why?'

The man stared fixedly at Andy, then nodded slowly, as if he'd come to a decision. 'It's about money, Andrea. Dollars. Millions of dollars. Hundreds of millions of dollars.'

Andy frowned, not understanding.

The man waved his gun around the office. 'Look around you. What do you see, Andrea?'

Andy said nothing, not sure what he was getting at.

'Prime City office space? The sort of office you could rent to a bank or a broking firm? An appreciating asset?' He shook his head. 'Appearances can be deceptive. It's worthless, Andrea. The whole building's fucked.' He gestured at the floor with his gun. 'The steel's corroding. It was built on the cheap and now the whole structure's almost ready to come down.'

Andy put a hand to her head. She was confused and finding it hard to breathe, as if something had been tightly wound around her chest.

'The people I work for bought the building last year. They're Chinese – they thought they were getting a good deal and they paid in cash. A lot of it was dirty money. Corruption. Drugs. Triad money. Just over two hundred and fifty million pounds. Four hundred million dollars. The vendors were Russians, but the Chinese didn't know that because the deal was handled by a German middleman. As soon as they handed over the money, the German disappeared. So did the Russians.'

'I don't understand,' said Andy. 'You're confusing me.'

'Try and focus, Andrea. They were conned. The Chinese were taken for a quarter of a billion pounds. What they thought was a solid-gold investment turned into a millstone around their necks, if you'll excuse the mixed metaphors.'

'Didn't they get it surveyed?'

'Oh, yes. By a partner in a big City firm. He's disappeared, too.'

'So what's that got to do with all this?'

The man shook his head impatiently. 'The building has to come down, Andrea. It has to be rebuilt, which will cost almost as much as they've already spent. And since the meltdown in Asia, they don't have the money. But if it should be destroyed in a terrorist bombing, then the government becomes the insurer of last resort. They get paid in full.'

Andy stood transfixed, the remote control in her out-stretched hand. 'That's what this is all about? You took my daughter. You kidnapped me. You're going to kill God knows how many people . . . just for money?'

The man laughed harshly. 'For a lot of money, Andrea. A hell of a lot of money.' He nodded at Green-eyes. 'That's not why she's doing it, of course. She wants revenge. But she's getting paid, too. So, if you do push that button, if you do set the bomb off, you'll be doing us all a favour. The Chinese'll get their money back, she'll get her revenge on the country that killed her brother, and I'll be paid in full.'

'Except you'll be dead, of course.'

'What if I were to offer you money, Andrea? What if I were to give you half a million dollars? What's that in your money? More than three hundred thousand pounds? I'll give you three hundred thousand pounds to put down that remote control and walk out of here.'

Green-eyes turned angrily to the man in the ski mask. 'What? You can't be serious.'

'It's none of your business.'

'It's totally my business.' said Green-eyes.

'You work for me. If I want to hire Andrea, that's up to me.'

Green-eyes walked over to the window and stood staring out over the City, her arms folded across her chest.

'Half a million dollars, Andrea.'

'No.'

'How much, then? How much to buy your co-operation?'

'I want my daughter back. And I want to go home.'

The man stared at her in silence. He clicked his fingers at Green-eyes and she looked over her shoulder at him. He clicked his fingers again. 'Give me the phone,' he said. Green-eyes handed over the mobile and he used his thumb to tap out a number. 'I'm calling your daughter,' he said.

Andy narrowed her eyes, suspecting that he was trying to trick her. She held the remote control above her head again.

The phone started to ring and the man put it to his face, keeping the gun pointed at Andy's chest.

Patsy and Hetherington looked at each other in astonishment. 'Do you believe that?' asked Hetherington. 'That's what this is all about? An insurance job?'

'There's no reason for him to lie,' said Patsy. 'He doesn't know we're listening in.'

'It's hard to credit. That they'd be prepared to kill so many people for money.'

Patsy shrugged. 'I've heard of shipowners scuttling ships with their crews on board to get insurance. This is just on a bigger scale, I suppose.'

'I didn't follow what he said,' said Martin. 'They're blowing the building up for money?'

'They want to make it look like a terrorist incident,' said Patsy. 'If the building was uninhabitable because of structural faults, the owners would have to bear the cost. As they've recently acquired it, they probably haven't got insurance. But if it's damaged in a terrorist bomb, then ultimately the government will pay. If what he says is true, the Chinese investors would get their money back in full.'

'So now it's over. We know what he's up to. He can't get away with it. All you have to do is to tell them that and they'll give up. They have to.'

'It's not as simple as that,' said Patsy. 'They've got a four-thousand-pound-bomb over there.'

'But don't you see,' pleaded Martin. 'If you tell them we know what they're up to, they have to give up.'

Over the loudspeaker, they heard the man call out to Andy. 'They're on the line,' he said.

'I want to talk to her,' said Andy. Her voice sounded strained, as if she was close to tears.

'We should go in now,' said Captain Payne.

'No!' said Martin. 'Wait until she speaks to Katie.' He looked at Patsy. 'They'll be monitoring the call, right?'

Patsy nodded. Martin kept the gun aimed at the captain, but turned to look at the thermal image monitors. As he did, something hit him in the small of the back, pushing him forward. As he fell, Patsy grabbed the gun and twisted it out of his hand. She shuffled sideways, keeping the weapon away from Martin as he struggled to regain his balance. Payne swiftly moved over to her and took the gun from her.

It was Tim Fanning who'd hit Martin, creeping up behind him while his attention was focused on the monitors. Fanning grabbed him around the neck and wrestled him to the ground. The two men rolled over on the floor. Fanning was younger and stronger and within seconds he was on top, his knees pinning down Martin's arms.

Captain Payne grabbed his phone. 'Stand by, stand by,' he shouted. 'Move in on my word.'

'No!' Martin bellowed.

Patsy looked at Hetherington, and he pursed his lips and nodded. Patsy opened her mouth to give the SAS captain the go-ahead, but before she could speak Denham stepped forward.

'Patsy, they're using the mobile. We can trace the call within a minute. We can find out where Katie is.'

Patsy glared at him, then turned to Payne again.

'One minute, Patsy,' said Denham. 'You can give her one minute, can't you?'

'Please,' begged Martin from the ground.

Patsy looked down at Martin. He was straining to get up but Fanning was too strong. Blood vessels were standing out on Martin's temples and there were flecks of saliva on his lips. He looked like a wild animal in fear of its life.

'Please,' he said again.

Patsy gritted her teeth. 'Damn you,' she said. 'Damn you

both.' She held up her hand to Payne, gesturing for him to wait. 'Tim, call the telecom people, right away. Trace that call.'

Fanning climbed off Martin and rushed over to a phone. Martin got slowly to his feet and wiped his mouth with the back of his hand.

The captain pressed his lips together tightly, impatient to get the operation under way. He put the phone to his face again. 'Stand by, stand by,' he said.

Everyone in the room stared at the bank of monitors.

The man in the ski mask kept the gun aimed at Andy's chest as he listened to the phone. 'Yeah, it's me,' he said. 'Hold the line, yeah?'

'Let me speak to Katie,' said Andy.

'Then what?' asked the man, holding the phone by his side.

'Then you let her go. Then we walk out of here.'

The man shook his head. 'I don't think so.'

Andy waved the remote control. 'You don't have a choice,' she said. 'If I press this, we all die.'

'You don't want to die, Andrea.'

'Neither do you.'

'Who'll look after little Katie? Who'll watch her grow?'

'My husband. At least she'll know that I did what I could to save her. I won't have died for nothing.'

The man smiled thinly, then slowly raised the phone. Andy stepped forward, thinking that he was about to hand it to her. He didn't. He put the phone to his mouth. 'Listen to me,' he said into it, speaking loudly so that his voice echoed around the office. 'Listen to me carefully. If the line goes dead, if I get cut off for any reason, kill the girl and get the hell out of there. Do you understand? If the line goes dead, you kill the girl.' He listened, nodded, then held the phone down by his side again. He sneered at Andy. 'Right,' he said flatly. 'Go ahead and press it. If we die, she dies.'

*　　*　　*

Lisa Davies pressed the button to keep the lift doors open as the ten office workers piled out. Two MI5 agents guided them through the carpark like collies marshalling a small flock of sheep. One of the agents, a thirtysomething man in a dark suit and highly polished shoes, whispered that the office workers weren't to run, and that they were to turn right as soon as they left the carpark exit. Other agents would be there to advise them where to go next.

Lisa stabbed the button to close the doors and watched the floor indicator rise slowly through the numbers. The four floors above the bomb were already clear. So were six of the floors below. She looked at her wristwatch. The seconds were ticking away. The lift reached the ninth floor, the floor where the bomb was. A four-thousand-pound fertiliser bomb. Lisa shuddered. She wondered if she'd feel anything if the bomb went off. Would the shock wave kill her instantly, or would it blow her into the air in a hail of shattered steel and glass? She stared at the floor indicator, willing it to change. Ten. Eleven. What would happen if the bomb exploded while she was on one of the higher floors? Would the building collapse in a shower of debris, crushing the life out of her? Would she die instantly, or would the life slowly drain from her as rescuers searched in vain through the thousands of tons of rubble?

Lisa shook her head, trying to dispel the tormenting images. There was no point in worrying about what might happen. She had her orders, and she'd follow them. She'd been told to evacuate the building, to get everybody out, and that's what she would do. The floor indicator reached fourteen and the lift juddered to a halt. The doors rumbled open. Gordon Harris was there with the next ten office workers. They were mainly women; Lisa saw just two men standing at the back. She ushered them all inside with urgent whispers. 'Come on, come on.'

'What's happening?' asked one of the women, grey-haired with a pair of spectacles dangling around her neck from a thin silver chain. 'Is there a fire?'

'No, there's no fire,' said Lisa. 'But we have to get you all out as quickly as possible.'

'But what's happening?' repeated the woman, her voice trembling. She dabbed at her eyes with a lace handkerchief.

'That's the lot,' said Harris. 'I'll head up to the fifteenth.'

Lisa pressed the button to close the doors. The grey-haired woman burst into tears. Lisa looked at her watch again, even though she was aware it was a futile gesture. She didn't know how much time they had, and she realised that it was probably best that she didn't know.

Patsy tapped her foot impatiently. It seemed to be taking a lifetime for the telecom experts to trace the call. Martin looked hopefully across at her and she gave a small shake of her head.

The SAS captain walked over to her. 'We have to move in,' he said. 'The clock's still ticking, remember? I make it fifteen minutes so far.'

She looked at him icily. 'I'm hardly likely to forget,' she said.

'Just a few more minutes,' Martin pleaded.

'We don't have a few more minutes,' said the captain. 'We have to get in there so that the explosives officers can get to work on the bomb. If we leave it much longer, even if we go in we won't be able to prevent the bomb going off.'

Martin pointed at the monitors. 'Don't you understand what's going on there?' he thundered. 'If you go in and that phone gets cut off, they'll kill Katie. We have to know where she is.'

'And if that bomb goes off, hundreds of people are going to die!' shouted the captain. 'Including my men.'

The two men stood just feet apart, glaring at each other.

'Easy, gentlemen,' said Hetherington, quietly but firmly.

'We're not fighting each other here. The enemy's over there. Let's not forget that.' He raised an eyebrow at Patsy. She shook her head. 'It's a mobile,' she said. 'Southern Ireland. That's all they know so far.'

Hetherington went over to Martin and put a hand on his shoulder. Martin could see in the man's eyes what he was going to say, so he spoke first. 'No!'

'If you're going to hate anyone for this, Mr Hayes, you have to hate me. It's my decision.' He turned to the captain. 'Send in your men, Captain.'

Payne took two steps over to the phone he'd been using and picked up the receiver. 'Can you hear me? It's a green light. Go, go, go.'

Patsy slammed down the phone. 'We've got a location!' she shouted.

'So it's your call, Andrea,' said the man. 'Press the button and everyone dies. Including your daughter.'

'Let me speak to her.'

'It's too late for that.'

Andy held the remote control in front of her, her hand shaking uncontrollably. He'd beaten her. There was nothing she could do. Whatever she did, she'd lose. And she could see from the look of triumph in the man's eyes that he knew it, too.

'It's over, Andrea.'

He pointed the gun at her head and took a step towards her. Andy took a step back. She looked around in panic. There was nowhere to run.

'Give me the remote control, Andrea. You know you're not going to press it.'

Green-eyes aimed at Andy's head, her finger tightening on the trigger. 'Let's shoot her!' She shouted. 'Let's just fucking well shoot her.'

The man in the ski mask ignored the outburst. He kept

his eyes totally focused on Andy, his arm outstretched towards her. 'Give it to me, Andrea. It's over.'

Captain Crosbie dropped the phone and adjusted his respirator. He raised his arm, his fist clenched. 'Go! Go! Go!' he shouted.

His men had split into two teams and had removed windows from the north and west sides of the building in preparation for the assault. On his command, each team dropped a shaped charge down on ropes, while Sandy and Coop pulled pins out of the top of stun grenades, holding the triggers in place as they stood on the window ledges, abseiling ropes around their waists. One trooper on each team was holding the trigger to detonate the shaped charge, and they nodded to each other and pressed their triggers at the same time. There were two loud explosions from below, and immediately Sandy and Coop dropped down, stun grenades at the ready.

As they disappeared over the edge, the rest of the troopers took their places, Heckler & Kochs at the ready.

The window to Andy's left exploded in a shower of glass. A fraction of a second later, the window behind her also erupted inwards, spraying her back with glass. Two metal cylinders bounced off the floor, the size and shape of cans of beer. Time seemed to stop for Andy. Everyone seemed to have frozen to the spot. The man in the ski mask's mouth was wide open. Green-eyes had her hands up in front of her face to shield herself from the flying glass, the gun forgotten in her right hand.

Andy had no idea what had happened. She wondered if the bomb had gone off, if she was already dead and it had happened so fast she didn't know it. She tried to move but her limbs were locked in place. She couldn't move. She wasn't conscious of breathing or of her heart beating.

The man in the ski mask started to react, swinging his gun around, bringing it to bear on the window closest to him, his mouth open as if he were about to scream.

The two cylinders exploded at exactly the same time. There was a flash of light, so bright that Andy was instantly blinded, then her world exploded.

Martin jumped at the sound of the explosions. 'What the hell was that?' he shouted.

'Flash-bangs,' said the SAS captain. 'Stun grenades.' He moved closer to the monitors, pushing Martin out of the way.

On the eight screens, three green figures were staggering around the office. One of them twitched and fell. Over the loudspeaker came the muffled rat-tat-tat of rapid fire from a silenced Heckler & Koch. More green figures were flowing into the office, moving quickly and purposefully.

'Who's that? Who's been shot?'

'I don't know,' said Payne. 'We've no radio contact.'

Martin peered over the captain's shoulder. 'Is it Andy?'

'I don't know,' said Payne sharply. Two single muffled shots barked from the loudspeaker. The sound of a silenced handgun.

Green-eyes was in spasm on the floor, though she was obviously dead. The right-hand side of her head was missing, exposing white skull and pink brain matter, and there were four blossoming red patches on the front of her overalls. Her gun, unfired, lay close to her twitching right hand. Andy stood transfixed, unable to comprehend what was going on around her, her ears still ringing from the stun grenades. To her left, two men dressed in black overalls and with black submachine-guns strapped to their chests were swinging in through one of the broken windows. They had respirators and dark goggles on and black webbing belts around their waists. The man in the ski mask was facing the other way, both hands on his pistol. He'd fired twice at three more SAS troopers who had come swinging in through another window in the wake of the grenades. He'd hit one in the chest with one of his shots, but the bullet had made a dull thudding noise as it had smashed into the soldier's body armour. The troopers were bringing their submachine-guns to bear on the man, but he threw himself to the side, rolling behind a desk.

There was a crashing sound from reception and the stamping of boots. Andy held her hands up in surrender, the remote control still clasped in her right hand. 'Don't shoot!' she screamed. Her voice sounded far away, as if it belonged to someone else.

The man in the ski mask rolled again and came up in a half-crouch, taking aim at Andy's chest. With his free hand he ripped off his ski mask. He had, Andy realised, a very ordinary face, devoid of distinguishing features. There was no expression of anger on it, nor fear. His features were totally blank as he pointed the gun at Andy's chest and tightened his finger on the trigger.

Andy sprang to her right and fell against one of the ovens. The two men who'd just piled in through the window to her left were unclipping themselves from their ropes. One of them swung his submachine-gun towards her. She wanted to scream that she wasn't a threat, that the man was about to kill her, but the only sound she could make was a low growl.

The man's silenced gun coughed and a bullet zipped by her head as she fell to the ground and scrambled away on all fours. The remote control dropped from her hand as another bullet thwacked into the ovens behind her. Four more soldiers came hurtling down the corridor from reception, guns at the ready, their boots beating a rapid tattoo on the floor.

She stood up, and one of the SAS troopers fired his submachine-gun. His aim was off and bullets raked the ceiling above her head, shattering the tiles. Chunks of polystyrene cascaded around her like a heavy fall of snow. The man with the handgun fired at the troopers and hit one in the respirator. The trooper slumped to the floor, blood pouring from around his face mask.

Andy dropped to the floor and rolled over, broken glass cutting into her flesh. She slammed into something soft and yielding and found herself face to face with the Wrestler, his eyes wide and staring, blood congealing between his teeth.

Andy groped for his gun. Her trembling hand made contact with the handle of the weapon, but when she pulled it wouldn't come free of the holster. She remembered the strap around the hammer of the gun and felt around with her thumb. There was a rat-tat-tat of silenced gunfire followed by two distinct shots, and she heard a body crash to the floor. She looked up. The man was only feet away from her. His face split into a malevolent grin and he fired at her, point blank. Andy twisted to the side, throwing out her hands for balance, and felt the bullet sear along her outstretched arm and into her shoulder. She screamed in pain and fell backwards.

The SAS troopers were shouting staccato commands at each other, but she couldn't make out what they were saying. There was another burst of automatic fire and the sound of bullets hitting metal.

As Andy hit the ground she saw the man fire at an SAS trooper and hit him in the neck. The trooper twisted around as blood sprayed from the wound.

Andy rolled, pain lancing through her injured shoulder, came up on all fours and crawled under one of the tables. Ahead of her was Green-eyes, blood pooling around her chest, her head twisted grotesquely to one side. Andy saw her gun and grabbed for it as another burst of bullets sprayed along the ceiling above her, ripping out tiles in a shower of polystyrene.

The handle of the gun was wet with blood, and Andy seized it with both hands, rolling over until she was on her back. The man was bent low, the gun turned almost upside down so that the handle was pointing up at the ceiling. Andy squeezed the trigger, praying that the safety catch wasn't on. Her ears roared as the gun fired, again and again as her finger tensed instinctively on the trigger. Blood spurted from the man's chest and Andy kept firing. The man staggered backwards. He tried to straighten up but his body began to twitch as if electrocuted. As the room began to spin around Andy, she became dimly aware of the sound of multiple gunshots coming from all around her. The upper half of the man's body turned scarlet and the phone shattered as bullets raked across what was left of his chest, then his face disappeared in a shower of red and white and he pitched sideways.

The last thing Andy saw was three troopers with goggles and respirators staring impassively down at her like giant insects considering their next meal.

The loudspeaker was suddenly silent. Then there was a man's voice. A gruff Scottish accent. 'Area secured!'

'They're in,' said the captain, relieved.

'Thank God for that,' said Hetherington.

'Andy. What about Andy?' Martin peered at the monitor closest to him. There were three figures sprawled on the ground. Around them moved a dozen or so flickering green shapes.

Captain Payne put his phone to his ear and listened, nodding and grunting. He turned to Patsy. 'Tango One and Tango Three are dead, Tango Two is dying. Tango Four is wounded but will survive. You can send in the explosive officers now.'

Martin's mind whirled. Tango Four was alive, the others dead or dying. But which was Andy?

Patsy came up behind him and squeezed his shoulder. 'It's okay,' she said. 'Andrea's alive. Your wife's okay.'

McEvoy took the mobile phone away from his ear. 'Shit,' he said.

'What happened?' asked Canning.

'Gunfire. Then the line went dead.'

Canning glowered. 'Gunfire? Are you sure?'

McEvoy looked contemptuously at his partner. 'I've heard guns before, Mick.'

Canning ran his hands through his unkempt hair. 'Maybe he'll call back.'

'I don't think so.' McEvoy put the phone down on the coffee table. 'I think it's over.'

Canning paced up and down. 'Shit. Shit. Shit. What the fuck are we going to do?'

McEvoy looked at the .38 Smith & Wesson which was hanging in a nylon shoulder holster on the back of the sofa. Egan's instructions had been crystal clear. If the connection was cut, kill the girl. But Egan was probably dead. 'We go,' he said quietly. 'We pack up and go.' He picked up the holster and fastened it across his chest.

'You clear the cottage, I'll check the girl's okay.'

'I'll do it,' said Canning. 'She's still scared of you.'

McEvoy sighed. 'You're a sad bastard, Canning. Okay, you sort the girl out, I'll put the gear in the car.'

Canning went into the kitchen. He opened the fridge and took out three cans of Coke and a bottle of Ballygowan water. His woollen ski mask was on the kitchen table and he pulled it on. He picked up the drinks, went over to the door leading to the basement and pulled back the bolts. He groped for the light switch and found it, but when he flicked the switch the light didn't come on. He cursed under his breath and moved slowly down the stairs, softly calling Katie's name.

He reached the bottom and peered into the gloom. 'Katie. Come here. Stop messing about.' He could just about make out the bed in the light from the open door at the top of the stairs, and he headed towards it. He heard a scuffling sound behind him and turned to see the little girl scampering up the stairs.

Canning dropped the cans and the bottle. The glass smashed and water splashed over his feet as he rushed after her. 'George, she's coming your way!' he shouted. He took the stairs two at a time and hurtled into the hallway. McEvoy was standing there, his arms outstretched. The girl was frantically trying to pull the front door open. She hadn't noticed that it was bolted. The bolt was high up, way out of her reach. She turned and tried to run to the kitchen, but McEvoy was too quick for her. She skidded to a halt and turned, but her face fell when she saw Canning. He strode over to her and picked her up around the waist. She kicked him and beat him around the head with her little fists. 'Stop it, damn you!' Canning shouted as he carried her back down the hallway to the basement door.

He took the stairs slowly, allowing his eyes to get used to the gloom. Katie carried on kicking him, but she was tiring and the blows didn't hurt. His shoes crunched over the broken glass and he dropped her on to the camp bed. She lay there sobbing, her knees drawn up against her chest. 'Jesus, girl, no one's going to hurt you. We're going.' He wiped his mouth with his sleeve and glared down at her.

He heard McEvoy come down the stairs behind him. He turned to look at him. McEvoy's face was set hard and he had the .38 in his hand. 'What are you doing with that?' asked Canning.

McEvoy pulled back the hammer with his thumb. 'She's seen my face, Mick.'

'We'll be well gone by the time the cops get here. She's a seven-year-old kid – she's not going to be able to tell them anything.'

'It doesn't matter,' said McEvoy, pointing the gun at the girl.

Canning stepped in front of the gun so that the barrel was levelled at his stomach. 'George, listen to me. If you kill her in cold blood, they'll never stop looking for us. We'll be branded as child-killers. If they catch us, they'll throw away the fucking key.'

'I'm not happy about this, but she saw my face. You shouldn't have let her get away from you.'

'So it's my fault, is it?'

'I just call it the way I see it,' said McEvoy. He moved to the side, trying to get a clear shot at the girl.

'You've wanted to off her from the fucking start,' said Canning. 'No way are you going to do this.' He grabbed the gun in McEvoy's hand, forcing his thumb between the hammer and the chamber.

'What the fuck are you playing at?' McEvoy shouted. 'Egan said do her. We've got to do her.'

'No,' hissed Canning. 'It's over.'

'She's seen me.'

'She's a fucking kid, George.'

McEvoy tried to pull the gun away from him, but Canning held firm, keeping the barrel pointed down towards the floor. Katie was sitting up on the camp bed, watching them nervously.

'It's all right for you, you've got your fucking mask on. She's going to tell the cops everything. And you've just told her my name.'

Canning seized McEvoy by the throat and pushed him back against the wall. He put his masked face right up against McEvoy's ear. 'Walk away, George.'

McEvoy glared at him. 'They're going to be coming for

384

us, Mick. I heard what happened. Gunfire. Hecklers, Mick. The fucking Sass. Egan's dead. They're all dead – the Sass don't take prisoners. If we don't kill the girl, she'll identify us and the Sass'll be after us.'

'There's a big difference between kidnapping and killing. If we leave the girl alive . . .'

'What? They'll forget all about us? Yeah, and maybe we can go and live with Elvis.'

'We've got enough time to run. They'll look for us, sure, but they'll be a hell of a lot more determined if we've killed her. It'll be no stone unturned if we're child-killers, George. You wanna be a child-killer, George? You want that on your conscience?'

McEvoy nodded slowly. 'Okay,' he said.

'We lock her in the basement, then we piss off back to Belfast,' said Canning. 'We can make a call on the way.'

'Okay,' said McEvoy.

Canning slowly released his grip on McEvoy's throat. 'Let's get our stuff together,' he said.

McEvoy drove his knee into Canning's groin and hammered the butt of the handgun against the side of his head. Canning staggered back, bent double. McEvoy hit him again with the gun, slamming it against the back of his neck. Canning fell to the floor, stunned.

'It's all right for you, you piece of shit,' McEvoy hissed. 'She hasn't seen your fucking face.' He turned and pointed the gun at Katie. She rolled off the camp bed and ran to the bottom of the stairs, but McEvoy moved to intercept her. 'Stand still!' he shouted.

Katie skidded to a halt. 'Please don't,' she said, her voice quivering with fear.

McEvoy aimed at her face and his finger tightened on the trigger. Canning lurched to his feet, roared and threw himself at McEvoy's gun arm. He kicked the man's legs from underneath him and McEvoy hit the floor, hard.

The gun went off but the bullet went wide and buried itself in the ceiling. Canning dropped down on top of McEvoy, fumbling for the gun. He seized McEvoy's wrist with both hands and twisted, but he couldn't loosen the man's grip.

McEvoy bellowed like a bull in pain. He tore at Canning's woollen ski mask with his left hand and ripped it off Canning's head. Canning locked eyes with him. McEvoy grinned. 'Now she's seen us both, what are you going to do?' McEvoy hissed.

Canning said nothing. He grunted, twisting the Smith & Wesson around, towards McEvoy's chest. Behind them, Katie edged along the basement wall to the stairs, her arms outstretched like those of a tightrope walker fighting to keep her balance.

McEvoy threw Canning's ski mask away and clawed at his face, hooking his nails into the man's eyes. Canning yelped and thrashed his head from side to side, continuing to hold on to the gun. He forced the barrel towards McEvoy's chin. The gun went off again, the bullet grazing Canning's cheek and slamming into the wall, where it sheared off a hand-sized piece of plaster. Canning's ears were buzzing and he could feel blood dribbling down his cheek.

McEvoy stopped scratching at Canning's face and used both hands to struggle for the gun. He pushed Canning with his knee and the two men rolled across the floor and banged into the table. McEvoy got on top and used all his weight to force the barrel down towards Canning's neck. Spittle peppered Canning's face. McEvoy was breathing heavily and his eyes were wide and staring, all his efforts concentrated on the gun.

Canning twisted to the side, and as McEvoy lost his balance Canning pushed the gun into the man's chest. He managed to get his own finger inside the trigger guard and the gun went off twice. McEvoy stiffened, then blood seeped between his teeth and he rolled on to his back. Canning lay gasping for breath. He pushed himself up off the floor, still holding the .38, and looked around the basement. Katie had gone. He heard footsteps running along the floor above his head and rushed up the stairs. He found Katie in the kitchen, trying to pull open the back door.

'It's locked,' he said.

She stopped fumbling with the handle and slowly turned to look at him. Her lower lip was trembling. 'There's blood on your jumper,' she said. 'And on your face.'

Canning put his hand up to the bullet wound on his cheek. It was smarting and still dripping blood. The blood on his pullover wasn't his. It was McEvoy's. He grabbed Katie by the shirt collar and led her back down into the basement. She didn't struggle or protest, and when he told her to sit on the bed she did as she was told.

Canning flipped out the cylinder of the .38. Two shots left. More than enough. He clicked the cylinder back into place. He pulled back the hammer. 'Close your eyes, Katie,' he said.

'I won't tell anyone,' she said. 'I promise.'

'Yes you will.'

She shook her head firmly. 'I won't. You can run away. I won't tell the police what you look like. I won't tell them what you did to him.'

'They'll find out anyway.'

'You could bury him outside.'

'The police will find me, Katie. They'll find me and then you'll identify me.'

'I won't. I promise. Please don't kill me.'

Canning pulled one of the wooden chairs closer to the bed and sat down on it, facing the girl. 'Katie, you don't know what the world's like. You're just a kid.'

'I know that adults aren't supposed to hurt children,' she said sullenly.

'I don't have any choice,' he said.

'It's not fair,' whispered Katie.

Canning smiled despite the enormity of what he was going to have to do. 'Life isn't fair,' he said. 'When you get older you'll . . .' He left the sentence unfinished. She wasn't going to get any older. Her life was going to end here and now. In the basement.

Katie pointed at the door. 'You could lock me in and go away,' she said. 'When the police find me, I'll tell them you didn't hurt me.'

'It won't work like that,' said Canning. 'They'll keep looking for me until they find me. What we've done is so bad they'll never stop looking. If you hadn't seen my face, it wouldn't matter, but you know what I look like. And the police will make you tell them.'

'They won't. I . . .'

Canning held up his hand and she stopped talking, waiting to see what he had to say. 'Let me tell you what would happen, Katie. They'll catch up with me eventually. Maybe in a week. A month. A year. But they'll get me eventually. They'll send policemen to talk to your mum and dad, and they'll all take you to the police station. They'll be really nice to you and tell you what a brave girl you are. They'll probably give you a Coke or a 7-Up or something, then one of them will sit down and talk to you. Probably a policewoman. Young. She'll talk to you like a big sister. She'll tell you that they've caught me but that you've got to identify me. She'll tell you not to worry, that they'll put me in prison for a long, long time, and that I'll never be able to hurt you or any other little girl again. Then the nice policewoman will take you to room and she'll show you a window. She'll tell you that there's a line of men on the other side, that you can see them but they can't see you, and she'll tell you to look carefully at all their faces and to tell her which one I am.'

'I won't tell them,' said Katie.

'You're seven years old,' said Canning coldly. 'You won't be able to stand up to them. You'll look along the line of men and you'll see me and you'll point me out. Close your eyes, Katie.'

Katie did as she was told. 'I won't tell,' she said. 'I promise.' She kept her eyes firmly closed and made the sign of the cross over her heart. 'Cross my heart and swear to die.'

Two green-overalled paramedics were wheeling a trolley through a police cordon as Patsy, Martin and Denham walked up. Martin ran over to the trolley. It was Andy. She was paler than he'd ever seen her, her hair tied back in a ponytail, dark patches under her eyes. She reached out with her hand and he interlinked his fingers with hers. A large dressing had been taped to her left shoulder and there were two dressings on her arm which had been placed in an inflatable splint. Blood was seeping through the dressings and she winced in pain as she tried to sit up. 'Katie . . .' she said.

'Lie down, miss,' said one of the paramedics, a stocky thirtysomething woman with short permed hair. 'We have to get you to hospital.'

Andy gripped Martin's hand, her nails digging into his flesh. 'I'm not going anywhere until I know that Katie's safe.'

'She's losing blood,' the paramedic said to Martin.

'I'm okay,' said Andy. She gritted her teeth as a wave of pain washed over her.

'Andy, you have to go to hospital,' said Martin. 'I'll come with you.'

'But Katie . . .'

Denham appeared at Martin's shoulder. 'Our people are on their way to Katie now,' he said.

'Liam?' said Andy. Her eyelids fluttered. She was obviously close to passing out.

'Yes, Andrea. It's me. You did well. We'll take it from here.'

'I want to stay here until I know what's happened to Katie.'

Patsy took her mobile phone from her jacket and pressed it into Andy's hand. 'As soon as we know where she is, we'll call you,' she said.

Denham nodded at the paramedics and they wheeled her towards the ambulance. Martin went with them.

'Do you think she's still alive?' asked Patsy as they watched the paramedics lift Andy into the vehicle. Martin climbed in, the doors were slammed shut, and a few seconds later the ambulance drove away, sirens wailing.

'God, I hope so,' said Denham.

A uniformed policeman examined Patsy's credentials and waved her through the cordon. Denham shrugged. 'I'm with her,' he said.

'That's fine, sir,' said the constable. 'I could tell you were in the job.'

Denham smiled to himself as he followed Patsy into the lift. Retired for ten years and he still looked like a policeman. He wasn't sure if that was a compliment or not.

They rode up to the ninth floor in silence. The doors opened and two more uniformed constables stepped aside to allow them into the office. Half a dozen Scene of Crime Officers in white overalls were moving around like silent ghosts, fingerprinting and collecting fibre samples with pieces of tape, all their evidence going into labelled plastic bags.

Two SAS troopers stood by the window, their automatic

weapons clasped to their chests. One was smoking a cigarette, the other was laughing. There was broken glass everywhere, and Patsy and Denham crunched over it as they walked to the pile of black garbage bags in the middle of the main office area. Two Metropolitan Police explosives officers were crouched over the bags, gingerly moving them apart. Both men were wearing olive overalls, and Patsy was surprised that neither of them was wearing protective armour. In Belfast, the EXPOs never went anywhere near an explosive device without full body armour and protective helmets. She realised that it was probably because the bomb was so big that if it did go off, no amount of protection would help.

'Everything okay?' she asked.

One of the EXPOs looked up and grinned at her. 'Safe as houses,' he said. He was barely out of his twenties, with a shock of red hair and acne scars across his cheeks. 'SEXPO's got the detonator. You could drop this lot out of the window and it wouldn't go off.'

'SEXPO?'

'Senior Explosives Officer.' The redhead nodded over at an older man in overalls who was standing by one of the desks. 'Our boss. Dave Hoyle.'

Patsy and Denham went over to Hoyle. He was peering at a digital display through a magnifying glass, examining the wires that protruded from the back of it. There was a tangle of wire next to the digital display and four small cylinders, the size of Parker pen refills. Patsy had seen detonators before, in Belfast.

She introduced herself and Denham, but Hoyle just grunted. He was a big, bear-like man with thick fingers that dwarfed the delicate electronics he was examining.

'It was live?' asked Ellis.

'Oh, yes. Timer was set. Twenty minutes left on the clock before we got to it.'

'No problems?'

'Simple circuit. Nice work. A woman, they said?'

'That's right.'

'They always do neat work, women. Tidy. Precise. Just look at the soldering.'

He handed the magnifying glass to Patsy, and she used it to examine the wiring. She had no idea what she was looking at and she gave it back to Hoyle none the wiser.

'No booby traps?' asked Denham.

'No, it was a simple enough circuit,' said Hoyle. 'No photoelectrics, no tremblers, no collapsing circuits. EXPO-friendly, it was.'

'What about the remote control?' asked Ellis.

'The what?' Deep frowns creased Hoyle's forehead.

'The infrared remote control. She had it rigged so that if she pressed it, it would go off.'

Hoyle's frown deepened. 'No way,' he said. 'Timer, batteries, detonators. There was nothing else in the circuit. Pressing the remote control wouldn't have done a blind thing.'

'Are you sure?'

Hoyle looked offended. Patsy began to laugh, and Hoyle stared at her in surprise. She shook her head, still laughing. 'She was bluffing,' she said to Denham. 'She was bloody well bluffing.'

Denham's mobile phone warbled and he took it out and put it to his head. Patsy stopped laughing as Denham listened, then frowned. 'Yes, Eamonn.' Patsy watched Denham's face, wondering if it was good news or bad.

Denham put his hand over the bottom of the phone. 'They've found Katie.' A smile spread across his face. 'She's okay. They locked her in a basement. She's scared but she's okay.'

Patsy grinned. She took a quick step forward and hugged

Denham, burying her face in his chest and squeezing him so hard that he gasped.

Denham hugged her back, then pulled away. 'I have to call Andy,' he said, then he smiled. He held out the phone to Patsy. 'Why don't you do it?'

THREE MONTHS LATER

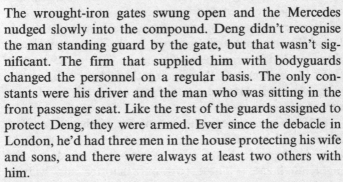

The wrought-iron gates swung open and the Mercedes nudged slowly into the compound. Deng didn't recognise the man standing guard by the gate, but that wasn't significant. The firm that supplied him with bodyguards changed the personnel on a regular basis. The only constants were his driver and the man who was sitting in the front passenger seat. Like the rest of the guards assigned to protect Deng, they were armed. Ever since the debacle in London, he'd had three men in the house protecting his wife and sons, and there were always at least two others with him.

He climbed out of the Mercedes and went into his house. The maid wasn't there to take his cashmere coat from him, so he hung it up himself and went through to the sitting room.

His two sons, the elder aged twelve, the other just eighteen months younger, were sitting together on the sofa, an expensive white leather model that Deng had had flown in from Milan. He glared at the boys. 'Didn't we tell you not to sit on the sofa in your school clothes?' he said. 'Why haven't you changed?'

The boys said nothing. The younger one was close to tears.

'What's wrong with you? And where's your mother?'

'She's with me,' said a voice behind him.

Deng froze. He turned slowly. Michael Wong was standing at the door to the kitchen, Deng's wife at his side. Her eyes looked at Deng fearfully, then over at her sons. She gave them an encouraging smile and made a small waving motion with a neatly manicured hand, trying to reassure them that everything was going to be all right now that their father was home. Deng took a deep breath. It wasn't going to be all right. Michael Wong had come for his revenge.

Wong pushed Deng's wife into the room and she tottered forward on her high heels, then ran to Deng and grabbed him around the waist and buried her face in his chest. Two big men in cheap suits and red-and-black-striped ties followed Wong into the sitting room. As the door swung back, Deng could see three bloodstained bodies on the kitchen floor. His bodyguards. And against the fridge, sitting up but with her head slumped against her chest, the maid. Her throat cut wide open.

The two men who came out of the kitchen were Red Poles, Triad heavies, but they weren't the two men who'd been in the love hotel when Wong had murdered the nightclub hostess. These two were shorter and heavier and had the rough skin and bad haircuts of mainlanders. One of them was holding a silenced automatic. The other had a roll of insulation tape in his hand. Deng looked at them over the head of his sobbing wife. 'I'll pay you ten times what he's paying you,' he said to them.

They laughed at him.

'Twenty times,' said Deng. 'I'll get you new identities, new passports. Hong Kong passports. I can do it. Plus twenty times what he's paying you.'

They laughed even louder, and Wong laughed along with them. The front door opened and the bodyguard who'd been in the Mercedes walked into the sitting room. The Red Pole with the silenced gun shot the bodyguard twice in the chest and he dropped to the floor without a sound. The driver never came into the house. When he wasn't working, he stayed in a small flat above the garage, too far away to hear what was going on in the main building.

The two Red Poles went over to Deng. The one with the gun pulled his wife away, grabbing her by the hair and throwing her over to Wong. The other heavy pushed Deng in the chest and he staggered backwards. The heavy seized him by the lapel and spun him down into a chair, and then quickly wound the insulation tape around his legs and arms, tying him fast.

'I thought I'd run through the programme I've planned,' said Wong. 'Just so you know what's coming.' He ran a hand down Deng's wife's breasts and between her legs. She squirmed in his grasp but he tightened his grip around her throat. She was looking at Deng with pleading eyes, but he knew there was nothing he could do. Nothing he could say, either, to her, or to Wong. There were no words with which to apologise to her for the horrors that lay ahead, nothing he could say to Wong to make him change his mind. The only option was acceptance. 'I'm going to fuck your wife,' continued Wong. 'Not because it'll give me pleasure, you understand. She has the face of a pig, and her body's not much better. I can see why you're always screwing hookers whenever you go to Hong Kong.'

Deng's wife moaned in despair and Wong twisted her head around so that he could look into her tear-filled eyes. 'Oh, poor baby,' he said. 'Didn't you know? Didn't you guess? Young girls. Pretty girls. He takes them to a love hotel in Kowloon Kong. He's probably thinking about them on the rare occasions he screws you.' He grinned at Deng and released his grip on the woman and kicked her over to two of the Red Poles. They grabbed her, an arm each, supporting her because the strength had gone from her legs and she could barely stand. 'Then my men will fuck her. In any way they choose.' Deng's wife began to sob uncontrollably. The two boys were staring at their mother in horror.

Wong gestured at the large man standing at the door to the kitchen. He was big and broad-shouldered, with close-cut hair and a round, line-free face. He had thick lips which he kept licking with a square-shaped tongue. 'Cheung here, he likes boys. It's all I can do to keep him out of prison.'

Cheung laughed throatily.

'He really likes your sons,' said Wong. 'So he's going to play with your boys for a while. Then he's going to kill them.'

Cheung opened his jacket and pulled out a curved knife. He ran his finger along the edge of the blade, still chuckling.

Deng kept his eyes fixed on Wong, his face impassive. There was no point in showing any emotion. That was what Wong wanted. A reaction. Appeals for mercy. He wanted to see Deng on his hands and knees, begging for his life and the life of his family. Deng knew that any such appeals would be ignored, so he kept his teeth clamped together and waited for the end.

Deng's elder son started to cry, and the younger boy put his arm around him and tried to comfort him. Deng was suddenly immensely proud of the young boy, not yet a teenager but already behaving more like a man than he could ever have imagined.

Wong held out his hand and one of the Red Poles gave him a baseball bat. Wong swung it by his side, the end brushing against the carpet that Deng's wife had had specially woven in Bangkok, to a design of her own. She was so proud of the carpet, it was the first thing she pointed out to visitors to their home.

Wong took a couple of steps towards Deng, then smacked the bat hard against his left knee. The knee-cap cracked like dry wood and his leg felt as if it had been thrust into a fire. Deng bit down on his lower lip, fighting not to scream as tears stung his eyes. For a few seconds he thought he was going to pass out, but then the pain subsided a fraction and his mind cleared.

'Then, Deng, you thieving bastard, I'm going to beat your wife to a pulp with this bat. Every bone in her body. From her toes up. Then, when her brains are all over the carpet, I'm going to do the same to you.'

Wong grinned, waiting for a reaction, but Deng said nothing. Then Wong slapped his forehead theatrically. 'But how stupid of me,' he said, taking a mobile phone from his jacket pocket. 'There's someone who wants to talk to you first.' He tapped out a number and listened until it was answered. 'Yeah? You can start now,' he said. He held it against Deng's ear. 'Your brother,' said Wong. 'And his family.'

The screaming was terrible, more than Deng could bear, and he tried to twist his head away, but Wong kept the phone pressed to his ear. There were three gunshots in quick succession. Then another two. Then two more. Then silence. Wong took the phone away from Deng's head. 'Your brother. His wife. Their daughter.' He put the phone away, then made his hand into a gun and pointed it at his own head, mimicking the hammer with his thumb. He grinned. 'They raped your sister-in-law, and your niece. While your brother watched.'

Deng's left leg had gone numb from the knee down. Totally numb. He couldn't feel his toes, or move them. Wong slapped the baseball bat into the palm of his hand. 'Right,' he said, nodding at the Red Poles. 'Let's get started.'

One of the Red Poles began ripping the shirt off Deng's wife, while another unzipped his trousers. Deng's sons began to scream at the men to leave their mother alone. Cheung stepped forward and slapped the elder boy across the face, hard, and blood streamed from his nose. Deng looked away. There was no point in watching. He closed his eyes and tried to blot out the screams and cries of pain. His wife called out his name, but he kept his eyes firmly shut. There was nothing he could do to stop what was happening. All that lay ahead over the next few minutes, hours maybe, was acceptance. Then death.

SIX MONTHS LATER

The doorbell rang and Martin Hayes put down his copy of the *Irish Times* and went to answer it. It was Saturday morning and he wasn't expecting visitors. It was James FitzGerald, the Garda detective inspector. Behind him stood Sergeant John Power. It had been raining all morning and both policemen were wearing dark blue raincoats.

'Mr Hayes,' said FitzGerald, nodding. 'Sorry to bother you.'

'What's happened?' Martin asked.

'It's about Katie,' said FitzGerald. Before he could continue, Andy appeared at her husband's shoulder.

'What's wrong?' she said.

'It's about Katie,' said Martin.

'We think we've got one of the men who kidnapped her,' said FitzGerald.

Andy reached out to hold her husband's hand. 'You're sure?' she asked.

'Well, he's denying it, but his fingerprints match some prints we found in the cottage.' He gestured at the car parked at the end of the drive. 'We'd like Katie to come to the station with us, to see if she can identify him. If that's okay with you.'

'She won't have to face him, will she?' asked Andy.

FitzGerald shook his head. 'She'll be able to see him, but he won't be able to see her.'

'I'll go and get her,' said Martin. He went down the hall and through to the kitchen, where Katie was kneeling on a stool and stirring a bowl of cake mixture with a wooden spoon.

She grinned up at him and held out the spoon, which was dripping with chocolate. 'Do you want some?' she asked.

'I'll wait until it's cooked,' he said. 'Katie, the police think they've found the man. The man who kept you in the basement.'

Katie put down the spoon and wiped a stray lock of blond hair away from her eyes with her forearm. 'Are they sure? Are they sure it's him?'

'They want you to look at him. To check they've got the right person.'

Katie frowned. 'I don't want to, Dad.'

Martin ruffled her hair. 'It'll be okay. I promise.'

He helped her climb down from the stool and held her hand as they walked to the front door, where Andy was already putting on her coat. 'I'll lock up,' she said.

She went through to the kitchen while Martin and Andy got their coats. FitzGerald smiled at the little girl. 'How are you, Katie?'

'I'm fine, thank you,' she said, buttoning up her coat.

'Thank you for helping us,' he said.

Andy came back into the hall. 'Right,' she said. 'Let's go.'

Power drove the blue Orion, with Martin and Andy sitting either side of Katie in the back. FitzGerald kept twisting around in the front passenger seat and smiling reassuringly at Katie.

Power dropped them at the front of Pearse Street Garda station and FitzGerald took them inside. Martin grimaced as they followed FitzGerald down the corridor past the interview room where he'd been grilled by the detectives the last time he'd been in the Garda station. He put his hand on

Katie's shoulder and gave her a small squeeze, as much to reassure himself as to comfort her.

FitzGerald showed them into a room. Martin was relieved that it wasn't the room where he'd been held before. It was slightly larger, with no recording equipment. FitzGerald asked them to wait, and they sat down while he went back down the corridor, returning a few minutes later with a young uniformed policewoman. She introduced herself by her first name. Teresa. She was in her mid-twenties, blonde with a pretty smile. She knelt down by Katie's side and asked her if she wanted a drink. Katie shook her head.

'What about a Coke?' asked Teresa.

'Okay,' said Katie. Teresa asked FitzGerald to get the little girl a Coke, then pulled a chair up close to her and sat down.

'Do you know why you're here, Katie?' she asked.

Katie looked down at the floor and nodded.

'Good. Now, I don't want you to worry. Everything's going to be all right. We think we've got the man who took you away from your mummy and daddy, but we have to be sure. Do you understand that?'

Katie nodded again. She began swinging her legs backwards and forwards.

'What we want you to do is to look at some men and see if you can recognise the one who took you away from your mummy and daddy. There'll be eight men. We want you to look at them, all eight of them, and then tell us which one is the man who took you. Do you think you can do that for us?'

Katie scowled. 'I don't want to.'

Teresa leaned forward and put her face close to Katie's. 'Why, Katie?'

'I just don't want to.'

'There's no need to be scared, Katie. The man can't hurt you. Look at me, Katie.'

Katie slowly raised her eyes and looked at the police-woman.

'Let me tell you how it works,' said Teresa. 'There'll be a line of men, and they'll be on the other side of a window. You look through the window at them, but they can't see you. It's a special glass. You can see through it, but they can't. They just see themselves.'

'Like a mirror?'

'That's right. Just like a mirror.' FitzGerald reappeared with a can of Coke and a plastic beaker. He put them down on the table and Teresa poured some of the soft drink and handed it to Katie. 'So they won't even know you're there. Each of the men will be holding a number. All you have to do is to look at all the men very carefully. Look at them twice. Then tell me which number the man you recognise is holding. You can do that, can't you?'

'I guess so,' said Katie quietly. She took a sip of her Coke.

'If you can tell us which one it is, we can make sure he'll go to prison for a long, long time. He won't be able to do anything to you again, Katie. You'll be safe with your mummy and daddy. You do understand, don't you?'

Katie nodded.

'If we don't put this man in prison, he might do some-thing to hurt another little girl. You wouldn't want him to hurt anyone else, would you?'

Katie put down her plastic cup. She looked at the police-woman for several seconds. 'No,' she said eventually. 'No, I wouldn't.'

'Good,' said Teresa. 'That's good, Katie. Okay, shall we go and have a look at these men?'

Katie nodded solemnly.

Teresa looked at Martin and Andy and they nodded too.

'Right,' said FitzGerald. 'It's this way.'

'You can both come,' Teresa said to Martin and Andy. 'Katie'll probably be more secure if you're with her.'

Andy took Katie's hand and they followed FitzGerald out of the interview room and along the corridor. Martin walked with Teresa. 'How's she been, since the kidnapping?' the policewoman asked.

'Fine,' said Martin. 'She saw a child psychologist for a few weeks afterwards, but there didn't appear to be any problems.'

'Perhaps she didn't realise the danger she was in.'

Martin shook his head. 'No, it wasn't that. She knew exactly what was happening. She just coped with it all, far better than we thought she would.'

FitzGerald held open a door and they all trooped in. It was a long, narrow room with a curtain running virtually the whole length of one side. FitzGerald motioned for Martin and Andy to stand with him. Teresa held out her hand to Katie and Katie took it. 'Right, Katie, let me explain what's going to happen. My friend over there' – she nodded at FitzGerald – 'is going to pull the curtain back, and you'll see the men sitting down on the other side of the window. Look at them carefully, look at every one of them at least twice, and then tell me the number of the man you recognise. There's no need to worry. They can't see you. Okay?'

'Okay,' said Katie.

'Are you ready?'

'I guess so.'

'Good girl. You're being very brave, Katie. I'm very proud of you. We all are.'

Katie looked over at her parents, and they nodded as if to encourage her. Teresa signalled to FitzGerald to draw the curtain back. He dimmed the lights first, then pulled on a cord. There was a ripping noise and the curtain parted in the middle.

There were eight men, all in their forties, sitting on wooden chairs and staring ahead blankly. They were all holding pieces of cardboard on which was printed a number, from one to eight.

'Take your time, Katie,' said Teresa.

Katie stared at the men. She walked slowly down the length of the room, gazing at their faces. The Nice Man was number five. He was wearing a black pullover and brown corduroy trousers and his hair was all messy, the way her dad's was when he'd just got out of bed. Katie walked back along the window.

'There's no rush, Katie,' said Teresa. 'Take all the time you need.'

Katie shrugged. 'He's not there.'

Teresa knelt down in front of Katie and put her hands on her shoulders. 'There's no need to be scared, Katie. He can't hurt you any more.'

Katie looked straight at the policewoman. She took a deep breath. 'He's not there.'

Teresa frowned. 'Are you sure?'

Katie nodded solemnly and made the sign of the cross over her heart. 'Cross my heart and swear to die.'